MAGGIE ALABASTER
JO BRADLEY

Saving Abbie

4 - 6

MUSE

SAVING ABBIE BOOK 4

Lock Me In
Written by Beau Pennington

Locked by reality,
Caught up in the flow.
Shaken by the maelstrom,
Ripped to the bone.

Shattered like glass,
Scattered dust and ash.
Pounded by the driving rain,
Torn by lightning flash.

Touched by hands that torment,
Held by arms that bind.
Soothed by words that have no meaning,
Mistaken by the past.

Take me by the heart,
Make me real again.
Heal my soul with something true,
Or let me cling to my imagination.

Give me something new.
Don't hold my scars against me,
Or mistakes I've made.
Lock me with reality, before I start to fade.
Lock me with reality, before I start to fade.

CHAPTER ONE

ABBIE

"I ASKED YOU A QUESTION." I turned around slowly. "What are you doing here, Pete?"

My former lover, owner of my old label, wore trousers and a button down shirt. They were longer than when I saw him last. His hair, once an inky black, was now grey at the temples. Fine lines surrounded eyes of faded blue. His skin was a shade or two darker than a tan. A day or two of scruff coated his chin.

Pietro Rossi was an attractive man. Even now, I saw why I fell for his charms.

At the same time, I wanted to deck the guy.

He gave me a lopsided smile that was too charming for anyone's own good. "Would you believe I got lost on the way to the men's room?"

"Considering the clear signage, no." I crossed my arms over my chest. "Try again. Or better yet, fuck off."

I made to push past him and head for the door.

He grabbed my arm. "I saw you come in here and followed you," he said quickly. "You know me, I'm impulsive."

I snorted a bitter laugh. "I remember."

One minute he was comforting me after I found out the man I thought I loved, Vance, only married me to further his own career. The next minute, Pete was kissing me and we were tearing off each other's clothes.

Yeah, okay, he wasn't the only impulsive one. I was just the one who got screwed over when Pete got back together with his wife and she insisted I be kicked off the label.

It didn't seem to have taken much persuasion on her part.

"Calista is dead," he said softly. "She…went for a swim and was taken by a shark."

He looked sad, confused, if not quite grieving. Their marriage was not what I would call rock solid, but that was a shocking, if incredibly rare way for someone to die.

I felt slightly bad for him for thinking that was how she died. Of course, I couldn't tell him she was very much *not* taken by a shark.

I saw her disembodied head in a box in Adelaide. Jackson, the manager of Wolf Venom, the band my guys were a part of, sent her head back to Melbourne to be dealt with by Asher's sister, Rose.

Evidently, Rose had dealt with it. I didn't know if I approved of her method, but it wouldn't cast suspicion on me or any of my guys. I had to give her credit for creativity.

It also wouldn't cast any suspicion on Pete, which I thought was the plan. Asher wanted to pin her death, and that of Vance, on Pete as retribution for screwing me over.

Okay, it was extreme but that was Asher for you. He only wanted what was best for me and the rest of the guys.

"That's terrible," I said sincerely. "I'm so sorry. That still doesn't explain what you're doing in a women's toilet in Singapore airport. Did you follow me just to tell me that?" I shook off his arm and stepped away from him.

His eyes tracked me across the room. He reminded me of some kind of predator looking for its prey. He wouldn't find it here. At least, not with me. Not again.

"I sold the label," he said. "Calista insisted. She said I was more interested in work than her."

"I detect no lie here," I said dryly.

I met her plenty of times when she was alive. She was the kind of woman who saw everyone and everything as competition that she needed to step over on her way to getting what she wanted. It was my understanding she broke up with him because he was at work more than he was at home. Of course, the moment she found out he slept with me, she wanted him back. She would have only played second fiddle to the label for so long.

"Yeah." Pete stared down at the immaculately clean, tiled floor. "My work was my life and now…"

"Now you regret selling the label, because the reason for doing it is gone?"

Were we having a therapy session now? I didn't sign up for any of this. What the hell was new? A lot happened when I was with Onyx Riot Records that I didn't sign up for.

He shrugged. "I'm at a loose end. I thought I would travel, but I didn't expect to see you—"

"Bullshit," I snapped. "A quick search on your phone and you would know exactly where I would be and when. Not to mention your industry contacts. What is this really about? Your wife died and you thought you would track me down and see if I would spread my legs for you again?" I wanted to high five him in the face, with a chair.

He narrowed his eyes. "You make it sound so sleazy. So what if I wanted to see you again?" He took a couple of steps forward, forcing me to step back until the side of my hip was pressed against the sink.

"It is sleazy," I said in disgust. "She's barely cold and you're chasing after me."

"This isn't about her," he said evenly. "Before I sold the label, I was talking to a divorce lawyer. I was done with her. I shouldn't have taken her back after she found out about us. I fucked up. What I did to you was shitty."

"You think?" I said sarcastically. That was one word for it. I had many others, and tons for him. It started with 'asshole' and went all the way down to...

Okay, I don't know any obscenities that start with Z, but if there was one, he was it.

"I'll understand if you never forgive me. All I want is the chance to prove I can be a better man. The kind a woman like you deserves." He gave me his best puppy dog eyes I knew all too fucking well.

"For the longest time I thought you were exactly the kind of guy I deserved," I said. "You and Vance. I figured I must be a crappy person to have people do crappy things to me like you two did."

He stroked the back of his hand down my cheek. "Abbie, you are not a crappy person."

I jerked my face away from him. "Oh, I know that now. I have more love and support than I know what to do with. I have guys who would do anything for me."

"Guys?" he repeated. He looked confused. "Plural? What the—"

"Abbie?" Asher's voice echoed through the bathroom. "Are you okay in there?"

"I'm fine," I said without taking my eyes off Pete. "I was just about to come out."

"We're coming in there if you don't." That was Zeke's voice.

"We might anyway," Tully said. "Did I hear a man in there?"

"It's no one," I said firmly. No one important to me anymore. Seeing him was actually therapeutic. Now I knew I put that part of my life behind me, once and for all. I could move on and stop looking back so much.

"It doesn't look like no one," Tully said as he stepped through the doorway. He was followed by Zeke and Asher, and then the other three members of Wolf Venom. Even Penn. All six of them were big, muscular, tattooed rock gods.

And none of them looked impressed to see Pete.

"He looks familiar." Asher cocked his head at Pete. "Have we met?" He stepped closer and held out his hand to Pete. "I'm Asher, one of Abbie's boyfriends.

Pete mouthed, "One of..." He didn't take Asher's hand. "I know who you are. Abbie is touring with you. You don't have to pretend—"

Asher dropped his hand to his side and shrugged. His ego was healthy enough the snub wouldn't make a dent.

"We're not pretending." Zeke moved to my side and placed an arm around my shoulders. "I know who you are and I know what you did to Abbie. You thought it was okay to destroy her career because you couldn't keep your cock in your pants. Fortunately, she had enough talent to overcome your crap."

"She's talented enough." Pete shrugged. "I'm sure it helps if she's fucking all of you. She was always energetic. And happy to put it out." Of course he would fall back on cheap insults when he was backed into a corner. That was typical Pete right there.

"You're not as smart as you look, are you?" Landon asked. The blue-haired bassist crossed his arms over his chest. "Because if you are, you would realise you're outnumbered." He raised one eyebrow, just slightly. He was adorable and threatening at the same time.

"Would six against one be fair though?" Channing asked.

Landon looked at him sideways. "I suppose not, but one of us could punch the shit out of him without breaking a sweat."

"Those would be fairer odds," Channing agreed. He seemed satisfied with that.

"Asshole looks like he's about to piss his pants," Penn remarked. "For the record, she's not fucking all of us."

"Yet," Tully said.

Penn didn't deny that but he didn't agree with it either. He just stepped out of the way when a woman entered the bathroom and gave them all a funny look.

"We should get out of here," Zeke said. "We wouldn't want to distract anyone from what they need to do." He jerked his head towards the door.

Judging by the way the woman was staring at them all with huge eyes, that was exactly what was happening already. It wasn't every day a person saw six gorgeous rock stars in the women's toilets.

Probably.

"Yes," I agreed. "Let's get out of here. I've said everything I need to say." I eyed Pete, daring him to try to add anything else. I cared about him once, but now it was like looking at a stranger. One who made his own bed. Now he could sleep in it.

Alone. Or at least, not with me in it.

In spite of the guys, Pete couldn't help himself. "Abbie," he started tentatively, "I'm sorry for the shit I did. I'm sorry you got caught up in it. I really do care about you. When these guys get tired of you, or you get tired of them, look me up. I know you remember how good we were together. I made mistakes, but I could make it up to you if you let me try."

I doubted that very much. "If they get tired of me—"

"We won't," Asher said.

"Nope, never," Zeke agreed.

"That's a matter of opinion," Penn muttered.

I rolled my eyes at the keyboardist and started again. "If they get tired of me, I still wouldn't go back to you. I can do so much better. Hell, I would do a lot better being on my own than being with you."

If I wanted to be with someone who only spent time with me at their convenience, I would get a cat.

"You say that now," Pete started.

"She's made herself clear," Tully said. Somehow, he managed to be pleasant and threatening at the same time. Was that something he learnt during his training as an assassin, or was that it just him? Maybe a little of both. You probably couldn't learn how to kill people without learning how to intimidate them as well.

"Come on, let's go." Asher took my hand and led me toward the door. "There's this restaurant I want to take you to. It'll blow your mind."

"Me too?" Zeke asked. As if he would be left behind.

"All of us," Asher said.

I stepped out of the bathroom surrounded by my six guys and didn't look back.

CHAPTER
TWO

ABBIE

"CAN YOU BELIEVE THAT GUY?" I said over a delicious bowl of rice.

"What guy?" Landon asked, an innocent expression on his face. "I don't remember a guy. Does anyone else remember a guy?"

"Not me," Channing agreed. He shoved the last of his apam balik into his mouth and started to chew around the huge mouthful.

I snorted, a laugh appreciative at their attempts to lighten the mood. "I don't want to remember the guy." My voice low, I told them what he said about Calista dying, and selling the label.

"Rose was always the creative one in the family," Asher mused. "Well, her and me. I would definitely have voted her most likely to come up with interesting ways to dispose of dead bodies."

Tully chewed thoughtfully on his roti. "He didn't say who he sold the label to, did he?"

I shook my head. "We didn't get that far. Why? Wait, don't tell me he sold it to Reuben Brantley?" I eyed Zeke. He was no fan of his mobster brother, or the rest of his family. Out of seven brothers, he was the only one not involved in the family business. Not for lack of trying on Reuben's part.

"No," Tully said. "He sold it to Xavier Lang. And he gave it to me."

I almost choked on my rice. Asher patted my back while Zeke handed me a glass of water.

When I finally got my breath back, I said, "I must be hearing things. Did you say you're the new owner of Onyx Riot Records?"

Tully shrugged. "Apparently so. That's what he said, but he was trying to distract me while his hired thugs took out Zeke."

"They weren't very good hired thugs," Zeke said.

"Judging by the fact you're still alive, I would say that's accurate," Asher said. "Thank fuck." He leaned over in his chair to give Zeke a side hug.

"What are you going to do with it?" Penn asked. "A record label, I mean. We're not looking for a new one, are we?" He glanced around the table.

"No, we're not," Zeke said firmly. "That's a good question though. What the fuck are you gonna do with a record label?"

"No idea," Tully said. "I guess I'll hire someone to run it for me and let it make me money. While changing the culture of bullying that went on there." He inclined his head towards me.

"There's certainly room for improvement," I agreed. "Lots of it. I'm happy to tell you who works there and doesn't suck. They'll be more receptive than some of the others."

"Sounds like you need to put together a list of people to get rid of," Asher said.

"And by get rid of, you mean fire?" I raised an eyebrow at him.

"Fire, if you insist." Asher pretended to look sulky.

I was sure he would take out a hit on anyone I asked him to, but, like Zeke, he left the violence to his family. For the most part at least. He hadn't flinched when he put a gun to the head of the man who tried to attack us in Perth. Nor had he flinched when he pulled the trigger, killing the man and sending blood and brains flying.

Just thinking about it made my stomach turn and my panties wet. I'd started to accept that I was fucked up in the head for being turned on by shit like that.

I punched him lightly on the chest. "There's no need for anything worse than people losing their job. Even then, I prefer to give people a chance. The worst of them are gone now anyway, for the most part."

"That's something we can work on, but after the tour," Tully said. "It might be fun to run it when I retire from playing. In the meantime, I'll have to find out if Xavier was telling the truth or not. There's no point making plans for the label if I don't own it at all."

"What are you going to tell your mother?" Penn picked at a piece of chicken with his fork.

Tully sighed. "Not the truth. At some point, she's going to call me to tell me he's dead. I'll tell her we had drinks, then went our separate ways. If she knew why he was in Perth, she'll figure out what really happened, but she won't point the finger at me. She would never be able to prove I killed him anyway. No one would."

He hadn't lost the haunted look he'd had on his face when he turned up at Perth airport. For a trained assassin, he hated killing. Especially his adopted father. That was understandable.

"Giving you the label should work in your favour," Zeke reasoned. "What excuse would you have for killing him when he gave you such a generous gift?"

"That's a good point," Asher said. "Plus, with all the attacker's bodies lying around, it'll look like one of them did it."

"And if it didn't before, then it will after my brothers have finished with the scene," Zeke added.

For guys who kidnapped me twice and threatened me with rape, the twins made themselves useful in cleaning up after us. Of course, that was only because the people who attacked us, hired by Dante Fiorelli, went after them as well. It was a strange alliance and was unlikely to last, but if it helped us to get out of that shit, then we would put up with them for now.

"I still can't believe you can say things like that and keep a straight face," I said.

Zeke grinned. "It's a knack we've all developed over the years. When you talk about this shit enough it stops feeling like a big deal. You're getting pretty good at it yourself."

"Shit." I frowned. "Am I really?" Was I already that desensitised to criminal activity and killing? I must be, because otherwise I would be having nightmares about Asher shooting a guy, and I'd be scared of the drummer.

Wouldn't I?

I couldn't imagine being scared of Asher. Underneath the big, muscular rock star exterior, he was a sweet and thoughtful guy. He would take out hits on people if I asked him to. No one said my guys and my relationship with them wasn't complicated.

Asher and Tully, on either side of me, leaned in and put their arms around me.

"You just roll with it," Asher said.

"You haven't had any other choice," Tully added. "You didn't ask to get involved with any of our shit, but that's what happened when you got involved with us. You could have walked away, but you didn't."

"Yet," Penn said.

"In spite of Penn being an asshole, you stuck around." Asher flashed a smile at the keyboardist.

Penn rolled his eyes in response and stabbed his fork into his chicken like it was Asher's eyeball. "Maybe she stuck around because I'm an asshole. She might have a type."

When everyone turned to stare at him, he looked up. "What? We all saw that Pete guy. We know what Vance was like. The rest of you all have your asshole moments. Sounds like a type to me."

"Are you hoping it is?" Landon looked at him curiously.

Penn just tore into his chicken and shoved some of it into his mouth.

"I think that's a yes," Channing said.

I pushed my empty plate aside and rested my elbows on the table. I gripped my wine glass in both hands and looked into the reddish-purple liquid.

"I'd like to think if I have a type it's not assholes," I said. "I don't think any of you are assholes. Not even Penn, although you have your moments."

Naturally, I said that when his mouth was full so he couldn't retort.

He might have rolled his eyes toward the ceiling though. His exterior was a tougher façade than Asher or even Zeke but it was just that—a façade. Once or twice, I saw past it. Deep down, there was a decent guy in there. I was determined to find him. If I couldn't, then we would have to learn to put up with each other.

Landon rubbed his chin. "I think if you have a type it's musical, badass, tattooed—"

"With lots of muscles," Channing finished for him.

"Who wants to fuck you, not fuck you over," Zeke said.

"And love you," Asher said.

"And keep you safe," Tully said.

All eyes turned to Penn. He washed down his chicken with a gulp of beer. "Who may or may not be assholes once in a while."

I found myself wiping a tear off my cheek. I waved Asher away when he looked concerned. "It's not a sad tear. It's happy tears. If that's my type, it sounds pretty fucking perfect to me. It sums up all of you. As long as the asshole part is only once in a while."

Who wouldn't want a group of guys like that? One of these days I was going to wake up and find all of this was a dream. A very long, very detailed, very hot dream, but still. How could any of this be real?

"I make no promises." Penn toasted me with his beer glass, then drank the rest down in a gulp.

We drank and finished eating in silence after that before I broke it with the question we were probably all thinking.

"So, do you think this—Fiorelli—will try to come after us again here in Singapore, or somewhere else in the world?"

I turned my gaze to Zeke, who was the official lead singer and unofficial leader of the band. And usually the one who had the answers to these kinds of questions.

"It's possible," he admitted, "but if they were trying to extend their influence across Australia, then probably not. They'll turn their attention to the rest of my family first. Either they'll try to kill Reuben or Reuben will try to kill them. Or they'll go after the Bells and vice versa. This shit gets ugly, if you haven't noticed."

I had. I really had.

"Any idea who might come out on top?" I asked.

"Ideas? A few. Answers? Not really. If someone does, it won't last. There's always somebody ready to step in and stir up shit. It's like that game where you hammer down one animal that pops up and another one pops up." He traced circles with the condensation on the table.

"Whack-a-mole?" Channing suggested.

Zeke pointed a finger gun at him. "Yeah, that. We weren't big on games like that as kids. We usually played hide and seek and ran around pretending to shoot each other with sticks."

"Why am I not surprised?" I couldn't quite imagine him as a little boy, but it was more plausible than his older brothers. Of the ones I'd met, they both seemed like they could use some childish fun once in a while. Maybe they wouldn't be such dickheads if they enjoyed themselves more.

Zeke grinned. "Because you've met four of my brothers. Believe me, Joshua and Lucas aren't any better. I don't think Joshua has ever smiled in his life. And Lucas, he's more like Reuben than the rest of us. He's ruthless when it comes to getting what he wants. He also has the same charm as the twins, which means never turn your back on him and don't trust what he says. Everything to him is a game with some kind of end goal."

"Lucky you have us as brothers now," Asher said. "And we have you."

"And we all have each other," Tully said. He looked thoughtful. It didn't take a genius or a mind reader to know what he was thinking.

I leaned into him. "I know you're not okay, but if there's anything I can do…" I didn't even know what to say in the circumstances. 'Hey, I know you killed your father because he was about to kill you, but you'll be fine.'

Yeah, even in my head it didn't sound right.

"Just keep being you," he said. "That's all I ask."

I smiled. "I can do that. I don't know how to be anyone else anyway."

"Me either," he whispered.

CHAPTER
THREE

PENN

"GOOD EVENING, SINGAPORE!" Zeke shouted into the microphone. "There's something I wanna know." He lowered the microphone to give them a moment to absorb what he said and cheer.

The guy could be a tosser at times, but he knew how to get the audience going.

Not that they needed it most of the time. I mean, we were Wolf fucking Venom. People were hyped up long before we got on stage.

Long before the support act, Blazing Violet, performed.

Before Abbie performed the few songs Levi Jones decided to shoehorn between the support act and us.

Yeah, okay, she wasn't *too* bad and she usually didn't kill the vibe Blazing Violet started, but when we were first told she was joining us on tour, I was as pissed as fuck. I expected her to be nothing more than an airhead distraction with her pretty face and gorgeous, fuckable body. We didn't need her along for the ride. We were fine as we were.

Sure my eyes followed her ass when she walked across the stage. Okay, so she was the one I thought about when I slid my hand up and down my cock. Women like her were still dangerous. They had a way of getting under your skin.

Just like she got under mine.

Because they suck, my asshole bandmates saw it long before I did. Long before I wanted to admit it to myself.

What good would come from admitting it anyway? She was fucking Zeke, Asher and Tully. It was only a matter of time before she fell into bed with Channing and London. That was the definition of handful and pussy full.

Where would I even fit into that picture?

The worst thing? It was more than lust. For weeks I've stood back, watching them fall for her, and her for them. They were all becoming dangerously intertwined, like a sticky spiderweb. And none of them could have been happier.

I shook my head and turned my attention back to Zeke.

He raised his microphone back to his lips. "I want to know if you can be louder than the audiences in Australia."

Fifty-five thousand people in National Stadium cheered, clapped and stamped their feet.

Zeke smiled. "Is that the best you can do? Come on, I want them to hear you back in Australia!"

The audience responded louder this time, just like every other concert ever. It never seemed to get old with crowds. Honestly, I wasn't sure it really mattered what Zeke said. It was his presence they wanted. To see the real Zeke Brantley, lead singer of one of the biggest bands in the world, standing on stage in front of their eyes. And their phones. He could have told them they were all goldfish with bowler hats and smelly armpits and they would have cheered.

I made a mental note to dare him to do that sometime.

"That's better." Zeke grinned. "I bet they can hear you in Sydney."

I snorted. If that was the case, we would all be deaf right now. Of course, he had to say shit like that. The audience ate it all up, even though everyone knew it was crap.

Zeke nodded and we launched into our first song of the night.

This was what I lived for. Literally sometimes. Being up on stage, playing for a huge crowd. People who were willing to part with a shit load of money to hear our music. We played covers here and there, when a song was good enough, but it's one thing to regurgitate someone else's creativity and another thing to put your own on display.

There was no bigger rush in the entire fucking universe then hearing a stadium full of people sing your lyrics back to you. They listened to songs I wrote on repeat. Over and over until they learned every word, because they wanted to. Because listening to it gave them pleasure. It was like fingering fifty thousand people at once, and knowing every single one of them would come.

Multiple times.

Nothing got me going more than this. A tiny voice in the back of my mind reminded me that Abbie got me going as much as this, but I ignored it. What did the little voice in the back of my head know about anything anyway? That same little voice would be happy if I let myself get lost in her like the rest of the guys.

Stupid prick.

My fingers caressed my keyboard. I let myself get lost in a much safer space. Notes, chords and tempo, the swell of the audience, the other instruments complementing mine. For about ten seconds, I was able to forget about Abbie.

Then the song ended and she came back on stage.

Fuuuck.

She was gorgeous in a short black dress that fit her in all the right places. Her ass looked like absolute perfection. The front showed just the right amount of cleavage.

I pictured myself tugging it down to expose her nipples. I imagined her looking down at me as I first sucked one, and then the other. I would roll the dress down her hips and off her long, shapely legs.

In my imagination, she wore a black lace G-string that was basically see-through at the front. Like the pair she wore in the hotel in Perth when I watched Tully fuck her while the other guys fucked each other.

And... if I kept thinking this way, fifty-five thousand people were going to see me get very hard. See, she's dangerous.

I grabbed my water bottle and took a few quick gulps. It wasn't a cold shower, but it would do for now.

I caught Asher's eye and the motherfucker grinned at me like he knew exactly what I was thinking. Hell, he could probably see from where he sat behind his drums. Dickhead.

I flicked the open end of the water bottle in his direction, but he only smiled wider as cold water hit his chest and face and trickled down his skin.

"Thanks, that was refreshing," he shouted.

I closed the bottle and put it back as Zeke and Abbie took centre stage, microphones in their hands.

On the signal from Zeke, I started to play the music to back up their singing. I didn't know why I bothered. I doubted anyone in the audience was aware I was playing at all. When those two sang together, no one seemed to notice anything but them. No one could deny they had chemistry. The way they had their hands all over each other while they performed, they might as will be fucking out there.

The crowd loved it.

I slipped back into my own little world until their second song was finished.

Then it was my time to shine. I mean, more than I already was.

The rest of the band left the stage, leaving me to my keyboard and the audience.

It was one song, but the chance to play by myself to that many people was huge for me. I didn't have as big an ego as the rest of the guys in the band.

Yeah, really. People would fucking laugh if I told them that, but that doesn't make it not true.

Ever since I first put my fingers on piano keys, playing was my entire life. I had a talent for it. A gift. At the same time, it was a curse. For years, I wanted to be seen past the piano. I wanted to be Beau Pennington, a kid. When I realised people were never going to look past my musical ability, I learned to embrace it.

Being alone out here was part of that.

I leaned toward the microphone. "Hey. How is your evening going?"

The roar of the crowd was like a tsunami of sound, washing over me, carrying me away to some other place. A place where only me and them existed. The rest of the world was gone, filtered out with a roar of appreciation.

Yeah, that's fucking poetic isn't it? That was how I felt. Sue me.

"I thought I'd play a little song for you. You might know it." I told the guys I didn't know what song I was going to play until I played it, and I didn't for the most part. Tonight, though, I wanted to play something I wrote. Something that spoke of the guy I kept deep down in the darkest parts of me. The guy I both wanted Abbie to touch, and was terrified she'd learn existed. The guys knew about him but not how deep he went, or how dark he really was.

I put my fingers on the keys and started to play "Lock Me In".

I didn't have quite the calibre of vocal talent Zeke did, but what I lacked in ability, I made up for in feeling the lyrics and putting all of my emotion into them. There were a lot of those. This song was about the darkest time in my life. A time when I had no idea if there would be a tomorrow, or if I even wanted there to be one.

If it wasn't for the guys, there wouldn't be.

In the corner of my eye, I saw fifty-five thousand phones with their lights on, waving back and forth in the air.

That was it. No one shouted, cheered or clapped. The audience got lost in the song the same way I did. For those three and a half minutes, the whole stadium shared the same perfect moment.

I let the notes die away and slumped forward a little. A second or two of silence was followed by rousing applause and shouts for more.

There wouldn't be more, not tonight. This was my moment, but it was enough. If I wanted to, I could go off by myself, solo, but this one song was plenty to satisfy my ego. The rest of the night, I would happily hide amongst the guys out here on stage.

"That was awesome." Zeke slapped me on the back on the way past.

"Yeah, never better." Tully slipped the strap of his guitar back over his head.

"You should do your own songs more often." Asher slipped behind his drums and picked his sticks back up.

"Maybe," I said noncommittally. I glanced towards the hydraulic stairs that lead backstage, but they were already closed. I couldn't even admit to myself I was hoping for a glimpse of Abbie.

I liked their approval, thrived on it, but that little voice in the back of my head wanted hers as well.

Hell, if I was her, I would flip me off, not give me praise. I hadn't been subtle in my annoyance at her joining the tour. And I was happy to tell her when I found her irritating. Only, that happened less and less often those days.

Not that I would let her know that, no way. The sooner she realised I really was an asshole, the better off we would all be.

No one ever said I wasn't as conflicted as fuck. In fact, they would probably tell you that was my default mode, conflicted and snarky, with a side of sarcastic asshole.

"You fucking killed it." Landon picked up his bass guitar, the bright purple and black one, and grinned at me.

I shrugged one shoulder. "It was okay." It was more than okay. It felt really fucking good. Better than sex. That was another good reason to stay away from Abbie. If sex with her was better than this, I'd be spoilt for life.

At least, that was what I told myself. I told myself a lot of things. Some of them made more sense than others.

"You're a rock god and you know it," Channing said. He picked up his saxophone and placed his hands on the keys, ready for the next song.

"Get it on a bumper sticker," I said. "Or a T-shirt."

Channing laughed and put his mouthpiece to his lips. More of the guys should play woodwind instruments. It was a good way of shutting them up.

I shifted on my stool to make myself comfortable and waited for the signal from Zeke.

CHAPTER
FOUR

ABBIE

"I'VE BEEN SPEAKING TO LEVI," Jackson said slowly.

His tone was ominous, or maybe I was paranoid. He pinned us down at breakfast while we all sat in the hotel restaurant eating bacon, eggs and toast, and drinking too much coffee.

If too much coffee is actually possible. Is it? Let's go with no.

"About?" Zeke prompted. He gave the band's manager the side eye. His fork was poised over his eggs as if he might use it on Jackson instead.

Jackson cleared his throat. Yep, that was definitely ominous. "I was thinking it's time we took Penn's performance to the next level."

Penn scowled. "It doesn't need… wait a minute, am I getting that mother-fucking grand piano I've been asking for for years?" He pumped the air with his fist. The expression on his face was the closest thing to a smile I ever saw on him. He actually looked excited.

Jackson appeared to be less enthusiastic. "Not exactly, no."

"A baby grand is fine," Penn ventured. "Or an upright." He was grasping at straws and from the expression on his face he knew it. "Raised platform?"

Jackson shook his head. "I was thinking, and Levi agrees, that you could sing with Abbie."

What the fuck?

Penn stared. First at Jackson, then at me. He had FUCK LIFE tattooed across his knuckles. Right now, he had his L finger pointed at my chest. "Did you put him up to this?"

I frowned at him. "What? This is the first I've heard of it too."

Penn dropped his hand to the table with a thud. Cups and plates rattled, and coffee nearly sloshed onto the table. "It's not fucking happening. That's my solo. You can screw with whatever the hell else you want, but not that."

He'd gone from ecstatic to furious so quickly I almost got whiplash.

At the same time, I understood why he was pissed off. Jackson hadn't even asked either of us. To spring something like this on Penn and me, in front of the whole band, seemed unfair.

"It would be awesome," Asher said tentatively. "You two would sound—"

"No." Penn slammed his fist down on the table so hard we all jumped. "We fucking wouldn't." He shoved back his chair so hard it screeched on the floor, then stalked away out the door.

"That went well," Channing said ironically.

Tully's eyes followed Penn until he was out of sight. "I should go after him. He might do something stupid."

"Give him some time," Zeke said. "He'll calm down. One of us can talk to him when he has his head on straight." He looked over to Jackson. "You didn't think he would be happy about that, did you?"

Jackson shrugged. "I figured he'd go off initially, but when he calms down, he'll realise I'm right. The audiences will love it."

"Does Abbie want to do it?" Asher gave me a questioning look. Apparently he was the only one who remembered I might have an opinion on the subject.

Did I?

"Not if it's going to create friction, no," I said. When it came to Penn, I hadn't done anything *but* create friction since I joined the tour. Most of it wasn't even the good kind of friction.

"Penn will be fine," Jackson said. "It doesn't even need to be an every night thing. You won't be on tour with the guys forever. While we are, we might as well make good use of you and lift your profile as much as we can."

"Right." Of course, it wasn't just about me or Penn. Like every aspect of this industry, it was a business decision. Whatever it took to make the label more money in the long run was what mattered. Including ensuring artists had career longevity.

I wouldn't complain if I had that, but I didn't want to feel like I was step-ping on Penn to get there. He certainly didn't need me to lift his profile. Unless he planned to go solo someday. In which case, this was a good move. Jackson and Levi might know things I didn't.

I mean, of course they did, it was their job to know.

"When he calms down, you can talk about what song you're going to sing and get in some rehearsal." Jackson looked like the matter was settled and we would have to deal with that whether we liked it or not.

I suspected he hoped it would be that simple, but I doubted Penn would come around that easily.

"I'll see you all later." Jackson gulped down the last of his coffee and slipped out of the restaurant.

"Well that was... different," Landon said. "You have to love it when your manager drops a bomb right in the middle of breakfast."

"It keeps life interesting," Asher said.

Zeke snorted. "That's one word for it, babe."

Tully was still watching the door, a worried expression on his face.

I chose my words carefully. "When you say Penn might do something stupid..."

Tully turned to me and the left side of his mouth drew back. "You know about his past?"

"Only what the tabloids mentioned," I said. "I also know how much they like to make things up." Most of those kinds of magazines should be in the fiction section.

Or better yet, not exist at all.

Zeke leaned forward and rested his elbows on the table. "Some of it is accurate. He did actually overdose." He looked down at his coffee cup and continued with glazed eyes, his voice a whisper. "That was during the early days of the band. We were the ones who found him. I thought he was dead when I first walked into the hotel room."

The memory clearly rattled him, even now.

I put a hand on Zeke's arm and squeezed his rock hard bicep. "That must have been terrible." Even if you got used to death, it would be different when it was a friend. And to find him like that... They all must have been devastated.

"It was pretty shit," Zeke agreed. "We were lucky we got him to hospital in time. Another hour or two and he would have been gone."

"And all his talent with him," Tully added.

"What a fucking waste," Asher said softly.

Zeke nodded slowly. "It would have been. It's not the first time he OD'd either. The first time, he was seventeen. He was full of rage because his parents planned his life out for him." The sides of his mouth tugged back.

"They gave him options," Asher said ironically.

Zeke laughed bitterly. "Yeah, concert pianist or lawyer. Nothing else would live up to their standards. They pushed him so hard, I'm surprised he didn't give up the piano entirely. Walk away to get them off his back."

"He loves it too much for that," Tully said.

"Lucky for us." Zeke curled his hands around his coffee cup. "And him. Anyway, he claims the first time was an accident, but I wonder if it really was."

"You think he tried to take his own life?" I asked as gently as I could. I was starting to understand why Penn was the way he was. It couldn't be easy having parents who made life choices for you. Who pushed you so hard, even if it was in a direction you might want to go. Who made you think you had no options left.

"Possibly." Zeke took a sip of his coffee. He must have found it cold, because he grimaced. "He was a pretty messed up kid. But, you know, how would he have known what the right dose was? That sort of thing is easy to screw up."

I nodded and squeezed Zeke's arm. "And the second time? Also an accident?"

"As far as we know," Asher said. "It's the last time he touched the stuff."

"It better be the last time ever," Zeke growled. "We signed with White Wolf Records shortly after that. There's a clause in his contract that if he even touches drugs, he's out."

"Out as in?" I asked.

"Out of the band," Zeke said. "Out of his contract. Out of his career, unless another label will touch him. He agreed to it. I'm not sure if he was the one who suggested it in the first place, to make sure he had extra incentive to stay clean."

"Levi Jones smokes weed," I pointed out.

"Levi isn't addicted to it," Asher said. After a moment, he frowned. "Not that we know of anyway." He looked around the table but no one disagreed with him.

"Penn hates the smell of weed," Zeke said. "It's other shit he was into. Harder stuff than dope. For the record, he would be just as out if he smoked weed. These days it's just Ibuprofen and alcohol for the boy."

"I've noticed he doesn't drink very much," I remarked. "Not excessively anyway."

"I'll get plastered when I know I won't wake up in Sydney working for my brother," Zeke said. "Until then, we all keep it low key."

"Besides, hangovers suck," Asher said.

"Truth," Tully agreed.

I turned to the lead guitarist. "So when Penn stormed out like that, you're worried he might find some drugs and...use them?"

"It crossed my mind." Tully started to stack the empty plates in a neat pile for the server to collect. "He's more likely to do something stupid when he's angry."

"That solo means a lot to him though," Landon said. "He wouldn't risk that. At least, I don't think he would." His brow wrinkled adorably.

"He better not," Zeke growled. "Otherwise Abbie can take his spot and he can float around as a pissed off ghost." He smirked in the direction of the door.

"Just what I need." I grimaced. "To spend the rest of my life haunted by the ghost of Penn. I'd wake up in the middle of the night to the sound of piano music."

"At least he doesn't play the tuba." Channing grinned. "Not professionally, I mean."

"I couldn't replace him if he did," I said. "I can't play the tuba." I wouldn't want to replace him anyway. I could play the keyboard, but nowhere near as well as him. Nor did I know the band's songs well enough. Nor did I want anything bad to happen to Penn.

"It's never too late to learn," Asher said. "I've always wanted to play something like that. But then I remind myself I already play an instrument that's loud and potentially obnoxious." He grinned.

"That sums you up perfectly," Zeke teased. "Loud and potentially obnoxious."

Asher laughed. "I think obnoxious but potentially loud might be more accurate. That sums up all of us."

"Speak for yourself," Tully said dryly. "I'm not obnoxious."

"Says you," Landon said.

I sat back and listened to them talk about who was obnoxious and who wasn't. Insults and teasing flew this way and that, but their banter made me smile. They were so comfortable with each other, even after Penn stalked out.

I have to admit, after what they told me about him, I was worried too. I would have to find some time to talk to him and work things out. I didn't want him to throw away his life and career because of me, and I didn't want him angry at me anymore. I would have to make him realise this wasn't my idea. Never in a million years would it have occurred to me that Penn's solo was anything other than his moment.

Now the idea was out there, it was hard not to think about it. Singing with Penn would be interesting, to say the least.

CHAPTER FIVE

ABBIE

"HEY, ASSHOLE." I crossed my arms and stood watching Penn play.

It didn't take a genius to realise where Penn stomped off to. I didn't know him as well as I knew some of the other guys, but when music was someone's happy place, it tended to be the place we turned to when we needed comfort.

It was a short walk to the stadium for our sound check for tonight's concert, our only one in beautiful Korea. Shame. I loved Korean food and K-pop. Korean dramas too, when I had the time to watch them. It would have been fun to stay here for a while longer. I'd have to find time to come back when the tour was over and spend a week or two.

In the meantime, we had a sound check to do, but I asked the rest of the guys to stay backstage while I spoke to Penn.

He didn't even look up. "Fuck off."

If we became friends and actually liked each other, we would probably still talk to each other the same way. The insults were strangely comfortable, like the guys' banter, or an old pair of shoes. The kind you should throw away but just can't bring yourself to do it.

"So eloquent." I didn't recognise the song he was playing, but when he stopped to scribble on a piece of paper beside him, I realised he was writing it. Usually, I would leave someone alone while they were in the midst of the creative process. In this case, he would have to suck it up. Things needed to be said.

"That's me," he said. "I'm all about being classy as shit."

I snorted, because I was also really classy. "A part of that is right."

He looked up at me and smirked. "Yeah, the classy bit." He leered unashamedly at the way my cleavage was pushed up by my arms.

"Keep telling yourself that." I lowered my arms to my sides.

"This might surprise you, but I don't need your permission to do a fucking thing," he said coldly.

"No you don't," I agreed. "Except listen to me for one minute."

The motherfucking smartass raised his smartwatch to his lips and said, "Set a timer for sixty seconds." He lowered his arm and raised an eyebrow. "You're on the clock."

I rolled my eyes. Since he was probably being literal, I said, "You know I had nothing to do with Jackson's suggestion, right? I didn't go to him and say, 'Hey, you know how Penn drives me absolutely nuts? Well let's screw with his day by making his solo a duet instead.'"

"Because it didn't occur to you to do that?" Penn asked. "You would have sooner or later."

I barked a laugh. "If I wanted to mess up your day, I would think of something more creative. Like putting lemon juice in your water bottle, or filling your shoes with confetti. Now I'm thinking about it, I still might do both of those things. But I had nothing to do with this. It—"

The timer went off.

"Time's up. For what it's worth, I didn't think you would come up with the stupid fucking idea. It's exactly the kind of shit Jackson and Levi pull."

"Because they're smart businessmen." I didn't realise what I walked into until Penn raised his eyebrows.

"Because they're *smart*," he said.

"Meaning I'm not." He knew exactly what to say to get under my skin and get a response from me. Being called a dumb blond was certainly one of those things, and he knew it.

"You said it, not me," he said easily.

He looked so smug, I was tempted to punch him in the face. Since I'd only hurt myself, I wondered if Tully would mind if I hit Penn with his guitar. He would understand if I explained the context. Hell, it wasn't as though Tully didn't have half a dozen more guitars he could use.

Lucky for Penn, I didn't want any musical instruments to be damaged in the process of this conversation. No guitar deserved that.

"You've really embraced the whole tortured rock star thing haven't you?" I asked. "Like you're the only person in the world who has ever been through stuff."

His eyes flashed with anger. "You haven't got a fucking clue."

"Don't I?" I challenged. "Why don't you enlighten me?" Did I really think he would open up to me? No, not really, but one of us had to open a channel of communication. It might as well be me.

His jaw moved a couple of times, then he shook his head. "I see what you're trying to do."

I crossed my arms again, not caring I was showing a bunch of cleavage. Let him leer. "Yeah? What's that?"

"You think I'm going to tell you my life story, so you can tell me I'm full of shit and everything that happened to you is so much worse." He slapped his pencil down on his piece of paper and got up from his stool.

"Absolutely," I said sarcastically. "Because everything with me is a competition. Every shit thing in my life is twice as bad as every shit thing in your life." I laughed bitterly. "Is it so hard to believe I just want to listen to what you have to say?"

The look he gave me said it was.

"Are you going to insist on this duet bullshit?" He stepped away from his keyboard.

"What are you going to do if I insist?" I asked. "Let me guess, you'll sit on your stool, cross your arms and refuse to play or sing. Will you pout too?"

He gave me a venomous look and stalked away towards the back stage.

I should have let him be, but I followed him instead. "See what I mean?" I said to his back. "You can't even have a civil conversation without storming off like a spoilt child. This might be news to you, but you can't always get what you want."

He turned around so fast I took a step back.

"Can't I?"

I was hardly aware of him moving again, but he grabbed my wrists, pulled them up and pinned me to the corridor wall. He pressed the length of his body to mine and slammed his lips down onto my mouth.

I was so surprised I didn't even think to protest. By the time I regained my breath, I realised I didn't want to. I kissed him and held nothing back. All of the anger and frustration became a burning desire. I wanted to feel every part of him on every part of me.

As he kissed me, he rubbed his body up and down against me. His already hard cock grazed my hip through the layers of clothes.

I let out a soft, needy moan.

He let my hands go and slid his up the front of my shirt to cup my breasts. His palms rubbed my nipples until they quickly became stiff, aching peaks.

I wound my arms around his neck as he moved his mouth from mine, down to my throat.

"I still hate you," he murmured against my skin.

"Got it." I snaked one arm from his neck down his chest, over his rock hard stomach to his equally rock hard cock. "I hate you too." Since we were more or less alone, but not caring if we were anyway, I undid the front of his jeans, releasing his erection into my eager fingers.

"Fuck." He seemed to be resisting the urge to pump himself into my hand. He slipped his hand down my side, over my ass, and pulled up my thigh until my knee was at his hip. He held it there while his hand ghosted across the front of my panties and delved into the gap at the side.

"Figures you're as wet as fuck already." He pressed two fingers into me and stroked my insides until I was panting. "Practically dripping."

I didn't know how he had words because I had fucking none right then. Even fewer when he pulled aside my panties and grabbed my wrists to pin them above my head again. He carefully placed his cock outside the entrance to my pussy and, with no restraint or hesitation, pressed all the way, balls-deep into me.

I bit my lip to keep from screaming out in pleasure. For a guy who could behave like a big cock, he also had a big cock. He certainly knew how to use it. He drove it into me hard, but at the same time angled perfectly.

He massaged my clit with his fingertips like he knew exactly what he was doing. Hell, he'd undoubtedly had a lot of experience doing it. Whatever, I wasn't going to complain.

I rolled my hips in time with his thrusts and watched his face. His expression was a mask of concentration and pleasure. There was nothing hotter than a guy mid-fuck. Especially when I was the one getting fucked.

I half closed my eyes as the pressure started to build. "Shit, yeah."

"I know you're close, but wait," he ordered.

I groaned. "I don't think I can." I didn't think I *wanted* to. He played my body like he played his keyboard. Did he think he could bring me to crescendo and then hold me there as long as he wanted?

Yes, of course he did. Like always, he wanted to be in control.

"You can because I say you can," he said with certainty. "For once in your life, shut the fuck up and do as you're told."

"Yes, sir." It was meant to be sarcastic, but it didn't come out that way. It sounded breathless and submissive.

His eyes snapped up to my face and for the first time ever, he smiled at me. "I like the sound of that. Say it again."

I was even closer to coming, but I managed to scrape together enough breath to say, "Yes, sir."

He groaned, a deep, guttural, animalistic sound that pushed me so close to the edge I might as well have been standing on a cliff with my toes poking off.

I screwed my eyes shut with the effort of not coming. "I need to..." I begged.

"Me too," he grunted. "Okay, you can come."

However he did it, he timed our orgasms to perfection. We were in sync like an orchestra who had played together for years. Like a band who knew each other so well, their music blended together to create something incredible.

Our voices were matching moans of pleasure and ragged pants of effort.

The storm that washed over me was better than any music. It started in my core and spread to every part of my body until my toes curled and my hair stood on end.

When the waters finally started to recede, they washed over me again. And again.

By the third time, I was completely out of breath and could have sworn I'd seen stars in another universe, in another time, for an eternity.

We slumped together, sweaty and sticky, but oh so fucking satisfied. We stayed like that for a couple of minutes before he slid out of me and pulled my panties back into place. He even put my skirt back down, although the front was crumpled.

I didn't care. We hadn't done anything to be ashamed of.

At least, that was what I thought until he said, "I can't get everything I want, can I? Seems to me, I can." He looked smug, but this time I didn't buy it.

"We should choose a song if we're going to have time to rehearse," I said.

He paused from taking his cock back into his jeans. "Really? You're going to insist we do this?"

I shrugged. "Yes, sir," I said with the slightest quirk of an eyebrow.

He pressed a hand to his forehead. "Fuck, you're going to be the death of me, woman." He actually looked amused.

What were the chances he would lighten up after this? Did I want him to? Maybe just a little.

"Big tough asshole like you?" I teased. "You can deal with it."

"I still really, really hate you." He lowered his hand and sighed. "Fine, but don't fuck this up for me. If you do, I'm going to make you say *yes, sir* around my cock until you suck me dry."

"Noted," I said. I wasn't sure if he intended that to be a threat or incentive to screw up.

Whatever. If he wanted to threaten me with a good time, then I was here for it.

CHAPTER SIX

PENN

I RUBBED my temple with my fingertips. "Jackson is fucking nuts if he thinks this would be ready tonight."

"He'd probably be surprised we actually agreed on a song," Abbie said dryly.

"Not as fucking surprised as I am," I thought she'd bitch and be difficult until she got her way. Apparently giving her orgasms lightened her up a bit. It should have done the same for me, but I was more on edge than before. Fucking her should have gotten her out of my system, but I wanted to touch her all over again.

Sitting beside her on my keyboard stool, I was very aware of her. She smelled intoxicating. Soap, shampoo, perfume. Whatever it was, I had to take shallow breaths so I didn't inhale too much. It was like a drug and I'd done enough of those in my life. Too much.

"Me too," she said. "I expected you to shoot down everything I suggested, just because I suggested it."

"I thought about it," I said unapologetically. "Pissing you off is fun."

"You need to get out more if you think being an asshole is fun," she commented. She toyed with the keys in front of her, smoothing her fingers over them rather than trying to make music.

I tried not to think of her touching my cock like that.

"I would suggest you try being more of an asshole to see what it's like, but you're already annoying enough." I resisted the urge to smile at the look on her face. I wouldn't be me if I didn't give her shit every chance I got. She gave back every drop of it and then some.

"Fuck off," she retorted. "You know, something occurred to me."

"You finally figured out why people don't wash coloured fabric with white?" I knew it irritated the shit out of her when I pretended I thought she was dumb. She was definitely not stupid. She might be one of the smartest people I ever met. Maybe I was lame for trying to get a rise out of her, just because I could, but I couldn't resist doing it every chance I got.

She poked me in the chest with a fingernail. "How the hell do the other guys put up with you?"

"I ask myself that every day," I said. "I guess they've learned to accept they will never be as hot and talented as me." I wanted to grab her finger and pull it, and the rest of her, closer to me so I could kiss her silly.

Instead, I batted her finger away.

"Are you going to tell me what occurred to you, or do I have to keep guessing?" I asked.

"I should keep you guessing, but since you're only going to come up with dumbass suggestions, I might as well come out and say it." She pressed down on the keys like she was trying to play chopsticks.

"Do you think Jackson really wanted us to perform together?" She dropped her hands to her lap and twisted around to look at me.

"That depends what you mean by perform." I didn't smile often, but I gave her a slight upward tug of my lips. Enough to show I was amused without looking happy. Let's not go too wild here.

She snorted. "Both meanings of the word."

I frowned. "You might have to draw me a picture, because I don't know what you're trying to say. You think he wanted us to fuck?"

A fascinating blush crept up her cheeks. For a woman who was very much *not* afraid of her own sexuality, there were still parts of her that held back, that were reserved but thankfully not embarrassed. No one should be embarrassed about sex.

I sure as fuck wasn't.

"Maybe not specifically that," she said slowly. "Think about it though. We've been hanging out for, what, three hours? And we haven't killed each other yet. He might have thrown out the suggestion just to get us to start talking to each other."

I scratched the side of my head. "That would be the kind of devious bullshit Jackson would pull. Levi too. This might have been some nefarious plot to try to get us to stop hating each other." Those two were all about team building exercises. I'd seen it tons of times with other bands. They even did those executive camp out week things.

I shrugged. "Shame it didn't work. We still can't stand each other."

I wanted to drag her down to the front of the stage and fuck her brains out in front of all the roadies who moved back and forth, getting everything ready for tonight's concert, but I still didn't like her.

No way. She was like the little brother's annoying best friend or something like that. She thought I was a shithead. I didn't plan to do anything to change her point of view.

Yeah, okay, I didn't believe it either.

"Of course we can't," she agreed. "But now we know we can spend time together without anyone losing a limb or an eye."

"Only because my cock didn't go anywhere near your eye," I said jokingly. "Something that big can cause damage." I placed a hand on my groin and wiggled it back and forth a couple of times. I didn't want to brag, but what I had was a good mouthful.

She laughed. "How many eyes have you poked out with your cock?" She glanced down towards it.

"None, but there's a first time for everything." I nodded. "If you're right about Jackson's motives, then I guess we can stop trying to practice."

"Trying to practice?" She frowned. "I was practising. What were you doing?"

"Resisting the urge to grab a couple of Asher's drumsticks and poke my eardrums out every time you opened your mouth." I pushed the pile of sheet music in front of us into a pile and tapped it down on the stand to tidy it.

She rolled her eyes. "You're such an asshole."

"Did you just realise that?" I asked. "I thought you knew that since we met. I haven't been trying to hide it. Maybe I haven't been enough of an asshole if you haven't noticed."

She barked a laugh and turned to straddle the end of the stool. I couldn't see up her skirt, but the memory of the look and feel of her pussy was fresh in my mind. I wanted to push her skirt up and take another look, just to be sure my memory wasn't faulty.

"I noticed all right," she said. "I just think you're not as big an asshole as you try to act like you are."

"Hey." I pretended to be offended. "I'm a card-carrying member of the asshole club, thank you very much. A proud one." I left the whole being nice thing to Asher and Tully. They were better at it than I was, and seemed to enjoy it for some reason.

Ironic, since Tully was a trained assassin and Asher's family would kill you and not think twice. Zeke's family was worse. If there was a competition for the worst family, mine would still be in the running, just for different reasons.

"Keep telling yourself that." She turned around and swung her leg over the stool.

"I will." I nodded. I wasn't going to change for her or anyone else. Being brutally honest with people kept them at arm's length. I didn't want anyone getting close to me, because it just led to disappointment.

Usually theirs.

I had a lifetime of experience in not living up to people's expectations. Fuck doing that anymore. It was easier to let the music speak for me. If people didn't like that, then they wouldn't come to our concerts. And they did. Lots of them. Over and over.

"Can I ask you something?" She turned back around.

"Can I stop you?" I grimaced at her. If there was anything I knew about Abbie, it was that nothing I said or did would shut her up when she didn't want to be shut up. She didn't take any shit from anyone, not even me. I certainly gave her a lot of it. I vaguely wondered what it would take to make her really, truly angry. So angry she couldn't think straight. If it led to more amazing hate sex, then maybe I should try to push her to that limit. She hadn't complained about it. Yet.

"Nope," she said lightly. "That song, 'Lock Me In'."

Every muscle in my body stiffened. No, not my cock, just everything else. I mean, my cock was an organ, not a muscle, but whatever.

Everything in me was on alert. That song was intensely personal and I didn't mind sharing it with the world, but I hated talking about it. It came up once in a while during interviews. They always want to know if it was about my past, my overdoses, my addiction. The whole fucked up mess. If you really want to piss me off, then ask about that time in my life.

"What about it?" I closed my eyes tight and braced myself for the barrage of questions I didn't want to answer. Would I answer them? I wasn't sure. I itched to get up and walk away, off the stage, right now. Walk and keep walking until I couldn't hear anything she said.

"Can I sing it with you?" she asked.

My eyes snapped open and then my brow fell into a frown. "You want to sing it with me?" Okay, I was *not* expecting that. "Why?"

"I don't know, I just…wanted to." She shrugged. "It's a beautiful song and it clearly means a lot to you. If you can handle my screeching, I thought it might be fun."

She knew it as well as I did that her singing voice was not a screech. I could have listened to her sing all day. Maybe alternating that with listening to her come. Both were beautiful music.

I eyed her doubtfully. "This isn't where if we end up sounding so good together you insist we sing it on stage, is it?"

"Technically we would be singing it on stage," she pointed out.

I rolled my eyes at her. "You're such a motherfucking smartass."

"Right back at you," she said. "So, how about it?"

For a good couple of seconds, I forgot she was talking about singing. All I could do was stare at the curve of her face, the colour of her eyes, the blush of her cheeks, the lines of her mouth. I wanted to kiss her so badly it was like an ache deep down.

More than that, I wanted to open up my heart and soul to her. I wanted to let her kiss and heal every wound, and push back all of the darkness until there was nothing left but me, laid bare and whole.

I forced my eyes away from her face. "Right. Sure. Just one more song. Then I need to eat, I'm fucking hungry." I hadn't finished breakfast and it was almost lunchtime. A big boy like me needed to keep up his sustenance.

"Hungry, yes," she sounded vague.

I wasn't sure if either of us were actually referring to food.

CHAPTER
SEVEN

PENN

"THAT MIGHT HAVE BEEN the best concert yet," Asher remarked.

"Yeah, it was okay." I shrugged and repositioned my feet on the chair in front of me. The view across Seoul from the roof of the hotel was beautiful. Especially since no one else was up here to enjoy it but us.

Thank fuck, because people splashing around in a pool behind me would be irritating.

I glanced sideways over to where Abbie and Tully were snuggled up on a reclining chair.

Check that, they were making out.

I supposed the lead guitarist deserved some cheering up after having to kill his adoptive father. I tried not to watch too much when he slid his hand up her shirt and caressed her breasts.

It was nothing I hadn't seen them do before, but it felt different somehow. Like he was touching something that was partly mine.

There was no jealousy on my part, not really. It was like having the rest of the guys play a song I wrote. Or me playing on one written by them. They belonged to all of us in a way. As long as we didn't share Abbie with the entire audience.

"Are you all right dude?" Asher asked. "You seem weird tonight. Weirder than normal." He grinned.

"I'm fine." I tore my eyes away from Abbie and Tully, and looked back at the view. I sipped my beer and watched the lights twinkle.

"You're definitely off," Zeke said from the other side of Asher. "Usually you would have given him the finger for that."

Belatedly, I gave Asher the finger.

Zeke leaned over the drummer to peer at me. His eyes widened. "You and Abbie did it, didn't you?"

Asher snapped his fingers. "That's what it is. He's got that, 'Penn got laid,' aura about him." He actually seemed excited.

I shrugged. "What if we did?"

"We told you you would," Asher said, as if he'd somehow won a prize by knowing I would want to fuck a beautiful woman. It wasn't exactly rocket science.

"Next time I see a trophy shop, I'll drop in and buy you one," I said sarcastically. "Would you like it engraved?"

"Yes please," Asher said, the grin never leaving his face. "She's amazing, isn't she? When did it happen? When you two were alone together before the sound check?" His eyes widened. "Did you fuck on the stage?"

"You sound like a fifteen-year-old boy whose friend lost his virginity and you need to live vicariously through him," I remarked.

"Hey, I do not," Asher protested.

Zeke chuckled. "You kinda do, babe."

Asher turned to him. "Don't tell me you don't want to know the answer too, because I know you do."

"I never said I didn't," Zeke said.

Both of them turned to me.

I rolled my eyes towards the sky. City lights and cloud cover meant the stars weren't visible, just an inky blackness. I wanted to lose myself in it.

"It's none of your fucking business, but no," I said eventually. "The stage was full of people at the time."

"So?" Asher asked.

My gaze slid back down to where Tully and Abbie lay. He'd rucked up her skirt—the woman did love her skirts—and had a couple of fingers deep in her pussy. Her eyes were closed but her lips were apart. Her expression was one of concentration and ecstasy. It was hard not to get hard seeing her like that.

On the other side of them, Channing and Landon were making out. They both had their jeans undone, cocks in each other's hands. At the same time, they were watching Abbie and Tully.

"Not everyone is an exhibitionist," I said. I didn't mind watching in a public place, but these days I preferred to keep my fucking in private.

Asher laughed. "Who are you and what have you done with Penn? I've seen you fuck groupies up against the tour bus."

"Then there was the time he fingered that make-up artist when we were supposed to be getting ready for a photo shoot," Zeke said.

"Yeah, Jackson wasn't impressed," Asher said.

"She was," I said smugly. Tiffany and I had been there several times before but not for a couple of years now. She was a nice enough woman, but she wanted to settle down and have kids.

I was definitely not the guy for that. Not with her, anyway.

"There's no accounting for taste," Zeke teased.

"Ain't that the truth," I retorted. "I was thinking that about you too."

"For the record, I'm adorable." Asher sat forward and pretended to fluff his hair.

"Yes you are," Zeke agreed. He leaned over and gave Asher a kiss on the mouth. At first, it was just a light kiss, but it quickly became deeper, until they looked like they might swallow each other whole.

The feet of their chairs scraped on the floor as they put their arms around each other and drew each other closer.

"That's my cue to turn in for the night," I said to myself.

I doubted anyone heard. I put my half-drunk beer down on the table and slipped away to the elevator that led down to our rooms.

A clock on the wall said it was one o'clock in the morning. I stripped off my clothes and stepped into the shower. I turned up the heat until it was just below scalding and let the water cascade over me.

I grabbed the bar of soap and ran it over myself, starting like I always did with the needle scars in the crook of my elbow. Some people liked to hide them, to forget that part of the past, but I always acknowledged them. They were a sign that past me was a fucking idiot. I probably shouldn't be here right now. I did a pretty good job of almost making sure I wasn't.

That wasn't something I wanted to forget. If I forgot, I might get complacent. And if I got complacent, I might give in to the cravings. Some days I wanted to.

Badly.

If it wasn't for the band and the music, I might have.

At times, the only thing that stopped me was knowing how much I'd regret giving in. Climbing out of that hole was hard enough the first time. The second time would be more difficult and a lot more public.

The fucking press would *love* to tell the world about me screwing my life up again.

I didn't want to acknowledge it yet, but Abbie was a vital part of that now too. The anchor that kept me in place when I wanted the tide to wash me away.

Of course, thinking about her got me hard again.

I put the soap back, placed a palm on the shower wall and gripped my cock in my other hand. I slipped my fingers and up and down my length while I pictured her on her knees, her mouth around me.

She probably felt hotter and wetter than the shower. Her pussy certainly did.

I pumped myself slowly at first, letting the pressure build bit by bit. I closed my eyes and got lost in the fantasy of her lips and tongue working me, while her eyes looked up at me. Watching me to be sure I liked what she was doing.

I doubted she could do anything I wouldn't like.

I imagined her here in this shower with me. Water rushing down her face, drenching her hair, shining on her breasts. The water trickled between them, sliding down her belly, down to the folds of her pussy. I wanted to pull her to me, to feel the slide of wet skin on wet skin, my mouth on hers. My cock slipping deep into her. Her moans of ecstasy through parted lips.

I rocked my hips and pumped myself harder. I heard the way she moaned in the corridor, and called me sir. Why that got me going, I don't know, but it fucking did.

Then and now. I wanted to hear her say it over and over again. Especially when I was telling her what to do and she was obeying me.

Fuck, that made my cock harder than ever.

I grunted as I came, spilling pearly cum over my fingers and into the cascade of water. In moments, it was washed away, down the drain. My hand was rinsed clean.

I slumped and let my cock slip out of my hand.

I should have felt at least somewhat satisfied, but for some reason I felt edgier than ever.

No, I knew the reason. My hand was not Abbie. There was no substitute for the touch of another person, however I felt undeserving of it. Honestly, I was pretty fucking undeserving most of the time.

I claimed to be an asshole, but I didn't always like being that way. It was a lonely way to live.

Chill out, I don't want any pity for it. No fucking way. I made my own bed. It was my fault if I had to lie in it alone. Let's be real though, most of the time I hadn't. For years, I shared it with whatever willing groupie was around.

There was always at least one.

Since Abbie came along, the groupies went away disappointed. Or with the roadies or whoever else was around. There was always someone willing to take what they were offering.

I turned the water to ice cold and rested my head on the tiles on the side of the shower. My skin protested the sudden change of temperature, but I ignored it.

Some people got cock piercings as a penance for doing bad shit, I tortured myself in different ways. Like leaving when everyone else was getting it on, on the rooftop. No one would have cared if I watched again. I even thought about seeing if Abbie would take my cock into her mouth. Would she have? Possibly.

But like I often did, I walked away instead. I was good at doing that.

Running away and avoiding my feelings. I lost myself in things like drugs, music and groupies. One of these days, I was going to have to stop and face all of this shit.

That day wasn't today.

I turned off the water, grabbed a towel and wrapped it around my waist. I stepped out into the room as everyone else was filing through the door.

I ignored any looks of concern and changed into a pair of boxers, right there in front of everyone. If they wanted to look, who was I to stop them?

I caught a glimpse of Abbie in the corner of my eye, taking a good look while the guys hurried around, getting ready for bed.

I turned to face her just before I pulled my boxers over my cock.

She gave me a secretive smile that made my stupid heart do a somersault.

Did she have to be so fucking gorgeous? This would be a lot easier if she looked like a potato.

Hell, no it wouldn't. She would still have found a way under my skin, and all the other guys' skin too. It wasn't just about how she looked, it was her. She was smart, talented, sweet and badass, fragile and tough.

She had all six of us wrapped around her little finger, and she didn't even seem to know it. If she did, she wasn't conceited about it. She just...went on being her.

The woman I was not worthy of. Not in a million years. I asked myself how I was going to deal with her being in our lives, in my life, and keeping her at arm's length when all I wanted to do was touch her everywhere.

I had no answers for that, I just turned away and wished I had something stronger than alcohol to get me through the rest of my life.

CHAPTER
EIGHT

ABBIE

"HEY." I had to trot to catch up with Jackson, who seemed determined to avoid me since Singapore. Tonight's concert in Mumbai was the last on our Asian leg, I didn't want to leave the continent without getting some answers from him.

He paused mid-step eight before the stairs that led up to the stage. His brow shone with sweat from the sticky, humid air.

I was starting to get used to it, but I'd had a lot of cold showers in the last few days to rinse off and cool down.

He turned around and looked at me with an expression that suggested he was distracted at best. Maybe he was busy and not avoiding me. He had a lot on his plate keeping two bands and a tour in line. That was a lot of ducks to keep in a row.

Not that we got too unruly. Most of the time.

"Is something wrong?" He massaged his temples with his fingertips. "Please tell me there's not another... *gift*. We're not about to come under attack again are we?"

He kept his voice down, but his brow creased. He certainly went above and beyond the normal duties of a band manager. Poor guy.

"No," I said quickly. "There haven't been any more *gifts*, thank God, and Zeke hasn't said anything about someone coming after us."

We hadn't even seen any sign of Hunter and Parker. Yet.

Jackson sagged slightly with relief. "Good. Any problems with the press? They seem to be behaving themselves for the most part."

"The occasional question about Vance's death, and Calista having been taken by a shark, but nothing I can't handle." I shrugged.

"Great." He made to step towards the stage.

"I wanted to ask about the duet you suggested Penn and I do," I said before he could move too far.

He stopped and sighed. "The one you both keep claiming isn't ready?"

"It isn't," I said with a faint smile.

"I haven't seen you rehearsing." He cocked his head at me like he thought I was trying to get away with something.

"Were you trying to push Penn and I together?" I said in a rush.

"Ahhh, that." He straightened his head.

"Yes, that." I crossed my arms over my chest, comfortable in the knowledge he was the only one who didn't stare at my breasts. At least, not that I noticed.

"He's been a lot less snarky with you lately," Jackson said. "I would like to see you perform together, but if all I get is a bit of peace and quiet between you, then I'll take it. That might be something to work out before the next tour."

I blinked. "The next tour?"

"Yes, well." He placed his hands on his hips and furrowed his brow. "Your tour, their tour, co-headliners, whatever. It won't be the same as this tour. Since you and the boys seem to be joined at the hip now, no doubt I'll be bitched at if you don't see each other once in a while."

"That would be nice," I agreed. I thought a lot about after, but it hadn't occurred to me Jackson might have thought of it too. It was nice of him, but I doubted it would be that easy. We would be told where to go and when, and we would go.

"So us not killing each other was a side-effect of you asking us to sing together," I concluded. "Not the main reason for it."

"Well," he said slowly, "that might have been a small part of it. Penn gets mad, and he's possessive of his solo."

"I noticed," I said dryly.

"At the end of the day, all he wants to do is make music." Jackson hesitated. "More than that, he doesn't just accept that he's talented and leave it at that. He's always pushing himself to get better. To write more complex songs. To push the boundaries. Working together was always going to be a challenge. For both of you. Once he realised that, he wouldn't have been able to resist doing it."

"You're much more devious than I realised," I said. He knew how to play Penn as well as Penn knew how to play his keyboard.

Those were some mad skills right there.

Jackson grinned. "Sometimes you have to be when you're dealing with temperamental rock stars. If you're not a step ahead, you'll be several steps behind."

"Tell me about it," I said dryly. "We are the worst." I didn't mind admitting I was just as bad as the rest of us. Okay, some of the rest of us. I would never demand peeled grapes or chocolate covered ants with gold leaf or any of that crap. But I had my moments.

"You're not so bad," Jackson said generously. "I've certainly managed worse. Of course, I've signed NDAs, so I can't give you any details, but you can imagine."

"I can," I agreed. "Like getting married for publicity."

He winced. "That was a crappy thing to do, but people have done worse things for publicity. Like have children."

"That *is* worse." I made a face. What a horrible way to come into the world. Especially if their parents treated them like a commodity.

Sometimes people sucked. Thank fuck neither Vance or Pete got me pregnant.

I tilted my head and gave him a speculative look. "Of course, now I'm wondering who you're referring to."

He snorted a laugh. "I'm sure you are, but I can't tell you. If you look it up on the internet, don't ask me to confirm or deny, because I can't do that either. Besides, the kid doesn't deserve to be the object of conversation."

"That's true, they don't," I agreed. "It's sad what people think they need to do to succeed."

"Right." He nodded. "It would be nice if people were recognised just for their talent. This industry gets more cutthroat every year." He grimaced. "Sometimes literally. Sorry, that was a bad choice of words."

"You're not wrong though," I said. "Although, I don't think whoever is behind the *gifts* is interested in furthering their own career. Unless they have a very specific skillset and audience in mind." That was a twisted fucking idea right there.

"I don't think there's much market for those kinds of skills," he said. "At least, I hope not." He looked a little green, presumably at the memory of Poppy's head in the box.

Fair enough, it wasn't something anyone wanted to see every day. Well, not normal people.

I wondered if he knew about Tully's assassin training. Probably. There wasn't much that went on that Jackson didn't know. This wasn't the time or place to ask about it.

"I've kept you for long enough," I said. "I should grab something to eat before soundcheck."

He nodded. "We don't want one of our stars fainting from hunger."

"I certainly don't," I agreed. "I'll make sure they eat too." I knew he was referring to me, but I couldn't resist pretending I didn't understand.

He chuckled. "I'm sure you won't have too much trouble there. Some days,

I don't know where they put all that food. If they're not careful, we'll have to roll them onto the stage."

I giggled. I knew what he meant. The guys did eat a lot. They burned it off on stage or exercising whenever they had the chance, but if I ate as much as they did I wouldn't fit into any of my clothes after a week or two. Well, unless I took up the drums as well as singing. Asher probably burnt off a big meal after only a song or two.

Jackson patted my arm and headed up onto the stage.

I watched him for a moment before turning and starting back to the green room.

Halfway there, a strange sound echoed through the narrow corridor. I stopped and frowned.

What the—

It was high-pitched and odd, but not unpleasant. If I didn't know better, I'd think it was some sort of child's plastic toy. That wouldn't be the weirdest thing to have happened since I met the guys, but it was still odd.

I stepped into the green room as one of the guys laughed.

It took me a moment to realise it was Penn. He was actually smiling. I hadn't realised until now he had a dimple in his left cheek.

How would I have noticed; he rarely smiled. He was even more gorgeous when he did. He actually looked relaxed and happy.

"It's gonna take more than that. Better luck next time." He tossed a plastic whistle onto the table in front of him. It was bright pink with holes down the top, and a mouthpiece. Exactly the kind of thing kids loved and parents hated.

Penn glanced up and saw me standing in the doorway. His smile evaporated and his expression shut back down to his usual scowl.

If I hadn't seen his smile for myself, I wouldn't have believed it. Not to mention the laugh.

"What's going on?" I asked awkwardly. I felt like I'd walked into a party I wasn't invited to. For some reason, that stung a bit.

Asher turned and grinned. "Everywhere we go, we try to find an instrument Penn can't just pick up and play. The more absurd the better."

"Fucker does it every time," Zeke said. He shrugged and picked up the whistle to give it a closer look before handing it to Channing. "This is more your thing."

Channing wiped the mouthpiece on his T-shirt and put the whistle to his lips.

The sound he made was closer to the one parents dread than the one Penn was making a minute ago. He grinned and tossed the whistle back onto the table.

I frowned. "Wait, you got an actual musical sound out of that?"

Penn shrugged. "Yeah."

"He can get an actual musical sound out of anything," Zeke said. "No practice, nothing. He just picks it up and plays."

"That's...incredible," I breathed. "I've heard of people who could do that, but I've never met anyone."

Penn looked smug. "I have skills. Something like that whistle is pretty basic, but the lip placement is different from the saxophone. Channing could do it if he played it properly."

Channing flopped down in a chair. "I'll stick to my sax. It's sexier than that thing anyway."

"Everything is sexier than that thing," Tully said. He stepped over to me and slipped an arm around my waist. "Especially you."

"Thank you," Asher said as if Tully wasn't looking straight at me.

"You too," Tully said over his shoulder.

"So you guys search around for weird and wonderful instruments to try to catch Penn out?" I asked. "Including things like drums and harmonicas."

"Even castanets," Tully agreed. "And spoons."

"There was a beerphone once," Zeke said, referring to the instrument that was basically a stick with beer bottle lids nailed to it. "That was especially fun."

"Can you play a lute?" I asked Penn.

"Yep." He crossed his arms over his chest.

"Oboe?"

"Yes."

"French horn?"

"I've only tried once, but yes." He was completely unruffled.

"Violin?" Surely he couldn't have played everything, ever.

"Since I was four," he said. "You can stand there all day and throw instruments at me, but the answer is yes."

"It really is," Asher said. "At least in this, he is as good as he says he is."

"In every way, I'm as good as I say I am," Penn said.

I caught a flash of doubt in his eyes, but it was gone as quickly as it arrived.

"We'll keep trying to find something he can't play," Zeke assured me. "One of these days, we'll find something." He stepped to the other side of me and kissed my mouth.

"Good luck with that," Penn said. "In the meantime, don't we have a sound-check to do? With real instruments."

CHAPTER
NINE

PENN

"I'M GOING FOR A RUN." I needed to burn off this morning's breakfast and a bunch of excess energy. Okay, and some frustration. At this rate, I would be more fit than ever. Was that mentally healthy? Probably not. Did I give a shit? Kinda. Whatever, I could run that off too.

"I don't know if anyone should go out alone," Zeke said as if he could actually stop me.

"It's India. It's kinda hard to be alone," I pointed out. Any of them could have come with me, but apparently an hour in the hotel gym this morning was enough for them. Whatever. That was their choice.

Zeke scratched the side of his head. "Okay, but be careful. Don't forget we fly out to London tonight."

"Yeah." I sat down and pulled on my running shoes. "Don't leave without me this time."

Abbie looked up from where she sat by the window reading a book. Some kind of hockey romance by the look of it. I could just make out the author's name, TB Mann, and a half naked guy on the cover.

"This time?" she asked. "They left you behind once?"

Asher snorted. "Penn is full of shit, as usual."

"We didn't leave him behind," Landon said. "He was running late and almost missed the plane."

"If it wasn't for Jackson telling them to wait, he would have," Channing said.

I shrugged. "Like I said, you would have left without me."

"We would have," Tally said. "But we didn't. You would have caught up with us, sooner or later." Like Abbie, the guitarist was nose down in a book. It looked to be the same series she was reading.

I might have to sneak a peek when no one was looking. Of course, I couldn't be seen reading romance novels, even though I did for my own enjoyment. Besides, they're a good way to learn what women really want. And I enjoyed the smut.

"I'll be back in an hour." I tightened my laces and headed out the door. Even though it was still early in the day, the heat was sticky and oppressive. Just what I liked. The hotter the better. And if it wasn't stinking hot, then I liked it freezing cold, like my showers.

I chose a direction for no particular reason and started at a slow run. That was as fast as I could go here, dodging people and slow-moving vehicles. Like any city, some of the people moved like they had to be wherever they were going yesterday.

The other half moved like they were in a competition with a snail to see who could move the slowest. With the traffic this thick, most of them couldn't go much faster anyway.

I swerved around a moped carrying two people that was doing its best to weave around the traffic. The driver didn't look like they minded if they hit a couple of people on the way through.

"Watch where you're going," I called out after them. They probably didn't hear me over the sound of the traffic and their own engine.

I coughed on their fumes and slowed to a walk.

I liked the hustle and bustle of cities, but this one was almost too much. A person would either get used to it or get overwhelmed by it. I was glad we were only going to be here a few more hours.

I'd worked up a sweat by the time I reached a park where a group of guys, all dressed in white, were playing cricket.

It was a sport I enjoyed watching more than playing. Mostly because, believe it or not, I wasn't good at it.

Yeah, there are things I haven't managed to nail. Hitting a ball with a bat is one of them. I could catch okay, but I was better at running and tackling than swinging.

Of course, my asshole parents didn't let me play any sport where I might get injured. They saw dollar signs the moment I picked up my first musical instrument. A football injury would have put an end to all of that. So I played when they weren't around to see.

Yeah, I had a rebellious streak. Shocking isn't it? All I ever wanted to do was live my own life and make my own choices.

I never thought that was too much to ask. One day I might sit down and talk to them about why they thought it was.

I leaned on a low fence and watched as the bowler sent the ball flying towards the batsmen. The batsmen swung and hit the ball with a crack. He dropped the bat and started to run. A small audience cheered him on.

"Fancy meeting you here," a voice said to the side of me. "What a coincidence."

"It really is," a voice said from the other side of me.

I didn't flinch when Hunter Brantley appeared on one side of me and Parker Brantley on the other. It was inevitable they would pop up sooner or later. They were like the shit you just couldn't get off the bottom of your shoe.

"I don't believe in coincidences," I said. "Especially since you two have been following us since Perth. Or is it since Sydney?"

"I think it's fair to say a bit of both," Hunter said. "You know how it is. We go where we're told to go."

"Great." I turned around so my back was to the fence. "In that case, go away."

Parker chuckled. "As much as we'd love to, we don't follow your orders."

I rubbed my chin. I needed to shave, the stubble prickled my fingers. "Maybe you should. You might get into less trouble that way. Or cause less of it."

"Hey, that's not very nice," Parker said, with totally fake hurt that didn't make me feel bad at all. "The last time we interacted with any of you guys, we helped you."

"We saved your asses," Hunter added.

"Zeke and Asher did that," I said. "You two dragged a dead body away." I didn't bother to keep my voice down. No one was close enough to hear us anyway.

"See, we helped," Parker said. He gestured over at Hunter, who nodded. "By the time we were finished, they couldn't have implicated any of us. You're welcome."

I snorted. "Okay, whatever. What the fuck do you want?"

"Some respect wouldn't go astray," Hunter said. "But since we're not going to get that from you, we might as well get straight to it."

I didn't like the sound of that. These idiots had kidnapped Abbie twice and threatened her with rape. They helped us when it served their purpose, but they weren't friends or allies. They were a pair of dangerous criminals. I doubted there was anything they wouldn't do if their big brother, Reuben told them to.

If they wanted to idolise one of their brothers, couldn't they have chosen Zeke? He was the only reasonable one amongst them.

"Get straight to it then," I said. "I have things to do and places to be." Mostly a shower and packing for the evening's flight. If I was lucky, I might find a moment to talk to Abbie. If I was really lucky, we wouldn't talk.

"We heard you had a little problem back in the day," Hunter said. "One that could have killed you."

I shrugged as if I didn't know what they were referring to. "We all have problems once in a while. You both have one in that you can't think for yourselves. Shouldn't you both be in university, getting an education? Getting out into the world on your own? You might even find there's a better life away from Reuben and the rest of them." That wouldn't be hard, surely. As brothers went, Reuben was a shitty influence.

Yeah, okay, I was a pretty crappy role model myself, but I don't pretend otherwise. Reuben struts around like he's king shit.

Parker smiled, but it wasn't a pleasant expression. It was so chilling I had to force myself not to shrink back away from him. Or punch him in the face.

I wasn't going to let on how disconcerted they made me. Pricks like this could probably smell fear.

"We like curry," Parker said. "And your company. We often say that, don't we Hunter? No one is more pleasant than Beauregard. Can we call you Beauregard?"

"No," I snapped. Not even my mother called me that. Thank fuck. The other boys at school called me Pennington from day one. I can't remember when that became Penn, but it was a shit ton better than Beauregard. What were my parents thinking?

"Great," Parker said as if he hadn't heard me. "Reuben has been on us about getting Zeke to quit the band. I know, it's probably starting to sound like a broken record. We're a bit over it ourselves, to be honest." He sighed dramatically.

"Good, then tell Reuben to fuck off and get over himself," I said. "It's about time he gave it up." Way past time, frankly.

"Oh, he hasn't given it up," Hunter said. "He just wants us to put an end to it once and for all. Since Zeke won't break up the band, we'll have to."

I frowned. "What the fuck are you talking about?" I shook my head. "You know what, I don't care. You've wasted enough of my time with your bullshit." I took a step away.

Hunter grabbed my left arm, Parker the right, their fingers bruisingly tight on my skin.

"What the—" I jerked my arms back and tried to pull away.

They were surprisingly strong. Their grip was like a pair of clamps screwed down hard. The more I struggled, the tighter they became.

"We're not done, Beauregard," Parker said. He still sounded pleasant, like we were old friends having a chat about nothing in particular.

I hadn't ruled out the possibility he might be a psychopath. Both of them. In fact, it seemed pretty clear they were.

"Don't fucking call me Beauregard," I growled. I wanted to grab both of their heads and smash them together as hard as I could. It might knock some sense into them. Honestly, right now I might not feel bad if I killed them. They were a pair of screwed up little boys.

Hunter pulled something out of his pocket. A syringe full of something clear. "This won't hurt a bit."

I writhed and tried to break away from them, but the asshole pulled the cap off the needle. Parker held me tighter while Hunter slid the tip under my skin.

"Don't you dare," I snarled. Was I asleep and having a nightmare? If so, I wanted to wake up now.

The way the needle pricked my skin as it entered... I was all too fucking awake.

Hunter depressed the plunger and the clear liquid was forced under my skin and into my vein.

"Motherfuck—" The site went numb so quickly, I could guess what it was.

"Don't worry," Hunter said. "It's not enough to kill you, just mess you up for a little while. Embarrass the band. Make things a bit difficult. The press is going to have a ton of fun." They both released my arms with a shove and stepped back before I could knock them on their asses.

I whirled around to face them. "Stupid cunts," I growled. "You have no fucking clue."

A bit difficult? These guys were out of their fucking minds. They wouldn't just mess me up a little bit, this bullshit could end my career.

I presumed from the way they talked, they didn't know about the clause in my contract, but if anyone found me like this, it was over.

Fucking *over*.

Neither looked even slightly sorry. If anything, they seemed to find this whole thing funny. Like it was a game to them. Like trying to end my career was something they did for shits and giggles. Like injecting shit into someone's veins was a laugh. How did they even get their hands on it anyway?

Yeah okay, that wouldn't have been the hard part. Shame they didn't get arrested and thrown in a cell for carrying it around. They could be another inmate's bitches for a while. I wouldn't shed a tear.

Parker smiled like we were friends or something, and they both stepped away. "We'll leave you to it. Maybe stay away from any bodies of water."

I muttered something that wasn't even coherent to myself. My vision was already starting to blur. I was feeling a strange combination of relaxed, euphoric and pissed off as hell. The anger faded though, blurring into the muddle of sensations like melting marshmallows.

Yum, marshmallows. Thinking about that made me feel like a marshmallow. Soft, squishy and boneless.

Marshmallows didn't have bones, right? What was mallow anyway?

What was coherent thought right now too? Who cared? Not me. I didn't care about anything right now.

I sat down on the ground with a flop and leaned my back against the fence. The crack of the ball and the roar of the crowd sounded strange in my head, like an echo being heard by someone else.

I blinked a couple of times, but everything made less and less sense. Something told me I couldn't stay here, but I couldn't remember why. I grabbed onto the fence palings and managed to pull myself to my feet.

Squinting against the glare—was it that bright before?—I started walking.

CHAPTER
TEN

ABBIE

"IT'S BEEN THREE HOURS." I put my book aside after realising I read the last paragraph three or four times.

"Long enough for a good nap," Asher remarked. I frowned at him and he shrugged. "I'm not wrong."

"I guess not, aren't you worried about Penn?" I uncrossed my legs and sat forward in the chair.

"Usually, I'd point out he can take care of himself," Zeke said slowly. "But it has been a long time, and with all the shit that's gone down recently…"

He picked up his phone from the table in front of him and pressed the screen.

Another phone rang from the vicinity of Penn's bed. The ringtone was one of the generic ones preprogrammed into the phone.

I would have guessed Penn would have something more interesting but that wasn't as strange as the fact Penn left without his phone.

Zeke pressed his screen again and shoved his phone into his back pocket. "I'm going to go and look for him."

"I'm going with you," I said. I gave him my best, 'don't try to talk me out of it,' face and he nodded.

"Fine. Asher, come with us."

For once no one made any jokes about sex. Evidently they were more worried than they let on. That immediately put me on guard. If anything got to them it must be bad. Hopefully we were worrying for no reason.

"Tully, Channing and Landon, stay here and let me know if he turns up. Keep your eyes open."

We all knew what that meant. Zeke was expecting trouble of some kind. I didn't know what kind of skills Landon and Channing had, outside of playing bass guitar and saxophone, but Tully's skills would keep them safe if they had none of their own.

"Got it." Tully nodded. "He probably just got sidetracked at a strip club or something."

"Why would he need to go to a strip club when he has us?" Asher asked. When everyone turned to him questioningly, he grinned. "What? We're all hotter than any stripper I ever saw."

"No offence to any strippers, but you guys certainly are," I said.

"So are you." Asher slipped his hand into mine and squeezed gently.

Zeke opened the door and peered outside into the corridor. "It seems safe enough, but don't let your guard down. My lead singer senses are tingling." He flashed a smile over his shoulder.

"Do you also slay vampires?" I asked, mostly joking.

"I've been known to impale people from time to time," he said. He wiggled his eyebrows at me and pressed the down button for the elevator.

I laughed. "Yes. Yes you have." I put my other arm around him and leaned into him while we waited. After a minute or two, the elevator doors slid open and we stepped inside.

"Any other day, and I would distract both of you in here." Zeke sighed with undisguised frustration.

"We could always come back once we find Penny," Asher said. "I bet he's not too far away. He probably got lost. I would if I went out there without my phone."

"You'd be more likely to leave a lung behind than your phone," Zeke said.

"Hey," Asher said in protest. "Just because that's accurate doesn't mean you should come at me like that." He looked like he was struggling to hold back a grin.

"I'll come at you some other way later then," Zeke said. He leaned in to give Asher and then me a kiss on the mouth. "You're right though, he probably is lost."

"Is that what happened the first time?" I asked. "When you almost left him behind?"

They exchanged a glance.

"It's a long story," Zeke said finally.

"And it changes every time he tells it," Asher said. "I think the original version involved a redhead. Then it was twins. Then it was three, but they weren't related."

"I think those were two different times," Zeke said. He scratched the side of his head and led us out of the hotel and onto the street. "Penn—he used to get around. We all did. But that's in the past."

"None of us were celibate before we met," I said with a shrug. I didn't care what they did back then or who they did it with, as long as they didn't do it now. If they wanted other women, or men, then they could break up with me or each other first. I would sooner let them go than be cheated on. If they needed something that the rest of us couldn't give, then it was what it was. There was no point clinging to something that wasn't working.

"Okay, in a city full of millions of people, where could one keyboardist be?" Zeke mused.

"Is it possible he *is* in a strip club?" I asked tentatively. Did I have any right to ask that question? Just because he and I had sex and were almost getting along didn't mean we had progressed into relationship territory.

That may never happen. He was free to do whatever and whoever he wanted.

Asher and Zeke looked at each other.

Zeke shook his head. "It's never really been his jam."

"Brothel?" I ventured, trying to hold back a wince.

"Slightly more likely," Zeke agreed. "But not when dressed in running clothes. Any place like that he'd go into would have a better dress code than that."

I'd have to take his word for it. My knowledge of brothels was exactly zero. I wouldn't judge anyone for working in one, but I'd never been so needy for sex that I've gone to one. Not yet anyway. Hopefully not ever.

"Let's hope he didn't get run over." The traffic got thicker as we walked.

Although, it also got slower. If he was hit, he stood a reasonable chance of walking away with only a few bruises.

I didn't hear Zeke's phone ping, but he pulled it out of his pocket and frowned at the screen.

"What is it?" Asher asked. "Don't tell me, he got arrested for something? Let me guess, public nudity?"

Zeke glanced over at him, confused. "What? No. It's a tipoff as to his whereabouts." He looked pissed off.

My heart sank. "Please say it's not..."

"The evil twins," Zeke confirmed. "No explanation, just a location."

"Can we believe he's actually there?" I trusted the twins as far as I could throw them. Just thinking about them reminded me of the way they touched me. Hands slithering up the inside of my thigh. Pinching my nipple.

I suppressed a shudder.

"There's only one way to find out," Zeke said. "It's not far. I'll send a message to Tull, in case this is some kind of diversion."

"What would it be like to have a normal family?" Asher mused.

"No idea," Zeke said. "My birth family and my present family are both insane." He flashed us both a quick grin, then tapped on his screen.

"Even normal families are a special kind of crazy," I said. Mine was pretty ordinary, in that they weren't involved in organised crime, that I knew of. But they were still a long way from perfect.

They hadn't had much to do with me since the first scandal with Vance. They gave me the old, 'we don't know what to say,' then said nothing. It could be better, but I got it. Sometimes there were no words to express how fucked up things were. Or how bad we felt about them.

Whatever. The guys were my family now.

"Stay close," Zeke said. He grabbed my other hand and we walked in a chain through the crowded streets.

People glanced at us in annoyance for taking up so much space, but I ignored them. Since the twins more or less confirmed their involvement in whatever happened to Penn, I was a lot more wary and a bit more scared.

I was not letting either of the guys go. For all I knew, this was a distraction so the twins could get a chance to kidnap me again. I wasn't going to let that happen no matter what it took to stop it.

"It's just up ahead," Zeke said.

The streets emptied out onto a long, wide park. An unexpected splash of green after the greys and browns of the road.

Maybe a hundred metres away, a group of people looked to be packing up a game of cricket. It was a sport I knew very little about. As a kid, I was good at hitting a ball with a bat, but I couldn't catch for nuts.

I scanned the area. There were plenty of people here, but I couldn't see any sign of a six-foot-three, muscular keyboard player. Or a pair of six-foot-two, identical assholes.

"I'm starting to get a really bad feeling about this," Asher said.

"Really?" Zeke asked. "Because I've had a really bad feeling about this since we left the hotel."

"Yeah, well, I'm just catching up." Asher turned a slow circle, worry on his gorgeous face. "Do you think he would hear if we shouted for him?"

"We should have brought that whistle," Zeke said. "He'd hear that."

"Like a dog whistle?" I asked.

"No, one of us could play it really badly and he would get so irritated he'd come and punch us out." Zeke half-smiled, but his expression was laced with as much worry as Asher's.

"I could try singing really loudly," Asher said. "That would have the same effect."

"That would get you arrested for causing a public nuisance," Zeke teased.

Asher flipped him off. "I'm not that bad."

"No, you're not, so it wouldn't work anyway." Zeke pressed his fist to his hip and shook his head. "He's got to be here somewhere. Let's take a look around. Before anyone asks, we're not splitting up."

"I think I speak for Abbie and me when I say neither of us was going to ask," Asher said.

"Definitely not," I agreed. "I keep expecting your brothers to jump out from behind a tree or something." Not just the twins, but the other two I met as well. I assumed Reuben and Caleb were in Sydney and Melbourne respectively, but who knew what the truth of that was?

Zeke turned his concerned expression on me. "Fuck. I should have left you behind in the hotel with Tully. Asher could always take you back—"

"No he can't," I said firmly. "Firstly that would be the definition of splitting up. And you just said that wasn't happening. Secondly, I'm here now and I want to help. Thirdly, it was my choice to come."

Which then reminded me of how Penn made me wait before I came. I wanted to feel that again with him. I had to believe that whatever was going on, he would be fine.

I was going to be really cranky with him if he was dead.

Zeke held up his hands in surrender. "Fine. Let's look for Penn. Just...keep an eye out for the little pricks too. I would bet just about anything they're around here somewhere."

He didn't need to explain which little pricks he was referring to. Whatever ground they made up with Zeke by helping in Perth, they were losing if they did anything to Penn.

I wasn't sure if any of us would be able to stop him from killing them if he saw them again. I also wasn't sure if any of us would try. Penn was one of us. He was family. Even if he could be a massive pain in the neck.

We crossed most of the park before we saw the bridge. It spanned a narrow stretch of water which didn't look especially clean. It wasn't fast flowing either, which meant it was probably deep. The smell of it was certainly unpleasant.

I noticed all of that right before I noticed Penn. He was standing at the railing looking down at the water.

I raised my hand to point.

Before I could speak, Penn started to climb up onto the railing.

CHAPTER
ELEVEN

ABBIE

"FUCK." Zeke started towards the bridge at a flat run. "Stay together," he called out over his shoulder.

Hands clasped tight, Asher and I followed as fast as I could run. The drummer could have kept up with Zeke; I thought about telling him to, but I knew he wouldn't. Just in case this was a setup, he'd choose to stay with me.

Penn climbed higher. He reached the top and straddled the railing. He stayed like that for a moment or two before trying to place his foot on the thick railing at the very top. He wobbled dangerously and teetered over the water.

My heart stopped. Zeke wouldn't reach him before he fell. And when he did...

Penn windmilled one arm and wobbled back the other way.

My heart restarted but sat firmly in my throat. People were starting to notice what was going on. For the first time in I don't know how long, I didn't give a shit. There was so much more at stake than reputations. I didn't realise how much I cared about the grumpy guy until right now.

I opened my mouth to shout at him to get the hell down, and that I needed him, but Zeke reached before I got a coherent sound out.

Zeke growled and grabbed for Penn's leg. He missed the first time, when Penn wobbled again.

He swiped his hand back the other way and clamped his hand around Penn's knee. With a yank, he tugged the keyboard player back toward his shoulder.

Penn slipped sideways and tumbled, slamming into Zeke. Zeke grunted and they both fell with a thud of arms, legs and dust.

Zeke shoved Penn off him and stared, hands out to either side. "What the hell are you doing, dude?"

Penn rolled over and sat up. He looked confused. He blinked heavy lids over glazed eyes.

"Fucking hell," Asher muttered.

I murmured something in agreement. That was exactly what I was thinking. Worry gave way to frustration. What had he done? More importantly, why?

Penn pushed himself to his feet and staggered back towards the railing. "I can fly," he declared.

Zeke scrambled up and grabbed his arm. "No you fucking can't. If you go off that railing the way you are, you'll bloody drown." He glanced at us frantically. "We have to get out of here. Before anyone starts filming him."

Shit. I'd forgotten about the clause in his contract. If anyone pulled out their phone, videoed him and uploaded it to the internet, the whole band would be screwed. Especially him. There would be no coming back from that kind of broken loose hell.

"Could Jackson—" I started.

"Jackson can't do anything," Asher said evenly, but clearly unhappy. "Not in this case. He'd have no choice but to go straight to Levi. We have to deal with this before Jackson or anyone else sees him."

I nodded. That might be a big ask in a crowded place. A few people stood around watching, but if anyone recognised us, I couldn't tell. It was possible people tried to climb all over the bridge on a regular basis. Stranger things had happened.

Zeke pulled Penn's arm around his shoulder to support him. "Asher, get on his other side. We'll have to pretend he's drunk or injured and hope people buy it."

He looked furious. With good reason. Whatever Penn took, he could have put the whole tour in jeopardy. We might end up on a plane back to Sydney tonight, instead of London. Not to mention, Penn could have died. And for what?

"Personally, I'd be happy to beat the snot out of him to make it look more convincing," Asher said dryly.

"Me too," Zeke said with a grunt.

Penn jerked away from him. "What are you doing? Hey, why is there a bunny rabbit?" He squinted towards the ground a few metres in front of him.

"The bunny is telling you that you need to come with us," Zeke said with no hint of amusement. "You need to sleep for a while."

"No, I need to fly." Penn tried to turn back around.

"No you don't," Asher said. "Look, the bunny is hopping away. We need to follow it." He waved in the vague direction of the road.

"Follow the bunny," Penn said with a silly smile.

This might have been funny if it wasn't so bloody serious.

"Where are we going to take him?" I asked.

"No idea," Zeke admitted. "Somewhere quiet. Keep an eye out for anyone who looks like press. Or an evil twin."

He didn't need to tell me that. I was already looking. Anyone with a phone in their hand was suspicious, as far as I was concerned. As for the twins, I always had half an eye out for them anyway.

"I want to fly," Penn said miserably. "Don't care if I don't land."

"It's wearing off," Zeke said. "He always gets morose near the end."

"And then sleepy," Asher said. He patted Penn on the chest. "It's okay, buddy, we've got you."

Penn squinted at him. "Why?"

"I ask myself the same question," Asher said. "You're a pain in my ass but you're my brother."

"Pain," Penn echoed as if he couldn't quite understand the word. "Lots of pain."

We got him out to the street across to a narrow alley between two tall, skinny buildings. There was nothing in the alley but rubbish and a few sheets of cardboard that suggested people slept rough here from time to time.

The guys lowered Penn to the cleanest of them, so he was sitting with his back to the wall.

Zeke crouched beside him. "Why the fuck did you do this?" he growled. "Why now? You've been kicking ass for four years. Why today?"

He looked so disappointed, my heart hurt.

Penn screwed his eyes shut. "I didn't. It wasn't… Fuck." He shook his head. "Didn't want to."

Zeke snorted. "That's what they all say. It's all about the excuses."

Penn looked like he was going to cry. He started to stand but Zeke put a hand on his chest and shoved him back down.

"You can screw up your own life, but you don't get to screw up everyone else's. You need to stay here until you come down. If Jackson sees you high as a kite, you know what he's gonna do."

"Yeah, they knew," Penn said like a lost little boy.

"What does that mean?" Asher asked.

"They," I echoed softly. I crouched down on the other side of Penn. "They who?"

"There is no they," Zeke said. "Just like there was no rabbit. Like he can't fucking fly." He gave Penn a dirty look. "It's a hallucination because of whatever he bloody took."

"I don't know about that," I said. "Look at his arm." I put a hand over bruises that looked like finger marks in the crook of his elbow. Fingers that were bigger than mine.

Asher and Zeke both looked doubtful.

Zeke shook his head and opened his mouth to say something before he realised what I was getting at. "Shit."

"Penny," Asher said slowly. "Are you saying someone did this to you?"

Penn frowned. "They looked the same, but there was two of them."

"In any other context that wouldn't make any sense," Asher said with a sigh.

Zeke rubbed his forehead with his fingertips. "Are you saying the twins did this? Held you down and injected some shit into your vein?"

"Yeah." Penn leaned his head back against the wall and closed his eyes again.

"If that's a handprint, it's at the wrong angle for him to have done that to himself," I pointed out. "How else would they have known where he was?"

"But why tell us?" Asher asked.

"If I tried to make sense of what they do, I would end up with a raging headache," Zeke said darkly. "It could be something as simple as Reuben wanting to remind us he could reach us whenever he wants to. He could have called all of the newspapers in Mumbai, but he *generously* chose not to."

He rolled his eyes. "This bullshit though—this is a new low. Messing with someone's addiction just to make a point is all kinds of fucked up."

"He doesn't need the press to know," I said softly. "Just Jackson. Would Reuben know about the clause?"

"The twins might not, but Reuben definitely would," Zeke said. "He makes it his business to learn things like that. People's weaknesses, so he knows how to exploit them. Still, he must be getting desperate to try this."

He flopped down beside Penn. "Whatever we do, we have to make sure Jackson never finds out." He pinched the bridge of his nose. "Shit, I hate lying to him, but we don't have a choice."

"If we can get Penn back to the hotel and into his bed for a couple of hours, we should be all right," Asher said. "Between us, we can distract Jackson long enough."

"If anyone can do it, we can," I agreed. I didn't bother to hide how appalled I was that any member of Zeke's family, or anyone else for that matter, would do this to another person.

Penn might be an asshole at times, but he didn't deserve this. Honestly, right now he didn't look like an asshole. He looked normal and very, very vulnerable.

I hoped like hell this wouldn't put him back on the path he'd worked so hard to get off. As far as dick moves went, this was way worse than what

Vance did to me. Sticking poison into Penn's body... They could have killed him. What the hell were they thinking?

Were they thinking at all? The lengths these people would go to, to get their way was, frankly, terrifying. If they'd do this to Penn, they'd do anything to any of us.

Anything.

"Are you up to walking, Penny?" Asher asked. He stood and offered Penn his hand.

Penn looked confused for a moment, but took it. He was still clearly under the influence of whatever the twins gave him, but he wasn't as high as he was when Zeke pulled him off the railing. His eyes were no longer glazed, but he looked tired and not quite present.

While Asher pulled, Zeke gave Penn a shove to his feet that was so hard the keyboardist staggered a few steps forward. If it wasn't for Asher's steadying hand, he would have plopped down on the other side of the alley.

With Asher supporting him on one side and Zeke and I following behind, we started the slow walk out of the alley and up the street.

"If he didn't do this to himself, then would Jackson—" I started tentatively.

Zeke shook his head. "He wouldn't risk it. Penn under the influence was too unpredictable. He would still have to tell Levi. Whether or not Levi would understand... It's just not worth it."

"They understood gifts in boxes," I pointed out.

"Those were problems they could deal with," Zeke said. "This... this better not become a problem again. We have enough of those right now as it is."

"It won't be a problem," Asher said over his shoulder. "We'll take care of Penn, even if we have to handcuff ourselves to him for the rest of his life."

"Yeah," Zeke said vaguely. Apparently Asher had more faith in Penn and the band than Zeke did right now.

I slipped my hand into his. "What is it? Is this just about Penn?" I suspected he was troubled by something more.

"This shouldn't have happened," Zeke said after a moment. "It's my fault for letting him go by himself. I should have made sure someone went with him, or that he didn't go at all."

"You couldn't have stopped him," I pointed out. Penn was determined to go. So hell bent on it, he'd forgotten to take his phone.

"I could have tried," Zeke insisted. "I could have gone with him. Hell, I could have had a tracker inserted into his right butt cheek."

I snorted a laugh. "I don't think that would have done anything. He still would have gone by himself, because that was what he wanted to do. He is as stubborn as they come. Like you. Like me. No one expected the evil twins to pop up and do something...evil. How could any of us have predicted that?"

"We knew they were around somewhere." Zeke's mouth twisted to the side with annoyance. "They were probably waiting for one of us to be alone."

"Right," I agreed. "They could have given any of us whatever they gave Penn."

"PCP," Penn muttered. "That's what it feels like. Fucking bad shit."

As far as I could tell, it was all fucking bad shit, but I would take his word for it that this was worse than anything else.

"It might have just been bad luck for Penn that it was him," I said. I hated to think what would happen if they did it to me. Or any of the guys. Just because the twins promised not to rape me didn't mean they wouldn't do other things while I was stoned off my head. I didn't know what. I didn't *want* to know, frankly.

"Lucky it wasn't me; I really would have sung," Asher said. He'd moved away a little, so Penn was walking on his own, but kept a hand out to catch him if necessary.

Penn walked with a slight stagger every few steps, but under his own power at least. He looked like he was ready to fall face-first onto the pavement. That made me angrier than ever. If I saw the twins again, I'd kick them both in the groin while wearing heels. Imagining the pain on their faces was more satisfying than it probably should be, but I was okay with that.

"Small mercies," Zeke muttered. He flashed Asher a smile when the drummer glanced over his shoulder.

"Zeke would have tried to play the drums," Asher said.

Zeke let out a short laugh. "I know better than to try. Those things are harder than they look."

"I like hard," Asher said.

"Me too," I couldn't resist saying. I hoped sneaking Penn into the hotel wouldn't end up being hard.

That was the kind of hard I didn't like.

CHAPTER
TWELVE

ABBIE

IN THE END, no one paid us much attention. By that, I mean staff who work in hotels like the one we were staying in, know to look the other way, and not comment on what famous guests are up to. They might gossip later, but no one stopped to take any pictures or incriminating videos.

Zeke, who made a note of where the internal CCTV cameras were, led us through the foyer, making sure one of us was between them and Penn, even inside the elevator.

I found myself beside the keyboardist, our arms touching.

"Are you okay?" I looked up at his face. He looked like he'd been run over by half the traffic in Mumbai.

"What do you think?" He sounded more like himself. I wasn't sure if that was a good thing or not.

"I think maybe we should have let you fly," I retorted. It felt good to banter with him. I was grateful to the universe, fate or whatever that I could. No thanks to the twins, in spite of the fact we might not have found him in time if they hadn't told us where he was. If not for them, we wouldn't be in this predicament at all.

"You fucking would," he grunted. "I'm surprised you didn't push me."

"I thought about it, but Zeke got to you first." I shrugged.

"I thought about it too," Zeke said. "But that water looked dirty enough without you ending up in it as well. You would have polluted the crap out of it."

"Sounds about right," Penn said. He scrubbed his face with his hand.

"Zeke would have jumped in after you if you went in," Asher said. "And so would I."

"I would have looked after their shoes to make sure no one stole them," I said. "Assuming they had the sense to take them off before they jumped." Their shoes were expensive and would have weighed them down.

They both glanced at their feet.

"Priorities," Asher said. He looked back up and grinned. "You know what they say. Shoes before dudes."

Zeke looked at him sidelong. "Who says that?"

"I do now." Asher wiggled his eyebrows.

"That's the dumbest saying I've ever heard," Penn said from behind his hand.

"I bet it's not," Asher said. "There are some pretty dumb sayings out there."

Penn spread his fingers and frowned at Asher. "That's true." He closed his fingers again.

"I think we're doing a pretty good job of acting normal for the cameras," Asher said softly.

"It's not going to be normal in a minute," Penn said with a groan. "I need to get out of here. I'm gonna be sick."

We all took a step back away from him, which would have done absolutely nothing if he was sick. The elevator was tiny.

"Hold it in," Zeke ordered. "We're one floor from ours."

Penn lowered his hand. His face looked several shades paler than normal. "You know that's not how reflexes work, right?"

"Make it work," Zeke said in a growl. "Everyone is going to notice if you puke in here and on us. Let's not give Jackson a reason to request a drug test. Okay?"

"I'll do my best," Penn said. His face twisted in an uncomfortable grimace.

I put a hand on his arm.

Before I could say anything, he said, "If you're thinking of saying something sweet, don't. That really will make me sick."

"In that case, swallow it the fuck down or I'll kick your ass," I growled.

"That's better," he said. "It would be even better if you call me sir again."

Zeke and Asher looked at us both in surprise.

"What?" Penn asked. "Everyone has their thing. Why not me?"

Before anyone could say anything else, the elevator pinged and the doors drew open.

Saved by the bell.

We stepped out into the empty corridor and hurried to our room, all of us on alert for any sign of Jackson. Just to look at Penn, it was clear he was still affected by the drug. His face, his speech and the way he walked would all give him away.

Asher pulled out a key card and unlocked the door.

Penn was the first one inside, hurrying towards the toilet just in time to be sick.

"Is he okay?" Tully asked.

Zeke closed the door behind us. "He will be." He told the other three what happened in as few words as he could manage. They all looked predictably outraged.

"What the hell?" Landon asked. "Who does things like that?"

"People who had the needle broken off their moral compass," I said dryly.

I walked over to the bathroom door to make sure Penn wasn't going to pass out and drown in his own vomit. That would really top off an amazingly crappy afternoon.

He stood from where he'd knelt in front of the toilet and grabbed his toothbrush. He must have noticed my reflection in the mirror.

"What?" He started to vigorously brush his teeth.

"Just making sure you're all right," I said. "From one victim of the evil twins to another."

He spat. "No, I'm not fucking all right." He rinsed his mouth and put his toothbrush away. "I'm going to have a shower. You going to watch that too?"

"Is it an invitation—" I started to say.

I froze at the sound of knocking on the hotel room door. I twisted around to look.

It was Channing who peered through the peephole. "It's Jackson," he mouthed.

Shit.

I acted without thinking. I closed and locked the door behind me.

"I guess I am watching."

Penn's eyebrows twitched, but he quickly undressed and left his dirty, sweaty clothes on the bathroom floor. Evidently he didn't mind me staying around to look.

I didn't either. I especially didn't mind when he stepped under the water and it started to cascade down his body.

There were definitely worse sights in this world than hot, naked, wet rock stars.

"You could always join me," he offered.

I put up my hand and pressed my ear to the door. I heard the guys talking and laughing, but couldn't make out what was said. It didn't sound intense or like anyone was in trouble. Not yet at least.

"They're probably out there telling Jackson you and I are in here fucking," Penn said.

I turned back to face him. "Yes, chances are that's exactly what they're doing."

Whatever it took to throw off any potential suspicion. I hated having to treat Jackson this way after how well he looked after me and the rest of us. Even if Penn took the drug by himself, I wouldn't have wanted him to wear the punishment for a moment of weakness.

I was far from perfect. The mistakes I made almost cost me my career. I knew how he'd feel if the same happened to him. I would kick his ass into next week, and so would the rest of the guys, but we would have his back.

I tilted my head. "It's good to see you weren't adversely impacted for too long."

Steaming water rushed over his erect cock.

"You can't keep a good man down," he said smugly.

I snorted softly and closed the distance to the shower. I leaned in so he could hear me when I lowered my voice.

"You know you scared the crap out of us all, right?"

He leaned out until his nose was almost touching mine. "I wasn't fucking enjoying myself."

"You also know Zeke is not going to let you go anywhere by yourself ever again." I raised one eyebrow at him.

"He does the same to you and you don't seem to mind," he pointed out.

"Bad shit happens when we're alone," I said.

He smiled slowly. "Good shit happens when we're alone." He reached out with one dripping hand and tangled his fingers in the front of my shirt. He pulled me to him until his hot, wet lips found mine.

I stepped into the water, not caring that my clothes got drenched all the way through in seconds.

He pressed me against the side of the shower and kissed me like he was starving.

On some level, I suspected he realised if we hadn't reached him in time, he might be lying in that dirty water right now, not standing in hot, clean water. With hot, clean me.

He pulled back and his eyes me raked up and down . "That's a good look for you."

I glanced down at myself. Every centimetre of fabric was plastered tight to my body. It left absolutely nothing to the imagination.

"I seem to be overdressed for the occasion." With his help, I wriggled out of all the wet fabric and left it in a heap in the corner of the shower.

"Even better," he said. "Now," he tangled his fingers in my hair and pulled my head back far enough to kiss my neck, rough and with a grazing of teeth and stubble, "get on your knees and suck my cock." He let go of my hair and gave me a push down.

I didn't resist, but I did look up at him and smile. "Yes, sir."

He groaned. And once more when I circled his tip with my tongue. He gripped my hair again and held me in place while I teased him with my tongue on his cock and my hands massaging his hot, wet balls.

"Stop teasing and suck," he ordered.

"Yes, sir," I said, my words muffled by my tongue licking precum from the seam in his tip. I slipped my lips around him and took him in as deep as he could go. My eyes on his face, I started to suck.

He tilted his head back and groaned loud enough they undoubtedly heard it out in the room. At least we were being authentic. And having fun doing it.

"Good girl," he said breathlessly.

For some reason, his words made me hotter than the shower water. I wasn't really used to that kind of praise, but I liked it, especially in this context. If he wanted to be the dominant partner and me the good, obedient partner, then I was here for it. It was arousing as fuck.

I closed my eyes to keep out the water when it brushed across my face, and sucked like his cock was the most delicious thing I ever tasted. It was certainly right up there. At the same time, I kept a gentle pressure on his balls, caressing and massaging in time with my sucks.

"Fucking hell, woman, your mouth feels even better than I imagined," he ground out.

I opened one eye and looked up at him, wondering how many times he'd imagined this. More than once by the sound of it. I was glad I lived up to his expectations. There would be nothing worse than being told I give a bad blowjob. Although, according to most guys I knew, there was no such thing.

He gripped my hair tighter and I knew he was close to coming.

I opened the other eye and watched the ecstasy on his face. The shower and now this, seemed to have washed away most of the effects of the drug. He was certainly not as sluggish as I might have expected.

Anything but.

He looked down at me. "I'm going to come in your mouth."

I nodded as best I could with a mouthful of cock and sucked a little harder.

He grunted and his hips pumped him deeper and deeper into my mouth. Finally, he let out a low groan and squirted hot cum into my throat. He held me there and panted for a while until he caught his breath.

Finally, he managed to say, "Swallow it."

I was intending to do just that, but I pulled my head back from him, locked my eyes on his like I had when I sucked off Tully in Perth, and swallowed down every drop. It was tasty, mercifully with no hint of any strange, illicit substances.

"Good girl," he said. He reached out to pull me to my feet. "Let's get dry." He traced a finger lightly around one of my nipples, making me shiver. "It's time for bed."

"Do we still hate each other?" I asked as I stepped out of the shower and reached for a towel.

He smirked. "Definitely."

"Good." I started to dry myself. "I would hate to think anything's changed."

CHAPTER
THIRTEEN

PENN

"ARE YOU GETTING ENOUGH SLEEP?" Jackson squinted at me critically. He didn't look like he thought anything suspicious was up. If anything, he seemed amused, like Abbie wore me out. Which was accurate.

"Not today," I said lightly as I could. My head was pounding like a jackhammer. All I wanted to do was to curl up under a few blankets with a couple of painkillers and a cup of coffee.

The last thing I felt like doing was boarding a flight. The couple of hours of sleep I got after giving Abbie three orgasms wasn't nearly enough.

Thank fuck by the time we got out of the shower, Jackson was gone. By the sound of it, he made a quick escape so he didn't have to listen to any more groaning.

I have to give Abbie credit for saving my ass. And blowing me off. The woman's mouth was next level perfect. She put my imagination to shame.

Yeah, I sighed mentally. Fucking her was better than being on stage. I was in big damn trouble now. Was it healthy to trade one addiction for another? Probably not. Did I care? Nope. She was better than any drug.

"I'll sleep when we get to London," I said. "Or on the plane." Or both.

He gave me a hard, companionable clap on the arm, just missing the bruises and puncture wound covered by my shirt. "You do that." He got up from his seat and moved across the boarding lounge to where Violet sat with her guys.

"He's like a mother hen sometimes," Tully remarked. He slipped into the chair Jackson vacated and handed me a cup of coffee.

I nodded my thanks. "He got me worried he suspected something, but I think he just wanted to catch up on the gossip."

Tully chuckled. "There's plenty of that going around right now." He glanced over to where Abbie sat between Asher and Zeke, and smiled.

"You don't think this is weird at all?" I frowned lightly. "All of us guys and one woman?"

"Have you ever worried about what other people thought about you?" he countered. "Outside the band, I mean. I know you care what *we* think." He gave me a lopsided, ironic smile.

I snorted. "I don't give a shit what anyone thinks. This thing could get ugly if it falls apart. What if she decides she doesn't want one of us?"

"Are you scared she'll reject you?" He opened the lid of his coffee and took a sip.

"Hell no," I lied. "It's more likely I'll get sick of her. Then I'll have to put up with her being a pain in my ass while she hangs out with you clowns."

"You weren't complaining too loud when you had your face between her thighs," Tully said. "It's good to see, and hear, you making progress with each other."

"Pervert," I said. Of course, we were on my bed, in the middle of the room, in full view of everyone.

"Same to you," he said with no hint of shame. "You seem to enjoy watching."

"I do." I shrugged. It wasn't as much fun as taking part, but there were worse ways to pass the time. Like sitting in an airport, waiting for a plane, while your brain tried to burrow out of your skull.

I sipped my coffee and enjoyed the way it burned down my throat. "Have you thought about what comes next?"

He cocked his head at me. "You know me, I like to live in the moment. Let the universe figure out what's going to happen from here. Are you worried about something in particular?"

He sounded like my therapist.

"After the tour," I said. "When we all go back to our more or less individual lives." We spent a lot of time together, probably more than was healthy, but Abbie changed things. We were becoming more than a band, more than brothers. We were becoming a polyamorous group. All the guys with Abbie and then two pairings within that. Wherever we went from here, things would be different forever.

This could either be amazing or end up a massive shit storm.

Tully nodded. "Okay, yeah, I wonder about that too. Zeke and Asher were practically living together before. Landon and Channing too. Both of us live pretty close to them. Maybe nothing changes, and maybe we buy a mansion and all live in it together, I don't know."

He paused for a moment, then added, "I'm surprised you're the one asking these questions. You seemed to be the most resistant to…all of this. I know it's not really because you think Abbie is a pain in the ass." He looked at me over the rim of his cup.

"Are you sure about that?" I asked.

He grinned. "One hundred percent certain. She's the least pain in the ass person I've ever met."

"Except for me," I said jokingly.

He laughed. "Right, yes. Except for you." He rolled his eyes toward the ceiling and grinned.

"Sarcastic bastard," I muttered.

He looked unapologetic. "How are you feeling anyway?" He glanced over to make sure Jackson wasn't listening.

"Like shit," I said. "I can't believe I used to do that on purpose. It's not worth it." Then again, people always said that when they had a hangover yet they still drank alcohol. No one ever said humans made sense. Most of us were dumb as fuck.

"So, no chance of backsliding then?" he asked pointedly.

I honestly didn't know how to answer that. I didn't become an addict on purpose. No one did. At the time, I needed something to help me deal with life. I didn't realise how bad it got until I overdosed the second time. In retrospect, it was fucking obvious, but at the time it wasn't. It crept up on me like a spider, then bit me in the ass.

"I don't want to," I said finally, honestly. "It's the last thing I want. It's screwed up enough having to sneak around and lie to Jackson when I didn't do it to myself."

Stupid as it might sound, I didn't want to see the look of disappointment on our manager's face. If the guys were like brothers, then Jackson was like a father. More than my biological father was. Or like an uncle. Jackson gave a shit. He was a good guy. A better guy than me. Like that would be hard.

Tully nodded. "Good. If you ever feel like you might, you know you can talk to any of us, right? We'll be more than happy to hold you down and kick your ass if we need to."

"Thanks," I said awkwardly. "I think." Their support was a major factor in me getting through the last couple of years, but I wasn't sure if I could, or would go to them if the cravings got too bad. I was used to dealing with that shit by myself. Which was basically the problem in the first place. Me and my stupid, fucking pride.

"You're welcome. I mean it, bro. We're family. If we don't look after each other, who will?" He gulped down the last of his coffee.

"You're not gonna try to kiss me are you?" I asked. I held my arm up in front of my face.

"Nah, you're not my type," he said lightly. "I prefer cute, blond and female."

"I'm cute," I protested. "I'm definitely not the last two." Confident that I was safe from his lips, I lowered my arm.

He grinned and shook his head at me. "Yeah, you're adorable."

"Is that sarcasm again?" I asked. "Careful dude, you know how fragile my ego is."

He laughed so loudly I winced.

"Dude. Go easy on my brain."

"Sorry, dude, but your ego is not even close to being fragile." He looked like the least sorry person I ever saw. Asshole.

"Says you," I retorted. "I keep shit bottled up."

"Now that part is true," he agreed. "Except when you're writing songs. Then you let it out."

"Are you going to become a therapist when you give up guitar?" I asked dryly. "I feel like I'm being psychoanalysed right now."

"Maybe I will," he said with a shrug. "People are fascinating."

"That's a matter of opinion," I said. "I find most people annoying."

"I've noticed." He barely contained a smile.

"Is this where you tell me I should try to be more tolerant?" I asked. "Because fuck that. People should be less annoying." After a moment, and in a bid to change the subject, I asked, "How are you? These last couple of weeks have been a bit shit for both of us."

He sighed. "Yeah, I'm okay. My mother called while you were out. She's upset, but I got the feeling she had a fair idea of what happened. Not the exact details, but what he was up to."

"Not minding if you ended up collateral damage?" I asked. That was some crazy, messed up stuff right there. My parents sucked, but I didn't think they wanted me dead. Hell, even Zeke's family cared if he lived or died. Of course, he couldn't go back and play the dutiful son if he was a corpse.

Tully looked down at the floor. "Yeah. I think she was surprised I answered the phone."

That knocked the breath out of me for a moment. "Shit," I said softly, once I could form the words. "That's fucked up."

He looked back up and blinked away a glaze of tears. "It could be worse. I could actually *be* dead."

"With your ninja skills? No way," I said with certainty.

Zeke and Asher were kinda scary and had scary families, but if I was really going to be afraid of anyone, it would be Tully. If he wanted to, he could kill me and I would never see him coming. I tended to do my best to stay on his good side, just in case.

He smiled faintly. "Even with ninja skills, I can be outnumbered."

"Not with the rest of us around," I said. "Whatever happens, we've got your back just like you've got ours." I offered him a fist bump.

He accepted, then went in for a bro hug. "You guys are the best."

"Hell yeah we are," I agreed. "Don't you fucking forget it either." I patted his back awkwardly.

"How could I forget it? You're always reminding me," he teased.

"You guys are so cute together," Asher called out.

I turned to see him grinning at me and flipped him off. I think he lived in some shiny little fantasy world where we would all couple off like a little package, with Abbie right in the centre.

If I was into men, it might be someone like Tully, but I wasn't. Unfortunately for Asher's fantasy, I wasn't going to fuck him to tie up some kind of imaginary loose end.

"At least we can have a fine bromance," Tully said.

"I can work with that," I agreed. Tully was easy to like, compared to most people. That is, he was somewhat less annoying.

That bar was pretty low though.

"Would you believe me if I told you I was worried about you earlier?" he asked.

"Nope," I said lightly. "You know me, I always pop back up sooner or later."

I could easily have *not* popped back up. I didn't want to admit it, but I was worried about myself as well. I still was. There was only a very small chance anyone would want to pull any of us over for a drug test, but that shit would be in my system for days. The longer it was, the less chance people would believe the truth. The bruises on my elbow would fade. The needle site would become one of many similar scars. Just because it was the truth didn't mean anyone other than the guys would believe it.

I'd be figuratively holding my breath for the next couple of weeks at least. And thanking fuck I wasn't some kind of sports star. There was no way in hell I would avoid a drug test then.

"I'm going to the toilet then going to buy a couple of books," Channing declared.

I looked over as he stood. Landon was frowning at him. He looked comfortable stretched across a few chairs, reading the same book Tully read the other day. It must be good if he was into it too.

Zeke swivelled around in his seat. "Not by yourself, you're not," he said. "What did I say about that?"

"The bathroom is just there." Channing pointed to a door maybe ten metres away. "And the bookshop is right there. You'll be able to see me the whole time." Before Zeke or anyone else could protest, the saxophonist jumped up and hurried across the room to the toilet.

I exchanged glances with Tully and shrugged. Even after what happened to me, it was hard to keep us in line. Channing was right though, we would be able to see him and there were lots of people here in the airport.

What could go wrong?

Yeah, famous last words.

CHAPTER
FOURTEEN

ABBIE

"HEY." Violet dropped into the seat beside me when the guys went to stand at the window to admire the planes. "It's like they never grow up, isn't it?"

I watched as Asher and Landon talked enthusiastically about some kind of aircraft. They all looked the same to me. Two wings, engines and windows. As long as they could fly, I didn't really care.

Zeke stood near them, looking about as interested as I was. Tully was deep in conversation with Penn, who looked exhausted.

I surprised myself by how scared I was for the keyboardist, but he made up for it with his tongue on my clit. He knew how to play me perfectly there too.

I laughed softly. "I guess it is. From what I've heard, growing up is over-rated anyway."

"That's funny. I've heard the same thing." She sat back and crossed her legs. "How is it that we're on the same tour, but I hardly get a chance to talk to you? I've been meaning to see how you were after what happened in Perth. That shit got crazy, didn't it?"

"That's one word for it," I agreed. An understatement, but it didn't matter what you called it. We were lucky to get out of it in one piece.

"I'm okay, but thanks for asking." I gave her a quick hug. Honestly, I'd been meaning to check up on her too, but between the guys and work, I'd been too busy and distracted.

"Thank goodness things settled down after that." She pulled out a block of chocolate from her bag and opened it before offering some to me.

I broke off a row and took a bite out of it. "Thank you. Settled down, yeah."

I resisted the impulse to look over at Penn. Things had settled until today.

For half a moment, I thought maybe all the shit would leave us alone. Forever would be good.

I should have known they wouldn't, but no one saw what the twins did coming. Of course not, who would guess someone would do something so horrible, much less anticipate it? What's the expression? 'You can't make this shit up.'

"Just between you and me, I'm really looking forward to the European leg." She bit into her own row of chocolate. "I like that we get to travel in tour buses and cars instead of flying everywhere. And the scenery is just gorgeous." She drew the word out. "It's one of my favourite parts of the world."

"Mine too," I said. "Although, we'll see most of that out the bus window."

People thought touring was glamorous, but it was mostly a blur of locations and faces, and working. Not so much sightseeing and going to parties.

I wouldn't change it for anything.

"True, but looking out the window is pretty awesome," she said. "And meeting new people. I'm always up for doing that." She glanced around. "I've heard you're getting along well with all of the guys these days."

"Are you asking for gossip?" I teased.

She gave me a cagey look. "Maybe just a little bit." She held two fingers half a centimetre apart. "I mean, six guys is pretty impressive. I'm busy enough trying to keep up with four and we're not even, you know, fucking."

I felt my face heat a little. "I'm not sleeping with all of them." Yet.

Landon and Channing made it clear they wanted to, but the opportunity hadn't arisen. So to speak.

Of all the guys, I knew them the least. I'd have to remedy that at some point soon. Right now, I was still coming to terms with the fact Penn and I were finally starting to form a relationship. If you could call it that. I was ninety-nine percent certain he didn't hate me. I didn't hate him either, even when he was being an asshole.

"Oh?" Violet asked. She gave me a sidelong look. "What does that mean? Only one or two of them? Let me guess, Zeke and Asher?"

"Well, yes," I agreed slowly. "And Tully." After a moment I added, "And Penn."

Her eyes widened. "*Girl.*" She drew the word out slowly. "You're my hero. We need to find time to have drinks so you can tell me all the details."

"All the details?" I echoed.

"If I can't live the dream, at least I live it vicariously," she said.

She must not have noticed the way Blaise, Ryan, Sharkey and Danny looked at her. Even Blaise, who had a bigger chip on his shoulder than Penn, as far as I could tell, looked at her like he wanted to gobble her up. She could have them all eating out of the palm of her hand if she wanted to.

"I'd certainly like to find time to have drinks." I could agree to that much. I wasn't sure the guys would appreciate me sharing details of our sex lives, even with her. Okay, some of them wouldn't mind, but I might.

"There's something else I'd like to talk about," she said.

I frowned. "That sounds ominous."

She shrugged one shoulder and looked suspicious as fuck. "It might be."

She waited just long enough that I started to worry, then said, "I was hoping we could sing together. Actually, I was kinda hoping I could convince you to join Blazing Violet, but I don't think Wolf Venom is going to let you go any time soon."

My frantically racing heart slowed and I blinked. "Okay, I did not expect you to say that." She made my head spin. "You're right though, the guys probably wouldn't, unless you want to be their support act until the end of time." At least that way we could tour together.

She laughed. "Fuck no. Next tour, it's our time to shine. In the meantime, I'd love to do a collab. Maybe we could write a couple of songs together and throw them on our next album?"

"I'd love that," I said sincerely. I found myself looking at her through a haze of tears. I fanned my face.

"Sorry, it's been a while since anyone wanted to work with me." Levi hadn't really given the guys a choice. Before that, people didn't want to risk their reputations to work with me. Yeah, it sucked, but I got it. There's a fine line between doing anything for publicity, and tarnishing your image with someone the whole world seemed to love to hate.

"You know I'm me, right?" I pulled out a tissue and dabbed at my eyes before I ruined my mascara.

Violet snorted. "That's the best thing about you." She paused for a moment. "Look, I have to admit, when we heard you were touring with us, I thought it was a mistake. A publicity stunt." She winced apologetically.

"But then I met you, and I realised you're the bomb. The good kind of bomb," she added quickly. "You're one of the most genuine people I've met in this industry. Yeah, I know, it's a low bar sometimes. Watching you perform, I've learnt a lot from you. And behind the scenes too. I think we can make amazing music together."

"I think we can too," I agreed. "Thank you for being honest with me. I thought all of those things at first as well." It hadn't occurred to me to wonder how she and her band felt about me tagging along. Granted, I had a lot of other things on my mind at the time. It was nice to clear the air before it became a problem.

"You guys have all been so welcoming. It's made a world of difference to how this all could have gone." If they treated me like shit, like Penn did at first, the tour would have been a nightmare for all of us. Especially me.

"Most of the acts at Onyx Riot Records were in it for themselves, even when we collaborated. Everything had to be their way or not at all. They hated to share the spotlight with anyone. Except Vance." I grimaced. I didn't like saying his name. "Touring with him would definitely have sucked." Not in the good way.

"Pete encouraged us to work together, but you know how it is." I didn't like saying his name either. "Musos and their egos."

"Let me guess, someone always acted like they were the star and the other person was a backing vocalist?" Violet asked.

"Basically," I agreed. "The amount of backstabbing at that place was next-level ridiculous. I guess that will change now." Tully wasn't ready to think about it yet, but he'd do a great job running a label. And if he didn't want to, I wondered if he'd thought about merging Onyx Riot with White Wolf Records.

If anyone could handle the extra workload, it was Levi. Or rather, he'd know who to delegate it to. Jackson maybe.

"Anyway, I would love to collaborate with you," I said sincerely. "I can't wait. You, me and Candy in the recording studio sounds like the dream team." I couldn't suppress the excitement that passed through me. The experience would be incredible. Would I be able to convince Penn to play keyboard?

For the first time, I almost looked forward to the tour ending. Things would change, yeah, but now I had something amazing to look forward to.

I spent a lot of time listening to Violet's music over the last few weeks and just her suggestion of working together gave me so many ideas about how we could blend our styles.

Violet grinned. "Great. I can't wait either. They might as well book a spot at the number one on every chart in the world for at least a year."

I grinned. "They're going to have to mine for more platinum."

She laughed. "Yes! They definitely will. Multi-multi-multi-platinum. Were all going to need really strong walls in our houses to hold up the plaques."

"I'm going to need a house," I said.

My bank account was a lot healthier now than it was the night Zeke and I met. I could almost afford to buy somewhere decent now. But how would that work? Would I invite the guys over for a night each? No, that wouldn't work for Landon and Channing. I wasn't sure it would work for Zeke and Asher either. I could give them two nights each, but then the other guys might be pissed.

I suspected the whole world wouldn't agree if I suggested we went to eight day weeks, just for my convenience.

Although, I had a compelling reason for it. Right?

Violet sat up a little higher in her chair. "I'm happy to help you find a place if you need it." She slumped back down. "But I guess the guys would want to do that too."

"I could use all the help I could get," I said firmly and with sincerity. "I'd probably choose a place that's about to fall down around my ears because I don't know what to look for. Or I'd fall in love with how pretty the tiles in the bathroom are, and not notice how dysfunctional the kitchen is."

"A functional kitchen is only useful if you actually cook," Violet pointed out.

I grinned. "That's true. Still though, I might learn how at some point. Or I could hire a cook. It would suck if they told me they weren't going to work for me because my kitchen was shit." It felt nice to have a silly conversation like this with another woman. Or anyone, really. Everything got so intense so often lately.

Death and chaos tended to have that effect on people.

"If they won't cook for you, then they'll have to take you out to dinner," she reasoned. "But if you insist, I'll make sure a functional kitchen is on the list. Between all of us, we'll find the perfect place for you. How many bedrooms do you need? I'm thinking—four?" She gave me a sly smile. "Or one really big one?"

I started to answer, but then had to stop and say, "I'll have to think about that. There's a lot of conversations I have to have and things I need to work out."

Things that got more complicated the more I thought about them. At some point, the guys and I would have to all sit down and talk. I had no idea what they wanted and they probably had no idea what I wanted either.

I mean, I didn't know what I wanted. No, that's not true. I knew what I wanted but it might not be what the guys wanted. I hoped like hell we could figure it out so we were all happy. Was that too much to ask?

I didn't think it was. After everything we went through, we deserved some peace and contentment. And a huge soundproof room where we could practice together. And a cuddle puddle where we could watch movies. And—

Yeah, my dreams were bigger than my bank balance could manage right now. I might have to dial it back a bit. Or a lot. Maybe forget the cuddle puddle. Although, a home recording studio would be pretty fucking cool.

Violet nodded. "You know where to find me when you need someone to talk to and help with that. And anything really. Us girls have to stick together after all, right?" She offered me her pinky finger, which I took with mine and shook it.

"I don't think I've done that since I was about seven," I said with a laugh.

"You need to live a little," she said. "Everyone should pinky shake at least once a week."

"What was I thinking?" I threw up my hands. "Clearly I've wasted all of those years."

Violet giggled. "It sounds like we have some catching up to do then. When we get to London, I'm buying us all water pistols. Then I'm going to drag you all out somewhere for a water fight."

"If you're not careful, I might learn to have fun," I warned her.

"You should definitely have fun," she said. "We all should."

She opened her mouth to add something, but whatever she was going to say was interrupted by a man's shout of alarm.

I shot up in my seat. What the fuck?

I exchanged glances with Penn. He looked about ready to crap his pants.

A couple of security guards came running from some other part of the airport. Instead of stopping at us to grab Penn, they bolted past us and skidded into the men's toilets.

"I have a feeling they didn't just need to pee," Violet said.

The crowd outside the facility was growing. Murmurs passed through them, both worried and horrified. What the hell happened in there?

I caught a glimpse of Zeke, his expression intense, eyes scanning the area. I didn't need him to tell me what he was looking for, or who.

Where the hell was Channing?

CHAPTER
FIFTEEN

ABBIE

"FUCKING HELL," I muttered.

I pushed myself up out of my seat and stepped over to Zeke's side. "Do you think—"

He shook his head and spoke with a tightly controlled voice. "I don't want to think it, I need to go and look."

The security guards were trying to move people on from the area.

"It's too late for an ambulance," one of them said, his expression grim.

I put a hand over my mouth. "Oh God," I whispered softly.

If something bad happened to Channing… I couldn't finish that thought. Didn't want to. Like Zeke, I had to see for myself. "I'll come with you."

"Me too," Landon said. He looked terrified, his face pale. He and Channing were practically joined at the hip. If anything happened to him the one time they weren't…

Zeke looked at us both, then nodded. "Fine, but stay close to me. And keep an eye out for identical felons."

Any other time, I would have laughed at his description of his brothers, but there was nothing funny about this.

My heart heavy, palms sweaty, I walked across the boarding lounge with a gorgeous but scared rock star on either side of me. It took me a couple of moments to realise Asher, Tully and Penn weren't far behind.

"I'm sorry, you can't go in there," one of the security guards said.

Zeke looked like he was ready to shove the man out of the way. "One of our party is missing. We heard something bad happened to someone in there and we're worried it was him." I would have been convinced if I was one of the guards. Zeke was charismatic, even when times were desperate, like now.

The security guard must have had a stone cold heart, because he wasn't budging. "I'm sorry, sir, you'll have to wait for the ambulance to arrive." Judging by his composed tone, he was used to dealing with people like us, and situations like this. Emergencies in general, not dead bodies in particular, I hoped.

"Is someone helping him?" Zeke demanded. His face was red, eyes full of barely contained frustration. He'd looked less angry when he pinned his brother, Caleb, to the wall in Melbourne. He was clearly struggling to keep from lashing out.

The other guard looked apologetic, but unmoved. "I'm sorry, sir, he's beyond help." He didn't elaborate. He didn't need to. His simple words told us everything we needed to know.

My heart sank. For the second time in half an hour, I blinked back tears. This was seventeen kinds of screwed up. What the hell happened in there? I kept expecting the evil twins to appear and have a chuckle over their latest escapade. If they did, the next ones dead around here would be them.

"Fuck," Landon said softly. "I should have gone with him. Why didn't I?" He let out a whimpering, moaning breath.

I laced my fingers through his and lowered my head to his chest. I felt his heart racing.

Or breaking.

"I'm sorry, sir," the first guard said again. "I have to ask you to step back, away."

Reluctantly, Zeke waved us back a couple of steps. He looked like he was ready to lose his shit. Landon too. The rest of the guys looked gutted and lost. The guards could tell us to move away all they wanted. We couldn't, wouldn't, go too far, not until we knew for certain.

I sniffled and held back tears.

"You guys look like you're at a funeral," Channing said. He approached us, a smile on his face, a pile of books under one arm and a chocolate bar in his opposite hand. "What's going on?"

With a choking sob, Landon threw his arms around him. "Thank fuck. We thought you were dead."

Channing had to tighten his grip on his books to stop from dropping them, but he managed to get his other arm around Landon.

"Why would you think that? I told you I was at the bookshop. I've basically kept you guys in sight the entire time."

"We couldn't see you," Zeke growled, but he patted Channing on the back. "I watched you go into the toilet, but I didn't see you leave."

"You were looking out the window at planes." Channing shrugged. "I was fine."

"This time you were," Landon said. "I shouldn't have let you go by your-self." He looked miserable.

I doubted he'd ever let Channing out of his sight again.

"Hey," Channing said gently, "we talked about this. We agreed that five or ten minutes apart once in a while wouldn't hurt. I'm fine, you're fine...and you still haven't told me what's going on out here."

Landon quickly filled him in.

"We're all accounted for," Zeke said. "So is Violet and her guys."

"I haven't seen Jackson for a while," I pointed out softly.

Zeke froze, but then nodded tightly. "I'll try him. If it's him in there, we'll hear his phone ring."

He pulled out his and tapped on the screen.

I held my breath and waited.

No ringing came from inside the men's room. Just a voice from inside Zeke's phone.

He put it to his ear. "Where are you?" He listened and nodded. "Okay, just checking. No, nothing. Everything is fine. Yep, see you in a minute."

He mashed his finger on the screen. "Jackson is getting a sandwich."

"Great," I said, my tone hollow. Not so great for the family of whoever actually died.

"Yeah. We should go and sit down again. The plane should be ready to board soon."

It couldn't leave soon enough as far as I was concerned. I loved India, but enough bad things had happened today that I just wanted to get out of here.

This was getting to be a bad habit. Needing to get out of a country, or off a continent before something else happened. I wasn't looking forward to leaving Europe at the end of that leg.

"So you were worried about me, huh?" Channing seemed to have surrendered the other half of his chocolate bar to Landon and was now teasing him as they walked back to the chairs, their arms around each other.

"They're cute, aren't they?" Asher asked. He wound his arms around me and I stepped in closer to absorb his warmth and comfort.

"Very cute," I agreed. "You're all cute."

"Especially me," Penn said as he walked past us and flopped back into a chair.

"Especially all of you," I said firmly.

"But really especially, especially me," Tully said with a grin.

I shook my head at him. "Don't make me change my mind."

His smile softened. "As if you would."

With Asher holding me firmly to keep me from falling, I leaned over to kiss Tully lightly on the mouth. "Don't tempt me."

"I will tempt you every chance I get," the guitarist said unapologetically. "As will the rest of us."

"One hundred percent accurate." Asher pulled me back and slanted his mouth across mine for a tender, but heated kiss.

"They aren't wrong," Zeke said.

"Nope, they aren't," Penn said, his eyes on his phone screen. "We'd all fuck you right now if we could."

That statement made me feel as hot as hell all over. Any more of that and I would have to change my panties before I boarded the flight.

"Fact," Asher said. "If the men's toilet wasn't out of commission..."

I wrinkled my nose. "Yeah, hard pass on doing anything in there right now." I looked over to see a couple of ambulance officers arrive, pushing a gurney. They didn't look like they were in any particular hurry. I supposed they wouldn't be if, as the security guards said, it was too late.

They wheeled the gurney past the security guards and disappeared.

"Rather them than me," I whispered.

Asher shrugged. "I hate to say it, but when you've seen a few dead bodies, it stops bothering you after a while. They've probably seen hundreds of them."

I grimaced. He was probably right, which didn't make me feel any better. It wasn't something I wanted to become desensitised to.

I turned around in Asher's arms, so my back was pressed against his chest. I watched the crowds go by.

Some of them hesitated and stared at us. A few gave me envious looks. Others just got excited to see Wolf Venom in person in the airport. A few took photos before moving on.

I saw Jackson coming back from the kiosk, sandwich in hand, coffee in the other. I was pretty sure he drank more coffee than the rest of us combined.

He started towards us when the ambulance officers pushed the gurney out of the men's room. One of them was just pulling the sheet over the poor victim's face and head.

Jackson stopped mid-step, frozen, and stared. I could almost feel the heart pounding in his chest.

I frowned. "What the fuck?" Whatever it was, he looked as rattled as hell. It wasn't one of us. Maybe it was an evil twin. Could we be that lucky?

He shook his head and hurried over to us, the stunned expression on his face not changing.

"What is it?" I asked when he got close enough. "You look like you saw a ghost."

It took him a moment to respond. "It was Pete Rossi," he said in a hoarse whisper.

My heart stopped. "What the hell? I thought you just said..." I must be hearing things. Surely he'd only caught a quick glimpse?

"I did," he said. "The former owner of your old label. From the look of it, he hit his head." Jackson looked slightly pale. At least he wasn't running to vomit. Yet.

If it wasn't for Asher holding me, I would have hit the floor. I shouldn't have been surprised. I really shouldn't. Pete was the last in the line of people who screwed me over before I met the guys. If whoever killed them was going to go after anyone else, Pete was an obvious choice.

"Are you sure?" I said. My head spun.

"Yeah, it was definitely him," Jackson said regretfully. "I've met him several times before."

"Holy shit," I breathed. Was this really happening or was it yet another bizarre nightmare? I forced a few breaths in and out and tried to clear my head.

"I presume they think it was an accident," Asher said lightly. He didn't sound anywhere near as shocked as I felt.

"Accident, my ass," Zeke said. "At least this time there's no chance of them trying to pin it on us." He rubbed a hand over the back of his head. "I hope."

"It's a little cleaner than a gift in a box," Asher agreed. "And the local authorities get to do the cleanup instead of us." He sounded very cheerful about that.

For some reason, that irritated the shit out of me.

"Yeah, those are the important things," I said sarcastically. "Let's not worry about the fact he's dead." I stepped out of the circle of his arms and turned to glare at him.

"Abbie," Zeke said softly. "You can't be freaking out right now. Freak out later, when we're alone. If you do it here, people will notice."

I wanted to shout at him but he was right. At some point, people were going to realise Pete and I were in the airport at the same time and wonder at the coincidence. Why was he here anyway? Had he followed me?

That was a chilling, sickening thought.

I closed my eyes and sucked in a deep breath. "Fine, but I will freak out later."

"Noted." Asher drew me back to him again and tucked me against him, under his chin. "We'll freak out with you, if you like. Or hold your hand. Whatever you need."

"Thanks." My voice was muffled by his shirt and pecs. "I'll think about that."

He traced circles around my back with his hand, soothing me like I was a child.

"There has to be some explanation for why he was here, and what happened," Tully reasoned.

Zeke shrugged. "He was obsessed with Abbie. Wanted her back. Followed her around Asia and met his end with a nasty accident. If I had to guess, I'd say he has a ticket to London on his phone. He might have been looking for an opportunity to get her alone, but never found one. He seemed like the persistent kind."

I reluctantly drew my head back from Asher's chest. "He was. I just... I was starting to think this shit had stopped. I hoped it had."

Asher gave me a squeeze and nuzzled his face into my hair. "Maybe it has now. There's no one else left that's pissed you off. Except..." He lifted his head and looked straight at Zeke.

"The evil twins," Zeke finished for him.

CHAPTER
SIXTEEN

PENN

"HELLO, LONDON!" Zeke said as he stepped from the luggage carousel to the main entrance area of Heathrow airport. He strutted in front of us like he was on stage.

People stopped to stare, and a few even clapped.

"Don't encourage him," I muttered. I caught Tully's gaze and rolled my eyes toward the ceiling.

Tully grinned. "He just really, really likes London."

"Yeah, who the fuck doesn't? He doesn't need to announce it to the world." I stopped to look back at two gorgeous women who were staring at me unashamedly.

"Oh my God, he's even better looking in person," one of them said.

I responded with my trademark smirk and kept walking. Yeah, okay, maybe London was all right. At least the women here had good taste.

Those two anyway. Plenty of them were staring at the other guys instead. And just as many were staring at Abbie, although it was mostly guys doing that. As for the beautiful woman herself, she walked in the middle of us like a queen, Zeke in front of her, Asher behind. Tully and I were on one side, Channing and Landon on the other.

She had her chin raised like she didn't give a fuck if anyone was looking at her not. I wasn't fooled though. I knew that little twitch in the side of her mouth, the way her eyes blinked a little faster. She liked the spotlight as much as the rest of us, but the spotlight had screwed her over and left her uneasy at times. It was bullshit. She should bask in it like the rest of us did. If anyone said anything bad about her, I might punch the shit out of them.

After sleeping most of the way here, I was feeling a lot better. My head still ached slightly, but it was a tolerable level. I had enough energy for a good right hook.

"I think there's a couple of people in London who didn't know Wolf Venom have arrived," Jackson remarked as we headed to the sliding glass doors at the front.

"Isn't it your job to make sure everyone knows we're here?" I asked.

He looked at me sidelong. "Yes, well." He cleared his throat. "The last couple of people who didn't know, now do, thanks to Zeke."

"Right, got it," I said.

We stepped out of the front doors into a media shit storm. For maybe a fraction of a millisecond I thought they were there for all of us, as they should be.

That was until they started to shout, "Abbie! Abbie! Did you know your former lover was found dead a few hours ago? Did you see him in Mumbai airport?"

Fuck.

She froze like a groupie caught with a mouthful of cock.

"I beg your pardon?" she asked the closest member of the press. In this case, a man I suspected was from a trashy magazine. "Vance died weeks ago."

And the acting award goes to Abbie Hart. She looked genuinely confused.

Frankly, I suspected she didn't fully believe Pete was dead until now. Jackson *had* only caught a quick glance. He could easily have been wrong about who it was.

Just quietly, I was glad he was right. This Pete guy sounded like a total prick, a shitty businessman and an even worse lover. Not to mention potentially stalking Abbie. If it wasn't him, it would have been some random dude who might have been a decent human being. If any of those existed. Naw, better that it was Pete.

"Not your former husband," the journalist, if you could call him that, said patiently. He gave them the impression he thought she was stupid. Asshole. "Your former lover. Pietro Rossi."

Abbie blinked even more rapidly than before. "Pete is dead? How? What the heck happened? I had no idea. Are you sure?" Her luscious lips dropped apart in shock.

Tully and I stepped in to grab her when she started to look like she might faint. She was turning it on for the cameras now.

"Yes, I'm sure," the sleazeball journalist said. "It's been announced officially."

Abbie shook her head and leaned against me, her face on my chest. Her own ample chest heaved as she drew in several thick breaths.

"So it's just a coincidence he died in the airport at the same time you were there?" someone else called out.

"Okay, enough," Jackson said. "We're getting out of here." He bulldozed his way through the press pack to the van, which was waiting for us. He slid the door open and waved us inside.

Zeke climbed in first, then turned to help Abbie before the rest of us followed.

"Fucking vultures," I said as I was getting in. I made sure to be loud enough so they could hear me. Lowlife, bottom feeding, blood sucking leeches.

Yeah, I really hate the tabloid press. I wished they'd leave us alone and let us live our lives.

Instead, they excuse themselves by saying they're just doing their jobs, but it's a shit job. They should do something more useful with their time than follow celebrities around like a pack of hungry dogs. Like inventing a fitted sheet that folds up the way it came out of the packet. How hard could that be?

"Tell them how you really feel, Penny," Asher said. He patted me on the shoulder as I slipped into the seat beside him.

I shrugged. "Okay." I raised two fingers to the press as the van pulled away from the curb. "Is that eloquent enough for you?"

Jackson scrubbed his face with his hand. "You should probably not antagonise them like that."

"How would you like me to antagonise them, then?" I put my hands on the button of my jeans as though I was just about to pull them down and moon everyone out the window.

"How about not at all?" Jackson suggested. "I know that doesn't sound like much fun, but they did confirm what I saw."

"Yeah." That brought me back to earth.

I looked over to Abbie, who sat opposite me. She was looking out the window with eyes as glazed as mine must have been when I tried to climb up on that bridge railing. "You okay?"

It took a moment for her gaze to turn to me. "I don't know," she said softly. "I think I'd convinced myself it wasn't him after all. Or that maybe he was alive and the ambulance guys got it wrong. Or something."

I nodded and leaned over to put my hand on hers. "I know it's fucked up, but we'll get through it."

She nodded. "I know we will, it's a lot to deal with. After..." Her eyes flicked to Jackson and back to me. "After everything that's happened, I wish it would stop. You know?"

Yes, I sure did know.

"Yeah," I said simply. "Hopefully it's over now." Whatever happened to all the people who died, they were all easier targets than Zeke's evil twin brothers. Those two little cockroaches would be a lot harder to kill, even if someone was willing to piss Reuben off by trying. Even I wasn't dumb enough to want to get on the wrong side of big brother Brantley. He was a mean ass dude.

"For what it's worth," Tully said, his eyes on his phone screen, "while we were in the air, the police looked into what happened to Pete. They've ruled it an accident." He raised his eyebrows and looked up at Abbie.

"What?" she asked.

"He had a ticket to London and then one to every other city on the tour," Tully read from his screen. "And a bunch of photos of Abbie on his phone. Some from different locations in Asia, including one taken inside the airport. According to this, they are looking into his involvement with the death of Vance, Calista and Poppy Newton. Sounds like you had an obsessed fan. Apparently they believe he slipped on a puddle of water and hit his head on the sink. Nothing more than that."

"Fuck," she said softly. "He was following me around?"

"Can you blame him?" Asher asked lightly. "Personally, I would follow you anywhere."

I gave him a funny look. "Dude, do you realise how fucked up that sounds?"

He shrugged. "I didn't mean it in a weird way."

"That was how it sounded," I said.

"It was a bit weird, babe," Zeke told him.

"I would follow you too, babe," Asher told him.

They shared a quick kiss while I made gagging sounds at them.

"These guys stalking you aside," Tully said slowly. "I'm glad we made sure you're not alone for the last while. If he was the one doing the killings, then who knows what he might have done to you?" Even with the seatbelt on, he managed to get his arm around her. She leaned into him in a way that made me slightly envious of him.

Only slightly though, because I am obviously better looking and taller than him anyway. And I can play his guitar at least as well as he can.

Abbie shuddered. "I guess it's true what they say, you never really know someone, but he seemed so normal. Although..."

"Although what?" Jackson prompted.

"Even before he signed me with his label, he made no secret of the fact he wanted to sleep with me," she said. "Sometimes I wonder if that was why he signed me at all."

"That's bullshit," I snapped. Even when he was dead, the motherfucker was making her feel bad about herself. He was a piece of shit, dead or alive.

"I'm with Penn on this one," Zeke said. "He signed you because you're talented. End of story." He gave her a look as though daring her to argue.

"Zeke and Penn are right," Channing said. "And I don't say that very often. Especially that both of them are right. It's one or the other..." He cleared his throat. "Anyway, you are as talented as the rest of us. It's not okay that he was sleazy and made you feel that way."

"Right," Asher agreed. "If he wasn't dead, I would punch him."

"I would punch him anyway," I said. "Dead or not."

They all looked at me funny, but I meant it. If anyone laid a hand on Abbie, I would hurt them, even if they were dead. Okay, I didn't give a shit if that made no sense. It was what it was.

"It's probably lucky you didn't get the chance," Jackson said. "I have a funny feeling Levi wouldn't take it very well. I know I wouldn't."

"Not to mention those security guards would have been pissed," Asher said. "Shit would have gotten ugly." He nodded like he was suddenly the wise guy of the group. Wise ass, more like it.

"It wouldn't have helped anything," Abbie said. "Except you getting arrested."

She didn't need to add anything about me getting drug tested, I saw it in her eyes, and knew it myself anyway.

"I'm starting to think I should put you all on one, long leash," Jackson said.

"Did you just suggest tying us all up?" Asher asked. "Because I might just be here for that." He grinned and wriggled his eyebrows.

"TMI," I said.

Jackson leaned forward, pinched the bridge of his nose and shook his head. "Remind me again why I wanted to manage you guys?"

"Money?" Landon suggested.

"Our good looks?" Channing said.

"Our personalities?" Zeke said. "Except Penn, who doesn't have one." He grinned at me teasingly.

"Fuck off," I said. "At least my personality isn't over the top with glitter on the side."

"That pretty much sums up the rest of us," Asher said. "The glitter part in particular."

"Only you guys would take an insult as a compliment," I said.

"That's not true," Tully said. "You do the same thing."

"I feel so attacked right now," I said with a dramatic sigh.

"Poor baby." Abbie leaned over to pat my knee.

I grimaced. "You didn't call me asshole." I didn't want to be called baby. At least, not in that context. I was supposed to be a badass rock star dude, not a marshmallow.

Asher leaned over and patted my other knee. "Poor asshole."

I grunted. "That's better. Don't forget it and start thinking I'm nice or some shit."

"Never," Asher said. The smile he gave me said otherwise.

Fuck, I was going to have to work harder or I would lose my asshole card.

CHAPTER
SEVENTEEN

ABBIE

THE MEDIA CONTINGENT around the hotel was even bigger than the one at the airport.

Jackson gestured for the driver to wait and let the van carrying Violet and her guys pass us. All the while, he was tapping on the screen of his phone, his brow creased in a frown.

"I'm going to have to talk to them, aren't I?" I pressed myself down as low as I could and let the wall of muscle that was Wolf Venom be my shield. I didn't want to hide behind them, but they were all drawing themselves up taller and sitting around in their seats so I couldn't be seen anyway.

"Absolutely not," Jackson replied. "Levi has his assistant putting together a statement." He read off his phone screen. "You're horrified to learn that your former lover was following you. You're shocked that he might have played a role in the deaths of several people. Your condolences go out to their families. You'd like it if you could process all of this in private and focus on the continuing tour. Which you have no intention of withdrawing from. You urge people to seek help for any mental illnesses."

"That sounds accurate," I said. "Nothing about his death?"

"We could say you're saddened by it, but that contradicts your response to his potentially being a stalker," Jackson said. "We can't exactly say you're glad he's dead because you're safe now. That wouldn't go down very well."

I snorted softly. "Not so much." I wasn't sure how I felt about him being dead but I couldn't say I was happy about it. Was I sad? Not exactly. Mostly, I was conflicted because, in spite of the things he did to me, I thought he was a decent human being. Clearly that was all wrong.

"This isn't a gag order," Jackson said. "Levi won't ban you from speaking to them if you want to, but he'd prefer you didn't. As far as he is concerned, the matter is closed. You need to concentrate on work now. He's going to fly out in the next day or so to catch up with us. Read—check up on you and make sure you're okay. All of you."

I caught Zeke glancing at Penn and hoped Jackson didn't notice.

"All of us?" Zeke asked.

"If Pete was killing people, any one of you could have been next," Jackson pointed out. "Or me." He glanced around the van. "I see by the looks on your faces that hadn't occurred to any of you."

Penn grunted. "We're all harder to kill than that."

I looked over to see him gazing out the window. It didn't take a genius to understand what he was thinking. If Pete happened to see him when he was high, he would have been easier to kill.

Zeke cleared his throat. "Lucky for us, we're all fine. I suppose there's no point in telling Levi not to come out here?"

"Levi will travel to Europe using any excuse he gets," Jackson said.

"So it's not just about us," Tully said.

"I can neither confirm nor deny." Jackson smiled slightly.

We drove past Violet's van, which was parked in front of the hotel. She and the guys were getting out and greeting the press.

At a brief glance, the journalists weren't interested in Blazing Violet. They waved at our van as we slid past, but we were driven around the back and let into a gated area. The gate was shut and locked behind us.

"It's nice of Violet to run interference for us," Asher said. "We owe them one after that."

"Yeah, we do." I picked up my bag from where it lay at my feet, and pulled out my sunglasses. They wouldn't do anything to disguise me, but they'd reduce the value of any photos the press took through the gate. That wouldn't deter them, but I was fucked if I was letting them get rich from this.

Jackson opened the door of the van and I was herded out in the middle of the guys. I lifted my chin and pretended nothing was amiss, while trying to ignore the shouts of the journalists who had run around the back to see us there.

"Fucking vultures," Penn muttered. This time, he didn't stick his fingers up at them, and he didn't moon them either. He ignored them the same as the rest of us.

"Can we throw our suitcases at them?" Asher asked jokingly.

"I'd like to see you throw one over that fence," Zeke remarked. "Think you can do it? A full suitcase."

Asher turned to appraise the fence in question. "Absolutely, but it might damage the suitcase."

"There is no way in fuck you could get a suitcase over that fence," Penn said scathingly. "And you say I'm full of shit."

Thankfully several hotel staff came out to take our suitcases inside for us, before anyone tried throwing any of them. None of the staff gave us more than a brief glance. No doubt they were used to celebrities staying there and having to deal with crap from the press.

"I could, but I'm not going to try," Asher said. "Although, Penn's suitcase is a good size." He eyed it as a man dressed in the hotel uniform rolled it past.

"Touch it and I'll throw *you* over the fence," Penn growled.

"Hands up who wants to see Penn try that." Landon raised his hand.

Asher batted it back down. "Dude, that wouldn't end well for anyone. Mostly Penn, because he'd hurt himself trying to lift me up."

"Unlike Asher, I'm not dumb enough to try something like that," Penn scoffed.

I turned and shook my head at them. I was going to suggest they be nice to each other, but then realised banter was their attempt to take my mind off things. All of our minds. Unfortunately, it was going to take a lot more than that.

We hurried inside and followed Jackson and a concierge to the elevator and up to our rooms. In this case, two adjoining rooms with a door connecting them. A door that would probably stay open most of the time. None of them seemed to like to take their eyes off me for too long. Would that change now Pete was dead?

Presumably not, especially while the evil twins were still a threat.

"I'll leave you to it for a while," Jackson said. "I need to get Blazing Violet settled and make sure all the tour staff got into the country. You're on your own for the rest of the day. I suggest ordering in for meals and alcohol. And don't trash the room." He said that last with a smile.

"When have we ever trashed a room?" Asher asked with mock hurt.

"Never, but there's a first time for everything." Jackson pointed two fingers at his eyes, then pointed them at Asher before he stepped out the door and closed it behind him.

"Talk about being attacked," Asher complained.

I slipped off my sunglasses and shoved them back in my bag. The hotel rooms were big and warm with rich colours and opulent furniture. Both of them had a king-sized bed and two singles. Both of the bathrooms were huge, and each had a jetted tub. Even the minibar was fully stocked with alcohol and snacks.

I'd forgotten what staying in places like this was like. Up until now, the accommodations had been more modest, which was fine with me. For the most part, they were nothing more than a place to sleep.

"This will pass over." Zeke stepped up behind me. He placed his hands on my shoulders and started to massage lightly.

I dropped my chin to my chest and sighed.

"Why is it always something? Just when I think we might be able to catch our breath, something else happens. When do we get a break?"

"Right now," he said firmly. "We can lock ourselves away in here and forget the rest of the world exists."

Asher moved to stand in front of me and took my hands in his. "Except when we open the door to people delivering food and alcohol."

"Except for then," Zeke agreed. "But someone else can open the door." He slid his hands from my shoulders, down my sides to my hips. "We can get busy in other ways."

"Yes we can," Asher agreed. He drew us both into the second room and Zeke closed the door behind us.

"Oh? Like what?" I asked teasingly. As if I didn't know exactly what was going on.

"Like this." Asher pulled me to him, tilted his head and pressed his mouth to mine. His stubble tickled my lips and chin, but I liked the way it felt.

I kissed him back, hungry not just to forget the world, but to be touched and to touch them. I pressed the tip of my tongue to his lips and inside his mouth when he opened it to me. He tasted like the cola he drank on the plane, with a hint of salt I guessed came from the tiny bag of peanuts. He'd complained they weren't big enough and ate them in a mouthful or two.

Zeke slipped his hands up the back of my shirt and unhooked my bra. The cups dropped, letting my breasts fall free under the fabric of my shirt.

The sudden rush of cool air made me shiver and my nipples hardened into points.

Zeke's arms snaked around me, rucking my shirt up past my navel. He cupped my breasts and rolled my nipples between his thumbs and forefingers.

My knees already wanted to give way at the hot heat that coursed through my body.

Asher's lips left mine and he started to nibble my neck and my throat.

"Abbie," he said softly. "I love you."

A flutter of butterflies did a dance around my stomach. Had I heard him right?

Without hesitation, I whispered back, "I love you too."

Asher pulled back and smiled at me, then over my shoulder. "Zeke, I love you."

Zeke leaned around me to kiss him. "I love you too, babe." He kissed me next. "I love you."

Even though we'd said it to each other before, this was the first time saying it in front of someone else. Of all people, Asher should be included in moments like this.

"I love you," I replied.

"Perfect." He gripped the hem of my shirt and pulled it up over my head. My bra quickly followed, along with the rest of my clothes.

And then all of theirs.

I would never get tired of seeing their bodies. Firm chests, rock hard abs, the Vs of their hips, broad shoulders, strong, veiny arms, big hands with long, thick fingers. They looked like gorgeous statues, with tattoos to add to the chiselled, perfect artistry.

And here I was, right in the middle. For the millionth time I wondered how I got so lucky.

Between both of these rock gods, they manoeuvred me over to the bed. They lay me down so I was stretched out, on my back, on Asher's firm chest and stomach.

Asher wound his arms around me to hold me in place and take his turn working my nipples.

Zeke bent my knees and placed each of my feet to the side of Asher's legs, opening me up to him. He propped himself on one elbow so he wasn't resting too much weight on Asher, and lowered his mouth down between my thighs.

His eyes on my face, Zeke started to lick at my pussy. Lightly at first, teasing with the tip of his tongue. Then faster and firmer, with ever-growing pressure and urgency, like he was starving for every drop of the juices he could get from me.

Asher's cock pressed into the side of my ass. I reached around behind me to curl my fingers around his thick, rock hard length. I was certain I could feel the blood throbbing through him with as much need as Zeke's mouth.

Zeke slowly slid a finger into me. Then another. "You're so wet," he said, his voice muffled by my pussy. "You're always so ready for us. Such a fucking goddess."

With six hot guys around to ruin my panties on an hourly basis, it was difficult to be anything but ready. As for goddess, I'd take that any day. Goddess and my six smokin' hot gods.

Hell yeah.

He worked me inside and out until I was ready to scream the whole hotel down. Between his tongue and the way Asher pinched and rolled my nipples, all I could do was shatter into a thousand rainbow shards and shudder and buck.

I bit my lip as wave after wave of firework-filled pleasure washed over me. Stars glittered in my vision. My hips moved, grinding my clit against Zeke's face, frantic to keep the high going for as long as I could.

I threw back my head and moaned and sobbed with how fucking good it felt. I wanted to stay right here in this place for eternity, but the tsunami crashed over, then slowly withdrew, leaving me to pant and whimper before the last drops left.

Like the gods, and gentlemen, they were, they let me catch my breath before Asher rolled us over and knelt between my legs.

Zeke moved up the bed and kissed me with his shining lips that tasted of me. Then he kissed Asher.

Asher traced his tongue all around Zeke's lips, then his own. "Yummy. I'd like to have the taste of both of you in my mouth. If you want to." He gave Zeke's cock a hungry glance, like he was looking at a juicy, perfectly done steak.

"I want to." Zeke scooted up a little further until his cock was a centimetre from Asher's nose and close to my face. "I want to a lot."

Far out, that was hot.

My body throbbed, heat pulsing in my core, when Asher eagerly opened his mouth and let Zeke slip his tip between his lips.

The sight, and wet smacking sound of Asher sucking, made me groan with renewed urgency.

"Asher, please," I begged. "I need you to fuck me." I wanted him inside me, yesterday.

His eyes flicked down to me and he nodded. His brow creased in concentration, Asher slid his cock into my wet but still very thirsty pussy.

Zeke and I let Asher set the pace of sucking and fucking. He slid his mouth off Zeke's cock and on again, as he slid out and back into me.

Zeke tangled his fingers in my hair while his other hand lightly cupped the back of Asher's head.

Zeke let out a guttural groan of pleasure. "You two are so *fucking* amazing." He punctuated his words with strokes into Asher's mouth.

"No, you," I said breathlessly. I reached over to ghost my fingers around Zeke's balls and the base of his cock. I ran my other hand over Asher's back, lightly raking my nails down and around his firm skin.

When Asher groaned, I dug them in firmer. If he wanted scratch marks, I was happy to oblige. The guys all wore them like a mark of honour when I did it. Like they'd fucked a wildcat and survived.

I was vaguely aware of the door opening and closing. The bed dipped as Penn sat down beside us.

"Is this a private party or can anyone join?" His gaze flicked over to the guys, then back to me. Judging by the heated look in his eyes, he liked what he saw. All of it.

"You're welcome to join in, sir," I said, a smile on my lips.

He eyed my mouth. "Cute that you really thought I was asking." He undid his jeans and slid them down his hips, freeing his erection. He lay on his side, his hips beside my face. "Suck my cock."

Aware that Zeke and Asher were watching with wide eyes, I said, "Yes, sir," and opened my mouth to let him press his tip inside.

"Mmmm, yeah," Zeke groaned. "You guys are all amazing."

"Yes, we really fucking are," Penn agreed. He started to thrust slowly in and out of my mouth, his eyes half closed.

Asher and I both made sounds of agreement around our mouthfuls, and Asher started to pound into me harder and faster.

Two sets of wet sucking sounds, coupled with moans from Zeke and Penn, and the way Asher filled me with his thick length, drove me toward the wild, ragged edge of pleasure.

I came with a soft wash of orgasm, that whispered through me like sinking into a warm bath. It made my toes curl and my breath come in pants out my nose. A faint shudder passed through my core before it was gone. Barely a second later, another, more intense orgasm flooded through me. This one had me gasping, but it was the third that followed in its wake that had me crying out around Penn's heated flesh.

I saw stars a thousand universes over and drew an orgasm out of Asher at the same time. He rolled his hips, grinding into me, while at the same time choking on Zeke's cock. He must have clamped his mouth around the singer's dick, because Zeke swore and grunted as he too came.

Penn was last, but not far behind. He wound his fingers around a section of my hair and said, "Suck harder."

I couldn't have called him sir, or anything else, if I wanted to. My mouth was too busy and my mind was still coming down from the heights.

So I sucked harder.

"That's it," Penn said approvingly. "Good girl." He tugged my hair and slid in and out faster between my lips. "Take all of me, dirty girl." He thrust to the back of my throat again and again. "Fuck yeah."

He wound his fingers so tight into my hair it hurt, but the pain was exquisite, like Tully's paddle.

I sucked as hard as I could, as deep as I could, loving the sensation of him sliding in and out, the taste of him, the heat of his body. Blowing a guy, especially one I cared about, was hands down one of my favourite things to do. I could do it all day, happily. That and sing. Okay, and come. If I could do all three at once, I'd be a happy girl.

"I'm going to come in your mouth," Penn said. "You're going to take every drop of my cum down your throat and you're going to swallow it."

"Shit, that's hot," Asher said. Zeke must have slipped out of him, since he could talk again.

"It really is," Zeke agreed.

I wished I could see all of their faces, but the view of Penn's chiselled, rock hard stomach wasn't bad either.

Penn's fingers tightened and his hips rocked before convulsing as he came. As promised, a fountain of hot cum blossomed in my mouth. I held it while he milked himself for every last drop and ragged pant.

Finally he slid out of me and locked his eyes on my face.

I looked back at him and swallowed.

He smiled. "Good girl. You blew me like a dirty, obedient whore."

That made me feel warm all over. And aroused again.

CHAPTER
EIGHTEEN
ABBIE

"I REMEMBER before we got big, I always wanted to play at Wembley," Tully said. He stood behind me, his arms around me, head resting lightly on my shoulder.

"It is pretty much the holy grail of places to play," I said. "Literally, because a grail is actually a bowl, not a goblet."

The place was enormous. For the first time in a while, I was actually scared of the idea of stepping out there.

As usual, Blazing Violet had the audience hyped up into a frenzy, but would that last when I stepped out onto the stage?

"I know it's hard to keep the stresses of the last couple of days from getting to you," he said in my ear. "You're going to knock their socks off, just like every other night."

Thankfully he didn't tell me not to let it get to me, because I couldn't have kept that from happening if I tried. The press was still outside the hotel this morning when we left for the soundcheck. They were also outside the stadium when we arrived. Some of them shouted questions to the guys about the tour, so there was some hope they might move on from me sooner or later. Most, though, were directed at me.

"I keep thinking about Pete," I said. "We first assumed someone did something to him." That was an easy assumption, under the circumstances.

"Now—now, I don't know what to think. The police said it was an accident. Maybe they're right and that's all it was." They were the experts in these kinds of things, right? In theory anyway.

"And if it wasn't, was it the twins?" Tully asked.

"Right. What reason would they have for doing it? And why didn't we see them?" I twisted around to look at him.

"Do they need a reason? After what they did to Penn, I would think they're capable of just about anything, including that. In Pete's case, he was friends with my father."

I blinked. "And anyone who was friends with Xavier Lang—"

"Is an enemy of Reuben Brantley," Tully finished.

"So...not an accident," I concluded.

Shit.

"Potentially not," he agreed. "They might have also have thought they could score some points with Zeke by getting rid of someone who was stalking you."

"How sweet," I said sarcastically. "They're the last people on Earth I want romantic gestures from." After a moment, I added, "Except maybe Reuben. And every journalist that's been outside everywhere I've been for the last two days. And... Okay, the list might be longer than I thought." I sighed out my nose.

"They can leave the romantic gestures to us," Tully said.

I almost asked if he would kill someone for me, but I knew the answer. If that was something he had to do, then he would do it. I freaking hoped it will never come to that.

"I'm sorry, I didn't mean to be a downer," I said. "We should be enjoying this, not talking about all the stuff that's happened."

"You could never be a downer." He kissed my cheek. "Sometimes you need to get things off your chest." He cupped one of my breasts and gave it a gentle squeeze.

Equally gently, I elbowed him in the chest. "Yes you do."

He chuckled. He took his hand off my breast to clap when Blazing Violet finished their last song.

I joined in the applause and added a whistle and a shout of appreciation. The guys all screamed and clapped almost as loud as the audience.

Violet and the guys waved their goodbyes and headed down off the stage.

I gave each a high-five as they passed, except Violet, whom I hugged.

"Knock 'em dead," she told me before she hurried off to have a shower.

"You're up," Zeke said with a grin.

That was the exact moment I froze.

I hadn't had stage fright since the first time I stepped out onto one, but I had it right now. More than a quiver of nerves, or a moment of second thought, my whole body shook. Sweat sprang out on my palms and under my arms.

I was glued to the spot with stone cold terror.

"Abbie?" Zeke frowned. "Are you okay?"

My voice trembled. "No. I am not o-fucking-kay. I don't think I can do it."

I was vaguely aware of the audience stamping their feet and getting restless.

The guys were all in front of me then, looking at me with five almost identical expressions of worry.

The sixth—Penn, of course—rolled his eyes.

"Of course you can do it," Asher said. "Listen to the fans. They want you out there singing to them."

Macquarie and Jewel, who backed me up, were already out there on stage, waiting. Probably wondering what the fuck I was doing. Honestly, I was wondering too.

"Do they?" I asked. "What if they don't?"

The stadium didn't allow concertgoers to bring in anything they could use as a projectile, even if they could get close enough, but they could throw insults and jeers. I could step out there only to be booed back off. What if they thought I had something to do with Pete's death? Or any of the other deaths? Or what if they hated the fact I was with the guys at all? Or hated my music? Or the little black dress I was wearing that the guys all seemed to like? Or—

I tried to take a step forward, but my feet wouldn't move. I wanted to cry but I wasn't sure if it was fear, frustration or a combination of the two. If I didn't step out there tonight, I may never step out anywhere ever again.

But I couldn't move. My feet were paralysed with anxiety.

"For fuck's sake," Penn growled. Without another word, he grabbed my hand and yanked me towards the stairs.

I stumbled a couple of steps, but had no choice but to walk, or be dragged.

"I can't—" I started to say.

"You fucking can, and you fucking will," he said. "This is what you do."

He raised his arm as we stepped out on stage, hand in hand. He gave the audience a bow as if all of this was rehearsed.

I thought he would dump me at the front of the stage and shove a microphone in my hand. Instead, he led me over to his keyboard.

"Sit." He pointed to the stool.

I sat.

Jewel frowned at me from where she stood behind her keyboard. Penn wouldn't let anyone else play his. She looked confused.

I shrugged. I didn't know what the hell was going on either. Well, I kinda did, but Penn was unpredictable, so who knew how this might end?

He slipped in beside me and moved the microphone over so it was between us both.

He leaned over and whispered, "Breathe," in my ear. "You know this song. All you have to do is sing it."

My fear gave way to anger at being dragged out here like this. At some point, that might become gratitude, but right now I was pissed off at him. He could have at least given me another couple of minutes to get my shit together. I would have... eventually. Maybe.

Rationally, I knew I didn't have a couple of minutes. The audience was waiting. Right now, they were cheering. Probably for him, but I would take it.

He put his hands on the keys and started to play the beginning of "Lock Me In."

I looked at him in surprise. Of all the songs I thought he might play, this wasn't one of them. Given how personal it was to him, I never thought he'd want to share it with me. Not like this.

I leaned towards the microphone and started to sing.

"Locked by reality,
  Caught up in the flow.
  Shaken by the maelstrom,
  Ripped to the bone."

In spite of how dark and intense the lyrics were, all of my fear melted away until I didn't even know why I had it in the first place. If anyone was shouting insults at me, I couldn't hear them. All I heard was ninety thousand people singing the words to Penn's song. Singing along to me.

Now I wasn't so pissed at Penn. Apparently he knew what I needed better than I did. A kick in the ass to get going. Singing with him didn't hurt either. Our voices blended so well together. Not as smoothly and practised as Zeke and I, but this was a rock concert. It didn't matter if we were a little rough around the edges. If anything, it was better that we were. If people wanted smooth and polished, they would go and see an orchestra play. If they wanted gritty and rough as fuck, they would come to us.

We finished singing and Penn sat back, a satisfied look on his gorgeous face.

Normally, I'd be tempted to punch him for looking so smug, but this time it was justified.

"There, now you won't steal my solo," he said.

He grunted as I elbowed him in the stomach. "Now get the fuck on your feet and sing, woman." He leaned in to speak right into my ear. "Enjoy standing up while you can, because after this I expect you to spend a lot of time on your knees."

I turned my head so I could talk in his ear. "Promises promises, sir."

"You can bet it's a fucking promise." He stood and helped me to my feet before he gave the audience a bow.

"I'm sure it is," I told him. "Now get the fuck off my stage." I waved him away.

I knew he hadn't done this so I would blow him off until my mouth hurt, but I might do that for him after this anyway.

I mean, we'd both enjoy it. Win-win.

He gave me a look like he wasn't sure if he should kiss me or fuck me in front of ninety thousand people. Since neither of those options was a good idea, and he knew it, he grinned and started towards the back of the stage.

Before he left, he couldn't help himself. He stopped, turned back around and gave the crowd another bow. The smartass even blew them a kiss.

He must have spent a lot of time watching Zeke; the lead singer was starting to rub off on him.

The crowd screamed and cheered as he headed offstage. He was certainly popular with audiences. And didn't he know it?

I grabbed a microphone out of one of the stands and brought it to my mouth. "Beau Pennington, ladies and gentlemen. He is shy, isn't he?"

I looked over my shoulder to see him roll his eyes before he disappeared from view.

I let the cheers die down, before I spoke again. "Some of you might know me. For those who don't, my name is Abbie Hart. I have a confession to make."

The crowd fell into an uneasy silence. As silent as ninety thousand people could be. Yeah, they'd heard of me all right. I had a feeling they were expecting me to say something horrible.

I raised the microphone again. "The truth is, London is one of my favourite places on the planet. No one else goes wild like you guys."

Of course, that was the cue to go wild. And they did.

I nodded to the Jewel and Macquarie. They nodded back. They were professionals. This probably wasn't the weirdest thing they'd ever seen by any stretch of the imagination. I bet they had some stories to tell. I'd have to ask them sometime.

In the middle of all the cheering, I started to sing.

CHAPTER
NINETEEN
ABBIE

I POKED Penn in the chest with my fingernail.

"If you ever drag me like that again, I'm going to rip off your balls and shove them down your throat." I poked him again but I was trying not to smile.

He stepped back through the door to our hotel rooms, grabbed my hands and pulled me toward him so my face almost bumped into his chin. "You talk a big game for a woman who was about to wet her panties." He leaned in and added, "I don't mean in a good way."

"I was not," I protested. I took a side step out of the way so Landon could close and lock the door behind us all.

"Were too," Penn said. "There's nothing wrong with admitting you were shit scared. It happens to the best of us."

"It happens to you?" I asked, an eyebrow arched in question.

The corners of his mouth tugged upward in a slight smile. "Shit no, but thanks for admitting I'm the best of us."

I tried to poke him again but he held my wrists too tight. "You are such a smartass."

He smiled a little more. "And smart, too. I'm starting to think you don't hate me after all." He caught my lips with his in a rough kiss.

"I still do," I said against his mouth. "Very much."

I didn't hate him. I never had, even when he was an enormous dickhead just after we met. He was being territorial. Considering all the things I learnt about the guys since then, I understood why. Surrounded by violence and death, it was easier to keep new people away. Safer for them and for you.

"Back at you," he said. His hands still on my wrists, he pulled away and looked down at me. "I made you a promise out there on the stage. I intend to keep it."

My heart raced. If my panties weren't wet before, they were now. In a good way.

"What promise was that?" I asked innocently.

Apparently not caring the guys were arrayed around the room, sitting on chairs and beds, he said, "The one where I said you'd be on your knees."

"Oh, *that* one." I nodded slowly, as though it slipped my mind.

Hell yeah, yes please.

"Yeah, that," he growled playfully. "Do it. Get on your knees." He pushed me downwards by my wrists.

Aware every eye in the room was on me, I knelt. "Yes, sir."

More than one of the guys groaned.

Slowly, I undid the front of Penn's jeans and drew down the zip. I pushed his pants down his hips and freed his erection. As I curled my fingers around his hot, thick length, I became aware of most of the guys slipping into the other room. Only Tully stayed.

I worked Penn with my hand, making him stiffer. I glanced up at him. Usually, I hated being told what to do, but when he did it, it was hot as hell.

"Suck my cock," he ordered, his tone bordering on a moan.

"Yes, sir." I lowered my mouth to him, but instead of licking and teasing like I usually did, I took in as much of him as I could and clamped my lips around him like a vise.

I drew back oh, so slowly, sliding my mouth all the way down to his tip, then back up again.

He muttered something incoherent, but it sounded as though he liked it.

Encouraged, I kept doing that, slowly at first, then gradually quicker.

He tangled his fingers in my hair, tugging lightly every few moments.

In the corner of my eye, I saw Tully approach. He was deliciously naked, slowly running his hand up and down his own cock. The piercing in his tip glittered in the light of a lamp in the corner.

"Suck Tully," Penn ordered.

With a wet smacking sound, I took my lips off Penn and turned my face to take Tully into my mouth.

While I sucked him, Penn stripped off. In a matter of moments, I was on my knees in front of two gorgeous, tattooed rock gods.

A girl could get used to this.

I alternated sucking one guy for a few moments, then the other. My hands ran up and down their lengths and massaged their balls while I went back and forth.

"I need to be inside you," Penn said finally. His fingers still curled in my hair, he encouraged me to stand up. "Put your hands up above your head."

I looked at him funny but did what he said.

He and Tully exchanged a glance before they both grabbed the hem of my dress and pulled it up over my head and off. Tully unhooked my bra and slid it down my arms while Penn pulled down my panties. I stepped out of them and let Penn lead me over to the bed.

"Kneel on the edge," he said. "On all fours."

I knelt.

Tully knelt in front of me, his body angled so I could take his cock back in my mouth.

Penn ran his hands over my ass, then leaned in to run his tongue from my clit to my rear hole.

I shivered deliciously.

He did that a few more times, then focused all of his attention on licking my clit and sliding his fingers inside me.

He brought me to the edge so quickly, I decided he knew how to play me better than any musical instrument. So well, it was almost not fair. I wasn't ready to come yet. At the same time, I didn't think I could stop myself.

Penn straightened up and leaned over me so his chest was curled over my back, but with none of his weight on me.

"You're so wet and so close, but you're going to wait," he said.

I responded with a noise of frustration muffled by Tully's cock. I looked up at Tully as though he might save me from the frustration, but he just smiled and went on watching me work him with my mouth. I could almost see him taking note of what I liked. He was all about people enjoying the sensations life has to offer.

"I could get a paddle," Tully said helpfully.

Shit. Yes please.

"Get it," Penn growled.

Tully slipped his cock out of my mouth and stepped away for a minute or two. He came back with the black leather paddle he'd used on me before. He offered it to Penn, who grabbed it and started to run it lightly in circles around my ass cheeks.

Just when I thought that was all he would do, he raised the paddle and slapped me lightly, only hard enough for the slightest sting. The sections of leather cracked together.

That was nearly enough to make me come, even without being touched anywhere else.

Tully put a couple of fingers under my chin to tip it back. "You like that, don't you?"

"I like it harder," I said.

"What's the magic word?" Penn asked.

"Please, sir," I said.

He brought the paddle down harder. This time the sting was sharper, more intense.

I gasped out loud. "Ohhh, yeah. Like that." After a moment I added, "Sir."

"Good girl," Penn said. He paddled me a few more times while Tully slid his cock back into my mouth. As the pain almost became too much, Penn tossed the paddle aside, gripped my hips and positioned his cock at the entrance to my pussy.

The feeling of him sliding into my body made me moan. He felt so good. Just as good as it felt to have Tully fuck my mouth.

Both of them got into a rhythm of firm, even strokes into my body. The world disappeared in a haze of wet thrusts and sucks. I could happily stay right here in this place forever.

Right before I thought he might come, Tully pulled out and moved to sit beside me on the edge of the bed. He kissed my mouth and let his hands wander down across my breasts, over my nipples and down to my clit.

I moaned the moment he slid his fingers across my folds. I bucked against his hand, desperate to find my orgasm.

"Don't let her come until I say so," Penn said. He leaned over me and grazed my back with his teeth. "Do you hear me? No coming until I tell you to."

I managed to grind out the words, "Yes, sir."

As if that was his cue, Tully started working me even harder.

I decided they were both cruel assholes. Lucky for them I cared about both of them a lot, otherwise, I might come to spite them.

I gritted my teeth with the effort of staying on the edge and not going over. That was hard with Penn pounding into me, and Tully's fingers expertly teasing my clit. Not to mention the fact I kept picturing Penn's cock bumping into Tully's hand every now and again. I knew they weren't into each other like that, but the mental image still did it for me.

Penn's thrusts became faster and more frantic. "Not yet."

I wasn't sure if he was talking to me or himself. Maybe both.

He grunted and his fingers dug into my hips. I rocked back into him, wanting to help him, so he would let me do the same.

"Not yet," Penn said again. His breathing was a ragged pant, to match mine. "Okay," Penn said finally. "You can let her come."

Like he flipped a switch, I was enveloped in an orgasm so intense I threw my head back and almost screamed at the ceiling. Somewhere in the back of my pleasure-flooded consciousness, I was aware of Penn coming too. Our moans and grunts were in sync like a symphony.

I left my body for approximately seven minutes. All I knew was where our bodies were all joined, and the ecstasy of an orgasm full of pink, purple and blue flashing lights. When I finally came down, I was gasping for breath and my head was feeling light.

"Lie back." Penn slid his now slick cock out of my body.

For a moment I thought he was talking to me, until Tully lay back and Penn guided me to straddle his hips. His hands on my sides, fingers almost touching my breasts, he lowered me onto Tully's cock.

"Ride him," Penn said.

"Yes, sir." I smiled down at Tully, who didn't seem to mind having the keyboardist boss us around.

Tully smiled back and gripped my hips to help me get a rhythm, sliding up and down his length.

Penn rolled one of my nipples between his thumb and forefinger while reaching down to rub my clit with his other hand. "You're going to come again."

I moaned. The way they were both touching me, I certainly was.

"What do you say?" Penn rubbed a little harder.

"Yes, sir." I glanced down where our bodies joined and saw Tully's cock slide past Penn's hand.

Holy shit.

I arched my back and rode Tully harder, until his breathing was a series of rapid gasps. I was already close to coming again.

"Not until I say so," Penn said, leaning over my shoulder so he could look me in the face.

I hissed at him playfully.

He chuckled and worked me harder. Asshole.

Tully groaned and thrust up into me harder and faster.

"Almost," Penn said. "Not yet."

I moaned.

"Okay, now," Penn said.

However he did it, I didn't care. Tully and I both came in unison, our bodies grinding together, slick with sweat and friction. I cried out louder this time, my voice mingling with Tully's moans and grunts.

"Fuck yeah," Tully ground out.

This time, my orgasm lasted longer, cresting several times until my whole body started to ache. Blood raced through every centimetre of me, taking tingles with it. My vision blurred. My heart pounded like a kick drum, louder in my ears than any concert I'd ever been to, or performed in. The pleasure reached a crescendo before finally starting to die away, like the last notes still echoing through a venue.

Exhausted, I slumped down over Tully until I caught my breath.

Penn flopped down beside us and we all lay there panting, satisfied.

For now.

CHAPTER
TWENTY

"HAPPY RELEASE DAY." Asher dropped into the seat beside me. Zeke sat on the other side. That was how it was when we went anywhere these days. They were on either side of me, or one was in front and the other behind. No one from the press, or anyone else for that matter, could get close to me except the other guys.

"Thanks." I clicked my seatbelt and pulled out my phone. "Do you think we'll slip away unnoticed?"

They both laughed.

After a moment, I joined in. No one would fail to notice a huge, double-decker bus with the words *Wolf Venom* down the side in huge letters. It was definitely not subtle, by anyone's standards.

"The windows are tinted," Zeke said. "They can try to look in as much as they want, but they won't see anything." He nodded towards my phone. "Well?"

"I'm too scared to look," I admitted. I nodded to Jackson as he climbed on board the bus and sat up in the front near the driver. If he knew anything, he wasn't saying. That made me more nervous.

"You have nothing to be scared about," Asher said. "Everyone is going to love it. They'll be excited for your whole album to drop."

"Possibly." Or they would hate it and the label would drop me like a hot, greasy spring roll. The kind that had too much cabbage and not enough of whatever it was that went into greasy spring rolls. Yeah okay, that wasn't the best analogy, but close enough.

The rest of the album wouldn't be out until after the tour was over. This song was a teaser. An announcement, of sorts, that I had a new label and wasn't beaten out of the industry yet.

"If you don't look, then I'll look for you," Asher said. He made a grab for my phone but I pulled it out of his reach.

"Fine, I'll look." I turned on my screen and did a quick search for my name and a review.

The first one I found, I read out loud. *"Abbie Hart's new single, 'Inside Out', is a reminder of her unique talent. Ms Hart is currently on tour with Wolf Venom. Rumours suggest she is romantically involved with at least one member of the famous band. That certainly won't hurt her future career."*

I snorted. "So apparently I'm fucking my way to the top. At least they liked the song."

Shit like this didn't worry me. It was standard for the last...ever. Since I started singing. My sex life always seemed to be more important or interesting than my music. This particular reviewer could have said a lot worse than they had.

"Of course they did," Asher said. "It's awesome. And the drumming and guitar on it aren't bad either."

"You and Tully playing on it are what made it so good," I said.

"That's bullshit and you know it," Penn said from the other side of the bus. "It's good in spite of them." He looked like he was trying not to smile. If he wasn't careful, he might actually do it at some point. He might even get used to doing it.

Tully and Asher both flipped him off.

"It's good because you're all awesome," Landon said. "Next time, I'm playing on your stuff too. We could be your backing band."

"Fuck that," Penn said. "We're nobody's backing band." After a moment he added, "That doesn't mean we can't help out if we have time."

"We'll make time," Channing said. "Jackson can always shuffle things around for us if he has to. Levi won't mind." Levi might, but it didn't sound like Channing was going to give him a choice.

I smiled appreciatively and tried not to look too surprised that Penn would make that offer. I was hoping he would, but it was always hard to tell with Penn. He'd probably want me to call him *sir* the entire time. Was it wrong that the thought made me tingly all over?

I clicked on the next review, and the one after that. Both made a brief, positive mention of the song, then either my supposed love life, or my alleged stalker and the string of deaths that followed me.

One went so far as to suggest the guys should be careful around me, even though Pete was dead. Evidently they thought I was bad luck. Even if I tried to tell the guys to stay away from me, they probably wouldn't.

What was I thinking? Of course they wouldn't. They certainly weren't going to listen to some random person on the internet.

"Social media likes the song," Tully said, his eyes on his own phone. "It's number two on that video making app. There's a ton of videos on here already of people dancing to it, and..." He frowned at his screen. "I'm surprised they let that much nudity on there."

Asher leaned over for a look. "Yeah, that's...probably gonna get taken down really soon. Shame, he's got some moves. Although, if he keeps dancing like that, he's going to end up with bruises on his thighs."

"I don't think I want to see," I said. If it was one of the guys slapping his cock on his thighs, I would happily watch. But not some stranger.

"He's cute," Asher said. "But not as cute as you and Zeke. And the rest of you," he added, clearly knowing the rest of the guys would say something if he didn't.

"Don't you forget it," Penn said.

"I wouldn't because you won't let me," Asher said.

"True," Penn said unashamedly.

The tour bus slid out of the hotel gates, past a smaller contingent of press than the one that was there two days ago. They took photos of the bus and watched it pass by.

That was their cue to get on with their lives. Those that wouldn't be following us to Cardiff anyway. With any luck, the Welsh press had better things to do than chase us around.

Or chase me around at least. If they wanted to report on the tour, we would all be down for that. It wasn't every day that a group of hot, Australian rock gods toured the country.

Even though they couldn't see me, I couldn't resist flipping them off before we were out of sight. Hopefully they would sense it. Okay, it was as petty as hell, but it made me feel better. I felt better still knowing they couldn't see it. They gave me enough grief without photographing me doing that.

The guys could get away with it, apparently, but I couldn't.

I turned back to my phone and read a few more reviews. Most were favourable, some weren't. One described it as nothing more than marshmallow for the ears, that will only appeal to people under the age of six.

Whatever, I couldn't please everyone. My style of music wasn't everyone's jam. I didn't mind that. I certainly didn't mind appealing to children. If they stuck with me for the next twenty or thirty years, I'd be set.

What I did mind was when critics got personal with their criticism, like the one who couldn't resist mentioning my weight, and suggesting I should eat fewer burgers. It's the same old story—it's easy to say nasty things when you're hiding behind a keyboard.

Realistically, some of these people would say the same things to my face. Oh well, they were the ones who had to sleep with their negativity at night.

I'm not going to claim I wouldn't dwell on it, because I always did. The bad stuff always stuck in my brain stronger than the good stuff.

It's true what they say about people being their own worst enemy. I shouldn't be reading reviews in the first place. They weren't for me, they were for people to decide if they wanted to listen or not.

Personally, I never paid any attention to reviews of other people's work. I listened and if I liked it, I listened again. If I didn't like it, then I didn't. Simple.

Why would anyone make up their minds based on a review anyway? It wasn't a three-hour movie. It was a three-minute song.

Asher started drumming on the seat beside him with his fingers.

I glanced over to see him looking out the window, obviously unaware of what he was doing. And the fact I was staring at him. He was so fucking gorgeous I could hardly believe I was on the same bus with him or the rest of the guys. How did an ordinary girl from the suburbs end up here? Was Tully right about it being fate, or some design by the universe? I couldn't think up a better explanation than that. Except luck, and I'd never been a big believer in luck, good or bad. We did shit and that shit had consequences. Sometimes bad, sometimes awesome, like this.

"Are we playing guess that song?" Zeke asked, breaking through my thoughts.

I turned to see him smiling past me to Asher.

Asher looked over at him and grinned. He was even more gorgeous when he did that. So much so, my heart did a little leap. How could I not be head over heels for these guys?

"We could," Asher said. He started to tap more intentionally.

"The Wheels on the Bus?" Landon suggested jokingly.

"Hot Cross Buns?" Channing grinned. "Or Mary Had a Little Lamb."

"Baby Shark," Penn said with a smirk. He clearly knew just saying those words would make the tune stick in our minds.

"No. No. And hell no," Asher said. "Don't you guys know any adult songs?"

"Like Fuck Your Face?" Zeke asked.

Asher frowned. "Is that an actual song?"

Zeke snorted a laugh. "I'd be surprised if it wasn't. If someone can put it in a song, they will." It wasn't the kind of thing Wolf Venom would get away with, but if they could, they'd try.

"True." Asher nodded. "Anyway, that wasn't the song. I thought you guys would be better at this than that."

"We know the song," Penn said. "But giving you shit is more fun than playing this game."

Asher stuck his tongue out at him. "Can we throw Penn off the bus yet?"

"Not while it's moving," Zeke said.

Asher craned his neck to look towards the front of the bus.

"What are you doing?" I asked.

"Looking for a traffic light." Asher smiled and wiggled his brows. "We have to hit a red one sooner or later."

"I vote we throw Asher off the bus while it *is* moving," Penn said. "But not yet. Let's wait to get out on the motorway and the bus is going a fuck ton faster."

"No one is throwing anyone off the bus," Jackson called out.

"Spoilsport," Asher said.

Jackson turned around in his seat. "Yep. That's part of my job description. You didn't know that?"

"I suspected it," Asher said. "You're always trying to stop us from having a good time."

"Maybe we *should* throw Asher off the bus," Jackson mused.

Asher laughed. "I know you love me."

"If you say so." Jackson turned around the other way.

"He just hides it well," Asher said.

"Very well," Penn agreed. "So well we'd—" He froze mid-word.

"What is it?" Zeke asked. "Penn?"

Penn was staring straight ahead at Jackson, who had turned back around in his chair and was staring at Penn.

Jackson had his phone in his hand and his face was pale. He undid his seatbelt and slowly walked through the bus towards us. "What is this?" he demanded.

"What is what?" Zeke asked evenly. "Whatever it is, I'm sure there's a logical explanation for it." He looked as confused and worried as I felt.

Jackson turned his phone around to show a photo of Penn in the park in Mumbai. It was taken from a distance, but he was clearly trying to climb the railing. Zeke, Asher and I were on the left side of the screen.

"What the fuck were you doing?" Jackson asked.

CHAPTER
TWENTY-ONE

PENN

"FUCK." I looked at myself on the screen.

It was obvious exactly what was going on. I knew it. Jackson knew it. We all knew it.

Jackson's expression was a combination of disappointment and frustration.

I thought about making up some kind of bullshit story, but there was no point. I was screwed.

"I was as high as fuck," I admitted. "I thought I could fly. They thought otherwise." I jerked my head towards Zeke, Asher and Abbie. "I didn't do it to myself. I had some unwanted help."

I didn't expect Jackson to believe me. Why would he? I'd screwed up enough in the past, he had little reason to trust me. Especially when it came to drugs.

"I know," Jackson said.

I frowned. "Huh?" What the hell? "What do you mean, you know?"

He swiped across the screen to the previous photo. It was one of me being held by the arm by twin pricks. My mouth was twisted into a snarl, but they looked amused. Assholes.

"None of you looked surprised," Jackson said slowly, with barely controlled anger. "Apparently I'm the only one in the dark about one of my guys getting assaulted." He shook his head and grimaced. "Why did I have to learn about this from a friend of a friend who works for Mumbai police? Lucky for you, they wiped these photos after they sent me copies."

"Thank fuck for that," I muttered.

"Yeah, thank fuck for that," he said sarcastically. He crouched down and grabbed the corner of the seat. "Did it slip your mind to mention this?"

I answered his question with one of my own. "Is my contract terminated?"

If that was the case, they wouldn't have to throw me off the bus. I might just as well jump.

"His contract clearly states no drugs," Zeke said. He looked worried and pissed off.

Jackson rounded on him. "Do you want me to tell Levi to terminate his contract?"

"Shit no," Zeke said. "We didn't tell you because —"

Jackson waved him off and turned back to me. "Do you think I'm not capable of exercising a bit of discretion?"

"Zeke is right," I said. I felt my career trickling down the toilet at the back of the bus. "My contract is clear." I was totally and completely screwed. If I saw those twin assholes again, I was going to rip both their heads off.

"Your contract states that if you do drugs it will be terminated," Jackson agreed. He swiped back to the photo of me climbing the railing. "Was any of this voluntary?" He looked like he was desperate for me to say it wasn't.

"Fuck no," I said firmly. "It was one hundred percent not consensual." I pinched the bridge of my nose. "I've worked hard to stay clean, you know that. I wanted to keep it that way. I don't know if they were targeting me or just any one of us." I shrugged and sighed. "I was in the wrong place at the wrong time."

"That's why no one is going anywhere by themselves from now on," Zeke said, his tone rock solid. He eyed Channing, who still looked unapologetic after going off by himself in the airport.

Jackson adjusted his position on the floor. "So you didn't tell me because you thought you'd be out on your rear immediately."

"Yeah," I said. "It's a pretty wild story when you think about it. People usually get shit slipped into their drinks, not their veins." I frowned. "Wait, were those photos from Pete's phone?"

"Yeah, they were," Jackson said. "Seems it wasn't just Abbie he was following. Lucky for you he took both photos."

"Because you wouldn't have believed me if you hadn't seen me with those assholes?" I asked.

Jackson shrugged. "Like you said, it's a wild story. I am going to have to explain all of this to Levi. If Pete took photos, then chances are someone else did. I need to deal with this before it becomes a problem. But for fuck's sake, the next time something like this happens, tell me. I can't help you if I don't know about it."

"Yeah." I felt like a kid who got told off by his parents for riding his bike too fast down the street. Luckily they only caught me once and it was totally worth it. Considering how steep the street was, it was a miracle I didn't fall off and break any bones.

What can I say? I've always been a live fast kind of guy.

"After everything we've been through, you really think you can't trust me?" Jackson asked. He looked hurt. "How many times in the last few weeks in particular have I helped you all to clean up messes?"

"We appreciate it," Zeke said. "You're right, we should have told you. We just..."

"Don't think of me as one of you?" Jackson finished for him. "I might not be in the band, but I think we can all agree I have a vested interest in everything you do. As much as all of you." He looked around at each of us, one after the other. "I'm not going to throw any of you under, or off, the bus." He managed a faint smile.

"We know," Zeke said. "We also know there are things you'd prefer not to get involved in. If it wasn't for that photo with the twins in it, what would you do? You'd have to decide between talking to Levi and covering for us."

"Or taking my word for what happened," I suggested.

"That too," Zeke said with a nod. "We didn't want to put you in that position if we could avoid it. You do a shit load for us as it is. Above and beyond. I don't think lying to Levi is in your job description, is it?"

"No, and I'd prefer not to do it," Jackson agreed. "If no other photos surfaced, then I wouldn't have to. I just...wouldn't tell him."

"I'm pretty sure that's still considered lying," Asher remarked.

Jackson shrugged. "I consider it as what he doesn't know doesn't hurt him. Fortunately, I don't have to do that in this instance. I'll tell him everything and he'll understand."

"How many things have you not told us so you don't hurt us?" Asher asked.

"That's a good question, Ash," I said. I gave Jackson a sceptical look.

"Thank you, Penny," Asher said. "I thought so too."

We both gave Jackson a sceptical look.

Jackson rose. "I'm going to plead manager's privilege on this one. Just like there are many things you haven't told me. We don't have to know everything about each other."

"We don't?" Asher asked. "I thought we did. I mean, we pretty much do, don't we?"

"Most things," Tully agreed. "We spend a lot of time together. Sometimes there's nothing else to do but talk about ourselves."

"Usually I just listen to the other guys talk about themselves," I said.

"That's true," Asher said. "Hey, Jackson, are you and Levi sleeping together?"

The question caught all of us off guard, Jackson most of all. His face turned slightly pink.

"None of your business," he muttered.

"You know who most of us are sleeping with," Asher protested.

"Which is none of *my* business," Jackson said. He shoved his phone in his pocket and hurried back to sit down at the front of the bus.

"I'd say that's a yes," Landon said. He was sitting sideways in his seat with his legs draped over Channing's lap.

"Sounds like a yes to me," Channing agreed.

"Me too," Abbie said. She shot Jackson an apologetic look when he glanced over his shoulder at her. "I just want everyone to be happy."

Jackson shook his head and turned away.

"At least we now know what to say when we want to distract him from yelling at us," I pointed out. Honestly, I was as relieved as fuck Jackson believed the truth. And that creepy Pete took the first photo, and didn't delete it off his phone. This whole conversation would be different if he had. Ugh, great, I got to be grateful to a creepy-ass stalker asshole. It was better than flying home in disgrace and the rest of the guys hating me forever.

And me hating myself forever.

"I wonder what else he took photos of," I mused. Probably all sorts of inappropriate shit. I was sure his family were sad he was dead, but I couldn't say the same. He seemed like one fucked up dude.

Okay, that was hypocritical of me, because so was I, but I didn't take photos of people without their knowledge or consent. I didn't stalk anyone. I didn't murder anyone. Maybe I wasn't such a bad guy after all.

Nah, yes I was. I was okay with that.

"I'm more concerned that anyone else took photos," Zeke said. "If those leak, we're going to be right in the middle of another shit storm." He ran a hand over the back of his head and exhaled deeply.

I shrugged. "Nothing I can't deal with. And if they get busy hassling me, they might leave Abbie alone for a while." I was perfectly capable of telling pushy tabloid assholes to fuck off.

"I'd like that," she said. After a moment, her face turned red and she added, "I mean, I hope they leave me alone. I don't want them to hassle you, or anyone else."

I knew that was what she meant, but I couldn't resist giving her shit about it.

"Sure. You could have a good laugh over the things they say about me online. Why not? I've had a good laugh about stuff they say about you." I gave her the slightest twitch of my eyebrows.

She snorted. "You're so full of shit. Do you even read the stuff they write about me online?"

She had me there. "Nah. I prefer to read about actual celebrities. You know, like the ones who are famous for being on reality TV shows. Rich people behaving badly are more entertaining than you are."

"The irony," Zeke said.

I turned to him and frowned. "Are you suggesting I'm a rich person behaving badly?"

Zeke grinned. "If the hat fits."

I sneered at him. He wasn't wrong though. That description fit me pretty well, especially the part about being rich.

Abbie laughed. "I think you just got called out, Penn."

"I'm a *big* boy," I said. "I can handle it." Before Asher made any remarks about me handling myself, I said, "Almost as well as Abbie can handle me. Right, Tully?"

Sharing with the lead guitarist was a little weird at first, but it worked. Instead of just getting to boss Abbie around, I got to boss both of them around. Plus it was just the right combination of watching and taking part.

I fully intend to do it again. Often.

"Abbie is very good at handling all of us," Tully agreed. "I'm not even trying to get the image of her red ass out of my mind."

Yeah, paddling her was one of my favourite bits. That and…all the rest of it.

I might have to get myself a paddle so I didn't have to borrow one from Tully. I surprised myself by how much I liked using it. Then again, I always liked it a bit rough. Thankfully, she seemed to enjoy it too. From what I saw, she enjoyed everything all of us guys had thrown at her so far.

I was curious as to what she would do with Landon and Channing and when. All three of them seemed to be taking their time, knowing it would happen when they were ready.

Whatever. The longer it took, the more time I had with Abbie. A part of me wondered if it should feel weird to share a woman with five other guys, but we shared everything else. Why not a woman? Especially one who seemed turned on by the lightest touch. I loved that she wasn't afraid of her sexuality or that of the rest of us. She just slotted in like another piece of our crazy puzzle.

The best piece.

CHAPTER
TWENTY-TWO

ABBIE

"BRITISH PUBS ARE THE BEST." Asher lowered a tray of fresh pints of beer to the centre of the table, and handed me my vodka and lemon.

I nodded my thanks and tried to smile around a mouthful of chicken schnitzel. There was enough food on my plate for about three of me. If I ate like this every day, there would quickly be three times as much of me. In spite of that, I was still eyeing the dessert menu.

"Are you knocking Australian pubs?" Zeke asked.

"No, but if I'm not careful I'm going to knock my head." Asher looked up to the low ceiling above us. Low compared to how tall he and the other guys were.

A hundred years ago, when the pub was built, people were my height, so it suited me just fine. Sometimes it paid to be short. Or petite, as I preferred to describe myself.

The tour bus driver managed to find us a pub in a small town somewhere in Wales.

I couldn't remember the place name and stood no chance of pronouncing it. It was the kind of town where most people didn't know who any of us were, so apart from a couple of stares, we were left alone. It was exactly what we needed after a hectic few weeks and a buttload of unwanted attention.

"You'll only do it once, then you'll learn how to duck," Zeke told him teasingly. He leaned over to give Asher a kiss. Then the other way to give me one.

"I'll learn or I'll knock myself out cold," Asher said. "Either way, you're right, I'll only do it once."

"Don't knock yourself out cold," Jackson said. "We need you conscious for tomorrow night's concert."

"I'm sure Kyle would fill in for him," I teased. I ducked my head over to the table where some of the tour staff sat.

Kyle raised his glass in a toast of agreement. He was one of those guys who had a lot of experience playing and working on different tours and albums, but always had half an eye out for a more permanent gig with a band. Hooking up with an established act would be easier than starting from scratch with a new one.

"Back off, Kyle," Asher said in mock warning. He held up his fists as though he was going to fight the other guy for the privilege.

"Let's not have a drummer-off," Jackson said dryly.

"I'd win," Danny said from where he sat with Violet and the rest of their band.

"Hey, Abbie," Violet called out. "Can't you just imagine them all comparing cock sizes?"

I laughed. "I totally can." As long as they didn't ask me to judge. Whoever won that would have the biggest head in the room. Both kinds of head.

"There's no need for that," Penn said.

"There isn't?" I asked. For a moment, I thought he was going to say something sensible like size didn't matter. I should have known better.

"No," he said. "I'd win." He looked smug.

Considering they'd all seen each other naked, they had a fair idea of who had what if they'd cared to look.

"Keep telling yourself that," Landon said. For once, he was sitting on the other side of me.

Apparently, since I was sitting with my back to the wall, Asher and Zeke deemed it safe enough to let me sit beside someone else. It was a nice change.

Channing leaned forward to see around Landon and asked me, "Do women compare breast sizes?"

"Sometimes," I said. "Especially when they start getting them. Some develop earlier than others. Some take a while but catch up big time."

I certainly had. I stopped growing up at about the same time my chest started growing out. Lucky for me, I ended up with decent sized breasts but not too huge. Enough for a handful in each hand.

"And some never catch up," Penn said.

Asher patted him on the shoulder. "It's okay. You could always have implants."

"Fuck off," Penn told him. "If anyone needs implants, it's you. Ball implants."

"Ouch," Asher winced. "Why are you coming at me like that? For the record, there's nothing wrong with my balls. They're exactly what I need them to be. Right Abbie?"

"Right," I agreed. "There is also nothing wrong with people needing, or wanting breast implants. Whatever makes people happy and comfortable with themselves."

"I'll drink to that," Tully said. He raised his glass.

We all followed suit, meeting in the middle to clink. We even avoided breaking any glasses. Go us.

We finished eating dinner and the publican came to clear away our plates.

"We have a local band playing tonight," he said in his lovely Welsh lilt. He'd introduced himself as Alan when we first arrived. "Nothing of your calibre, of course, but I hope you will enjoy what you hear. They go by the name of Fandango Flit."

"I'm sure they'll be amazing." I hoped they didn't want us to get up and sing or play. I was pretty sure Alan was one of the few people who knew who we were. Personally, I would prefer to keep it that way.

The band set up in the corner of the room. They consisted of three men; one singing, one playing guitar and the other on drums. They had a basic set up, but when they started to play, they were pretty good. Perfect for a little Welsh pub and a relaxing night. Like most pub bands, they started out with popular songs we all knew. Before too long, people got up to dance.

"Would you like to dance with me?" Landon asked when they played a slow song.

"I'd love to," I said.

When he offered me his hand, I took it.

We stepped over to the makeshift dance floor, which was just an area where tables had been cleared after dinner was finished. Landon slipped his arms around my waist and I put mine around his neck. We didn't so much dance as sway to the music.

"This is the most normal night I've had since..." I had to stop and think about it. "Since Zeke and I met."

At least, the hour or so before we had a gun pulled on us was normal. If you can call giving a blowjob to a complete stranger under a table in a night-club normal.

I often wondered if I'd have done it if I knew who he was at the time. I doubted it. I would have been too scared of fucking up with Wolf Venom for it to have occurred to me.

"It's been a while for me too," Landon agreed. "Like, before the band got big. I used to go down to the pub on Friday and Saturday night and hang out with friends, just like this. Then I met Channing and the other guys and it's hard to go anywhere without being stared at. I think I forgot what it feels like. Kinda makes me wonder if all the fame is worth it."

"I can totally relate to that," I said. "I remember the days when I could go clothes shopping without being stared at." Granted, I did most of my shopping online, but I liked to try things on when I had the chance. And have coffee with my friends. Back when I had friends to have coffee with.

"I'm surprised you could do anything without being stared at," he said. "Even without being famous. You're beautiful." His hands slipped down so he cupped my ass while we swayed.

"So are you," I said. "Having blue hair makes you stand out a bit too." Just a *tiny* bit.

He grinned. "That's the point. I've always liked to be different. Not like a face full of tattoos different, but I've tried a lot of hair colours and I'm always thinking about new places to get pierced. Like maybe Jacob's ladder for my cock. Channing has a Prince Albert. I could go one better." He shrugged like it was no big deal. "Or maybe a magic cross."

I had a feeling it would be a big deal if he did it. Having three guys around with pierced cocks would be interesting. I wouldn't pressure the other three into getting them, but I wondered if they would consider it.

That was a conversation for another day.

"If that's what you decided to do, we would all support you," I said. "Maybe I should get a nipple piercing. Or one in my clit." Or rather, the hood. From what I'd read in magazines and online, that was the most popular piercing for women to get down there.

"I've heard those can make you feel really good," he said. "You'd look adorable with either of those. Or both. You know we would support you too if you decided to do any of that." He nodded firmly and his eyes shone with so much warmth my heart did a backflip.

I could easily fall in love with him too.

"That's sweet," I said with a smile. "I'll have to think about it." I may need a few more drinks of vodka before I was brave enough to have a piercing needle anywhere near my clit.

"You'd look adorable without them too." He lowered his mouth to mine in a kiss that started off soft and gentle but quickly became heated enough that I thought he would devour me. And vice versa.

We hadn't kissed until now, but it felt like our mouths were made for each other. Perfect size, shape and intensity. Even our tongues enjoyed dancing with each other. Sliding across our lips and brushing against teeth. He tasted like beer and steak. Delicious.

We finally came up for air before we forgot where we were. I doubted Alan would appreciate it if we started fucking on the dance floor. This wasn't that type of establishment.

Once I caught my breath, I asked, "Does Channing mind you doing that?"

"Not at all," Landon said lightly. "As long as we're completely open with each other and, usually in front of each other, we're both cool with it. It's like any good relationship. Communication is key. Like Zeke and Asher, we both want to be with you and with each other. As long as everyone knows what's what, I think we'll be okay. Don't you?"

"Yeah, I do," I agreed. "You guys are all something else. Most guys I know aren't big on sharing, much less like this."

"I don't really see it like sharing," Landon said slowly. "It's more like…we all want to be with each other one way or another. Like one big happy, crazy family. Y'know?"

"I do know," I agreed. "It's definitely crazy at times." I smiled. Happy? I could hope we would end up that way. Even now, there was so much hanging over our heads. The twins, Dante Fiorelli, the tour. After the tour.

It was enough to make my head spin.

"It'll be okay," he said as though he was reading my mind. "Whatever happens, we have each other's backs. Even if we decide to pursue solo careers, we will always be there for each other." He grinned. "You're not getting rid of any of us that easily."

"That's good, because I don't want to get rid of any of you," I said. I wasn't even sure I wanted this night to end. Tomorrow, we'd be back in the spotlight, for better or worse. For now though, I was going to enjoy being ordinary Abbie spending time with her extraordinary guys.

CHAPTER
TWENTY-THREE

ABBIE

"THEY'RE GOING OFF TONIGHT." I grooved along with Blazing Violet. By the sound of it, the Edinburgh audience couldn't get enough of them.

"The band or the crowd?" Zeke asked. He stood beside me with an arm around my waist and his other over Asher's shoulders. He seemed more relaxed since the night in Wales. As relaxed as he ever got that was. He still watched for trouble wherever we went. That was ingrained at this point. And contagious, since the rest of us were vigilant as well.

"Both." I leaned against him, but didn't stop grooving. "I love this place. Not to mention the accents." It was hard to resist a Scottish accent.

"Oh, really?" Zeke turned to me and raised his eyebrows. "Do we have to worry about you running off with some Scottish band?"

I pretended to think about that for a moment. "Maybe. There are some pretty hot Scottish bands out there."

"If they try to steal you away, we will end them," Tully said lightly.

"And dispose of the evidence," Asher added.

"And make it painful," Penn said.

"And messy," Landon said.

"Very messy," Channing said.

"I don't know if I should be horrified or turned on right now," I remarked.

"Both?" Zeke suggested.

"Definitely both," Asher agreed. "There's nothing we wouldn't do for you."

"Nothing," Tully agreed.

"There's nothing I wouldn't do for you either." We'd certainly gone through some crazy shit already. I hated to think what else we might have to do just to survive.

"Will you go out on stage and perform naked?" Penn asked.

"No," I replied. "I guess there's almost nothing I wouldn't do." After a moment I added, "Would you go out there naked?"

"I would if Zeke and Jackson would let me," Penn said.

"That's an easy claim to make since there's no way either of us would agree to that," Zeke pointed out.

Penn shrugged. "Not my fault if you two are too uptight."

"The world would never recover from seeing your cock," Asher said.

"That's a fact," Penn said. "Half the planet would want me and the other half would be jealous of me."

"Exactly," Asher agreed. "You don't need that added pressure on you."

Penn eyed him doubtfully. "I feel like you're being sarcastic but I'm not sure."

"Maybe I'm just being nice to you for a change," Asher suggested.

Penn grunted. He was obviously not convinced.

The crowd roared, signalling the end of Blazing Violet's set.

"You're up, gorgeous," Zeke said. He slipped his hand down to squeeze my ass.

Violet and the guys hurried down the steps, sweaty but grinning.

"Edinburgh is fucking awesome," Violet declared. "Best crowd yet."

After Penn helped me out in Wembley, I hadn't had even a hint of stage fright. It was almost like that night never happened.

Until I walked out on the stage in Edinburgh.

After hearing the crowd yell and scream, I expected, or at least hoped, to be greeted with enthusiasm. Instead, I got what sounded like a handful of clapping from the sixty thousand strong crowd.

I glanced back over my shoulder and gave the guys an uncertain look. They all gave me two thumbs up each. Then they were out of my sight.

I gave the audience a wave as I walked over to the stand and pulled out the microphone.

"Good evening, Edinburgh," I said into the mic.

The handful of cheers I got in response was underwhelming to say the least.

"How was Blazing Violet? Pretty fucking epic, right? They always know how to burn the place down." That comment usually got a laugh or two, but not tonight.

The crowd turned and started to chat amongst themselves. Those with seats sat down in them. Ouch.

Okay, it wasn't the first time that happened. I could deal with it.

I turned to Jewel and Macquarie as they settled in with their instruments. Macquarie gave me a shrug and rolled her shoulders.

Right, I would get no help from them. It wasn't their job to save me from falling flat. Nor could Penn come and save my ass again.

This time, Abbie, I told myself, *you'll have to save yourself.*

I nodded to the girls and gave them a subtle gesture by holding up three fingers. Change of plan. Instead of starting with the first song in the set list, we were going to start with the third. It was one I usually sang to the crowd after I got them going, but I needed to start with the big guns first.

That included talking to the audience like I knew they really came out to see me tonight, not the guys. It was all about me and the crowd. If I wasn't confident, I wouldn't win them over. I wasn't leaving the stage until I did.

"Did Blazing Violet wear you out?" I asked. "If you're that tired, I better tell Wolf Venom to go home."

That got the attention of some of the audience. They responded with some shouts and cheers.

"No?" I asked. "You still want to see them?"

They roared a little louder and some turned back to look at me.

"I don't know," I said. "They're backstage listening, and I don't think they're convinced. You're gonna have to be louder than that. Work with me here."

I lowered the microphone and walked from one side of the stage to the other.

I raised the mic back to my lips. "Let's try this again. Good evening, Edinburgh. How the fuck are you tonight? You don't mind me swearing, do you?"

The crowd got a little louder.

"You don't mind? That's fucking great. Did you come here tonight to have a good time or what? Excellent. Let's have a song or two and convince Wolf Venom that you guys are still awake."

Here goes nothing.

I nodded to the girls and started to sing.

I managed to sound like I wasn't even slightly rattled by their initial lack of interest. Go me.

Just as I hoped, the crowd started to get into the song. Bit by bit at first, then the rest of the stadium. By the end of the song, most of the place was back on their feet, dancing and clapping.

You've still got it, I told myself.

I gestured to the girls to go back to the top of the set list. We would stick to the same order for the rest of the set, but the change did what I hoped it would.

"Some of you might have heard this song," I said. "It's called 'Inside Out'. I think most of us can relate to feeling like that once in a while."

The crowd roared in response.

For a new song, most of the audience seemed to know the words. A few of the people at the very front started to do the dance from the video making app, which made me grin. Thankfully, they were all dressed, so no one would bruise their own thighs with their cock. I'd hate to be held responsible for someone doing themselves damage. Especially to delicate organs.

"My name is Abbie Hart. Thank you for hanging out with me tonight, Edinburgh. You rock harder than any crowd I've seen on this tour." They shouted their appreciation and actually sounded disappointed I was finished. That was good for a girl's ego.

"Be extra loud for Wolf Venom!" I said before I put the microphone back in the stand. When I left the stage, the audience was screaming and cheering deafeningly loud. Perfect.

Smiling, I trotted down the steps and ducked into the backstage area.

"That was fucking epic." Asher caught me up in a huge hug.

"We knew you would win them over," Landon said.

"Not a moment of doubt in our minds." Zeke grinned and hugged me and Asher.

"I had doubts," Penn said. "But you proved me wrong." He waited until the others stepped away and surprised me by giving me a hug and a quick kiss.

I could be pissed off at Penn for his lack of faith in me, but that was just him. At least I knew he would always be honest with me.

"Did you just admit to being wrong?" Asher teased.

Penn shrugged. "It happens once in a while. Come on, let's get the fuck out there."

"Yeah, hurry up," I waved them all away. "I didn't warm them up for you for nothing."

They all grinned and trotted up the steps to the stage.

"You did good." Jackson stepped over to me and placed a hand on my shoulder. "An indifferent audience is everyone's worst nightmare."

I shrugged and tried to pretend I wasn't a little bit freaked out at first. "Nothing I couldn't deal with. In comparison to all the other things we've handled lately, this wasn't even top ten on my shit list."

"You're not a good liar," Jackson said warmly. "It has to be at least top three."

"It really is," I admitted. "But this is the job that chose us, so all we can do is roll with it."

"And that is why you're still around, while others have stopped performing," he said. "If you can't take the heat, stay off the stage."

"I don't think that's the saying," I pointed out. "But I'll take it. I have to admit, I wondered about the wisdom of sticking around in the industry after everything that happened with Vance and Pete. I wasn't sure if it was worth it. I could have gotten a job working in a supermarket. Go back to school and become a music teacher."

"The world needs more good music teachers," he agreed. "But you would have been wasted on the checkout, scanning people's groceries and lube."

I snorted a laugh. "Yeah, maybe." I'd probably want to give them advice on the right lube for them. And get fired after the first day. "It's something to think about anyway. Now things are back on track, I might stick around for a bit longer."

"You absolutely should," he said. "Levi is already talking about trying to move up the release date for your album. 'Inside Out' is going so well, we want to keep up the momentum. Don't be surprised if you get a couple of days back home before you're headlining your own tour."

"No pressure," I groaned. I was exhausted just thinking about it. But elated at the same time.

He chuckled. "None at all. That's what you get for being talented and popular."

I couldn't complain about getting exactly what I wanted, could I now? I also couldn't help having a moment of self-doubt. It happened to the best of us. Yes, including Penn.

"Do you think people will come? To my concerts I mean." And the other way as well. I didn't mind being told my music was the soundtrack to people's fucking. If I could get them to feel things just by singing, then I was doing my job and winning at it.

"They better," Jackson growled. "Levi is banking on it. He wouldn't back you if he didn't think your concerts would all be sellouts. Or close to it anyway."

Even the biggest names didn't sell out every time. As long as each venue was as close to capacity as possible, Levi would make his money back. And then some.

I smiled. "Abbie is back, baby."

Jackson patted my shoulder. "She sure is. And better than ever."

That might be a bit of a stretch, but I'd take it. I felt better than I had in a long time. Years. Like finally everything I'd worked towards was starting to happen. Really happen.

I turned my attention to the stage where my guys, *my band,* were playing better than I ever heard them. At the same time, a song started to form in my mind. That was happening more and more often these days.

Every single one of those gorgeous guys was my muse.

CHAPTER
TWENTY-FOUR

ABBIE

"I LOVE DUBLIN," I said as I stepped down off the tour bus. "All of Ireland actually." Most of which I'd seen through the window of the bus, unfortunately. I added it to my list of places to come back to some day.

"In Dublin's fair city, where none of the girls are as pretty as Abbie," Asher said. He stepped off the bus right behind me. He took my hand and tucked me against his hip.

"You're going to make me blush," I said with a smile.

I felt light and relaxed after Edinburgh. Like maybe I could take on the world and win.

In the back of my mind, I reminded myself we had the rest of Europe and then America left on the tour. America in particular could be a very tough crowd. They tended to pay closer attention to celebrities' personal lives than some other parts of the world.

Some of the fans of Wolf Venom would take exception to me being in a relationship with any of them, much less all of them. Adoring fans were universal, and tended to get attached to their favourites. They would have photos of the guys on their phones and some may refer to them as their future husband, or whatever fantasy it was they had. Some would go as far as to hate me because I had what they didn't.

Obviously, there was nothing I could do about that. People thought whatever they wanted to think. I had no control over it and I wouldn't lose any sleep over it either. I'd just have to work harder to win them over before and during each concert.

No pressure.

"None of the girls are as pretty as me either," Penn said as he stepped down beside us.

Asher snorted a laugh.

"Of course they're not," I told Penn. "No woman is as pretty as you guys." I patted his cheek.

He grabbed my wrist and turned his face to kiss my palm. "Except you."

"And that was the exact moment we knew Penny melted like the rest of us," Asher said.

Penn shrugged. "You clowns wouldn't have stood a chance if I moved in first. Abbie wouldn't have looked at any of you."

"That's a load of crap," Zeke said cheerfully. "But if it makes you feel better to think that, go right ahead."

"Don't make me use my ninja skills on you three," Tully warned.

"All of you settle down," Jackson said. "You might not have noticed the press pack headed our way."

I stifled a groan. "Hopefully they'll play nice." They had in Edinburgh. We had a couple of interviews, but they were mostly interested in the guys. That was fine with me. At the end of the day, this was their tour, I was just along for the ride.

"What the—" Zeke frowned. "Is that the police?"

He was right. Two police officers were pushing their way through the press and telling them to stay back.

My heart started to race like crazy and my palms were suddenly sweaty. I tried not to glance at any of the guys. Whatever was going on, this could be about a number of things. Pete's death, Callista, Vance, Poppy. Penn's run in with the evil twins, even something to do with Dante Fiorelli.

Or maybe the tour bus driver went too fast at some point and they were here to give him a ticket. I could hope, right?

"Good morning," one of the officers said pleasantly. Well, pleasantly in spite of the fact they were clearly there for a reason.

"Morning," Jackson said in the same tone of voice. "Can we help you with something?" He'd managed to move so he stood between us and the officers.

"We won't keep you too long," the other officer said. "We need to speak to Mr Cole."

All of us turned to look at Tully. His face was expressionless. With his training, he wasn't given to panicking, especially when there wasn't anything to panic about yet.

He stepped forward. "I'm Tully Cole. I'm happy to help in any way I can."

The first officer nodded. "Good. You'll need to come with us. The police in Perth, Australia want us to ask you some questions about the death of your adopted father, Xavier Lang." He waved towards a police car parked by the side of the road.

Fuck.

"Tully." I put a hand on his arm.

He patted it lightly. "It's okay. I'll answer their questions and sort every-thing out." But when he looked at me I saw real worry in his eyes.

The officers led Tully to the car and got him settled in the back seat.

I could hardly breathe as the car pulled away, taking Tully with it.

RHYTHM

SAVING ABBIE BOOK 5

Before I Stay
  Written by Landon Flynn

You want to give me all of your soul,
  But your eye is on the door.
  Your hand is on the handle, ready to turn,
  But you step toward me.

You want to step beside me,
  But you're standing very still.
  You need to jump with your eyes open,
  But you close them anyway.

You know exactly what I need,
  Because you need it too.
  You know the words you want to say,
  But they won't come before you go.

You're lying here beside me,
  But you're never really here.
  You need to stop and hold me,
  Before I stay.
  Before I stay.

Come and walk beside me,
  So we can both stay.
  Can both stay.
  Can both stay.

CHAPTER
ONE

ABBIE

"YES, I REALISE THAT." Jackson ran a hand over his head and curled his fingers into his hair in frustration. He looked like he was ready to throw his phone across the hotel room.

"If it's just... Then why do they..." He listened and threw his hand up in the air. "Okay, I get that, but I need my lead guitarist for the sound check in the morning."

I sighed and leaned back against Asher's chest. The drummer slid his arms around me and nestled his face into my hair.

"It'll be okay," he said softly. "Jackson and Levi will get it sorted out."

"Yeah, I know." I had to believe that. The band's manager had been on the phone with the Dublin police, the Perth police and fuck knows who else for hours. By the sound of it, he was going around in circles. No wonder he looked pissed now.

"I can't stop picturing Tully getting into the back of that police car." I saw it over and over in my head on continuous repeat. My heart ached each time.

The guitarist had looked calm and composed as always, but he must have been a nervous wreck on the inside.

I was.

The police hadn't said he was under arrest, just that he needed to answer some questions about the death of his adopted father. If the authorities had an inkling Tully was the one who killed him, surely they knew it was in self-defence? Xavier Lang pulled a gun on him and would have killed Tully to prove his loyalty to Dante Fiorelli. That was some fucked up shit right there.

Almost as fucked up as Zeke's evil twin brothers, Hunter and Parker, helping clean up the mess of dead bodies left behind us. Right before they assaulted Penn.

Tully left Australia with us immediately after Xavier Lang's death. The police might consider that an admission of guilt.

"He'll be fine," Asher assured me. "They'll explore all the legal channels, then the illegal ones. Whatever it takes."

"If anyone can talk their way out of it, it's Tully," Zeke said. The lead singer of Wolf Venom looked a lot more chill than I felt. He usually did. Right now, he was leaning back against the wall, arms crossed, one eye on Jackson and the other on me. How could he look so fucking calm? Especially when it was a façade. He was on alert for anything, always. That was what came from growing up in a family whose business was organised crime.

"And if he can't talk his way out of it?" I put my hands on Asher's arms to cuddle him tighter. Assurances were nice, but I needed the comfort of physical contact. His hard, muscular body certainly gave me that.

"Then we start calling in favours," Zeke said with a shrug. "Or doing a few, if we have to." He looked less than impressed with that idea. That was understandable, considering he might have to ask his oldest brother for a favour, and Reuben Brantley didn't do anything without a steep price tag.

"I vote we stage a breakout," Landon said. "All in favour raise your hand and say fuck yeah." The rhythm guitarist grinned and put up his hand.

"Fuck no," Penn grunted. The keyboardist was leaning against a window frame, his ankles and arms crossed. "Then we'd all end up locked away. I spend enough time with you clowns."

"Right back at you, Penny," Asher said. "But if they lock us up, I vote for being locked up with Abbie and Zeke."

"I don't think we get to choose," Zeke said dryly, "but we're not breaking Tully out."

"Spoilsport." Landon pouted playfully.

Channing put an arm around him and patted his back. "It'll be all right. You can raise hell in some other way."

Landon's pout evaporated into a smile and he leaned over to give Channing a quick kiss.

"Don't call Zeke a spoilsport," Asher said. "That's Jackson's job."

"Thanks." Apparently Jackson got off the phone just in time to hear that remark. "The lawyer is with Tully now. All we can do is wait. And not stage a breakout." Evidently he heard that too.

"See," Asher said lightly. "Spoilsport."

I twisted around to glance at him. He looked as concerned as the rest of us. Asher used humour as a way to cope with stress. It usually helped, but today... Today everything was more difficult. More serious somehow. Ironic considering we'd spent weeks dealing with a stalker and killer who left severed heads in boxes for us to find.

Priorities.

"Did they elaborate on why they wanted to talk to Tully?" Zeke asked. "There shouldn't be a shred of evidence he had anything to do with it."

Tully was a trained assassin. He knew how to cover all of his tracks. So did the evil twins, assuming they cleaned up like they claimed they did. The fact we only had their word for that added to my unease.

"He had drinks with Xavier Lang before he died." Jackson pulled out a chair from behind the table at the side of the room and flopped down onto it. "If nothing else, Tull was one of the last people who saw him alive."

"He also gave Tully an extravagant gift," Zeke pointed out. "Killing someone isn't a standard reaction to that person giving you a record label."

"I think that's a rare enough occurrence that there is no standard reaction, as such." Penn uncrossed his ankles and crossed them the other way.

"True," Zeke conceded. "Any kind of extravagant gift. Unless they're trying to buy you off. From what Tully said, that's not the case here."

"Tully should give them Hunter and Parker's names," Penn said. "Even if they didn't kill Xavier Lang, those fuckers have plenty of blood and other shit on their hands."

No one could blame him for being bitter after the pair injected him with PCP. They left him beside a bridge he almost jumped off while high. If he ever saw them again, they'd be lucky to get out of that meeting alive. Or at least without getting punched in the face.

Hell, I'd be happy to give them a punch or two myself.

"Or Dante Fiorelli," Zeke said.

"Can we just tick an 'all of the above' box?" I asked.

"That could work," Asher agreed.

We all jumped at the sound of a knock on the door.

"I'll see who it is." Jackson sighed wearily and stood.

At this point, it could be anyone from the press, to more police, to mobsters or hitmen.

No one could say this world tour was boring.

Jackson looked through the peephole, then unlocked and opened the door.

"Levi, you're just in time for all the fun," Jackson said ironically.

Levi Jones, the owner of White Wolf Records, stepped into the room, a tired smile on his face. He was dressed in ripped black jeans, a purple T-shirt so faded I couldn't make out the logo on the front, and thick black boots. His hair was tied back in a man bun that was messier than usual. In spite of all that, he smiled and gave Jackson a bro hug.

"See, they're sleeping together," Asher whispered loudly.

I smacked him lightly in the chest with the back of my hand.

"Ouch," he said, although it couldn't possibly have hurt, since his body was rock hard. If anything, I was more likely to hurt myself by hitting him.

"I hear you guys have been raising hell," Levi said, his eyebrows raised. His gaze settled on Penn in particular.

"Not us." Penn shrugged. "We're innocent bystanders." His eyes flicked right and left as though daring us all to contradict him.

"We might not be innocent, but we're not guilty either," Zeke said. "The forces of the universe are working together to piss us off."

"It's working," Channing said dryly.

"It really is," Landon agreed. "Can't we just live our lives?"

"That doesn't seem like too much to ask," Asher said.

"It doesn't does it," I said softly.

Asher kissed my cheek. "Whatever happens, we'll deal with it like we always do. With music, alcohol and sex."

"All the good things in life." The side of Zeke's mouth tugged up adorably.

"Anyway," Levi said, having patiently waited for the banter to die down. "The lawyer thinks he can have Tully out in a couple of hours. It would be sooner, but apparently they have *paperwork*," he used finger quotes, "to do. Like any government department, the Dublin police are underfunded and under-staffed. Apparently, I could potentially face charges if I suggested a *donation* to move things along a little quicker."

"Levi Jones," Asher said, pretending to be shocked. "Did you try to bribe police officers?"

"Asher DiMarco, don't tell me you didn't think of it first," Levi retorted.

Asher chuckled and shrugged. "Of course, but Jackson didn't seem to like the idea."

"Legal channels first," Jackson said, his tone bland. He gave Levi the side eye, apparently not approving of the mention of bribery. The band's manager had dealt with a shit ton of things since the tour started. Probably before that too, knowing the guys the way I did now. If we didn't end up locked up before the tour was over, it would probably be because of him.

"Yes." Levi moved to sit in the chair Jackson had vacated. "Legal is a lot cheaper."

"Exactly." Jackson pulled out another chair and flopped down. "You wouldn't want to end up a mere millionaire."

Levi groaned. "Definitely not. That would be terrible." He rubbed a hand across his face and smiled briefly before his expression sank back into weary frustration. "What really happened with Tully?"

"Self defence," Zeke said firmly. "Lang and a rival family, the Fiorellis, came after us. After me and my twin brothers specifically. Evidently, Xavier Lang didn't mind if Tully ended up collateral damage."

Levi winced. "Lovely. So Tully had no choice?"

"None," Zeke said. "It was him or Xavier." He still looked pissed off that anyone would do that to one of us. One of the members of his band; his real family, as far as he was concerned. As our unofficial leader, I suspected he blamed himself, even though he shouldn't. Truthfully, if it wasn't for him getting us out of the hotel in Perth just in time, things could have ended differently.

Levi nodded. "Okay." It seemed that matter was closed. He turned to Penn. "Jackson tells me you had no choice either. I've seen the photos, but I want your side of the story."

Penn uncrossed his legs and leaned his head back against the wall. "I went for a run, met up with a pair of twin assholes who thought it would be cool to inject shit into my veins. If it wasn't for Zeke, Asher and Abbie, I would have jumped into some dirty water in Mumbai, and I wouldn't be here to grace you with my presence." He smiled sardonically.

"Don't do drugs, boys and girls," Asher said.

"Nope definitely don't," Penn agreed. "Zero stars, cannot recommend. Also, stay away from evil twins."

"Naughty twins are a lot better," Levi said. He gave a slight wiggle of his eyebrows, but he was obviously troubled by everything he heard. That was understandable, it was all very troubling. Not to mention how much money he would lose if the rest of the tour was cancelled.

I mean, that wasn't the most important thing here, but no doubt he would take it into consideration.

"Do we get to hear that story one day?" Landon asked. "About the naughty twins."

Levi laughed. "Not a chance. You'll have to use your imagination."

"My imagination is pretty good," Landon said. "Were they identical?"

"Were they male or female?" Channing asked.

Levi turned to Jackson. "I'm starting to think you're not giving them enough to do. Apparently they have nothing better to worry about than my sex life."

"I noticed that." Jackson nodded. "We could hire a personal trainer or two to make sure they get more exercise."

"They could probably practice more too," Levi said. "Wouldn't want them getting rusty, would we?"

"We definitely wouldn't." Jackson rubbed his chin as though in deep thought.

"Fine." Landon and Channing sighed almost in unison, then laughed.

"We're curious, that's all," Landon said. "Blame Asher, he's the one who started talking about it."

Asher shrugged, his chest rising and falling against my back. "I'm nosy, but

I'll keep myself contained. If you insist." He made it sound like a chore as boring as hanging laundry on the line.

"We insist," Levi said. He placed his palms on the table. "Okay, I'm convinced you guys didn't get yourselves into trouble on purpose. Just… Try to stay out of it from now on, please?"

"We'll do our best," Zeke assured him. "The last thing we want is trouble." He looked tired and over it. We all were.

Levi nodded sharply and stood. "Jackson and I are going to go to the police station and see if we can get Tully out a bit sooner. We'll also speak to the press. Footage of him getting into that cop car has gone viral, as you can imagine. We'll put out that spot fire and hope that's the last of them."

His eyes lingered on me. "Are you doing okay?"

"Yeah." I nestled deeper into Asher's arms. "I'll be better if things calm down, but hopefully after this they will." I would be ecstatic if we didn't have to deal with any more attacks, murders, stalkers, and could just enjoy the rest of the tour. A little bit of boring wouldn't go astray here and there.

"Good." He smiled. "Your new single, 'Inside Out', is making us all a lot of money. Radio stations and streaming services are already clamouring for a follow-up."

That was the best news I heard all day, by far. "Thank you. If you hadn't put your faith in me…" Shit, now I was getting choked up. I blinked back tears.

"You deserve it," Levi said. "Now, you guys concentrate on the tour and we will deal with the police and media." He nodded to Jackson and they both hurried out the door.

I hoped it was as easy as he made it sound.

CHAPTER TWO

ABBIE

"AT LEAST THEY got Tully's angles right," Landon remarked.

"He looks good," I agreed, nodding at the footage on the television of Tully leaving the police station. He gave the cameras a brief wave, but Jackson and Levi were the ones who did the talking.

"He was never a suspect," Levi said. "The Perth police were trying to establish a timeline of events. They might have gotten a little overzealous in bringing him in, but that's all there is to it. We won't be pursuing the issue further. Thank you." He herded Tully and Jackson to a waiting car and the news broadcast changed to another story.

"Do you think that's really all there is to it?" I sat on the end of one of the beds in the hotel room we all shared.

Landon sat behind me, a leg to either side of my hips, and massaged my back and shoulders.

Channing sat beside us, the remote for the TV in his hand. He changed the channel to some kind of cartoon and tossed the remote on the bed beside him.

"We'll find out when Tully gets back," Channing said.

"It won't be long now." Landon swept the hair off the back of my neck and planted a kiss there.

In one of the universe's giant coincidences, a knock on the door sounded about nine seconds later.

"I'll check who it is." Zeke got up from where he and Asher were cuddling on another one of the beds. He walked over to the door, each step careful, body angled back like it might explode in his face.

Hell, considering some of the shit that happened over the last few weeks, it might.

He put his eye to the peephole, then unlocked and opened the door.

By some miracle, none of us died, or were even attacked. There wasn't even a cardboard box lying in wait outside. Not one I could see anyway.

Instead, Tully strode in like nothing happened. "Hey."

"Tully!" Asher jumped up and gave him a big, warm squishy hug.

Tully hugged him back, slightly less squishy. "Anyone would think I was gone for a year."

"You could have been gone for life," Penn said dryly.

"Not a chance," Tully scoffed.

Zeke looked out into the corridor before closing the door and locking it again. "It's good to see you, bro." He also gave Tully a hug. "What did the cops want?"

Tully walked over to sit on the other side of me. "They wanted to know if I knew anything about what happened to Da... Xavier Lang. Apparently the police in Perth were aware he was into some shady shit. They thought I might know something about it. Of course, I knew nothing about it. I'm just a grieving son." He rolled his eyes and smirked.

I put a hand on his thigh. "You are, in a way. You cared about him." I searched his face for the truth of that. I found it in his eyes, but something else too. The beginning edge of acceptance. He'd started to put the night behind him, not let it haunt him any longer. Maybe the police did him a favour, pushing him to confront what happened in a way we hadn't.

He put his hand over mine. "I did, until he tried to kill me. You could say I'm grieving the man I thought he was, but if I'm honest with myself, I wasn't that blind. I mean, adopting a kid and then training him to be an assassin is a pretty big red flag." His wide mouth turned down.

"Just a bit," I agreed. I wanted to tell him that Xavier must have cared about him, at least on some level, but he was right. Trying to kill him was always going to put a dampener on that relationship. Attempted murder was something most people didn't recover from.

I held a grudge against people who did less to me. Although, they were all dead now, so I guess I could let that grudge go. Hopefully he could do the same.

"So the cops don't want anything else?" Zeke asked.

Tully turned to him. "No. They were even nice enough to apologise for the inconvenience they caused us all. They didn't go as far as to admit it, but they could have just taken me aside for a minute to ask me what they had to ask me. I think they felt bad about all the hassle."

"How big of them," Penn said sarcastically. He was lying on another of the beds, his hands under his head, knees bent and crossed. He could have been lying on a beach, not a hotel room in Dublin. "Are you going to sue their asses?"

"Honestly, I couldn't be bothered," Tully said wearily. "It would be a pain in ass, and I don't need the money. Besides, something good did come out of it."

"Yeah, you got a hug from me when you walked through the door," Asher joked.

"Two good things then," Tully said. He smiled at me. "If the press are talking about me, then they're leaving Abbie alone."

That was true, I supposed, if beside the point.

"I can think of better silver linings," I said. "Like they could talk about someone that wasn't anyone in this room, or known to anyone in this room. Or better yet, start talking about important things like climate change, or the price of bacon."

"Huh. I didn't realise you had a problem with the price of bacon." Landon cocked his head at me and frowned.

I laughed softly. "I don't, I just think it's more important than I am. I mean, it is bacon."

"I never thought I'd say this," Asher said, a frown on his face, "but there are more important things in life than bacon."

Grinning, Zeke pressed the back of his hand to Asher's forehead. "Are you feeling okay?"

Asher grabbed Zeke's wrist and pulled his hand down to kiss his palm. "I'm feeling fine. I just think Abbie is more important than bacon, that's all. Do you disagree?"

"Hell no." Zeke snaked an arm around Asher's neck and pulled him in for a kiss. "I think you're both more important than bacon."

"That's a stretch," Penn said. "Abbie's more important than bacon, but I don't know about you two." He smiled at the pair, who flipped him off.

"Zeke tastes better than bacon," Asher said.

Penn grimaced. "TMI. Waaay too much information."

"Asher tastes better than bacon too," Zeke said loudly.

"You're both right," I said.

Penn looked over at me. "But I taste the best, right?"

"Or me," Tully said.

I opened my mouth, but a knock on the door saved me from having to answer.

Zeke sighed. "I'll see who it is." He got back up and trudged to the door. A moment later, he opened it to Jackson and Levi.

Levi rubbed his hands together. "What are you all doing moping around? We're in Dublin! Let's go out, have a nice dinner and enjoy ourselves."

We all stared at him.

"We're allowed out?" Asher looked amazed, if a bit sceptical.

"I don't see why not," Levi said. "We might get a bit of interest from paparazzo if they're around, but it's past time they started to report on you guys being on tour. They seem to have conveniently forgotten that, amongst all the other shit that's gone on. Let's go and party like rock stars!"

Penn picked his head up and looked at Levi. "Can we get changed first?"

We were all dressed in the clothes we'd travelled to Dublin in. Some of the guys wore track pants or jeans, but a couple of us, like me, wore shorts. I preferred skirts, but it wasn't always easy to find somewhere to do laundry while on tour, so shorts it was for now. The ones I wore were bright pink with purple flowers. Definitely not a rock star look.

Well, unless you were the kind of rock star who entertained children with songs about dinosaurs and brightly coloured convertible cars. Then they were perfect.

"Sure," Levi said cheerfully. "Knock yourselves out. But don't take too long." He leaned back against the door and crossed his arms.

Jackson shrugged. "You heard the boss. It's time for some fun. And before Asher says anything, yes, I know how to have fun." He smirked at Asher.

Asher grinned. "I wasn't even thinking that."

"You would have," Jackson told him.

"Well… Yeah," Asher conceded. "I probably would."

"You definitely would." Zeke patted him on the shoulder. "That's one of the things we love about you." They both went for their suitcases and started to get changed.

I exhaled and moved down the bed a centimetre or two before Tully caught my hand in his.

"Can I talk to you for a minute?" he asked. His wide mouth was pressed in a line so tight his lips were pale.

"Of course you can," I said. I flashed Landon a smile of gratitude for his massage. The guy had magical fingers.

My hand in Tully's, I let him lead me over to the corner of the room.

"Are you okay?" I asked. It was strange to check in with him like that. It was usually the guys asking me. The expression on his face had me worried though.

What could he possibly have to tell me that would make him look like that?

"Yes, I'm fine," he said quickly. "When I got into the back of that cop car, I started to think about what would happen if things didn't work out all right. For all I knew, they had CCTV footage of me and Xavier. I knew they didn't, I looked, but you know how the mind likes to play tricks on us." He shrugged a single shoulder.

"I absolutely do know," I said wryly. "The twins could have done something again."

"That occurred to me too," he agreed. "Plus the Fiorellis and Brantleys have long arms. Dante Fiorelli in particular might be pissed I ended his new lapdog."

He sounded so bitter my heart ached for him.

He closed his brown eyes for a moment before he continued. "For a while there, I wasn't sure if I would walk away from the police station. And that got me thinking about not seeing you every day. That would have been the worst part of this. Even worse than never playing guitar again."

I wound my arms around his neck. "Thank goodness none of that happened."

He slipped his arms around me and buried his face in my neck. "I would have gone crazy. But worst of all, if anything happened to me, I wouldn't have told you I love you. I need you to know that. I'm head over heels, madly in love with you."

My heart skipped a beat. I held him tight, like I planned to never let go. "I love you too."

I hadn't thought about what would happen if I never see him again. I hadn't seriously considered the possibility. Now I did, my heart ached even harder. I resolved to do whatever I could to make sure that never actually happened.

"I don't know what I would have done if I hadn't met you guys," I said softly. "You've all become so important to me."

That was an understatement. I couldn't imagine not seeing them every day and being in their lives. And in their beds. In the short time I'd known them, they'd become everything to me. My world. There was nothing I wouldn't do to be with them, including giving up music.

A few weeks ago, nothing would have made me even consider thinking about that. Now, it seemed so insignificant, in the scheme of things. I loved music, but it wasn't my universe anymore.

"We would have tracked you down," Tully said with absolute certainty. "Something would have brought us together. It was as inevitable as breathing. As the sun rising in the morning."

"As you walking out of that police station," I said.

"More inevitable than that," he said. "It was the most inevitable of inevitabilities."

"That's almost as much a mouthful as you are," I said.

His chest rumbled against mine. "Almost. That's a pretty high bar."

I snorted. What was it with guys and their cocks? It was almost like they were really fond of them or something.

Okay, why shouldn't they be? I certainly was.

"Yes it is," I said. And it was.

All of the guys were impressive. I knew that from first-hand experience with four of them. I was sure I'd find the same with Landon and Channing when we got around to it. None of these guys could disappoint me if they tried. The best part about that—I knew they wouldn't try. They wanted to make me as happy as I wanted to make them.

"We should go and make ourselves pretty," I said finally.

"Too late," Tully said. "You're already pretty."

"No, you," I said back.

"No, you." He grinned.

We went on like that while we got ready to go out and enjoy the city.

CHAPTER THREE

"I FEEL like we've been let out of confinement." I sipped my beer and grinned at Channing and Abbie. What could be better than sitting in a genuine Irish pub in Ireland with my favourite people in the whole wide world?

Like always, I sat next to Channing, but we managed to snag a spot next to Abbie.

He and I were both as into her as the rest of the guys, but we agreed to sit back and take it slowly. Partly because we both wanted to get to know her and partly because we'd been so tight for the last two years, we didn't want to screw up our dynamic with each other.

Lately though, the three of us had become closer. The progression from friends to potentially something more felt natural and comfortable. Which was just how I liked things. Was a relationship real if you had to force it? Nah.

"I'm surprised Zeke let us out," Channing said. He gave our lead singer the side eye.

"Is Zeke the boss?" Levi asked. He looked and sounded buzzed already.

We looked at Zeke, then at Levi. In unison, we said, "Yes!"

Everyone at the table laughed except Levi, who was pretending to look put out.

"Wrong answer."

Zeke shrugged and sipped his bourbon and cola like, well, like a boss. "I've trained them well."

Asher slung an arm over his shoulders. "Yes, you have. So well that when Levi tells us to go out and have a good time, we do. But we make sure it's okay with you first."

They shared a brief kiss.

They were almost as cute together as Channing and I. Yeah, that was a very high bar. We were pretty fucking adorable. We also knew there was something between Asher and Zeke long before they did. It took meeting Abbie to bring them together, but they would have gotten there sooner or later.

Even if we had to give them a kick in the ass to get going.

"Do they do what you say?" Levi asked Jackson.

Jackson snorted. "Only if they were planning to do it in the first place. I didn't have any grey hairs until I started managing them."

"That's bullshit," Penn said. He was drinking cola without any alcohol.

I suspected his run in with the evil twins had him twitchy about any kind of drugs. As long as I'd known him, he'd never been a big drinker anyway, but now he seemed particularly cautious. Maybe he was on his guard against Hunter and Parker, who would undoubtedly turn up sooner or later. I wouldn't want to be them when they did. We all wanted to punch the shit out of them.

"You had grey hairs when we met you," Penn added.

The guy had absolutely no filter whatsoever. It was refreshing sometimes and irritating at others. I loved him like a brother, just like I loved the rest of the band.

I wanted to punch him out sometimes too.

"Thanks Penn, I appreciate it," Jackson said sarcastically. "You're as sweet as always."

"You're welcome." Penn gave him a sardonic smile. "I'm always ready to dish out a healthy dose of reality for anyone who needs it." He looked around the table. "Anyone else?"

"I think we've all had enough reality lately," Tully said. He looked tired. He hadn't been himself since that night in Perth.

I guessed killing the guy who raised you for most of your life would do that to a person. I wished I knew what to say or do to make it better. Apart from being a trained assassin, Tully was one of the gentlest people I knew. I also knew Abbie was helping him out a lot, being there for him and giving him cuddles. Sometimes, that was all you could do.

"More than enough reality," Abbie agreed.

She looked tired too, but as beautiful as ever. I never saw eyes that shade of blue before. They were an even better shade than my hair. I mean, my hair looked pretty awesome, but there was no comparison. Just looking at her made my cock hard. Looking at Channing did the same thing.

Although, I was twenty-two. Pretty much everything made my cock hard.

I leaned over in my chair and brushed my lips over hers. She tasted like citrus from the vodka and lemon she was drinking, only sweeter.

"From now on, let's make a pact to have as much fun as we can." I leaned the other way and kissed Channing. He tasted like beer, which was just as delicious.

"Hell yeah, I'm in," Channing said without hesitation.

I wouldn't have expected anything else from him. Whenever one of us suggested something, the other was right by his side, ready to jump feet-first.

The rest of the guys thought we were joined at the hip. We might as well have been sometimes. Tully would have said something about the universe making us for each other and bringing us together. That sounded about right to me.

The more I got to know her, the more I thought Abbie belonged in that picture too. And all the other guys, but them in a platonic way. Not that they weren't adorable, but I wasn't into any of them and they weren't into me either, as far as I knew. That arrangement worked for everyone.

"I'm always down for having fun," Abbie said. "We haven't had enough of it recently."

I smiled. "I was hoping you'd say that. While we were waiting for Tully, I did a search on my phone. I found a place you might find interesting. If the zookeepers will let us out, that is." I glanced over at Zeke and Levi.

It was Zeke who responded. "It depends what it is. And where it is. You know the rule about not going off anywhere by yourself."

It was difficult not to chafe at that and tell him to fuck off. I knew he was trying to take care of us all and keep us safe, but we were adults. We could make our own choices.

On the other hand, we also didn't want to end up dead or arrested. That would suck. Not in a good way.

"Just down the block," I said lightly. "We could walk there from here. We could all go." My gaze shifted to Abbie. I really wanted to have her and Channing alone for a while. And away from a hotel room or a stage.

On the other hand, if the others wanted to come and watch... That kind of was the point.

"There's enough of us," Channing said. "We can take care of ourselves and each other." The whole 'being locked away from the world' thing annoyed him more than it annoyed me. He didn't like being told what to do and he didn't like sitting still for too long. He preferred to be active and busy. He was always looking for his next distraction or adventure. If one didn't find him, he got short-tempered and edgy.

I loved him for it; it was who he was, but when he went off by himself in the Mumbai airport and we thought he was dead...

I was happy to follow Zeke's rules if it meant keeping Channing in my line of sight, and out of trouble, or a grave.

The thought of losing him scared the shit out of me. Honestly, the thought of losing any of them scared the shit out of me. That was one of the many reasons why Abbie was so perfect for us. If our lives centred around her, and each other, then we would never need or want to leave each other for other people.

If that was how it worked out, I'd be a happy boy.

Zeke sighed. "Fine, we'll go, but keep your eyes open for twin mother-fuckers who might have a passing resemblance to me, and don't talk to anyone who looks like paparazzi."

"When would we ever talk to anyone who looks like paparazzi?" Channing asked.

I pointed at my boyfriend. "What he said. Unless Jackson told us to." After a moment I added, "Or Levi."

"At least you got the order right," Jackson said. He smiled slyly.

Levi snorted. "I get no respect. None. Hey Tully, I hear you scored your own record label. Let's talk later."

Tully did a double-take at the sudden change of subject. "Right. Sure." He looked like he didn't have a clue what Levi would have to say, but in typical Tully style, he had an open mind. Honestly, when it came to Levi, that was the best way to be.

"Maybe he wants to tell you all about how you won't get any respect from anyone signed with your label," Asher said jokingly.

"Tully will totally get respect from them," Penn said.

Now we were all surprised. Since when did Penn start sticking up for Tully? Or anyone else for that matter? He was usually ready with an insult, not praise or support. Knowing Abbie must have changed him too.

Tully shrugged. "A guy can hope. Maybe we should start giving Levi more respect."

"Hell yeah," Levi said. He raised his nearly-empty glass at that.

At the same time, everyone else said, "Nah," and laughed.

Abbie leaned over and stretched out so she could put a hand on Levi's arm. "You know we all love you, right?" Of course, she'd be the sweet one and reach out to him.

"We really do." Asher nodded his agreement, but a cheeky smile tugged at the corners of his mouth. "If we didn't like you, we'd be nice to you." He gave in to the urge to grin broadly. His eyes shone with humour and sass.

"We wouldn't want that, would we?" Levi said ironically. "Lucky for you, I'm a big boy. I can take it. It's not like you assholes give me a choice anyway."

He gulped his drink, swallowing down so much, I was worried he'd choke on it. Somehow, he didn't.

"Not really," Zeke agreed. "You learn to roll with it after a while." He made a face like he was one long-suffering dude, and sighed dramatically.

"When do you not get respect?" I asked Zeke.

"All the time," Zeke said offhandedly. He frowned as though deep in thought. "I can't think of any specific occasions right now." A smile caught at the corners of his mouth and his brows twitched once, twice. Not quite a wiggle, but close enough.

"You're so full of shit," Penn told him scathingly. "Everyone respects you, and you know it."

"Being called full of shit is, um, a good example of not getting respect," Zeke pointed out. He cocked his head at Penn and raised his eyebrows to their full height. His mouth jerked to one side.

"Nah," Penn said. "I'm just being honest." He sipped his cola and shrugged. He would never be apologetic for calling someone a fucking idiot, much less telling them they're full of shit.

That was Penn for you.

Zeke and Asher exchanged a look and shrugged. We had all learned long ago not to take anything Penn said personally. Just like Penn didn't take anything we said personally. Giving each other shit was part of who we were as a group.

Brothers onstage and off. For better or worse. Richer or… even richer. And so on.

Channing caught my eye as he swallowed the last of his beer. "I'm ready to get out of here," he said

The side of his mouth twitched, a subtle sign of his agitation. When we made a plan to go somewhere, he pretty much had to go right now, if not sooner. It was an impulse for him, something he couldn't get past.

I learned to roll with it a long time ago. It was just another adorable thing about him. One of many.

I nodded and downed my last mouthful, then held the glass up for the last drop. I didn't want to waste perfectly good beer, did I now? Nope, I didn't.

I leaned over to Abbie. "Are you ready?" I gave her a look to suggest I didn't just mean ready to leave the pub. I was ready to have a good time with her and get closer to her.

Okay, I wanted to fuck her and Channing. My cock twitched at the thought of it. My balls felt so heavy they might fall off if they waited much longer. That would suck six ways from Sunday.

Her cheeks turned an adorable shade of pink. "I'm ready," she said softly.

"Don't worry," I said "We've got you."

"I know you do," she said. "I trust you."

That warmed my heart and my balls at the same time. Having her trust meant so much to me.

I was painfully aware I was the youngest guy in the band. The one everyone might assume would flake out, or do something stupid. To have her believe in me...

I might have puffed my chest out a little.

"I won't let you down," I promised.

CHAPTER
FOUR

ABBIE

"THIS IS THE PLACE," Landon waved towards a stairway that led down into what sounded like a basement club. Throbbing music pumped out toward us.

I admit to being a little nervous. I wasn't sure what Landon had in mind, except for one thing. I was at least ninety-nine percent sure it involved sex. With Landon. And Channing.

The guys told me right from the start they were never with a woman unless they were both involved. I'd seen myself how committed they were to each other. Being with someone else without the other around must feel like cheating to them.

What did that mean when it came to me being with the other guys without everyone being there? I hadn't been with only one guy since Penn and I had our hate fuck up against the wall in the stadium in Seoul. It was usually me with Zeke and Asher or me with Tully and Penn. Tully and Penn didn't touch each other, but they enjoyed sharing me as much as I did.

"This might be the seediest fucking place I've ever seen," Asher remarked. "I like it."

"That's because you're a degenerate," Zeke teased. He draped an arm over Asher's shoulders. "Just like me."

"Which is why we're so good for each other," Asher said.

"Does that make me a degenerate too?" I asked sweetly. I knew they weren't implying anything, but I couldn't resist stirring them up. Their constant banter and razzing was rubbing off on me. Or maybe I felt comfortable enough around them to be myself for the first time in a long time.

Landon put an arm around my waist and another around Channing's and tucked each of us against his hips. "It makes you whatever you want to be," he said firmly.

We started down the stairs in lockstep with each other.

The further we went, the harder the music throbbed. It pounded through my feet, pulsed through my stomach and the rest of my body.

I loved feeling music as much as I loved hearing it. There was something compelling about a bass so heavy you couldn't tell it apart from your own heartbeat. Maybe they were in sync. Maybe I was inside the music. Maybe it was inside me.

The bouncers on the door barely gave us more than a glance and a nod before we headed through the door. If they recognised us, they knew better than to stare.

I realised the reason for that the moment I stepped inside.

The lights were low, like you'd expect from a nightclub. It took my eyes a couple of minutes to adjust.

"Oh my," I said in a voice even I couldn't really hear.

Everywhere I looked, everything was either black or gold. A few people sat or stood with drinks in their hands, shouting to be heard over the music. Others were lying on couches, clothes half off, hands and mouths all over each other.

It reminded me of the club Tully took me to in Perth, but instead of private rooms, people were just… fucking.

"Like I said, my kind of place," Asher shouted over the music.

"Mine too," Penn shouted. He liked to watch, but not as much as he liked to take part.

Landon drew me to him so he could speak in my ear and be heard. "How do you feel about doing it in front of other people? It's kinda a thing for me. Don't worry about anyone here taking photos and telling the press. The owners of places like this keep a super close eye on everything. Besides, people would have to admit they were here too." He grinned.

"That's a good point," I said. I nodded and tried to tear my eyes away from the woman who was bent over a table, a slender man thrusting into her like he planned to take all night and then some.

People came to clubs like this to explore a side of themselves they wouldn't explore out in the real world. They certainly wouldn't admit to it. That explained why the bouncers didn't look too closely. Discretion was currency in clubs like this. See nothing, know nothing, tell the paparazzi nothing.

Fucking perfect. Mental chef's kiss to the establishment. More places should be like this.

"So… What do you think? No pressure to do anything you don't want to do." Landon squeezed my hand and gave me a reassuring smile.

Honestly, between the music, the people clearly enjoying themselves, and being surrounded by six hot guys, I was dripping wet already. All I wanted, right this moment, was to be touched and to touch.

The idea of doing that in front of strangers added an extra thrill. I liked screwing in front of the other guys. And there was that one time outside Zeke's place just after we met, when two guys walked past. They stopped to watch and clap.

Yeah, that was a fucking good memory. And a good fucking memory.

In the back of my mind, there was even the excited thought—what would happen if someone took a photo of us and it leaked out? No, I didn't want that to happen, but at the same time…the forbidden was arousing as hell.

"I'm game," I said finally.

Landon grinned. He took Channing and I by the hand and led us over to a corner. Zeke and Asher sat side by side on a couch nearby.

Tully and Penn went to the bar to get drinks, but made it clear they were also going to watch. Avidly, by the look of the tenting in the front of both their jeans.

They were pushed to the back of my mind as Landon sat me down between him and Channing.

I decided to let them guide me in this. Not the fucking part, I knew how to do that already. I'd even seen them do it with each other.

No, what I didn't want to do was overstep and get in the way of the relationship between the two of them. The thing between them and me was new and I was still finding my way with the boundaries. There might be things they would do with and for each other, that they wouldn't do with me.

I'd let them show me.

Landon put a hand on my cheek and kissed me lightly, then turned my face so Channing could kiss me too. Both of them had soft lips with a tickle of stubble and the taste of beer.

In spite of that, I could have closed my eyes and told you who was who from the way they felt. Channing's kisses were a little firmer, not quite possessive, but hard compared to Landon's. Landon's kisses were soft, but his tongue was more bold. It bobbed against my lower lip every time we kissed.

Both guys rested a hand on either side of my waist. In almost the exact same place. I got the impression they made sure whatever one did, the other did in equal proportion. It was sweet how considerate they were of each other, and of me.

When Landon slipped a hand up the back of my shirt, Channing slid one up the front. Landon unhooked my bra and Channing pulled down the cups to let my breasts fall free.

I guessed they'd done that move before. Like with the other guys, I wasn't judging their pasts. Instead, I admired how well they worked together. If they practised a lot to get there, I got to reap the benefit of it.

Win.

They gripped the hem of my shirt, front and back and lifted it up to expose my breasts. My nipples immediately pebbled with the brush of cooler air, and the need to be spoilt.

I swallowed hard, and glanced up. The only ones looking at me were the guys, their gazes eager and hungry. No paparazzi popped up to take photos.

Yet.

Landon slipped a hand around the front of me to cup my breast and palm one nipple until it was harder still. Channing lapped at the other with the tip of his tongue.

I shivered deliciously, so aroused already all I knew was that and the thud of the music. Fortunately, the couch under me was the kind you could wipe down. Otherwise I would have left a permanent mark in the shape of a puddle.

I hesitated for a moment, then grabbed the hem of my shirt from where it sat just below my neck. In a quick movement, before I changed my mind, I pulled it off the rest of the way. Then my bra with it.

I set them aside on the floor beside the couch and slipped my hands up the front of Channing's T-shirt.

Like the other guys, he was ripped. Rock hard ridges were smooth under my fingers except where I encountered several scars. What were they from? I'd have to ask him some time.

I slid my hands up higher, taking his shirt with me. I'd seen him naked before, but not up this close, not touching. Now I was, I saw and felt the criss-cross of scars across his torso, interspersed with tattoos and muscle.

With one hand, he gripped his own hem and pulled his shirt off over his head in a single movement. His nipple ring caught the low light in the club and glittered.

Sensing it was the right thing to do, I turned to run my hands over Landon's stomach and chest and help him out of his shirt.

He gave me a smile that let me know he knew I figured out how they liked things.

I smiled back and kissed his mouth, then Channing's.

They manoeuvred me so I was reclining against the back of the couch, my feet still on the floor, and both had one of my nipples in their mouth. They were almost close enough for the tops of their heads to brush against each other if they weren't careful.

I quivered under their touch. I half closed my eyes and looked over to see Zeke and Asher making out. Penn and Tully were watching me like I was the main event on a small, intimate stage. All they needed was a bucket of popcorn between them.

It shouldn't really come as a surprise that people who performed for a living weren't shy about what they did in front of other people. If we were, we wouldn't be very good performers. The ability to sing or play music was only one part of the job. Some would argue it's not even the most important part.

I wasn't going to get involved in that argument. As far as I was concerned, it was all important.

In sync as ever, Landon and Channing both slipped a hand up my thigh. Their fingers bumped at the apex of my thighs and they both rumbled with laughter. Channing's hand retreated to the inside of my leg, while Landon brushed feather light strokes over the base of my belly and the top of my folds.

I let my hands wander and dance over the front of each of their pants, finding twin bulges there. I wanted to feel both of them inside me.

They raised their heads and, with the stubble of their cheeks tickling my nipples, they kissed each other.

Holy shit that was hot.

Hotter still when they stretched over me and undid each other's jeans.

I looked down, watching as both erections sprang free, both dark with blood and desire. I wasn't sure if I should touch them, or if they wanted to touch each other. I got my answer when they went back to lavishing attention on my nipples and ghosting fingers over the gusset of my panties, and venturing underneath.

I curled a hand around each of their cocks and oh so slowly slid my hands down to their sacs and back up again. Landon's cock was slightly longer, and bent to the left, while Channing's was a little thicker. A Prince Albert piercing cut across the sax player's tip.

They were both hot as fuck and throbbing as though filled with the music too.

The guys exchanged a glance and a nod before putting their hands under me to lift my hips and pull down my panties.

Again, I swallowed and looked around. No one was looking at me, but two guys, women on their knees in front of them, sucking each of their cocks, looked close to coming. Their eyes were closed as they thrust their hips slowly, or we might have locked gazes.

"You're so beautiful." Landon sat up beside me and kissed my mouth. At the same time, Channing moved down to kneel between my legs.

Anticipating their next move, I slid down the back of the couch until I was lying with my head in Landon's lap, my shoulder beside his thigh.

He stroked my hair, before curling his fingers around a fistful and slipping his cock between my lips.

I tasted his pre-cum with my tongue, which I rolled over his tip and around the end of his shaft. I cupped his heavy balls lightly in my hand and massaged them before lowering my mouth fully, deeply onto his heated length.

I felt a groan pass through him, down his body, to the cheek I had pressed to the light hair of his rock hard belly.

I guessed he liked that as much as I did.

Channing started to flick against my clit with his tongue. It didn't surprise me at all that a saxophonist was good with his mouth. Better than good. He had me panting around Landon's erection in a matter of several teasing strokes

He teased me right to the edge of coming. Every nerve in my body was ready, racing toward that delicious peak. I bucked against his mouth and tightened my grip on Landon's balls. I sucked harder with every roll of my hips.

Right before the orgasm crashed over me, Channing pulled away from my clit. He kissed the insides of my thigh, down toward my knees, then back up my other leg.

I growled in frustration, slowed my sucking and caught my breath.

He smiled at me and wiggled his eyebrows. Yeah, he knew exactly what he was doing.

Clit tease.

He finally found his way back to my pussy, right before I suggested he get a map, but instead of spoiling my poor clit, he tickled my rear hole with his tongue, and lapped all around my folds.

Everywhere but my clit.

Should I order him around like Penn did to me? I would in a minute, if he didn't stop driving me crazy.

He glanced up at me, a knowing smile in his eyes, before he finally went back to lapping at my clit and sliding his tongue inside me.

I wasn't starting from scratch, but he'd neglected my clit for long enough that it took several minutes to work back to where I was. I decided it was worth it. The second time felt even better than the first. My nerves were singing in time to the music, more intense, more *ready* than before.

I ground against his tongue, moaning when he slid a couple of skilled fingers inside me to stroke my g-spot.

Fuck, yes. I would have shouted if my mouth wasn't full, but I did moan and graze my teeth over Landon's cock.

His hand tightened around my hair. He must be close too.

The orgasm slipped up like a tiger creeping through a darkened jungle, padding it way on huge, soft paws to find me. Just before it pounced, Channing drew back again.

"Fucking hell," I said around Landon's cock.

Laughter rumbled through Landon's belly and into my face. He was lucky I only bit down on him gently.

Landon bent down toward my ear. "That feels amazing, honey."

Well, if he liked that... I bit down a little harder, nibbling gently on his hot skin.

"Ah yeah," he groaned.

I glanced down to Channing, who didn't even look slightly sorry for frustrating the crap out of me. Instead, he was busy running his tongue over the tender flesh on the inside of my thigh and pretending he was innocent of any wrongdoing.

He even lifted his mouth just high enough for me to see his cheeky grin.

When he lowered his face again, it was to thoroughly kiss the insides of both my thighs.

I was so frustrated by now, I was ready to scream.

I dropped my hand toward my clit, intending to get myself off, but Channing caught my wrist and held it a couple of centimetres away.

He shook his head and gave me a scolding look, before finally returning his attention where it belonged, my poor hungry, begging clit.

This time it wasn't a tiger, it was a whole streak of them. They leapt on me so hard, I couldn't have fought them off if I tried. Every single nerve in my body exploded with a rush of pleasure that thundered louder than the pounding music around me.

Nothing—*nothing* existed in the entire world but the pulsing, throbbing heat of blood, orgasm, strobing lights and the shatter of my being into infinity, amazing fucking pieces. I shuddered and screamed and bit, maybe too hard.

I was barely down before the tigers pounced again, even more unrelenting than before. I sobbed and gasped, overwhelmed by sensation. The blood in my ears drowned out the thudding music. I arched my back and had to slide my mouth off Landon's cock so I could catch half a ragged breath before crashing back down to Earth in a puddle of boneless skin.

Channing went on licking and teasing until I came all the way down and wriggled with the sensitivity of my clit.

He lifted his face, shining with my juices, and smiled like the cat that licked up *all* of the cream. Which was basically accurate.

Like a tag team, Landon slipped away from me and they swapped places.

Landon knelt between my knees and positioned his cock at my entrance.

Channing replaced Landon's cock in my mouth with his.

Like their lips, their cocks tasted different. Landon's was sweeter, but Channing's had a unique flavour that made my tongue sing. Although, I was tempted to bite him hard for edging me. Okay, it was worth it, so he got a pass. This time.

Landon slowly slid his cock inside my body, all the way to the hilt.

I sighed with pleasure, tingled with the aftermath of coming, and the other people fucking around us. Add the pumping music and every nerve in my body was flooded. It could have overwhelmed me, but it was like a perfect symphony of sensation. It was..... freeing in a way I never felt before.

Like everything so far, when they fucked my mouth and pussy, they did it in near-perfect sync. At the same time, they angled their upper bodies so they could kiss, tangling tongues over my head. Landon had one hand on my hip and the other on Channing's arm. Channing had a hand on Landon's back and the other on the back of my neck. It was like being tied in a perfect knot.

I managed a quick glance over to see Zeke and Asher lying top to tail on their couch, cocks in each other's mouths.

Penn and Tully both had theirs in their hands, eyes still on me. Penn locked his eyes on me and came as I watched. My eyes widened and I almost did the same. It wasn't until a few moments later when Tully came that a light orgasm fluttered through me, making me tingle and convulse around Landon's cock.

He must have been close to the edge already, because he came right behind me, gasping and thrusting furiously, teeth gritted in concentration, lips apart. He let out a choked cry and dug his fingers into my hips. He scrunched up his face and thrust more slowly, before finally coming to a stop.

I sucked Channing harder, encouraging him to come too. He grunted and rolled his hips, thrusting faster, then slower, then faster again, like he was needing to come but wanting to delay it for as long as he could.

I was tempted to pull my mouth off him and let him be frustrated for a while, but instead I grazed my teeth along his length and pumped him with my hand and mouth.

"Oh, fuck," he shouted. "Fuck, fuck, fuck." He grabbed the back of my head in both hands and pulled me down harder onto his cock, until he was right at the back of my throat.

I sucked until my mouth hurt, then went and sucked until he exploded inside me, flooding my throat with his pearly juices.

He held me there while he milked himself for every last drop, then finally let me go.

I pulled off him, swallowed hard, and gasped for air.

"Wow." Landon nestled up against me on the couch, fully naked. "I knew you would fit with us."

"Yeah," Channing agreed. "Perfect fit." He flopped down on the other side of me, not beside Landon for once.

At that moment, their two became three. Another piece of our puzzle.

CHAPTER FIVE

ABBIE

"HAVE YOU EVER PLAYED BASS GUITAR?" Landon looked at me from under his ridiculously long eyelashes.

The only way I could have lashes like that would be with extensions. Mine were so short and light, they all but disappeared against my face unless I wore mascara.

"Never," I replied. "I've played guitar, but never bass. Is it hard?" I should know better than to ask a question like that, I really should.

The minute I did, he grinned. "Usually. Especially around you and Channing."

Channing, who was on the other side of the stage, changing the reed in his saxophone, must have heard his name. He looked up briefly and smiled before he looked back down again. The only time they weren't side-by-side, apart from the other night, was when they were on stage. Then they were all about the music.

I rolled my eyes playfully. "Sorry, I should have asked if it's difficult compared to playing a regular guitar?" Sometimes I felt like I was surrounded by a pack of horny boys. Then I remembered I liked that about them.

Landon picked up his bright purple bass and plucked a couple of strings. They left out a soft twang.

"It's not that much different, to be honest. It has fewer strings and a lower pitch, as you know." He glanced slyly at Tully. "And my instrument is bigger."

Tully arched an eyebrow at him and paused in tuning his own, black, electric guitar. "Only your guitar," he said dryly.

"Keep telling yourself that," Landon teased. He held his bass out to me. "You wanna try?"

I eyed him and his instrument—the musical one—with scepticism. "It's not that I don't want to, it's just that there's already hundreds of fans lined up outside the front of the venue. I wouldn't want to scare them away with my shitty playing."

It was a beautiful morning in Paris, if a little chilly. Europe was a refreshing change after Asia, at least in climate.

"They might shout 'merde' and run away." That was one of the few words I knew in French, apart from baguette, fromage and croissant. And oui, of course. All of the most important ones.

Landon laughed. "It's not plugged in. No one will hear it but us. I'll plug it in before the sound check starts."

The staff who worked on the tour were still busy running around, setting up the stage. The sound guys in particular were fiddling around with the speakers to take best advantage of the acoustics.

I liked to watch them work, their level of dedication was incredible, and of course they made us sound good. Some days, that was miraculous.

"Okay." I took the bass from him. "I better not break this then."

He gave me a face that suggested no, I fucking better not. Guys and their instruments were like guys and their cocks. Any damage to either would cause a lot of pain. Some of them looked after their instruments better than themselves. Fair enough, when your livelihood depended on it.

The bass was heavier than I expected, but still comfortable in my arms. When I was a kid, I used to accompany myself on an old acoustic guitar my parents bought me from a garage sale. It quickly became obvious I was better at singing than I was at playing, at least at a professional level, but I enjoyed it regardless. I mean, you don't have to be good at a thing to get pleasure from it. Right?

I strummed a few chords and managed not to make the guitar sound like a dying duck. Honestly, considering what it was worth, it wouldn't sound bad unless the player really sucked, but it would sound better in the hands of someone like Landon. Someone with talent, skill and dedication. Not to mention magical hands.

"When did you start playing?" I asked curiously.

"I don't remember not playing," he said, a faint frown on his brow. "Mum and I had instruments lying around from her boyfriends. A couple of them left them behind when they ditched on her." The side of his mouth pulled back and his eyes glazed.

"Assholes never stuck around for very long." They were clearly unpleasant memories. His anger at the past wasn't buried deep. Right now, he wore every moment of it on his face.

I paused in my strumming. I wanted to kiss away his pain, but the darkness wasn't so easily vanquished. "I'm so sorry. That must have been difficult."

My heart broke a little for the kid who must have wondered why people came and went from his life so quickly.

He shrugged. "I can't say I blame them. She was into a bunch of shit. Crack, usually. She used to leave me alone at night so she could go out and... Do what she had to do to get money for it. And to buy food once in a while. Took me the longest fucking time to realise she was selling herself." He swiped the back off his hand over his cheek, but not before I saw a tear glisten there.

My mouth formed an O. "That's terrible. How old were you?"

"I dunno." He flopped down on Penn's bench. "About eight or nine. One of the neighbours found out and dobbed on her. Cops came and I went into foster care. Lucky they let me take a guitar with me. I probably would have gone ballistic without it."

"Yeah, I'm sure you would." I placed his bass down as carefully as if it was mine, and sat beside him, my thigh touching his.

"I've always found music the best way to escape reality." I wound an arm around him and leaned against his shoulder.

"Exactly." He nodded his agreement. "Anyway, Mum tried to get clean and get me back. It worked for a while, but eventually she went back to her old ways." He sighed heavily. "I went back into foster care until I met this mob." He gestured briefly around the stage with his hand. "They kinda saved me, y'know?"

"I do know," I agreed. "They've saved me too. A few times. Them and you. It seems to be something you guys do. You might be superheroes in disguise." I gave him a teasing, speculative look, laced with sympathy for kid-Landon and even past me, who needed saving so badly.

He managed a faint smile. "That sounds about right. They're a good bunch to fall in with."

I smiled softly and kissed his cheek. "They really are. Even Penn."

Penn, who was lying on the front of the stage, his hands under his head, looked over at us. "Especially Penn," he said before he closed his eyes again. "Also, you're on my bench."

"You'll live, mate," Landon said, shrugging indifferently.

"Can I ask what happened to your mother?" I said gently. "Is she still..."

"Alive? Using?" He shrugged. "I couldn't tell ya. I tried to keep in touch with her, but she drops in and out. Last time I heard from her was about six months ago. She told me she was trying to get clean. I wanted to believe her but I've heard it a thousand times before. At this point, it is what it is. I've tried to help her, but she has to help herself first."

"She has to *want* to," Penn said. "No one could make me do shit until I was ready." He turned his face towards us. He would have denied it, but he had sympathy in his eyes. If anyone would have a clue what Landon went through, he would.

"The struggle is real," Landon said. "I just had to learn to get on with it and not think about it too much. Not dwell on it and shit."

I reached around with both arms and gave him a squeeze. "It sucks that you have to do that. People talk about how important family is, but so often family isn't people you are related to by blood. Is it?"

"Nope," he agreed. "My sperm donor wasn't much fuckin' help either. He skipped out before I was born. Fuck only knows what his name was, Mum would never tell me. Truth is, she probably didn't know." He exhaled as though he wanted to blow his frustrations out his mouth and away. "Honestly, I'm not gonna lose any sleep over it. Not anymore."

"You used to?" I asked softly.

"Totally," he agreed. He hesitated for a moment as though unsure how I'd react to what he was about to say. Finally, he continued, "I still lie awake at night and wish he'd come and take me away to some, I don't know, superyacht or fancy island, or superhero lair. Or, like, anything really. That probably sounds dumb as shit."

"It sounds totally normal to me," I said. "I used to wish the same thing. Not for a father to take me away. Mine was all right."

I smiled ruefully, embarrassed at kid-me. "I used to wish for some rich, hot guy who would carry me away and worship me." That wasn't too much to ask, right? After a moment I added, "Now I have six."

Hell yeah. Maybe kid-me wasn't so crazy after all.

"Fuck," Landon said, a frown on his adorable face.

I sat up. "What? Is something wrong?"

"Yeah," he said slowly. "I forgot to buy a superyacht. What a letdown." He smiled.

I laughed and smacked him lightly on the chest. "I don't need a superyacht. Or a fancy island. Or even a superhero lair. Although, that would be cool." I mean, who wouldn't want one of those?

"Oh, man. Now I want to get a superyacht to sail off to a fancy island that has a superhero lair on it." He grinned.

"You're gonna get kicked out of the band if you keep being nerdy like that," Penn remarked.

"You might get kicked out of the band if you're not nerdy enough," Asher said as he and Zeke stepped out onto the stage.

"Yeah," Zeke agreed. "There's nothing wrong with being nerdy. Or geeky."

"The fuck kind of rock gods are you guys?" Penn asked. He rolled his eyes, but smiled slightly.

"The nerdy kind, obviously," Asher said. He stepped over and gave me a kiss before moving to sit behind his drums.

"The kind who are ready for a sound check," Zeke said. He waved for everyone to get up and get into place.

Landon stood, but before I could, Penn waved me back down. "You can stay if you want to."

He'd come a long way from a couple of months ago, when he told me to get the fuck off the stage during Wolf Venom's sound check. Back then, he seemed to hate the sight of me. And I wanted to wipe the smirk off his face almost as much as I wanted to fuck him.

We'd both come a long way, now I thought about it.

"Okay." I sat around on the stool and played a few notes.

"Not worried about making me look bad?" He slipped in beside me and dropped a lingering kiss on my lips.

"No," I said lightly. My mouth twitched as I struggled to hold back a smile.

He raised his eyebrows. He didn't look like he believed me.

"Are you waiting for me to say you can do that all by yourself?" I asked.

"In a word, yes," he said. "I give you guys enough shit. I expect to get plenty of it back." He didn't look too worried about that happening. He was a big boy, he could deal with it.

"I decided to be nice." I kissed him back. It was nice to do that, especially given the fiery start to our relationship. "Don't worry, I'll think of something sarcastic to say soon."

"I wouldn't have it any other way." He touched his forehead to mine in a gesture that was surprisingly intimate and sweet. Sometimes, it was difficult to figure Beau Pennington out. I liked that. He always kept me guessing.

Zeke pulled the microphone out from its stand and turned it on. "All right ladies and gentlemen, boys and girls, are you ready to rock out, Paris?"

"Let's do it," Landon called out. He had the strap of his bass around his neck and a grin on his face.

I couldn't help smiling in response. He had a particularly contagious smile. The fact he still managed to do it after what he told me about his mother was even more miraculous. The more I learnt about these guys, the more I was amazed and besotted. How could anyone not fall head over heels in love with them?

I had, and I was loving every minute of it.

I grooved along with the guys as they started to play. It was only a sound check, but the guys held nothing back. That, of course, was why they were so successful. They put their hearts and souls into each performance and their fans, and I, loved them for it.

As I listened and enjoyed the performance, I couldn't help but dwell on what Landon told me about his mother. I understood now why it took longer for him to gravitate towards me, even when he was attracted. As well as his deep involvement with Channing, he must have assumed I would walk away, like so many other people in his life had. I had no intention of doing that. Not if I could help it.

I had a feeling I was going to have to prove that to him.

CHAPTER SIX

LANDON

"SO, you told Abbie about your childhood?" Channing asked softly. "How did she take it?" He sounded worried about me.

He was sweet that way, always putting my needs first and looking out for me. He'd been like that since we met. We clicked immediately, but like with Abbie, I held back, scared he'd walk right out of my life as quickly as he'd walked in. Equally scared he realised he was too good for a guy like me.

By some kind of miracle he stuck around, the one solid island in a sea of crazy. I loved him for it.

"As well as I expected." I nestled against my boyfriend's chest and debated leaning over to steal some of his croissant. I'd eaten mine already while he only picked at his. "She's sweet. I didn't think she would freak out. Especially knowing about the rest of the guys and their shit. Mine was pretty mild in comparison."

I hated feeling sorry for myself or making a fuss. Yeah, I went through shit, but other people went through worse.

"Hey." Channing caught my chin between his thumb and forefinger and turned my face towards him. "No one deserves to go through the stuff you did. Especially you. Breaks my heart to think about it." His gorgeous hazel eyes showed the truth of his words. He'd probably hide me away in a blanket fort if he could. With beer and too much cheese, if there was such a thing.

"Yours wasn't a bed of roses either." I pointed out. "Luckily, we both turned out okay. More or less."

Still gripping my chin, he kissed me. "We both turned out perfectly weird. That's the best way to be." He let my chin go and pushed his plate over to me. "I saw you eying it off. Might as well finish it. I'm not going to."

"You're the best," I told him.

He sat back to sip his coffee. "Hell yeah, I am. I'd tell you not to forget it, but there's no way you would. I'm that fuckin' epic." He tipped his head to the side and smiled.

"Yes you are," I said before biting into the croissant. "I swear they taste better here than anywhere else in the world."

"Everything tastes better in France than anywhere else in the world, because we're eating it here. Even greasy takeaway burgers."

"To be fair, greasy takeaway burgers taste good everywhere," I said. I tried to stick to a healthy diet, but once in a while I couldn't resist the lure of a good burger. They were like a siren, calling to me, begging me to stuff my face. Luring me with their delicious meaty juices...

Okay, I didn't need that much convincing. One of the guys suggests burgers and the rest of us follow along. We were super good at enabling each other when it came to food, music and sex.

Not necessarily in that order.

"You're not wrong, Lan," Channing said. He was the only one who called me that. Just like I was the only one who called him Chan.

Our fans called us Lanning or sometimes Chandon, which was super cute.

What would they call us if we both got together with Abbie? Whatever it was, I already couldn't pronounce it.

"Did you tell Abbie everything?" Channing put down his coffee cup and looked at me like he already knew the answer.

"Not everything," I admitted. "Not about that last time I saw Mum. It... kinda stings still. Y'know? I just wanted her to be happy for me." Even more, I wanted Mum to get her shit together. If I could, I would have dragged her off to rehab and made them lock her in until she wasn't a danger to herself. Or anyone else.

"Yeah, I know." He draped an arm over my shoulders. "At least my parents were just as shitty about it."

"Not surprising, given their strong views on LGBT folk," I said regretfully. His were the dictionary definition of homophobic. If conversion therapy was legal, they would have forced him to do it. Correction, they would have tried. Channing would have told them to fuck off.

"After everything my mother did, you think she'd be more understanding. The shit she did..." I hadn't expected her to be so harsh. So—bitter.

The worst part was, I didn't think she'd mind if I was gay, but somehow, for some reason I couldn't grasp, my being bi was offensive to her. It wasn't the first time I encountered shitty attitudes like that, but from my own mother...

At the end of the day, the best thing I could do would be not to sweat it too much. Her attitude, her words, they weren't going to change who I was, even if I wanted them to. Which I didn't.

I was attracted to who I was attracted to. End of story.

"She'll get over it," Channing said. "And if she doesn't, you have the rest of us. Forever." He lightly touched his nose to mine. "You know I love you, right?"

"Not as much as I love you," I said. That was our thing we said to each other. Our version of, 'I love you more.' "I don't know what I would do without you."

"Lucky for you, you'll never have to find out." He wiggled his nose against mine. "I'm not going anywhere."

"I don't think Abbie is either," I said carefully. "How do you feel about that?"

We talked about her lots of times in the last few months, but I always felt the need to check back in case his feelings changed. As busy as we were, it was easy to get caught up in everything and forget to communicate. The last thing I wanted was to lose anyone I loved because I hadn't taken the time.

Yeah, I was insecure as shit, but I had good reason to be.

"I feel the same way you feel," Channing said easily. "The same way the rest of the guys feel. There's something about her that draws us all in like a magnet. She just… Belongs. Like you and I belong."

I nodded, relieved to hear him say that. "You're right, that is exactly how I feel. But I worry about after the tour. How are things going to work then?"

"I don't know," he admitted. "But I know they will work out because we want them to. We'll do whatever it takes to make it happen. Right?" His expression was intense. He wanted Abbie as much as I did. As much as we wanted each other.

"Yeah, we will," I agreed. "Things are going to work out. I can feel it." I kissed him and then finished off the rest of the croissant while looking around the small café.

The rest of Wolf Venom, Blazing Violet and a bunch of tour staff sat finishing breakfast. Only a couple of people who sat at a table near the window had nothing to do with us. We'd pretty much taken over the whole place this morning. The café workers didn't seem to mind. Most of us were on our second cups of coffee.

My gaze was drawn over to where Abbie sat with Zeke, Asher and Violet, the lead singer of Blazing Violet. Violet's hair was as bright as mine, but purple rather than blue. She and Abbie seem to have formed a friendship during the tour. If she got sick of being surrounded by us guys, she had someone to talk to.

I couldn't not support that.

Abbie smiled and laughed at something Asher said.

I knew she had absolutely no idea how fucking gorgeous she was. Not just beautiful. Channing used the right word—magnetic. I wanted to look at her for hours on end. I wanted to listen to her talk and sing and laugh.

I wanted to touch her and fuck her like I had the other night. I wanted to curl up in a big bed with her and Channing and stay there for a year or ten. Maybe we could get the other guys to bring us essentials like coffee and croissants. That didn't seem like too much to ask.

Okay, they might get sick of that after the first year or two. They could just join us. A cuddle puddle for seven sounded perfect to me. With a huge movie screen at one end and shelves full of toys and rope at the other.

Channing handed me a napkin.

"What's that for?" I took it and frowned at him.

"For wiping up the drool on your chin." He grinned. "If you stare at her any longer, you're gonna start salivating."

I felt my face heat. "I stare at you just as much," I insisted. Was he teasing or jealous? I didn't want him to be jealous. I didn't want anything to mess up our relationship.

"You're adorable when you blush." He touched my nose with the tip of his finger, and traced the line up to my forehead and around the side of my face to my chin. "Even your ears turn red."

"I'm adorable all the time," I protested. "Just like you." I tilted my head so I could kiss the heel of his hand.

"Just like Abbie," Channing said. "I can't stop thinking about both of you the other night. It was pretty fucking epic."

"It was." We'd shared partners often enough to be in sync for much of the time. I knew a lot of them thought it was strange, but it made perfect sense to us. With Abbie, though, it was different. I felt like the three of us were extensions of each other. Like we all knew what was in each other's heads and what we all liked.

Granted, we'd watched her with the other guys a few times, and took mental notes, but doing it was a different story.

"What do you think she would think of..." I leaned over to whisper in his ear.

"I think she'd like it," Channing said, a glint in his eye. "I know I would. She seems game to try anything, as long as we're respectful and shit."

"We're always respectful and shit," I said with a nod.

Channing chuckled. "Yeah, we are. We're good dudes."

"The best." After a moment I added, "The best of the best." Our bandmates were pretty good dudes too. Most of the time. We were lucky to have found them. Even luckier to have had the success we had.

Okay, there was a shit load of hard work involved too, and a fuck ton of talent, but also some luck.

"Anyone would think we have healthy egos or something," Channing said with a laugh.

I snorted. "Pfft, not us. We're as humble as... I dunno what. Something fucking humble."

Okay, we weren't, but I'd met a lot of people worse than us. Some with good reason, others not so much. There was nothing wrong with having a good opinion of yourself, as long as you weren't a dick about it.

Channing's gaze fixed on something outside the window. He blinked and then frowned.

"What?" I turned and squinted, trying to figure out what caught his attention.

He shook his head slowly, then tore his eyes off the window. "It's nothing. I thought I saw someone I knew, that's all."

"You're in a café in Paris, which is, at this very moment, full of people you know," I pointed out. "And this isn't all of us. Was it someone from the tour?"

"No." He peered into his coffee cup like he wished it was still full and hot. "It's nothing. They just looked familiar, that's all. Nothing to worry about."

"Okay," I said slowly. I wanted to believe him, but he looked rattled. Then again, a lot of things got him rattled. Never for very long, but enough to be noticeable and to make me worry each time. I would never not worry about him if anything bothered him. No matter how big or small a thing might be.

"Do you want another coffee?" I asked.

"What I'd really like is to run all the way up the Eiffel Tower," he said, snapping back to his normal self again. "That would get the blood pumping."

"If anyone I know would, or could, do that, it would be you," I told him.

Him or Penn. They were both bundles of pent up energy that needed somewhere to go. "Maybe you should challenge Penn to a race up to the second floor."

He looked thoughtful. "I wonder if we could get Levi to convince them to let us race all the way to the top."

The stairs from the second floor to the top of the Eiffel Tower weren't open to the public. But we were Wolf Venom. Would they bend the rules for us?

"I would bet on you," I told him. Even if I didn't think he would win, I would still put my money on Channing. As much as I loved Penn, Channing was my person. I would support him no matter what he did.

He smiled, but he still looked troubled.

CHAPTER
SEVEN

ABBIE

"ARE THEY REALLY GONNA DO THIS?" I slipped on my sunglasses against the glare of the sun and straightened my black ball cap. Okay, Asher's cap, but I swiped it a few days ago and he hadn't said anything.

Jackson glanced down at me, and shrugged. He had his 'long-suffering manager' expression in place. "It can't hurt. Well, it shouldn't hurt us. It might hurt them when they're doing it, but if they're that silly, who am I to stop them?"

Because of tourists and safety concerns, Channing and Penn weren't allowed to race up the Eiffel Tower. Much to their disappointment and a non-zero level of swearing. Being the guys they were, once the challenge was on, they had to follow through. Because—of course they did.

They'd hunted for somewhere else ever since. They finally decided to race each other around the outside of the Olympiastadion in Munich.

It was as good a place as any, I supposed.

"Just another day in the life of Wolf Venom," Asher said lightly. He pulled his navy blue cap down to shade his eyes better. Like all the guys, he wore designer sunglasses. Mine were just a cheap pair I picked up in Sydney airport. It might be time for me to upgrade.

"Another day in the life of Channing and Penn," Landon agreed, nodding. He didn't wear a cap, just sunglasses with big rims, shorts and a singlet that showed off his muscular arms and tattoos. The arm holes were so wide, when he lifted his arms, his nipple ring glinted in the sunlight.

"I didn't realise they were so competitive with each other," I said. Of course, you didn't achieve a high level of success without a decent amount of mongrel in you, as they say. Determination, fight, whatever you wanted to call it.

"It's not that they're competitive with each other," Zeke said slowly. He was dressed from head to toe in black, including a cap the same as mine.

"It's that they're competitive with *everyone*," Tully finished for him. "They both came from families of overachievers that expected them to be over-over-achievers. Sometimes they like to rebel against their upbringing and sometimes they go along with it."

"And sometimes they like to be seen," Landon said. The crowd had already noticed us and started to gather, wondering what the hell we were doing.

"They're going to be seen all right," I said. I couldn't miss the paparazzi mingling with the crowd. They'd already taken several photos of us. Unfortunately for them, we weren't doing anything embarrassing or scandalous.

Yet. Give it a minute, that could change.

"Am I the only one resisting the urge to flip the paparazzi the finger?" Asher asked cheerfully.

"Nope, I'm resisting too," Zeke said.

"I was thinking about mooning them." Landon stepped closer to me, until his bare arm brushed mine.

I laced my fingers in his. I sensed he liked to have someone physically close by as much as possible. Part of constantly thinking people will leave you included struggling to let them out of your sight. Channing wasn't just his boyfriend, he was his emotional support saxophonist. Didn't everyone need one of those?

He squeezed my hand and I caught the look of gratitude on his face.

"You're not really thinking of mooning anyone are you?" I asked him.

"I would say not in public, but we both know I would." He grinned. "Not in front of paparazzi though. The whole world isn't ready to see my ass." He spoke with no hint of modesty. He'd probably run around naked and not blink an eye.

Why not, his ass was adorable.

"They aren't ready to see mine either," I agreed. There was exhibitionism and then there was getting yourself arrested for public nudity. Not to mention having photos of you go viral. It was a fine line.

"Let's save both for later," he suggested.

"Deal," I said. My stomach fluttered. I doubted there would come a day when I didn't want any of the guys. Or all of them. Part of me still wondered if that was greedy, but most of me didn't care if it was.

Before I met the guys, I wouldn't have dreamt about dating any of them. They were so far out of my league we weren't on the same planet. Now, a whole freaking rock band was mine. Six guys. It was surreal and magical. Whichever direction I turned, there was a guy who cared about me. Who I cared about.

I was beyond blessed, and grateful for every moment of it.

"Looks like they're ready," Jackson said.

Levi, who stood about ten metres away, raised his arm above his head. He'd travelled around with us since Dublin. Penn joked he'd stuck around just for this. Levi hadn't denied it.

"Ready. Set," Levi said loudly.

Channing and Penn jostled each other playfully, trying to put each other off. Or knock each other over.

"Remember," Levi called out, obviously trying to catch them off guard so one or both would break early. "No tripping each other, no trying to hurt each other, and no running into members of the public."

He didn't say anything about not running into paparazzi. That probably went without saying.

"Go!" Levi shouted. He dropped his arm and took a few hurried steps back as the guys leapt forward at a run, Penn slightly ahead due to having a height advantage.

The crowd, who cottoned on to what was going on by now, started to cheer.

It's not every day you get impromptu entertainment from a pair of rock gods. Especially hot ones who were going to be glistening with sweat by the end of this race.

Yum.

"They're going to need to shower after this," Landon remarked.

"You're right," I said. "I wonder if they'll need any help."

"Only the winner," he said with a sly smile.

"You're sure Channing will win, aren't you?" I asked.

I didn't think he'd help Penn shower, nor would the keyboardist want him to. Was it wrong that I pictured that anyway and liked what I saw?

No, I decided, it wasn't. Luckily I had plenty more fantasies to live out, and guys happy to help me fulfill them.

"He's quick," Landon said. "He's built more for running than Penn is."

"Penn used to run in school," Asher said. "If half of what he says is true, he was good at it. When his parents let him take part." The grimace on his lips showed what he thought about that.

"I guess we'll see," Zeke said. His expression matched Asher's. I suspected the Brantley family was as supportive as Penn's when it came to having fun.

I swung my gaze away the direction Penn and Channing went, but they'd already run out of sight.

"What if it's a tie?" I asked.

"The hotel has a big shower," Landon said without hesitation. He looked over at me and grinned, then leaned in to lightly kiss my mouth.

"We could all fit," Asher said. "Even Jackson."

The band's manager looked at him in surprise, then shook his head and looked away.

"I think that's a no," Zeke remarked.

Jackson didn't look back when he said, "That's a fuck no. You guys are enough trouble without going that far."

"You know you love us," Asher said. He pouted playfully at Jackson's back.

"You're okay," Jackson said patiently. "Doesn't mean I want to get naked with you all."

"Which one of us do you want to get naked with?" Tully asked teasingly.

Jackson sighed. When Levi walked over to join us, he said, "I think I should get a pay raise for having to put up with these guys' apparent fascination with my sex life."

Levi laughed. "If they're hassling you, they're leaving me alone."

"That doesn't seem fair," Asher said. "Fortunately, we have the ability to hassle you both. We're equal opportunity hasslers."

I smiled at the infectious grin on Asher's face. The whole vibe from White Wolf Records was so different to what I experienced at Onyx Riot. Everyone genuinely seemed to like each other. To say we were one big family was usually such a cliché, but in this case it was true.

Jackson and Levi were like big brothers or uncles to everyone else, rather than bosses and managers. Most bosses wouldn't let the guys get away with half the things they did, for a start.

"Levi, what were you saying about getting a drum machine?" One side of Jackson's mouth pulled up in a smile.

"I believe I said it would be cheaper and less trouble than Asher." Levi grinned.

"Hey!" Asher said in protest. "You wouldn't replace me. No drum machine could sound as good, or look as awesome, as I do." He didn't even look slightly concerned that they might follow through with the threat.

"I dunno." Jackson scratched the side of his head. "Technology has come a long way." He lost the struggle to hold back a smile.

"Fine, I'll stop hassling you. For now." Asher crossed his arms over his chest, stuck out his chin and looked at Jackson down his nose. He was too stinking cute when he was pretending to be serious.

"No doubt that will last about an hour," Jackson said dryly, clearly unmoved.

"An hour if you're lucky," Asher agreed. He craned his neck. "Any sign of them yet? How long does it take to run around one stadium?"

"It depends on the stadium, but more than five minutes, babe," Zeke told him. "Although, knowing them, they probably stopped for a latte." He gestured in the general direction of the other side of the stadium.

"If there's a place that sells coffee on the other side of the stadium," Tully said slowly, a frown on his brow, "then why are we standing here?"

"That's a good question," Asher said. "It's probably because we'd get distracted by the coffee and forget to watch the race."

"There's a race?" Zeke asked jokingly.

Asher turned to him. "So I've heard. I'm not sure if the rumour is accurate or not though." He rubbed his chin as though deep in thought.

"I think you missed your calling," Jackson said. "You all should have been stand-up comedians." He gave a playful half roll of his eyes.

"I think that's a backhanded way of saying we're fucking hilarious," Zeke said.

"That's what it sounded like to me," Tully agreed. "Thanks, Jackson."

Jackson snorted. "You're welcome. I think." He scrunched up his face and shook his head.

Asher hooked an arm through Jackson's. "Aren't you lucky to have the best job in the world? Imagine how many people wish they could hang around with us all day, everyday. You're basically living the dream right here."

"Lucky me," Jackson said ironically. In spite of his apparent lack of enthusiasm, he smiled. "Yeah, okay. I am fortunate to do what I do. There are definitely bands out there who are a lot worse than you guys."

"Like who?" Asher asked. His face lit up with curiosity.

"I would tell you, but I signed an NDA saying I wouldn't," Jackson said.

Asher groaned. "Fucking NDAs. They spoil all the fun."

"They also stop me from spilling all your secrets," Jackson pointed out.

"Awesome NDAs," Asher said, snapping his fingers. "They're the best thing since sliced bread."

"I've never seen you change your tune that quickly," Tully teased. "Even on stage."

Asher laughed. "Yeah, well, when you're wrong, you're wrong. Although, I bet sometimes Jackson would like to get shit off his chest." He gave the manager a cagey look.

"That's why Jax talks to me about stuff," Levi said. "You're not allowed to know things, but I am. You know, being the boss and all."

Asher turned and cocked his head at Tully. "Tull, if we signed with your label, would you tell us stuff?"

"Nope," Tully said lightly. "Not if there's an NDA in place. Which there would be. Besides, everything we do is more interesting anyway. Probably." He raised his hands to either side like he wasn't sure.

"Exactly," Jackson said. "If I told you, you'd be bored silly, instead of just the regular kind of silly."

Before Asher could respond, a ripple of excitement passed through the crowd. People started to chant either Channing's name or Penn's. It seemed like they had an equal amount of fans amongst those watching.

Landon squeezed my hand hard with excitement. He was standing on his toes and craning his neck to see over the crowd.

I didn't even try. If he couldn't see, I had no chance.

Not until Zeke said, "Want a piggyback?"

I barely had time to register what he said before the guys were helping me up to sit on Zeke's shoulders. I gripped on tight with my legs, feet hooked around each other, his hands holding mine.

"Are you sure this is okay?" I asked. Was that him wobbling or me? Or both?

"You barely weigh a thing," Zeke said. He was definitely not the one wobbling. "I could have you sit on me all day."

I snorted a laugh. "I bet you could." And not on his shoulders either.

"How's the view up there?" Tully asked.

I looked around. "Amazing. I can see the guys. They're neck and neck." Until I saw them, I hadn't realised how nervous I was to let them out of my sight. Security surrounded the stadium, blending in with the crowds, but I still liked them where I could see them.

I let go of one of Zeke's hands long enough to wave at a paparazzo as he started to snap photos of us. This was the kind of positive story I didn't mind them sharing with the world. Nothing scandalous, just sitting on the shoulders of one of my boyfriends.

"Where's the finish line?" I asked.

"Oh, shit." While we snickered, Levi trotted back over to where he'd started the race. He must have forgotten to get back into position until I reminded him.

He got back in place just in time to drop his arm and celebrate the winner.

CHAPTER
EIGHT

ABBIE

"THAT WAS AWESOME." Now we were inside the stadium and away from public scrutiny it was safe to push myself up on my toes and kiss Penn.

"Of course it was." He snaked an arm around my waist and pulled me until my breasts were pressed against his firm chest. "I won."

"And we're never going to hear the end of it, are we?" I teased.

"Nope." He slashed his mouth over mine and kissed me, rough and demanding. "What do I get for winning?"

"Bragging rights," Levi said as he slid past us in the stadium corridor.

"The promise of a rematch." Channing was close behind Levi, his hand in Landon's. He was still smiling. He might be as competitive as fuck, but he was a good loser. Probably because he knew there would be chances to beat Penn another day.

"Any time, dude," Penn said. "I'll wipe the floor with you again."

"You didn't win by that much," Asher pointed out.

"I'll take you on too," Penn told him. "You don't get to criticise if you won't put your money where your mouth is."

"That is a really weird expression," Asher said. He shrugged and hurried after Zeke as the lead singer disappeared into the stadium's green room.

"He's right, it is," Tully said. "Personally, I'd love to see who would win a race between you and Asher."

Penn drew himself up a little taller. "Me. Asher is too busy running his mouth off to outrun me."

Asher stuck his head out of the green room door. "I heard that." He ducked back inside.

Penn snorted a laugh. "I need a shower." He eyed me speculatively.

I looked back at him. In the corner of my eye, I saw Channing and Landon. They seemed to be having the same conversation.

"There's plenty of showers for everyone," I said.

"Good, because I wasn't asking." Penn took my hand and led me through the green room, to the bathrooms at the back.

All of our things were here already, including changes of clothes. I fully intended to have a shower anyway, but why not share? We might even take a moment to get clean.

"Of course you weren't." I gave him a long look before heading into one of the cubicles.

"We could conserve water by sharing," Landon pointed out.

"It would definitely be good for the planet if all four of us were in there." Channing nodded.

When he put it that way...

Penn shrugged and reached down with one hand to pull his shirt off over his head. "There's plenty of room."

There wasn't really, but that was kind of the point.

Faint heat in my face, and with the full knowledge all three guys were watching me, I started to shed my clothes.

Funny that, even after fucking in a room full of strangers, I was still self-conscious about my body. Less than I used to be, thanks to six guys who always seemed to like what they saw.

"You are so fucking gorgeous," Penn whispered. He waved to the other guys in and closed and locked the door behind him.

"I know you are," I told him. He was mouthwateringly hot as fuck.

Since fair's fair, I watched them strip off, until I was surrounded by naked, sweaty muscle.

Holy fucking yes please.

Penn turned the water on and kept his hand under it until steam started to rise. He nodded to himself, then grabbed my wrists and turned me around to face the shower wall. He pinned me to the tiles with one hand.

Water gushed down my hair and down my back, hot, but not as hot as Penn pressing the full length of his body against me so the shower poured down over us both. His cock poked into the back of my leg, hard and ready.

He ground against my thigh, his breath a ragged groan over the water.

"So fucking gorgeous," he muttered. With one hand keeping me in place, he reached around with the other, deft fingers nudging my thighs open and delving into my clit and folds.

I moved my feet further apart, giving him better access. He grunted in triumph as he found my clit and traced circles around and over it with two fingers.

I blinked water out of my eyes and turned so my sodden hair fell off my face.

Landon was on his knees right beside me. His fingers were cupped around Channing's balls, the saxophonist's cock right in front of him, thick and firm.

Landon ran his fingers up and over Channing's balls a few times, while teasingly flicking his tongue at his tip.

Channing groaned and looked ready to slam himself into Landon's mouth. Teasing must be their thing, because he waited until Landon was ready to slip his lips over him and started to suck. Then he curled his fingers in Landon's blue hair and pulled him closer, going deeper.

Forever, I'd always find that arousing as fuck. Muscular, masculine men being intimate. All the smokin' hot.

"You want to do that too?" Penn asked, his tone rough with desire, mouth right beside my ear.

He loosened his grip on my wrists. "Get on your knees." He pushed me down so I was half in, half out of the water, kneeling beside Landon. He tangled his fingers in my hair and positioned his cock in front of my mouth.

"What do you say?" He smirked at me.

"Yes, sir." Eagerly, I opened to let him slide between my lips.

I sucked him hard, using my lips and tongue, taking him all the way to the back of my throat while I cupped and stroked his balls with my hand.

He thrust into me a few times, then pulled my head back and guided me over to Channing's cock.

Landon sat back on his heels, eyes dark with desire while he watched me suck his boyfriend.

I watched him back, our eyes locked on each other.

After a minute or two, Landon rose and stood where the spray from the shower landed in droplets on his tanned skin.

Penn drew me back off Channing's cock and guided me over to Landon's.

"Fuck yeah," Landon breathed as I closed my lips around his hot length.

I teased his weeping slit with the tip of my tongue and sucked, my eyes still on his.

Penn muttered something incoherent and drew me back to him.

Landon crouched back down between me and Channing. He teased Channing's cock with his mouth, while stretching around my ass and running his fingers lightly over and around my pussy.

"You're so wet," he said. "Not just from the shower."

I laughed and tried not to get a mouthful of water. Of course I was wet. Between his touch and Penn alternating my mouth between his cock and Channing's, I was a matter of breaths away from coming.

When Landon swivelled my hips around and pulled me down onto his cock, I almost did. My whole body tingled with a surge of blood and passion.

Only Penn's barked order, "Don't come yet," stopped me from exploding then and there.

I groaned and looked up at him in playful defiance.

He gave me an arched eyebrow and a, 'Don't you fucking dare,' look.

With my eyes, I told him how much he sucked, but he smirked and kept on being smug. He knew I'd wait until he told me to come, whatever it took.

As if in on the game, Landon thrust into me slowly, taking his time, while he gave Channing's cock the same careful treatment.

What else could I do but join in? I slid my mouth off Penn's length and teased him lightly with the tip of my tongue.

He gave me an amused look, but I just smiled.

Takes four to play this game, buddy.

Finally, on some unseen signal, we all moved faster, sucked harder, thrust deeper. We went from languid to frantic in a heartbeat.

Channing was the first to come, his hands wrapped around the back of Landon's wet hair. His hips swung back and forth as he milked himself dry between the bassist's lips.

So. Fucking. Hot.

He slid his softened length out of Landon's mouth and sat on the tiles beside me. While Landon thrust hungrily, Channing's fingers hummed against my clit, barely touching at first, then firmer, as if searching for my orgasm.

Concentration on his face, he slipped past my folds and into me, so two of his fingers and Landon's cock were inside my pussy at the same time.

My eyes widened. That was... different, but I liked it.

They set a rhythm of pressing up into me, both relentless, as if wanting me to come to spite Penn.

At the same time, Penn's eyes were on me, ordering me to wait.

Blood roared through me, pushing me closer and closer.

Landon kept a hand on my hip and reached around to tease my nipple with the other.

I gasped around Penn's cock. I needed to come so badly it was almost an exquisite agony.

I turned pleading eyes up at Penn.

He hesitated for a moment longer, then nodded. "Okay, you've been a good girl for long enough. Come like a dirty whore."

On command, my whole body exploded with pleasure. I might have cried out and bit down on Penn's cock. He jumped, but didn't pull out. Instead, he came too, thrusting and grunting while water and orgasmic goodness washed down over me.

My juices gushed over Landon's cock and Channing's fingers, driving an orgasm out of Landon. He thrust harder, deeper, furious, gasping and moaning until the last delicious drop of pleasure was forced out of us both.

I pulled off Penn's cock, swallowed, then flopped down under the hot flow of water and let it wash me clean.

CHAPTER
NINE

LANDON

"HEY, I need to talk to you about something." I curled my fingers around Abbie's wrist and stopped her from taking more than a couple of steps from the tour bus.

I'd thought about this the whole way from Munich to Zürich. I could have talked to her on the drive, but the moment hadn't come. The mood was light the whole way. I didn't want to be the one to shatter it.

Now, I couldn't sit on it any longer. Shit, I was freaking out on the inside. On the outside too, judging by her expression. I was trying to play it cool. Seems I didn't pull it off.

Fuck.

"That sounds serious," she said, her tone deceptively light. She looked worried, scared even.

I should have thought this through better before I spoke. She always seemed so strong and confident, sometimes I forgot what she'd been through with Vance and Pete, and the assholes from the press.

"Shit," I said softly. I pulled her to me and kissed her nose. "It's nothing like that, honey, I promise."

I grabbed Channing's hand in my free one and laced my fingers in Abbie's. We walked slowly behind the others towards the door that led inside Letzi-grund Stadion.

"What is it about?" she asked. In spite of my assurances, she looked like she thought I was about to break up with her.

I was never very good at this stuff. The other guys had the charisma, the way with words. I was awkward as hell.

I exchanged glances with Channing. He nodded reassuringly and smiled. At least one of us had faith in me.

I swallowed down my nerves, part of them anyway, and spoke. "It's about my mother."

"Have you heard from her?" Abbie asked immediately. "Is she okay?" Of course she would be concerned and interested. I called her honey, but she was sweeter than that.

I shook my head. "I don't know. I just wanted to tell you about the last time I saw her. We had a fight. She..." I glanced at Channing again. "She wasn't accepting of him and I. She didn't understand how I could be into guys and girls. She..."

I felt like I was picking at my own scab with this. Opening wounds which were still healing.

I swallowed, then spat out the words, "She told me she wished she hadn't had me." That was the tip of the iceberg, but it was the main point.

Abbie winced and drew me to a stop. "I'm sure she didn't mean that."

"I'm sure she did," I said with equal conviction. It wasn't just the words, it was the truth behind them. More than once, the guys whom she was with wanted her to ditch me. Then they'd ditched her. She made me feel like a dead weight around her shoulders. The thing keeping her from living her life, or giving in and dying in the gutter.

She made me wish she'd never had me too.

"She was harsh," Channing said simply. "It's up to him, of course, I'll support him no matter what, but I'd be happy if he never saw her again. He deserves better."

He looked furious now as he had back then, six months ago. At the time, I thought he'd punch Mum out. If she was a man, he probably would have.

"Yeah," I said softly. "Channing was amazing." I gave him a soft look, trying to convey the love I felt for him. "He let me cry on his shoulder for about three days."

Okay, that was an exaggeration. It was two and half days.

After everything she put me through, the last thing I wanted to hear, needed to hear, was that she never wanted me in the first place. I shouted back at her that I'd never asked to be born and things went downhill from there. The things we said to each other...

I wasn't sure if I'd ever get a chance to make amends.

Or even if I wanted to.

No, that's not true, I definitely wanted to, if only for my own peace of mind.

"Anyway," I continued, "Mum and I didn't part on good terms. It was ugly as shit. I'm sorry to dump all of this on you, I needed you to know the whole story." I didn't want to hold back anything from her. It was why I needed to tell her about that fight. It was a small deal in the scheme of things, especially compared with what she'd been through, but it was a big deal for me. My mother made letting me down an art form. I didn't want to do the same to the people I loved. I needed Abbie to know that. I was all in. This was my round-about way of telling her that.

"Thanks for telling me," Abbie said softly. "There's nothing you could ever say to me that would make me turn my back on you like that. Either of you."

"You say that," I said, "but you don't know *all* our dirty little secrets." I managed a faint smile. Just most of them.

She smiled back and squeezed my hand. "There's nothing so dirty...or so little, that would make me run away." She grimaced. "I mean, you know I did some dumb things and none of you turned your back on me. That goes both ways. Always. Okay?"

"None of us has to worry about *little*." My smile got bigger and more genuine now.

"That's true," she said. "Little is definitely not a word I would use to describe any of you."

I swung their hands to either side of me while we walked. I could get used to this. Not just being able to open up to her, not just being with them, but the whole feeling of belonging.

In the back of my mind was still the thought she might walk away and break my heart. For the most part, I was able to ignore it, but it lingered.

Why would a woman like her want a guy like me anyway? Especially when she had five others to choose from? Not to mention a planet full of single guys who would probably do just about anything to get her.

I was sure she didn't even notice the stares she got when she walked down the street. It wasn't just because she was famous, or because she was surrounded by six hot guys. People looked at *her*. I looked at her a lot too. Some days, it was hard to tear my eyes away from both of them.

Insecure Landon, who sat on my shoulder like a dead weight, told me they were both too good for me. That they might hook up and run away together. That at the end, I'd be the one to end up alone. That—

Fuck off, I told him. *Let me enjoy myself. If shit goes down, I'll deal with it.* Even if they ripped out my heart.

"Don't look now," Channing said suddenly. "We have company." He nodded straight ahead.

I turned to look. Not surprising, a gaggle of paparazzi, cameras and phones in hand, waited outside the entrance to the arena.

"Want me to let your hand go?" I asked Abbie. Photos of her sitting on Zeke's shoulders went viral and fans seemed to love it. To then see her holding hands with me might confuse the issue.

She hesitated for a moment. "Not if you don't want to," she said finally. "Let them think whatever they want to think. It's not like they're wrong anyway. Relationships like ours are more normal than people seem to think. Maybe we can help to normalise it a bit more. It's way past time people stopped stigmatising polyamorous relationships."

"I couldn't agree more." I nodded and walked a bit more proudly. She wasn't just gorgeous and sweet, she was a badass.

I hoped she didn't end up regretting the choice. We all knew how vicious the paparazzi could be. A shiver of worry crept up my spine. What if they were so vicious she changed her mind and walked away from us?

Yeah, that was insecure Landon again. He didn't know when to piss off. Asshole.

I thought about letting her hand go anyway, but I didn't. I couldn't seem to make myself do it. The little boy in me who just wanted to hug his mother, wanted to hold on to her and Channing and never let either of them go.

Yeah, even big, bad rock stars have inner little boys and insecure assholes messing with their heads.

As soon as we got close enough, the paparazzi started to take photos. People stopped to stare and point when they realised who we were.

Lines and lines of people wound around barricades outside the stadium. By the look of it, a lot of them camped out overnight just to get a front row spot at the concert tonight. Sweet. I loved their dedication. It went a long way to bolstering my ego.

We waved, but the paparazzi stepped in front of the crowds to take photos.

"Get the fuck out of the way," one of the fans shouted.

"Yeah, leave them alone," shouted another.

Someone in the crowd started to chant and everyone else quickly took it up. "Wolf Venom! Wolf Venom! Venom! Venom! Venom!"

They started to push against the barricades. Security, dressed in black uniforms with radios on their shoulders, hurried in from all angles to hold them back.

"Let's get inside," Jackson said, urgency in his tone. "Before things get ugly."

The crowd shouted louder, more demanding.

Someone threw a water bottle. It slammed into the shoulder of one of the paparazzi.

The crowd cheered and jeered, pushed harder against the flimsy barricades.

Security waded through the crowds, trying to reach the person who threw the bottle. The fans immediately closed rank around them.

"Shit, this isn't how this is supposed to go," Abbie said. Her face was pale. Her hand was sweaty in mine.

I murmured my agreement and pulled her and Channing along a little faster. The sooner we got out of the area, the less chance there would be of a riot, or something else, happening.

That was the last thing we needed this close to the end of the European leg of the tour. Okay, that and a bunch of other shit that might happen. Fuck knows we'd been through enough already.

We were herded along, but I kept looking over my shoulder. I couldn't tell if they got the person who threw the bottle but I caught Abbie's expression in the corner of my eye. She was white as snow, her mouth pressed in a tight line.

I didn't need to be a mind reader to know what she was thinking. She was remembering the music festival in Queensland where someone threw a can and hit her in the face. A bunch of other people had thrown cans and water bottles onto the stage as well.

I had to grab Channing's hand to keep him from jumping down into the audience and start swinging. All of the guys were pissed, but him most of all.

Honestly, if he'd thrown a few punches, I would have joined him.

And we'd be locked up in jail right now instead of hurrying into the stadium in Zürich.

"Are you okay?" I knew she'd been asked that at least three hundred million times in the last few months, but I couldn't help asking again.

"Um, kinda," she said. "Just a little freaked out. I'm not a fan of when people start throwing things. Especially when they actually hit people with them."

I let go of her hand and slipped an arm around her instead. "Me either. At least they're not throwing things at us this time."

"Right, but that guy could have been badly hurt." She looked back over her shoulder as we hurried through the doorway.

"Only you would feel bad for paparazzi after what they've done to you," I told her.

She looked up at me and smiled. "I only hold a grudge against some paparazzi in particular, not them as a group."

"You're crazy," Penn said. "They all fucking suck. Not in a good way either."

"If they sucked in a good way, would you want them to?" Asher asked. He seemed genuinely curious, but grinned teasingly at the same time.

"Hell no." Penn grimaced. "Being an asshole might be contagious. I don't want to catch it." After a moment he added, "I'm enough of an asshole already. But at least I am a faster runner than Channing." He smiled slyly at the saxophonist.

Channing flipped him off. "I had an off day, that's all. Next time, I'm going to whip your ass." He rubbed the palms of his hands together like he couldn't wait to get on with the job.

"Promises, promises," Penn said. "Maybe I don't want to race you again after all. Gotta keep my reputation intact."

"If you don't race me again, you'll get a reputation as a chicken," Channing challenged.

"I don't have a problem with that," Penn said lightly. "But I'm going to race you again to prove that I can beat you again. But next time, let's have higher stakes."

"Like what?" Channing asked.

Penn shrugged. "I dunno. I'll think of something."

"Whatever it is, game on," Channing said. "I look forward to you eating my dust."

"At least it's never boring around here," I said to Abbie.

She snorted a laugh. "It certainly isn't." She was a tad less pale, but still clearly rattled.

I hoped it didn't give her doubts about staying on the tour with us. The thought of her leaving left me cold.

"Hey," I said, suddenly shy. "Would you have dinner with us tonight? I... have something in mind." Something I hoped she and Channing would like.

"Of course," she said. "Just the three of us?"

"Yeah. Dress all fancy. I'll arrange all the things."

CHAPTER
TEN

ABBIE

I HAD no idea what Landon planned, so it took forever to decide what to wear. I narrowed it down to my little black dress and a cute black skirt and red halter top. I lay them both out on one of the beds and looked back and forth between them about a million times.

"What do you think?" I asked Asher.

He sat on the edge of one of the other beds, watching me watching my clothes as if they would stand up and beg to be put on. I wished they would. That would make the choice easier. Of course I'd go with the outfit that lay there like it wasn't alive and freaking me the fuck out.

"I'm going to assume naked isn't an option?" he asked.

"I don't think so," I said dryly. I mean, stranger things, right? "I just saw Landon disappear into the other room with a bag that looked like it had a suit in it. Not a birthday suit," I added quickly.

Asher snapped his fingers. "Bummer. In that case I say you should go for…" He rubbed his chin and thought.

"The dress. Landon said fancy, didn't he? Dresses like that are universally fancy. Especially when they're lying in a puddle on the floor."

I laughed softly. "Do you think about anything other than sex?"

"Absolutely," he agreed. "Sometimes I think about drumming. Not very often, mind you. I wouldn't want to distract from all the thinking about sex."

Zeke came and sat beside Asher. "Did I hear someone mention sex?" He kissed Asher, then grabbed my hand and pulled me onto his lap. "Are we making plans? Or just getting down to it?" He kissed me lightly, but quickly deepened the kiss. His tongue grazed over my lip, enticing me to forget what I was doing. And maybe my name.

I kissed him back, but then broke it off. "I'm supposed to be getting ready for a date with Landon and Channing."

"Ah, the mysterious date," Zeke said. "He's been buzzing about it all day, but he won't give anyone any details." He didn't look pleased about that.

"Landon's not going to do anything stupid," Asher said. "He wouldn't risk Channing or Abbie."

"What are we going to do when we get back to Australia?" I asked. "Hole ourselves up in a hotel until the end of time?"

"I don't know," Zeke admitted. "We'll take care of it. Whatever it takes to do that. Even if we have to buy an island and hide out there."

"I'm down for that, if it has Wi-Fi," Asher said.

"It would definitely have Wi-Fi," Zeke said. "And place for a helicopter to land. And a yacht or two. And a bunch of staff to cook and clean for us."

I sighed. "That sounds heavenly. Where do I sign up?"

"Anywhere you like," Zeke said. "As long as you come with us."

"Wait," Asher said. "We need a recording studio too."

"Fuck yeah," Zeke said. "We can fly Candy out to produce our stuff. We're going to need to keep releasing if we're going to afford this island and all the shit on it."

"Blazing Violet and Cameo Orchid can come and record there," Asher said.

I leaned into Zeke and rested my head on his shoulder. If nothing else, it was a nice fantasy. At some point, we'd have to find a way to get back to living in the real world. Would it ever be safe enough to do that though? It had to be. If Zeke said we would deal with it, then we would. One way or another.

"Can we have our own chickens?" I asked. "I've always wanted to have chickens. They're so cute and fresh eggs are so nice."

"If you want chickens, then we're having chickens." Zeke nodded.

"I can see children chasing them around," Asher said. "Little blond-haired kids who look just like me."

"That would be sweet," Zeke said, his voice low. "But I'd like at least one to look like me." He looked at me with dark eyes.

What could I say to that? I wasn't ready to think about next week, much less children. One for each guy was a lot of children. Would they all even want that? That was a question for another day. Maybe another year.

"I don't think it's very nice to encourage children to chase chickens," I said. "Although, from what I know about chickens, they're more likely to chase children. Especially the roosters."

"Would we need a rooster?" Asher asked. "I think we have enough cocks as it is." He chuckled.

I laughed too. "We'll put a rooster on the maybe pile." Along with all of those children.

"And if the rooster chases any children, we'll put it on the barbecue," Zeke said, a broad grin on his face.

"Are you going to kill it?" Asher asked. "Or take a hit out on it? Maybe Tully could use his ninja skills to do it."

"What am I using my ninja skills on?" Tully sat down on the bed beside my two outfits, careful not to sit on them.

He shook his head after Asher explained. "I don't think I could kill an innocent animal."

Asher opened his mouth, but closed it again.

I guessed he was going to say Tully would kill a rooster if it tried to kill him first, but thought better of it.

Judging by the expression on Tully's face, he saw the same thing. His eyes took on a haunted look until he shook his head and managed to smile.

"I'm sure you can find someone to do the deed," Tully said lightly.

"Maybe we should just not get a rooster," I said. "While you're all here, I could use all your input on what outfit to wear tonight."

"We've already ruled out her going naked," Asher said helpfully.

"Shame." Tully clicked his tongue. "You could wear one of my T-shirts. You'd look cute like that."

"Yes I would," I said. "But I don't think that's what Landon had in mind when he said fancy." Or maybe he did and I had it all wrong. I didn't think so though.

"My T-shirts are very fancy." Tully sniffed and pretended to look offended. "You could put a belt around your waist and a pair of heels."

"Why does that sound so fucking hot?" Asher asked.

"It does, doesn't it?" Zeke asked.

"I don't have a belt." I shrugged. I had to agree, the outfit would look adorable.

"You could use the cord I use to charge my phone," Asher offered. "What could be hotter than a USB cord wrapped around you?"

"Just about everything?" I said tentatively. I made a face at him and laughed. "I'm not going to wear a cable around myself, but thank you for the offer."

"You're welcome," Asher said. "What about shoelaces?"

"What about I wear one of these outfits?" I gestured towards them. "Or I could go and buy something new, but that could take hours." I glanced at my watch. My shopping trips never took that long, but the implied threat that they would have to follow me around while I looked through clothes and tried things on, might hurry the guys up in making up their minds.

"I vote for the black dress," Zeke said quickly.

"Me too," Tully said.

Mission accomplished. I bit back a smile.

"Thank you," I said graciously. I hopped off Zeke's lap and folded up the skirt and halter top. I placed them back in my suitcase and closed the lid. "It really would be nice to go for a shopping trip one day."

"Take Penn." Asher jerked his head in his direction. "He loves shopping for clothes."

Penn, who was sitting on the couch watching cartoons on TV, looked over and nodded. "For once in his life, Asher isn't being sarcastic. I actually do like shopping for clothes."

"We knew there was something wrong with him," Asher said jokingly.

"You could do with a few new outfits," Penn said, looking him up and down critically. "Do you own anything that doesn't have a hole in it somewhere?"

"Of course I fucking do," Asher said in protest. "At least a couple of things."

"This whole conversation is ironic, since we all have clothes with holes in them," Tully said. "We wouldn't look much like rock stars if we were in three-piece suits or brand-new jeans. The kind that look new."

"No, then we would be crooners or pop stars," Asher agreed. "And we're neither of those. Although, we would look sharp in three-piece suits."

"No," Zeke said simply.

"No?" Asher asked.

"No, we're not wearing suits on stage," Zeke said for clarification. "At least, I'm not. You guys can please yourselves I guess." He shrugged. "It's too fucking hot out there for that. We get drenched enough as it is."

"In a word, no fucking way," Penn said.

"That's three words," Tully pointed out.

"Whatever." Penn changed the channel. "Well shit."

"What is it?" I glanced up to see him watching the news. That couldn't be good.

"To the surprise of absolutely no one, Sydney police have ruled the death of Calista Rossi not an accident," Penn said. "According to forensic evidence, she was dead before she was munched on by sharks. Who knew?"

"Right." I sank down on the bed beside my dress.

"Don't stress. Apparently they found a bunch of blood at Pete's place. They're testing it to see if it matches hers. How much do you want to bet it will?"

"Nothing," I said. "I didn't like her, but I don't want to bet on who or what killed her either." I massaged my forehead with my fingertips.

"Hey." Tully shifted over closer to me and put his arm around me. "At least they know it wasn't you. Her family would want answers, wouldn't they?"

"I guess so," I said. "I mean, I would if I was them." I hadn't met them. If she was anything like them, I wouldn't want to.

Still, they deserved answers. It wouldn't be fair to go around thinking an innocent shark did something they didn't. Poor sharks got enough bad publicity as it was. Even more than I did. They were just big fish who wanted to live their lives. Could they help it if sometimes people got in the way? My philosophy was that if they stayed out of my bath, I would stay out of theirs. So far, that worked pretty well.

"Someone got arrested for throwing a bottle at paparazzi before the concert the other night," Penn continued. "Apparently they got off with a warning. And a ban from attending concerts at the stadium for the next decade." He changed the channel back to cartoons.

"On one hand, that sucks," Asher said. "On the other hand, I don't have any sympathy for people that throw things like that. I'm so conflicted." He scratched the side of his head.

"Actions have consequences," Tully said. "I'm not conflicted."

"Me either," Zeke said. "It's lucky they didn't throw a bottle at us, or I would be facing some hefty consequences right now." He smiled but looked unapologetic.

"They wouldn't have hit us anyway," I pointed out. "We were too far away."

"Then they are the lucky ones," he said. "Because I'm not letting that happen again to any one of us. I'm still pissed off it happened to you."

I touched my cheek lightly. There was a faint scar there from where the can hit me and broke the skin. Asshole could have thrown an empty one. It would have done less damage.

"Me too," I said. Sometimes I dreamt I was on stage, dodging flying objects. Sometimes they were cans, other times heads. The heads were definitely worse. Each of them had a face: Jonah, Poppy, even Pete. My stomach turned just thinking about it.

I lowered my hand. "I should get ready for this date." I hoped I didn't bring the mood down.

I didn't want to ruin whatever Landon had planned for us.

CHAPTER
ELEVEN

ABBIE

"YOU LOOK BEAUTIFUL," Landon said at the same time as I said, "This is incredible."

We both laughed.

Channing, who was standing over by the table, grinned. "I think everyone likes what they see."

"I certainly do," I agreed, my eyes on both guys.

They each wore a suit, button-down shirt and no tie. Landon's suit was blue and his shirt bright yellow, while Channing's was black, over a crisp white shirt. That was their personalities, right there. Landon was flamboyant, Channing understated.

I dragged my eyes off them to admire the room.

Located on the other side of the corridor from our hotel rooms, someone had pushed the furniture off to one side and brought in a dining table and three chairs. Every surface was covered with candles, each a dancing flame flickering in the warm breeze that came through the open doors that led to a balcony.

Another section of the room was left empty of everything except a bunch of rose petals scattered over the hardwood.

"That's the dance floor," Landon explained. "In case we feel like dancing. There's also a really big hot tub. It's big enough for eight, so it should fit three just fine."

"You thought of everything," I said. This was by far the most romantic date I have ever had. Even more than the one with Tully in Perth. Although, the race was closer than the one between Penn and Channing.

Landon poured three glasses of champagne and handed me one.

"He always does," Channing said. "He's the undisputed master of romantic dates." He shot his boyfriend a proud, loving look.

Landon sipped his drink and shrugged, but he seemed to enjoy the praise. "I like to spoil the people I care about. We don't get many nights off, so we should enjoy it."

"It's beautiful," I assured him. "Did you light every candle yourselves?"

Landon glanced at Channing. "I'd love to say we did, but I'd be bullshitting. We had some help from the hotel staff. Otherwise we'd be lighting them for days."

"Hashtag fact," Channing said. "Thank fuck blowing them out is going to be easier. I tried to talk Landon out of having so many, but he insisted." He smiled indulgently.

"Go hard or go home," Landon said with a shrug. "Do you wanna sit?" He put down his drink and pulled out a chair.

"Thank you, kind sir," I said graciously, and sat. How different that would be if I was talking to Penn. For one thing, I wouldn't have put 'kind' in front of 'sir.' 'Harder,' maybe, but not, 'kind.'

Landon even pulled a chair out for Channing, who raised an eyebrow at him but sat. Could they be more stinking cute together?

The funny thing was, I never felt like the third wheel with them. Or with Zeke and Asher. I had a different kind of relationship with each of them and their relationships with each other were different again. No one was competition for anyone else. We all just enjoyed each other's company.

"Food won't be long," Landon said. "I can't take credit for any of that either. Except organising the menu with the kitchen. I hope you like what I chose."

"As long as it's not barbecued rooster, I'm sure I will," I said.

When they both gave me a funny look, I explained the conversation I had with the rest of the guys. I also briefly mentioned the bit about Calista and the person who threw the bottle. I didn't want to dwell on either of those things.

Evidently, neither did the guys because they quickly changed the topic to how good the champagne was.

A knock on the door announced the arrival of the first course. A a member of staff dressed in the hotel uniform wheeled in a trolley. On top were plates with a variety of small finger foods. Tiny quiches, tiny pastries, toothpicks with fruit and cheese. Everything was identical in portions and shapes. That kind of detail must have taken hours. It almost looked too good to eat, but at the same time, I was hungry.

I picked up a mini quiche Lorraine and bit into it. The crumbly, buttery pastry was cooked to perfection, the egg was light and fluffy.

"Mmmm, this is so good." I finished in two bites and reached for a pastry.

"One of the best parts about travelling the world is getting to taste food you didn't make yourself," Landon said.

"At least you can cook," Channing said. To me he added, "He's trying to teach me, but I'm not very good."

"Yes, you are," Landon said around a mouthful of fruit. "Scrambled eggs are tricky."

"They really are," I agreed. "It's easy to overcook them." I did it myself plenty of times. My mother had a knack for them, which I hadn't inherited or learned.

"See?" Landon said to Channing. "It's just a matter of practice. You'll get there, love."

"I'm better at making cakes," Channing said. "Unfortunately, Landon won't let me eat cake for breakfast, lunch and dinner." He grimaced playfully. He slid the fruit sideways off a toothpick and dropped it onto his plate.

"You'd get tired of cake after a while," I said. "Even if it was really good cake."

"That's what I keep telling him," Landon said. "Everything in moderation."

"Even champagne." I wasn't used to drinking the decent stuff, just the cheap drop from the local bottleshop. The one Landon chose tonight was delicious.

"Even champagne," Landon agreed.

The first course was replaced by the second. Not rooster cooked on a barbecue. Not even chicken. Instead, it was a fancy version of macaroni and cheese. It was absolutely delicious.

"If I eat much more than this, you're going to need to roll me out the door." I patted my stomach.

"Or we can work it off first." Landon winked.

"I should have guessed you'd suggest that," I said teasingly. "Lots of dancing then?"

Both guys laughed at that.

"Lots and lots of dancing," Channing agreed. "Speaking of dancing, should we work up an appetite for dessert?" He looked sideways at us, clearly not proposing we dance vertically. Or, not for very long anyway.

"Yes, we should." Landon jumped up and grabbed his phone from the table. He pressed the screen a couple of times before music started to play. "I was hoping for speakers in the ceiling, but the hotel couldn't get them installed in time. So this will have to do."

He set the phone back down and held out his hand for me to stand.

I took it and we all moved to the dance floor. Landon faced me, and Channing stood behind. They both stepped in close so their bodies were pressed full length against mine.

Channing placed his hands on my hips, just above Landon's. Together, we started to sway, me the meat in a hot-rock-gods-in-suits sandwich.

Fuck yes.

In a matter of moments, their erections were pressed against me. Just in time for me to be as wet as fuck. There goes another perfectly good pair of panties, I sighed to myself.

Honestly, my laundry bill for panties alone must be almost as big as the cost of the entire tour. If the label wanted me to pay, I was going to pass it on to the guys. Most of it was their fault anyway. Knowing them, they'd happily pay it.

Men.

"Hot tub, balcony, bed, or wait until after dessert?" Landon asked.

"Yes," Channing said. His chest rumbled against my back.

Landon snorted. "Okay, all of the above, but which first?"

"Why choose?" Channing asked. "Can we take the bed and hot tub out to the balcony and fuck while eating desert?"

"I admire your ambition," Landon said. "But the hot tub weighs about a million kilos and is tiled into the bathroom."

I giggled at how silly this conversation was. It was adorable how comfortable they were with each other. I liked how they fitted me into their lives without a second thought. At least no second thoughts I saw. They both seemed to be as all in as I and the other guys were.

"There's always—" I started to say. I was interrupted by the arrival of the dessert trolley. "Fucking hell." We all sprang apart.

"Long time no see," Hunter Brantley said. He was dressed in a dark blue suit. His twin brother Parker was right behind him, dressed in dark grey. "I offered to bring the dessert up and they were happy to let me help." He smiled.

"Actually, we swiped the dessert trolley," Parker said. "We thought we'd surprise you."

"It looks like we did." Hunter grinned.

"What the fuck do you want?" Channing growled. He'd turned so Landon and I were behind him.

"Honestly," Hunter said slowly, "I'd love some of the desert on this tray." He picked up a cloche and peeked at the plate underneath. "Looks good, doesn't it?" He poked a finger into the middle of the chocolate mousse, then stuck it in his mouth.

"Mmmm, that's really good. Park, you should try some."

"I'm trying to watch my figure," Parker said. He placed his hands on his hips and wiggled.

"What do you really want?" I asked coldly. Apart from ruining our evening and our dessert. There was no way I'd touch it after Hunter had. Truthfully, there's no way I'd touch it knowing either of them were anywhere near it. Fuck knows what they might have slipped into it. Probably something nasty, dangerous and illegal.

"Oh, hi Abbie." Parker gave me a little finger wave. "I didn't see you there hiding behind these two clowns. Funny, I would have thought they would hide behind you. How's Penn, by the way? No hard feelings there, I hope? We were just doing what we were told. Except the part about telling you where he was. That was kind of a peace offering, in case our dear brother decided to go to Reuben."

"Penn is fine, no thanks to you," I said. "I suggest you stay away from him unless you want your nuts ripped off and roasted over a campfire."

Hey, that was creative. Go me.

"Feisty, aren't you?" Hunter asked. He picked up a bowl of chocolate mousse and a spoon and started to eat. Not the one he'd struck his finger into. Fucking brat. "If you ever get tired of those losers, you should look Parker and I up. We'll show you how real men fuck."

"Don't you have a girlfriend?" I asked. "Real men don't cheat."

"No, but Lila wouldn't mind if you joined us," Hunter said without batting an eyelash.

"I'd rather fuck a potato," I said.

"As evidenced by your presence in the room with these two." Parker grinned.

Channing growled. Landon grabbed his arm to stop him from lunging at the evil twins.

"They're not worth it," Landon said. "Sooner or later, they are going to piss off the wrong people and end up in a shallow grave. I for one won't shed a fucking tear."

"Me either," I said.

Parker clicked his tongue. "That's not very nice."

"You're not very nice," I retorted. "Now tell us what you want and then get the fuck out of here. Before we call security."

"There's no need to be like that." Hunter put down the half-eaten chocolate mousse and stuck his spoon into the third bowl, which hadn't been touched until now.

What a prick.

"We just came to say hello," Hunter added. "And let you know we're still hanging around. Reuben wanted us to remind you that we exist and he exists and all that shit." He shrugged.

"We've been trying to forget, but we haven't managed it," I said. "Maybe next time send us a text message. Or better yet, go back to Sydney and tell Reuben to fuck off."

Parker winced. "Personally, I wouldn't do that. And I promise you, you don't want us to do that either. Reuben gets pissy when people tell him to fuck off."

"Is there anything he doesn't get pissy about?" I asked.

The evil twins exchanged a glance.

"Not really," Hunter admitted. "Anyway, we've delivered our message. We'll be on our way. Have a great rest of your night." He and Parker ducked out the door.

We all sagged against each other.

"We should tell Zeke," I said softly.

"Before or after we blow out all these candles?" Channing asked.

I sighed. We didn't need to talk about it to know we were in agreement not to stay here after that visit.

What I wanted to do now was hide under the blankets with as many of my guys around me as possible.

CHAPTER
TWELVE

ABBIE

"THOSE LITTLE FUCKERS!" Zeke growled. He started towards the door but stopped a couple of metres from it.

"They'll be long gone by now. I should have been there. I would have kicked their asses into the next millennia. Or the one after that." His face was red with fury.

Asher and I moved to comfort him and bumped into each other. He put out a hand to steady me, and we both half laughed.

"Sorry." I slipped an arm around Asher and another around Zeke. "I whole-heartedly support your desire to kick their asses. They freaked the fuck out of me when they walked into the room."

"I'll bet they did." Zeke pulled me closer so my head was resting against his shoulder.

Asher did the same on the other side, so we were all pressed together, sharing heat and muscle.

"Not to mention the waste of chocolate mousse," Asher groaned.

"That might just be the worst part of all," I said, grimacing against the smooth fabric of Zeke's shirt. It wasn't the worst part, not even close, but whatever it took to lighten the mood.

The twins scared the crap out of me without even trying, without even threatening us or waving guns at us. They'd assaulted me and Penn, I had no idea how far they might go on Reuben's orders. I didn't particularly want to find out. If it was worse than what they'd already done, then it would be pretty fucking horrible.

"I'm sorry," Zeke whispered so only we could hear. "I should have dealt with them somehow. They've been a thorn in my side for so long. If I'd known they were going to haunt us on this tour..."

"What could you do?" Asher asked. "You're not the kind of person who goes around killing indiscriminately. You did what you could to distance yourself from the rest of the family. What's left after that?"

Zeke's shoulder twitched when he shrugged slightly. "Beat the shit out of them until they promise to leave us alone?" He sighed. "Yeah, I know. I wouldn't have done that either. Even if it's a good idea. Maybe I need to rethink my attitude towards gratuitous violence."

"Reuben would love that," Asher said ironically. "Right before he welcomes you back into the family and closes the door behind you. That's the whole reason you walked away, remember?"

"Not the whole reason," Zeke said softly. He pressed the side of his face against Asher's and smiled down at me. "I wanted to know the people I love weren't going to get stuck in the middle of some gangland war. It happened anyway."

"If this is where you say, maybe we should break up to keep us safe, no deal," I said firmly. "We're in this with you until the end. No matter what happens. I'm not walking away from you."

Even as I said that, my heart raced. If he wanted to walk away from me, from us, I couldn't stop him. Not really. When it came down to it, we had only known each other for a few months. Everything was still new and fragile.

But fuck, losing either of them would break my heart.

"Hell no, we're not going anywhere," Asher said. "Whatever you do, no matter how stupid, we'll stand by you. I'll hold one of them down for you while you beat them up if you want. Whatever you need."

Zeke smiled a little broader, but still with restraint. "I'd like to think it won't come to that. But if those little pricks come near either of you again, all bets are off."

I had the feeling if the twins were in front of him right now, they'd both get a one way trip off the balcony. It wasn't high enough to kill them, but it might break a few bones. That would slow them down. Not to mention, it might be fun. For us.

I should probably not enjoy that thought as much as I did. Fuck it, you couldn't go around scaring the shit out of people without them thinking nasty thoughts about you. That was how the universe worked.

"Where's Channing?" Zeke asked after a couple more minutes of fuming.

"He took the dessert cart back down to the restaurant," Landon said. "He wanted to make sure they didn't kill anyone. I was going to go with him, but I thought it was better to bring Abbie back here first."

Zeke hesitated, but then nodded. "As long as he stays inside the hotel, he should be okay. But if he doesn't come back soon, we'll go looking for him."

Landon nodded, then jumped at a knock on the door. He hurried over to look through the peephole, then opened it to let Channing inside.

"Thank fuck," Landon said. "I was starting to worry." He wrapped his boyfriend in a bear hug.

Channing patted his back. "I'm fine. The kitchen didn't even notice the trolley was missing. All of the staff seem to be accounted for. They said they'd send up some more chocolate mousse for everyone."

"Fuck yeah," Penn said. He and Tully had stayed sitting on the couch, listening while Landon and I told them what the twins did. They looked equally pissed off as each other.

Okay, maybe Penn edged out Tully a little. He would hold his grudge against Hunter and Parker until the end of time, if not longer. Which was totally understandable. What they did to him was grudgeworthy, and then some.

"I love chocolate mousse," the keyboardist added.

"Doesn't everyone?" Tully rose and moved to grab a T-shirt from his suitcase. He tossed it to me. "In case you want to change out of that dress."

I caught it before it hit the floor. "Thanks. I think I'm ready to look a bit less fancy now." After the way the date ended, I might just stick to casual clothes and group activities from now on. Safety in numbers and all that.

"I can't guarantee you'll look less fancy." Tully grinned. "You could make a paper bag look sexy."

"Is it wrong that I'd like to see that some day?" Asher asked.

"I don't know if it's wrong," Zeke said. "But it is a bit weird." He gave Asher a funny look.

"Since I'm a bit weird, then that works out perfectly," Asher said cheerfully. "I'll keep an eye out for a paper bag the right size."

"That sounds like one of those fashion shows where they like to push the envelope," I said. I kicked off my heels and started to change. Since all of them had seen me naked several times before, I didn't even think twice about doing it in front of them.

Neither did Landon and Channing, who started to strip off their suits and put on boxer shorts for sleeping in.

"You might start a new trend," Zeke said. "Paper bag couture."

"Yeah." I snorted. "It's all fun and games until it rains."

"Why does that sound so fucking hot?" Asher groaned.

"You first," I told him. I pulled Tully's T-shirt down into place. It hung almost to my knees. The funny thing was, he probably thought he was getting it back someday. Ha ha, nope, it was mine now. I felt cute in it and it smelled like him. For some reason, that was incredibly comforting. It was like a block of chocolate, a glass of wine and a blanket fort, all rolled into one.

Penn laughed loudly. "Asher wearing a paper bag. That's fucking funny."

Asher flipped him off. "For your information, I'd look adorable." He also started getting ready for bed. "I don't think they make paper bags big enough to fit on me though."

"We could find one," Zeke said. He stripped off his jeans and actually folded them before he put them into suitcase. "Or have one made. What's the point of having money if you can't have people make weird shit for you?"

In spite of his banter, and the smile on his mouth, Zeke's eyes showed he was still worried and annoyed.

I hoped he wasn't planning to do something stupid. Partly because he might get hurt and partly because we would all follow him into it. I didn't think there was a person in the room who wouldn't follow him to the end of the Earth and back. Even if we all ended up in trouble because of it.

Fortunately, no one was naked when a hotel staff member knocked on the door and wheeled in a trolley with seven fresh bowls of chocolate mousse, cups and a pot of fresh coffee.

"Oh my God, that smells so good." I inhaled the heavenly scent, but stayed back until the woman left and Tully firmly locked the door behind her.

"I feel like we're having a sleepover party," Penn said. He had also stripped down to his boxer shorts.

Asher grinned. "It does feel like that, doesn't it? Zeke and I used to sleep over at each other's houses all the time."

"Or tell our parents we were sleeping over and then go somewhere else," Zeke said. He picked up a bowl and spooned some mousse into his mouth. It wasn't until he swallowed, waited and didn't die, that he waved for us to grab some too.

"Yeah, like to the park to get wasted on a bottle of cheap alcohol," Asher said.

"That sounds like fun," Landon said softly. He grabbed a bowl and a cup and went to sit on the end of one of the beds. He wore bright red boxer shorts with a superhero logo all over them.

I grabbed mine and sat beside him. "You didn't get to do sleepovers?" I asked as gently as I could. "Even in foster care?"

I could understand why he wouldn't want friends over with his mother around. Kid-Landon wouldn't have wanted his friends to see her like that, even if his mother allowed it. That was the kind of thing kids never let other kids forget.

"Not really," he said, his eyes down. "I never really wanted to. It was easier to let the other kids assume I lived with my parents and had a normal life like them."

My heart broke for him. "That must have been rough." I could just imagine the things the other kids would say if they knew what he was going through.

He would have been teased and ostracised. It was painfully sad to think he had to pretend just to get by.

The bed dipped as Channing sat on the other side of him. "You have us now and we can have all the sleepovers you want. You'll still have to pretend you hang out with normal people though." He grinned.

Landon snorted softly. "Nah, I gave up on that part of the dream a long time ago." He bumped his shoulder playfully into Channing's.

"Apparently normal is overrated anyway," I said. I dipped my spoon into my chocolate mousse and scooped out a mouthful. "Mmmm, this is the seventh tastiest thing in the room."

"That's very specific," Tully said. He cocked his head at me and slowly licked mousse of his spoon like he was fucking it.

I watched, mesmerised, until he dipped the spoon back into his dessert.

"Yeah," I agreed, blinking to break the spell. "Nothing could be tastier than you six." Their cocks, tongues and the rest of them.

"Then this is the eighth tastiest thing in the room," Landon said. "Because you are definitely delicious." He leaned over and kissed my mouth. He tasted of a divine combination of chocolate and coffee, with a little touch of salt.

If I could bottle that flavour, I would be a billionaire.

"Ninth," Penn said. "Because this mousse is good, but nothing beats coffee."

None of us could disagree with that.

While I ate and drank, I kept half an eye on Zeke. I could almost hear him stewing over his brothers turning up like that. I wanted to tell him not to worry about it, that I wasn't that scared. That was a flat out lie and we all knew it. Seeing them again had me rattled as fuck. That they could so brazenly walk into the room of a hotel in Vienna, without breaking a sweat, without even blinking...

Yeah, I got the message all right. They could and would turn up whenever and wherever they wanted.

That was what scared me most of all.

CHAPTER
THIRTEEN
LANDON

WHEN I WAS A KID, I used to think Vienna was some kind of desert. The fancy kind people only got when they were rich. It wasn't until I was in high school I realised it was a place. And now, here I was, standing on a huge stage in Vienna looking out at the crowd.

With a craving for chocolate-covered ice cream. Yeah, I have a sweet tooth. Especially when it came to chocolate.

Zeke moved back and forth across the stage with his usual energy. Some nights, he was exhausting to watch. Other nights, I itched to move around up there with him.

I glanced over at Channing and knew he was thinking the same thing. If he could, he'd be dancing around with his saxophone for the entire ninety minutes, until sweat dripped off him, drenching his clothes until they stuck to his body, to the ridges of his muscles, the hard plane of his stomach, the V of his hips.

The downside to him playing saxophone, was that he more or less had to stay put, like me. The two of us and Asher were the backbone of the band, but as the spine we had to stay at the back. That suited me.

Channing, well, he usually tried to fit in a workout before we went on stage. To work off that nervous energy.

"Vienna, you are fucking nuts!" Zeke shouted into the mic. "You're the best, wildest audience all tour! Maybe ever!"

Of course, the crowd loved hearing that. Just like the crowd loved hearing it every concert we'd done so far, even though they probably knew he said that every time. It was all part of the fun of going to a rock concert.

As far as I knew anyway. I'd only ever been to school concerts before I joined Wolf Venom. Even now, the ones I went to were by acts signed with our label. They were more than happy to hand a few tickets around to us. I'd never been to see anyone just for the hell of it.

When did I have the time? If I wasn't touring, I was busy with something else to do with the band. I was always the first to put my hand up for interviews, guest appearances, or playing on other people's albums. If I made myself indispensable, then they would keep me around for longer. Right?

Yeah, I know some people would think it was stupid that I was insecure. I played bass guitar for the biggest, best rock band on the face of the planet. I should have an ego as big as the sun. I tried to act like I did, but there was always that voice in the back of my mind that told me I wasn't good enough and that sooner or later everyone would leave.

Realistically, the band might break up some day. The other guys wouldn't have an excuse to hang out with me anymore. Except Channing. Him I was sure of.

Abbie—confidence in her might take a bit longer. I wanted to be sure of her, one hundred percent, but that same little voice told me I wasn't good enough for her.

Okay, that little voice told me I wasn't good enough for Channing either, but I had to believe him when he told me I was. I *wanted* to believe it.

I watched him put his saxophone to his beautiful mouth and make gorgeous music. Bass was the best instrument ever, of course, but some days I wished I could play saxophone too. Channing tried to teach me, but I didn't have his or Penn's talent for it. I could play both kinds of guitar so there was that.

Even my insecure brain could admit I was good at it.

I grooved as I played, lost in the music, my bass in perfect harmony with Asher's drums. If any of the others made a mistake, no one would notice, at least not as much. If Asher I screwed up, it would throw everyone off. Everything they played and sang was to the rhythm we made.

Asher liked to say that we were the unsung heroes of the band. I agreed with that. When the audience danced and clapped, they were doing it along with us, not Zeke, Tully or Penn. Not even Channing.

Not even Abbie.

I was still furious after those twin pricks ruined our date. The look of fear on her face made me want to hide her away somewhere safe forever. Not in a weird, stalker way, but to protect her.

Channing felt the same way. After chocolate mousse and coffee, he'd told me, in whispers, how angry he was.

"I was ready to take that spoon," he growled, "and shove it down until it came out his ass."

"That's very graphic." I snuggled into his side. "Is your arm that long?"

He snorted with half amusement, half annoyance. "It wouldn't need to be. I'd squash him down like an accordion, until his chin touched his feet. Then I'd do the same thing to the other one."

I chuckled, even though the conversation was slightly disturbing. "I don't know if that's hot or if you've just watched too many cartoons. Maybe you should stop watching TV with Penn."

"You don't think I can do it hmmm?" His fingers slid down my side.

"If anyone could, it would be you," I whispered. "Maybe Zeke. Zeke is pretty fucking strong."

"Yeah, but would Zeke do this?" He flicked his tongue against my neck.

"Not to me," I said. A shiver of desire passed through me. My cock had not forgotten that the twins interrupted at the worst possible time.

All right, even if we weren't interrupted, my cock would still stand up when Channing touched me like that.

"Are you guys still awake?" Abbie whispered.

"Yeah," Channing whispered back. "What's up?"

"Can I sleep next to you? Asher was snoring in my ear."

The sound of the drummer's roars was like a plane engine. I didn't blame her for not wanting to hear that up close.

"Of course you can, honey," I said.

Channing and I shifted over to make room for her.

"We might not sleep for a while," Channing warned.

After a moment, she said, "I wasn't tired anyway."

"The old men went to sleep and left you hanging?" Channing asked teasingly.

For a moment I thought that was what happened. She was only over here as a last resort.

"I wanted to finish what we started," she said. "Without the interruptions this time."

"Sounds good to me," Channing said.

The next thing I knew, he rolled her over until she was lying on her stomach on top of me.

"Um, hello there," I said. For someone with such presence, she weighed almost nothing. Well, not nothing, but she was light, her curves soft under my hands.

"Hey," she said before she kissed my mouth.

I slipped my hands up the back of her thighs and over her perky ass. I rucked up her shirt and slid my hands across her bare back. Her skin was so smooth under my fingertips. If my calluses bothered her, she didn't show any sign. She might like the way they felt. Channing did, as much as I liked his. Extra texture meant extra sensation.

In the faint light that filtered through the curtains, I saw Channing move around behind her. He hooked his hands through the top of her panties and slid them off her ass and down her legs.

She lifted her feet to help him pull them off before he tossed them aside.

He moved back up and his face disappeared between her legs. All I could see past her perfect, round ass, was the top of his head.

She let out a soft, sighing moan as he started to work her with his mouth. Her breasts brushed my chest, her nipples hardening with the contact. My cock hardened along with them.

She must have felt it because she wriggled against me. Her hand slipped down between us to grip my length. She had absolutely no mercy. She wound her hand up and down me like a corkscrew, firm and fast like she was determined I would come so hard I blew my head off.

I groaned and bucked against her driving fingers.

My eyes were half closed, but they popped open when she slid down my body.

"That's better," Channing whispered. He dove back between her legs, but he'd moved her so her mouth was beside my aching, needy cock.

"Just a little," I agreed as she licked at the bead of precum which wept from my slit, then teased down to my balls and back up again with the tip of her tongue.

I didn't even try to hold back the groan that slipped from my mouth when she drew my cock into hers. She felt so different to Channing. Apart from the fact she didn't have stubble grazing my body. Her mouth was smaller, but softer. Where his was firm and demanding, hers was giving and tight. One wasn't better than the other, they were just different. Awesomely so.

Her breath became a series of ragged pants and sighs before she gasped and shuddered on top of me.

Channing said something to Abbie that I couldn't hear past the blood pounding in my ears.

I figured it out a moment later when she let go of me with her mouth and scooted back up the bed. She rolled us over so I was lying on top of her.

Channing disappeared for a moment, before returning with a tube of lube in his hand.

Hell yeah.

I knelt between Abbie's spread thighs and rubbed my fingers lightly over her saturated pussy. She was so unbelievably wet and warm. Just feeling her like that made me harder than ever.

I positioned my cock outside her entrance and pressed myself slowly into her body. My cock was surrounded by the most incredible, delicious heat, like a velvet pocket. If pockets were between a gorgeous set of thighs.

At the same time, Channing liberally, but meticulously, spread lube around and inside my ass and over his cock. He took the greatest care to make sure I was as wet as Abbie. By the time he was done, I was aching for him, my body begging to be filled.

He tossed the tube aside and gripped my hips with firm, demanding fingers. His cock probed for my ass, hard and as needy as I was. He positioned himself and paused for a heartbeat or two.

When he moved again, he was as relentless as Abbie was with her hand. He pushed himself inside me, only pausing occasionally to let me stretch to take him until he was seated deep.

My whole body was a mess of sensation from front to back. If I even tried to talk right now, it wouldn't be coherent. The only thought I could manage was something about enjoying being so close to two people I cared so much about.

Love, the back of my mind whispered. *You love them both.*

I would unpack that later, at a time when I could think straight.

Slowly, I started to thrust into Abbie.

Channing, who was usually the dominant partner out of the two of us, matched my rhythm instead of insisting I match his. When I slowed, he slowed. When I reached the edge of the precipice and needed more friction, he went faster too.

Fortunately, I didn't have to decide what felt better, me inside her or him inside me, because I couldn't have. They both felt beyond incredible. Filling and being filled at the same time had never felt so...fulfilling.

Even our breathing was in sync, all three of us. Abbie's came in soft little gasps. Channing's was a deeper, heavier grunt and mine, mine was somewhere in the middle. The backbone of the band again.

I worked my hands under her knees and brought her legs up over my shoulders. At the same time, I bent over her more, to let Channing drive in deeper. With every stroke, we were both balls deep now.

"Fuck yeah," Channing grunted.

At least one of us was capable of speech. I may never be able to put a full sentence together again. Good thing I was the bassist, not the lead singer. For so many reasons.

Abbie trembled underneath me and I knew she was close to coming again. That brought me closer still, but I wasn't ready to let go yet. I wanted them both to get off first. Was that gentlemanly or just my need to please people?

Whatever, no one complained. Yet.

Abbie's breath got faster, and she was bucking against me, her clit grazing against my stomach each time I thrust. "Hell yeah," she breathed. "Oh my God, that feels so good."

She groaned and shattered underneath me, bucking harder and panting out her orgasm. Her breath was a series of soft pants out her mouth and nose. The noise alone was almost enough to make me come.

I bit my lip to stop myself, and went on thrusting, while at the same time clamping my muscles around Channing as hard as I could.

"Fucking hell, Lan, that's..." Apparently he couldn't speak much either, because he trailed off and pounded into me with even, forceful strokes. "I'm going to come, love."

"Please," I begged. "Please come inside me." Right now, that was the last thing left on my wish list; for him to feel good, for my body to do that for him.

He muttered something incoherent and came, slamming himself over and over again until it stung, but I wouldn't tell him to stop. Not until he was done.

He cried out, his fingers digging hard into my hips. He drove himself once, twice more, then fell still, gasping and sagging against my back.

I huffed out a gusty sigh and let myself come, the sensation like a rush of heat and fireworks that started in the base of my balls and erupted through them and out the end of my cock. Cum blasted from me, filling Abbie's gorgeous pussy to the brim.

I slumped over her, panting and tired, but satisfied.

I came back to myself as the song ended. Good thing I had a guitar to cover my groin until my erection softened again.

CHAPTER
FOURTEEN

ABBIE

"WELL THIS IS NEW," I said uncomfortably.

"It's the label's way of connecting better with fans," Jackson said.

"Yeah, I guess it will do that," I agreed.

The room was like a panel at one of those pop culture conventions. Instead of a table, the guys sat on chairs on the stage, while people who paid good money to see them had tiered seating in the small auditorium. A couple of the tour's support staff wore Wolf Venom T-shirts and carried microphones.

Lucky for me, I got to stand off to the side with Jackson and watch.

Landon and Channing looked as uncomfortable as I felt. Tully sat up in his chair like he was at school. Asher, Zeke and Penn all reclined in their chairs like they were couches. Zeke and Asher looked happy to be there. Penn had his usual scowl on his face.

"This is going to be interesting," I said softly. With any luck, Penn wouldn't offend anyone. Honestly, I doubted he'd give a shit if he did.

The host of the Q and A was a tall, model-gorgeous brunette, with big breasts and a perfect body. She had the kind figure I wished I had. Slender in a sporty kind of way. I could work out for a hundred years and still not look like that.

None of the guys seemed to notice her, but she definitely noticed them. Her eyes followed them around, attentive like a hawk.

She put a microphone to perfectly painted, bright red lips and smiled while looking at them through her lashes.

"Good afternoon." She spoke flawless English with an Austrian accent. "My name is Valentina Wagner. I would love to welcome you to this question and answer session with the fabulous band, Wolf Venom."

"Who is she again?" I whispered.

Jackson shrugged. "Some local entertainment reporter. Apparently she's famous in Austria." He sounded as impressed as the guys, but I'd seen the way he looked at her when we first walked in. Not that I could blame him. If I was into women, I'd drool over her too.

The audience clapped. They were obviously excited, judging by their smiles and the way they all looked ready to leap out of their seats, but they were more reserved than a concert audience. So far.

"Let us first let the boys introduce themselves." Valentina walked over on her stiletto heels and leaned forward to make sure the microphone in Zeke's hand was turned on. Of course in order to do that, she had to bend over so her breasts were right in front of his face.

He raised his eyebrows and moved his head back until she stepped away.

If she noticed his discomfort, she showed no sign. She was either professional, oblivious or both.

One by one, the guys said their names into the microphone and passed it on. Each time, the audience clapped and a couple of people wolf whistled.

"Now we'll open for questions," Valentina said when they were done. "Raise your hand and my friends will bring a microphone to you."

Almost every hand in the place rose.

The first to ask a question was a boy of about eight. He had pale blond hair, bright blue eyes and looked nervous as hell as he spoke into the microphone.

"What is your favourite song that you play?" His question out, he sat down with a plop.

"Do I have to pick a favourite?" Zeke asked, speaking first because the microphone was back in his hand. "Okay, um. 'Rock out with You'."

He passed the microphone on down the line until it reached Asher. Instead of answering, he looked at the boy and asked, "Which is your favourite?"

The boy, his face bright red, stood up again and said, "I watched on social media when Penn played 'Hallelujah'. That was my favourite." He sat down again.

Penn grinned and leaned over to speak into the microphone. "Good choice. You clearly have great taste."

The audience laughed.

The next question was from a curvaceous blond who couldn't have been more than about nineteen or twenty years old. "I have a question for Zeke."

Asher handed the microphone over.

"Hey, how are you?" Zeke asked. His gaze was on her like she was the only person in the room. He had a way of making people feel like he genuinely cared about the answer. Like in that moment he knew she existed and that she mattered.

"Good," she squeaked.

"You have a question for me?" he asked, his gaze unwavering. That look would make any girl ruin her panties. It was doing it for me.

"Yeah, I do. Will you marry me?" the young woman giggled.

"There's always one," Jackson muttered.

I rolled my eyes. "There always will be." Whatever. Her fantasy couldn't hurt me, or my relationship with Zeke. It made me more uncomfortable than I already was, but that would pass.

Zeke smiled. "That's very flattering, thank you, but I'm spoken for." He handed the microphone back to Asher without a glance at him or me. If the question bothered him, he showed no sign. It seemed likely he got proposals so often they were quickly forgotten.

The woman pouted and sat back down, but the smile never left her face. She got to speak to her idol. It wasn't something she'd soon forget.

The next question was from a man in his mid-thirties. The band had fans of all ages. The youngest person here was around five and the oldest looked to be in their seventies. You're never too young or too old to appreciate good music.

"Do you think you will ever retire from playing?" the man asked.

It was Asher who answered. "A couple of months ago, I would have told you I'll keep playing and touring until I die. But recently I've started to think that maybe there is a life after music. I'm not ready to step away yet, but I see a day in a few years' time that I might."

All of the guys nodded their agreement.

"Thank you." The man nodded back and sat down.

The next to ask was another young woman. She had pin straight black hair and lips that looked unnaturally plump. She wore the tiniest dress I've ever seen. I was almost certain she had no panties on underneath. If she bent over, the whole room would see her ass and pussy. I had a feeling there were six guys on the stage she wanted to have look at her.

"Hello," she purred into the microphone.

"Hey," Asher said back into the one he still held. "You have a question for one of us?"

"Actually, I have a question for Abbie," she said. She looked straight over to where I was standing.

Valentina looked uncertain. Clearly she hadn't expected this to happen and wasn't sure what to do. Like the professional she was, she rallied quickly. She turned to me and gave me the kind of smile a woman gives to another when they think they are beneath them somehow. As if she was certain she was thousand percent more gorgeous than I was.

She might be right, but she didn't need to be a bitch about it.

"Abbie Hart, darling, would you like to come out here?" she asked smoothly.

Resisting the urge to give a sarcastic smile and tell her to fuck off, I looked up at Jackson. I half hoped he would say no.

"It's up to you." He gave me an encouraging smile but looked questioning at the same time.

By that, I assumed he meant this event wasn't for me, but the publicity for the label wouldn't hurt. If I decided to stay over here, he would support me, I knew that. All of the guys would.

On the other hand, the audience would remember. No doubt it would get blown up later into something ridiculous. The press might suggest I had something to hide or some shit like that.

I smiled sweetly. "Of course I will."

I stepped out onto the stage and caught Landon's eye. He glanced towards the audience and gave me a secretive grin.

I had to hold back a laugh at his suggestion that we'd even consider fucking in front of them. That was definitely his thing all right.

Predictably, the moment I had that thought, a bolt of heat went right to my core. He knew how to get to me with just a look. Then again, they all did. These days, it didn't take much. At this rate, they'd have to empty the rig truck and make room for spare changes of panties for me.

I considered sitting on one of the guy's laps to answer the question, but thought better of it. Instead, I walked over to take the microphone from Asher. He let his fingers brush over mine a little more than they should, and grinned.

He was as big a brat as Landon.

I looked up into the audience to find the woman and gave her the warmest smile I could. Meanwhile, my palms were sweating and my heart was racing.

Please, please, please, don't say something horrible. It had occurred to me she might have asked me to come out here to tell me to fuck off and leave the guys alone. Nothing much would surprise me these days.

"You're touring with one of the most amazing bands ever," the woman said. "Six—I think we can agree—hot guys." She smiled down at them.

I had no idea where this was going, but I nodded.

"I am and, yeah, they're okay." I smiled at them and tried not to laugh when they made faces at me.

"How do you deal with that?" the woman asked. "I mean, it's difficult enough for women in the music industry anyway, right? Take today. They're on centre stage and you're off to the side. Shouldn't you be out there with them? A generation of girls is looking up to you and you're being pushed aside. Doesn't it make you angry?"

Okay, I hadn't expected any of that. She made a lot of very good points. Good enough that I had to take a moment to give her a genuine, thoughtful response.

"I'm not gonna lie," I said. "It is hard. A lot of the stuff that's happened to me over the last couple of years would have been different if I was a guy. If a man married a woman for twenty-six hours he probably did it because she wouldn't sleep with him, or because she told him she was pregnant, or whatever. That's the story the press would tell. She'd be the one vilified."

"Exactly," the woman said. "It's a double standard." She looked genuinely pissed off.

Shit, I felt terrible for judging her based on what she was wearing. Was I any better than the double standard we were railing against? I made a mental note to be less judgy from now on.

"It is, but I was standing on the sidelines because Wolf Venom are headlining this tour. When I'm headlining, if anyone tries to tell me I can't stand in the middle of the stage during a Q and A, I will kick their ass." I grinned.

The audience laughed and almost every woman there cheered and clapped.

"Thank you," the woman handed the microphone back to the support guy and sat.

I gave her a smile and was about to hand the microphone back to Asher when the guy with the next question spoke.

"You claim to know audiences are coming out to see Wolf Venom," he said, his tone pure acid. "Why are you touring with them when no one wants to see a washed up slut?"

Yeah, I should have guessed shit like that was coming. The audience muttered, some angry, some in agreement. The guys looked like they were ready to bound out of their seats and rip the guy's head off.

I held up a hand to let them know I could deal with this. I hoped.

"Excuse me for a moment, I have to ask my manager something," I said.

Still speaking into the microphone, I said to Jackson, "How many countries is 'Inside Out' currently number one on their music charts?"

"At least forty-two," Jackson shouted. He smiled with unbridled satisfaction.

"At least forty-two," I repeated into the microphone. "Nice. I think that answers the question." I handed the microphone back to Asher and walked off the stage to a deafening roar of applause.

CHAPTER
FIFTEEN

ABBIE

I SLIPPED out a side door of the auditorium, to a small waiting room close enough to hear but not see. Or be seen.

I flopped down on a couch in the corner to gather my breath and my thoughts.

Footsteps in the corridor outside made me startle, but it was only Jackson who appeared in the doorway. He walked over and sat down heavily beside me.

"According to the saying, there's one in every crowd." He leaned back and crossed his legs so his ankle rested on his knee and one arm lay across on the back of the couch behind me.

"In my experience, more than one," I said dryly. "They're usually not given a platform to stir up shit."

He looked over at me. "Next time I'll have the staff vet the questions before they're asked. That should head off the problem before it becomes one. For what it's worth, most of the audience was behind you."

Yeah, most. Not all.

"I shouldn't let it get to me." I sighed heavily. "I know that, but I've asked myself the same question... I don't know how many times. Why me? Why this tour?"

"Why *not* you? Why *not* this tour?" he countered. "Because Levi thought it would be a good fit. I happen to agree with him." He was the soul of calm and patience right now.

I leaned against the back of the couch, my face raised towards the ceiling, and closed my eyes. "I'm sorry. You have better things to do than nurse singers with fragile egos."

"Nursing rock stars with fragile egos is at the top of my job description," he said. "Just above dealing with drunk ones and ones who behave like dickheads, and being a spoilsport. Trust me, you have nothing on some of them. Most of them, if I'm honest. Some days it's Asher's smart mouth, or Penn's grumpy ass. Other days it's trying to stop Violet and Blaise from screaming at each other and throwing things. One of these days they're either going to fuck or kill each other. Hopefully not the latter. I wish they'd get on with it. I don't know how the rest of the band puts up with them."

"Sounds like you need danger pay," I said sympathetically. "Especially if people start throwing things. At least the guys only throw food at each other. And insults." That I've seen.

Jackson snorted. "Yeah, there's that. Although Asher once dumped a full pitcher of beer on Penn's head. You can imagine how well that went down."

"Cold and dripping?" I guessed.

He chuckled. "Something like that. Knowing Penn, he deserved it, but what a waste of perfectly good beer."

I'd have to remember to ask them what led to that. I pictured Penn's expression now as he sat drenched in sticky beer and smiled.

"What did Penn do?" I asked. "He would have wanted to get Asher back for doing that?"

"He chased Asher around the room and hugged him until they were both wet, and stank." Jackson smiled softly at the memory.

I grinned. "That sounds hilarious. I would have liked to see that."

"Do me a favour?" he asked. "Please don't ask them to recreate that moment. Levi wasn't happy to get the cleanup bill from the establishment." He rolled his eyes playfully.

"If they do, I'll ask them to do it outside, and maybe use water instead of beer," I said helpfully. It wouldn't be quite as funny, but seeing them with their clothes stuck to them would be worth it.

"Thanks," he said. "I think."

"I'm sure they've gotten up to all sorts of things over the years," I said, hoping to prompt him into spilling some juicy stories.

"Definitely." He nodded. "Most of them you'll have to ask them about, since I can't tell you. But I can tell you this." He locked his eyes on mine. "They've never been as happy as they are now. Even when they first signed with the label and started to get big. They were ecstatic but..." He frowned as he searched for the right words. "I think they were scared it wouldn't last, or that it was a dream. Whenever a song did well, there was pressure for the next one to do even better. Same with every tour. They handled it pretty well, but they were all insecure. Since they met you, they've, I don't know, become comfortable in their own skin? They don't, 'fake it till they make it,' any more. They've made it and they're enjoying it. Does that make sense?"

"Yeah," I said softly, "it does." I hadn't realised I had that impact on them. I cleared my throat before I got too emotional and cried.

"I can relate to trying to outdo myself," I said, changing the subject before I lost it. "I'm more competitive with myself than with anyone else. I hated the idea of letting anyone down, but I hate letting myself down more. I guess that's why questions like that get to me. I feel like I haven't done enough to prove myself." And if I hadn't, then what the fuck more could I do?

He placed an arm lightly around my shoulders and gave me a gentle squeeze. He watched me while he did it, clearly aware of overstepping any boundaries.

"What would it take to feel like it's enough?" he asked. "Number one in over forty countries? A sell-out world tour or three? Or four? Several Grammy awards? A dozen ARIA awards? A guest appearance with the Wiggles?"

I couldn't contain laugh at the last one. "All of the above? Especially the Wiggles. Who wouldn't want to work with them? When I was younger, I wanted to *be* one of them."

"Just between you and me, so did I," he admitted. "That dinosaur looks like a lot less work than most rock stars."

I laughed, but it faded to a faint smile as I thought about his question. I wanted to give him, and myself, an answer.

"I don't know what it would take," I said finally. "Maybe I'm always going to feel like I'm not good enough. Is that necessarily a bad thing though? It means I have to keep working to get better and better, instead of getting stale and complacent."

"I can't imagine you being either of those things," he said softly. "Especially not stale."

He looked at me with an unreadable expression before he drew his arm away. "I think you and the guys will keep pushing the boundaries until there are no more boundaries to push. Then you'll find some new ones and push those. Isn't that what living is all about? Challenging yourself to do things you never thought you could do?"

"I'd like to think some of it is about enjoying the things you know you can do," I said. "Without having to prove yourself again and again."

He shifted on the lumpy couch. "I sound like an old man, but one thing I've learned is that you can't please everyone. We're not tacos. Or cheese."

"You're not an old man." I twisted around sideways and sat with my knees on the couch. "And even cheese can't please everyone. Some people can't eat dairy."

He spread his hands. "That's exactly my point. Not even something as amazing as cheese can make everyone happy. What hope do people have? All we can do is be the best version of ourselves we can be and hope to survive the day without getting beer dumped on our heads."

"They would never do that to you, would they?" I bit back a laugh. I could certainly see them thinking about it, especially Asher, but dumping beer on your manager sounded like a really bad career move to me. Not as bad as Jackson doing it to them and getting fired, but bad enough.

Jackson raised an eyebrow. "I wouldn't put it past them. They like having fun, especially on tour, in the rare moments they get bored."

"Rare moments indeed," I said dryly.

The audience in the auditorium laughed and I smiled. "Sounds like everyone is having fun in there."

He looked down the bridge of his nose at me. "Do you want to go back?"

"No," I said. "This is their moment. You can go back if you want to."

"And leave you alone with the evil twins wandering around?" He grimaced. "Even if the whole band wouldn't be pissed at me, I wouldn't do it. Those two are trouble."

"That's putting it mildly," I said. Just thinking about them made my heart race and my palms sweat. Honestly, I was relieved Jackson was okay about staying with me, otherwise I would have wandered back into the auditorium after I caught my breath. Now I thought about it, coming here alone was kinda silly. Thank goodness Jackson had the sense to follow me.

"I have security watching for them everywhere we go," he said. "Although, from past experience, they are slippery and good at sidestepping security. I guess that's why their family gets away with so much shit. They know how."

"We've gotten away with a bit of it ourselves," I pointed out. "With their help, sometimes."

"That's unfortunately true," Jackson agreed. "I would prefer not to have to deal with…" His gaze flicked towards the door. "Things like that."

Given he was referring to disembodied heads and dead bodies, I could do nothing but agree with him. No one wanted to deal with shit like that. Except, presumably, whoever cut those heads off. Pete, according to the police. I still had my doubts about that. He could be a dickhead, but a killer?

"Yeah. We're lucky you're so chill about…actually, everything." Without thinking, I asked, "You don't think it's weird that I have a relationship with all of the guys?"

He seemed mildly surprised at the question. "Does it matter what I think?" he asked. "If I tell you it's weird, is that going to change anything?"

"No," I admitted. "So—do you?" I was genuinely curious now.

"Like I said, the guys have never been happier. You seem happy, apart from assholes asking stupid questions. What more is there to think about? Love is love and all that." He crossed his legs and cupped his hands around his knee. "If you feel like you need my blessing, you have it. But I don't think you need it."

"Maybe not," I said slowly. "But I feel better knowing you don't feel uncomfortable with the situation. I mean, you do get to hang around with us a lot and things could easily get awkward."

"If it wasn't for those NDAs, I'd tell you a whole bunch of times things got awkward." He made a face. "After a while, you learn to roll with it. Trust me when I say there's pretty much nothing I haven't seen. Or done, for that matter. It might surprise you to learn I've been around the block a time or two myself. I was a full-time touring musician for years before I gave it up and became a manager."

"Oh, I didn't know that," I said. "What instrument did you play? Wait, let me guess. Bass guitar?"

"Yep. Always destined to be in the background." He shrugged.

"The backbone of the band," I said firmly. He was the kind of guy who supported other people without needing a mountain of accolades himself. I could easily imagine him grooving on stage, bass in his hands, looking cool.

"That too," he agreed. "Don't worry, I'm not so insecure that I don't appreciate the role of the bass player. I was never meant to be out the front in the spotlight. It was never what I wanted. All I wanted to do was play and entertain people. When it became apparent the band was never going to be big, we broke up and I concentrated on helping other bands to entertain people." Wistfully, he added, "It's almost as satisfying."

My heart went out to him. Someone had to manage all of our craziness, but it must have been hard to step aside from something he loved to make room for other musicians.

"Do you still play?" I tucked my knees up under me. The couch was so hard it was difficult to stay comfortable for long. I tried not to think about what might have happened on its surface.

"When I can," he said. "If Levi and I are in the same town and have time." He caught the look of surprise on my face and smiled. "You didn't know Levi was in a band too?"

"I knew he was, but I didn't know you were in the same one," I said. "He played lead guitar, right?"

"Guilty," Jackson said. "And sax. Not at the same time. He always had to be the boss and the centre of attention back then, just like now." While other people might have been resentful of that, Jackson spoke fondly.

Unlike Asher, I didn't think Jackson and Levi were sleeping together, but I bet they had some good times performing together.

That gave me an idea. I just had to figure out how to pull it off.

CHAPTER
SIXTEEN
LANDON

"WHERE DO people get off being fuckheads?" I sipped good German beer out of a huge stein. A couple of these, and I'd be shitfaced. Right now, I was in the mood for it. Most of the Q and A went smoothly, but I couldn't get that asshole and his nasty question out of my head.

"Some people can't help themselves," Abbie said darkly. She handled it beautifully, but she was still as pissed off as the rest of us, I could tell. The guy had pinpointed her insecurities and attacked her with them. No one would blame her if she wanted to scratch his eyes out.

Hell, I wanted to scratch his eyes out.

"Some people should try harder," Penn said with a grunt.

That was ironic coming from him, but for a change, no one pointed it out.

"Want us to track him down and beat him up?" Asher offered.

I couldn't tell if he was joking or not. "I'd be down for that," I said, in case he wasn't.

"Don't give him the satisfaction," Abbie said reluctantly. "People like that want to feel good about themselves so they do it by trying to drag other people down."

"Is that all that's bothering you?" Tully asked her.

"Is it that obvious?" She gave him a wry smile.

He must be more astute than me, because I hadn't picked up on it until he mentioned it. Now he had, I squinted at her. Yeah, something else was definitely up. And the beer was going right to my head. If I wasn't half buzzed, I would have seen it sooner.

She took a moment to continue. "I feel like shit for assuming the woman who wanted to address sexism in the music industry was going to come on to one of you guys," she admitted. "Or all of you. I looked at what she was wearing, and figured..."

I squinted. How could anyone as beautiful as Abbie think for a moment we'd even notice another woman? Okay, I remembered her, and her tiny dress, but she hadn't even crossed my mind. Not like that.

"That other girl had just proposed to Zeke," Asher pointed out with a grin. He poked his boyfriend playfully in the chest. "When's the wedding?"

Zeke groaned. "To her? Never."

"Yeah, she's way too good for you," Penn teased.

Zeke flipped him off.

"Thanks," Abbie said sarcastically. "Nice of you to suggest he's lowered his standards all the way down to me. And Asher."

"You're too good for him too," Penn said unapologetically. "Asher is about right. They're both dickheads." He ducked when Asher scooped up a handful of peanuts from the bowl in the middle of the table and threw them at him.

"Don't get us kicked out," Channing warned.

"I can see the headline now," I said, a silly grin on my face. "Wolf Venom gets kicked out of Frankfurt beer hall for throwing snacks."

"Update at ten," Asher added.

We all laughed.

"It's all fun and games until someone slips on a peanut," Tully said.

Asher frowned. "I'm pretty sure there's a joke or a pun in there somewhere."

"Someone hurt themselves falling over your nuts?" Zeke suggested.

Asher pointed a finger gun at him. "There you go. That works. It's even plausible, given how big they are."

"It's more accurate to say you are a big nut than you *have* big nuts," Penn said.

Asher shrugged. "Any more than a mouthful would be a waste."

"Fact." I nodded. Although, if I died choking on Channing's balls, there were worse ways to go.

Channing grunted something incoherent.

I leaned against his side and put a hand on his arm. "Are you okay? You seem distracted tonight." It must be contagious.

He twitched and for a moment I thought he was going to pull away from me. "Yeah I'm just..." He let out a huffing breath from his nose. "Can we go somewhere? Just for a couple of minutes."

I started to make a comment about him wanting to take me away for a quickie, but then I saw the serious expression on his face.

"There's a spare table on the other side of the hall." I nodded towards it. "We should be able to talk there."

"Okay. Let's go." He pulled away from me and stood.

I gestured to Zeke that we wouldn't be long and followed Channing.

My heart sat in my throat. The beer lay heavy in my stomach. I couldn't say it wasn't like Channing to be serious all of a sudden, because it was. Every time, it made me anxious as fuck. I always assumed the worst. Like, this time he would break up with me or something.

I slipped into the bench beside him and placed my stein on the table in front of me. Depending on what he said, I might need to drink the rest of it quickly.

"Is everything okay?" I asked. "Did I... Do something wrong?"

Should I apologise for it now or wait until he told me what it was? Right now, I had no idea. Maybe I snored too much. Had he decided he didn't want to bring Abbie into our relationship? Had he decided to quit the band and go home? Had he...

Or I could listen and find out what he had to say.

"No, you didn't do anything," he said quickly. "I just feel like..." He looked down at the table.

Okay, here it came. Was I about to get my heart broken?

"Feel like what?" I asked gently.

"Like..." He hesitated again.

My heart beat so hard it was painful.

"Like I hardly get to see you lately," he said quickly. "I know we spend all day every day together, but I haven't had you to myself. Not with all the other guys around."

"And Abbie?" Was that what this was really about? Spending time with her?

"No. Yes. No." He scrunched up his face. Even troubled, he was absolutely adorable. How did I get so fucking lucky?

"Some of the above?" I suggested. Yes and no covered pretty much everything, without actually covering anything. He was making me more and more confused.

"You might need to help me out here," I said. "Is it yes or no?"

"Both." He sighed in frustration. "I see you with her and how happy you are. I wonder if..."

"I'm starting to think I should tickle it out of you," I said only half joking.

He managed a faint smile. "I'm just wondering if you still want to be with me." He said in a rush. "Sometimes I don't think I'm good enough for you, and if she makes you happy..."

My breath came out in a rush of relief. "Is that what this is about? You think she makes me happier than you do? That I'm gonna leave you for her?"

My relief might be premature. Just because he wasn't mad at me didn't mean we weren't headed for heartache. I almost held my breath until he spat out what he wanted to say.

Since passing out wouldn't be good for the conversation, I forced myself to breathe.

He looked down into his half drunk beer. "I'm not always the easiest person to get along with." He almost looked like he might cry.

"You're my person, and I love you," I said firmly. "I'm not always the easiest person either. None of us are. We're high strung rock stars. But I'm as sure as ever that we can all make each other happy. If that's still what you want?"

"It is," he said quickly. "I just wanted to make sure we were all reading from the same song sheet."

I covered my hand with his. "We are. Nothing will ever change that. You, me, Abbie, the rest of us, we'll make it work as long as that's what everyone wants. You and I, though, we are rock solid. Harder than my cock when I think about you."

"That's pretty hard," he agreed. He gave me a suggestive, lopsided smile that made my heart flip and my blood run hotter. Could he be any more stinking adorable?

I grinned. "Very hard." I took a moment to take a sip of beer. "Did something happen to provoke this? I've noticed you've been a bit moody since—" I thought for a moment. "Since Vienna? I figured you'd tell me when you're ready."

Which I supposed he had.

"It's been stewing for a while," he admitted. "Since before the tour, I guess. You're so, I don't know… you. You deserve better than someone like me."

"I don't know," I said slowly. "I've never met anyone better than you." Abbie being equally good as him, of course. They were the best two people I knew. The rest of the band weren't too far behind.

"See what I mean?" he asked. "You're beyond sweet." He pressed his forehead to mine. "How did I get so lucky?"

"Just by being you," I said firmly. I kissed his mouth and felt the tickle of stubble against mine. I could happily gobble him up right here and now in front of everybody. Literally. And have a fucking good time doing it.

He kissed me back, then sat with his nose lightly touching mine. "What if Abbie doesn't want me as much as she wants you and the other guys?"

"She does," I said with certainty. "I can guarantee you one million percent that she wouldn't suck your cock if she didn't want you as much as the rest of us."

She was as invested in this as I was. As all the rest of the guys were. I knew she wouldn't fuck any of us if what she felt for them wasn't strong and genuine.

"Would you like me to give you some time alone with her when we get a chance?" I offered.

His brow creased and smoothed out in thought. Finally, he shook his head.

"No. I mean, yeah I'd like to keep having one-on-one conversations with her. But you mean a date with just her and I, right? I kinda like it being the three of us. I'd feel like I'm cheating otherwise."

"Me too," I agreed. We'd been a duo for so long, it felt right to keep doing that.

"She's something special, isn't she?" he asked. "We shared a lot of women but no one has ever felt like…" He exhaled. "Like home. You know? Like you do."

"I do know," I agreed. "I feel the same way about you and her. We're just a trio of comfy throw pillows, or a blanket. Sexier than that though."

He chuckled. His breath brushed my lips. "I don't know, I've seen some pretty sexy throw pillows."

"Did we just enter an episode of confessions from teenage Channing?" I teased. "Did you used to hump pillows?"

He laughed again. "Didn't everyone?"

"No," I said. "But I did have this big plush elephant I got close to." I loved that elephant. The social worker who drove me to one of my foster homes gave it to me. I took it to the next two before the third one wouldn't allow it. Apparently it was too old and manky by then. That was the excuse I was given.

I left it behind with a younger girl who probably needed it more than I did anyway.

The first time I got any royalties from the band, I tracked down a similar plush elephant and bought it. It sits on my couch in my living room, taking up space. And not getting humped.

Channing must have seen how sad I got thinking about my past. He cupped my cheeks with his hands and slanted his mouth over mine. He kissed me, slow and deep and loving. It washed away every last bit of self-doubt the conversation gave me.

You love both of them, the voice in the back of my head said. I put all of that emotion into my kiss so Channing would know and feel it, but I wouldn't be ready to tell Abbie that for a while yet. We'd get there when the time was right, but that time was not right now.

If not now, then when? The back of my mind asked. I didn't have the answer to that. I would know when I knew.

I hoped our conversation put Channing's fears to rest. All I wanted was for everyone to be happy, whatever it took to get us there.

CHAPTER
SEVENTEEN
ABBIE

"I'M NEVER DRINKING BEER AGAIN," Asher declared. He lay down on the floor backstage and groaned.

"Sure you're not," Penn flopped down into a chair. "Until next time."

Asher groaned again. "Don't talk so loud." He pressed his hands to either side of his forehead.

"Poor baby." I stretched out beside him. "I thought you took something for the pain?"

"I did. It hasn't worked yet." He lowered one hand and started to trace circles around my upper arm.

Zeke sat beside us. "If you think he's bad now, you should see him when he gets sick. He gets the worst case of man flu I've ever seen."

"I do not," Asher protested, his voice full of discomfort. "I just get sicker than everyone else."

"Bullshit," Penn said. "You bitch and moan louder than anyone else. Anyone would think you are dying the way you carry on sometimes."

"I'm dying right now," Asher said. "Tell Blazing Violet when they go on not to play too loud, would you?"

"We could ask Danny to play in your place?" Tully suggested. "You can stay here and get some sleep."

"I thought you were supposed to get more seasoned as you got older?" Landon said to Channing. "You'd think at Asher's age—"

"I'm not old," Asher protested. He picked up his head. "Why aren't the rest of you hung over too?"

"Who said we're not?" I asked.

"I'm not," Penn said. "I only had one beer."

"I don't get hangovers," Zeke said with a shrug. He hadn't really drank that much either. Honestly, neither had I. It was difficult to let loose with the evil twins lurking around, ready to take advantage of it.

"By the way, I'll be fine to go on stage," Asher said. Evidently it took time for the words to filter into his brain.

"If you don't puke while you're out there," Penn said helpfully.

Asher grunted. "Don't talk about puke."

"Okay." Penn shrugged. "I won't mention chunks of carrot or corn. Or green mush." He smiled slyly.

"You fucking suck," Asher told him. "If I spew, I'm going to spew on you." He rolled over as though he was about to do just that.

Penn shot up out of his chair and moved to the other side of the room. "The hell you are!"

Landon chuckled and lowered himself down beside me. He lay propped up on his elbow. "You know what would be nice?"

Channing sat down beside him. "If Asher stopped complaining?"

"Thanks for the sympathy, guys," Asher said sarcastically.

"What would be nice?" I asked Landon. I wasn't going to give Asher any sympathy. Hangovers were one hundred percent self-inflicted. He didn't have to accept when that German guy challenged him to a drinking challenge. We were lucky he didn't pass out on the floor.

"A big comfortable nest," Landon said. "A bunch of pillows, blankets, stuff like that. Somewhere we could all have a nap while we wait to go on stage."

"Fuck yes," Channing said. "Maybe a big-screen TV and a movie."

"And a big juicy steak," Zeke said, deliberately speaking in Asher's direction. "The kind dripping with pan juices. And some fresh vegetables on the side. And chips, of course. You have to have hot chips with your steak."

"I thought you loved me," Asher groaned. "If you keep talking about food, I'm going to hurl."

"You might feel better if you do," Tully said. "Get the rest of it out of your system."

"I tried that twice already, it didn't help." Asher rolled over and pressed his forehead to the floor.

I exchanged glances with Landon, shook my head and smiled. "I guess he won't be drinking again."

"He will." Landon started to trace little circles over the bare skin between my chin and the neckline of my dress. "He's like this every time. In a couple of hours, he'll be ready to drink more than he drank last night."

"No way," Asher said, his voice muffled by the floor. "Never again."

Landon's circles got a little lower, until the tip of his finger slipped under the fabric.

I started to melt, although his touch was feather-light.

"You like that?" he whispered.

"Yeah, I do," I whispered back. In spite of the fact we were in a room where anyone might walk in, or maybe because of it, my pussy started to throb. When had I become such a risk taker? It was a recent thing, since I'd met them. They brought out my inner sex goddess.

"Good." He peeled back the fabric of my dress and the cup of my bra, letting a blast of cool air tickle my nipple. He quickly covered it with his mouth, sucking gently on my sensitive peak.

I closed my eyes, only opening them again for a moment when Channing did the same to my other breast. They really were one hell of a team.

"Can anyone join this party?" Tully asked. The other guys must have agreed, because the guitarist gently bent my knees and knelt down between them. He hooked his fingers into the gusset of my panties and pushed them aside. He lowered his face between my thighs and started to tease my pussy with his tongue.

Between the three of them, I was shivering and shuddering in moments.

The first notes of Blazing Violet's music echoed through the corridor and into the room.

Tully strummed me as Blaise strummed his guitar, starting slow but building quickly, driving the audience into a frenzy. Tully sucked my clit and thrust his tongue into me and around my folds. He lapped at me like a man dying of thirst. And I was the only well in sight.

Blood thundered through me to the beat of Danny's drums and Ryan's bass. The tempo increased, pounding around the stadium and right into my core.

I shattered into a million pieces. I arched my back and rocked against Tully's mouth. Violet held a high note that matched mine, long and intense until my breath was gone from my body.

I flopped down, gasping, as the song ended and another began.

Tully, his face glistening, moved up my body to the beat of the music, grooving as he went. He undid the front of his jeans, his eyes on me, searching for my reaction. For my consent to do this here.

I gave all of that and more with a long, lingering look laced with heat.

He nodded and pushed his jeans down just enough to free his erection.

Landon and Channing didn't stop lavishing attention on my breasts. They too moved in time with Blazing Violet's music, sucking and licking faster and slower with the tempo.

Tully positioned himself outside my pussy and slid inside during a long bridge. He let out a deep, low groan of pleasure that matched the cry of Blaise's guitar.

"You feel so fucking incredible." He was careful, as always, letting me get used to him note by note, before he slid all the way, balls deep, into my body.

"So do you," I said. When he started to thrust, my hips rose and fell in perfect harmony to meet each one.

Zeke abandoned his chair and came to sit beside us, eyes dark with desire. He glanced at us both before he slipped a hand under Tully's stomach and started to circle my clit with his fingertips.

I gasped, overwhelmed by the barrage of sensations from all four guys, and the pounding music from above. It was like the club Landon took us too, but more personal somehow. We knew the set Blazing Violet would play, and all the lyrics, all the notes. That became the soundtrack for this moment.

Four became five as Asher, apparently feeling well enough already, rolled over and opened the front of Zeke's jeans. He helped the singer's cock to pop free and lowered his mouth onto him.

"Holy crap, yeah," Zeke breathed. "Your mouth is incredible, babe. Don't stop doing that."

Apparently not wanting to be left out, Penn moved over, suspicious eyes on Asher until he knelt next to me. He leaned all the way over and kissed my mouth, all lips and teeth. He fucked my mouth with his tongue until I was breathless.

I reached the edge of the precipice again and hurtled over, unable to stop myself, even if Penn ordered me to. The blood rushing through my ears was louder than the pounding of the drums that poured through the speakers. It surged all the way through me lifting me up and dragging me down until every nerve in my body was screaming with pure joy.

My orgasm claimed Tully. My body convulsed around him until he came as well. He shouted a pure note of pleasure. He pounded frantically, then stilled and ground into me, my pussy milking him for every drop.

Zeke was close behind, thrusting frantically into Asher's mouth.

Watching his face scrunch up in concentration, his mouth open as he gasped and panted, then exhaled as he came, made me come again.

This time was even more intense and all-encompassing than before. If I thought all my nerves felt it the second time, I was wrong. This one, I swear I felt down at the end of my hair and into my toenails.

I screamed, this time in time with Sharkey's keyboard, backed by Ryan's bass. Danny's drums came back in as I hit my peak, driving me higher. I crashed down as he clashed his cymbals, ending the song to a storm of applause.

When I finally came down, I was floppy, boneless, panting.

Tully slid out of me and Landon took his place. At the same time, Channing positioned himself so he could slide his cock into Landon's mouth.

Inspired, Penn undid the front of his jeans and slid his cock into my mouth.

Zeke rolled Asher over the other way and did the same to him. It wasn't for the music on the stage, all anyone would hear was the sound of sucking and groaning.

"Thank you!" Violet shouted. "This next song is dedicated to a guy I once knew. It's called 'Blow Your Top'."

I snorted with the irony of us blowing to this song, and went on sucking.

Landon grinned and thrust faster and faster into my body, while Penn matched him stroke for stroke.

I sucked and teased him with my tongue, ran my hand up and down from my chin to his balls. Out of the corner of my eye, I watched the other guys. What was it about watching a guy blow off another guy that was as hot as fuck? Maybe because they were so big and masculine, but like this they were vulnerable and giving.

Or maybe I just had a thing for stubble and cocks. I mean, both of those were good things too.

I don't know if Penn agreed, but he fixed his gaze on my face and came next, flooding my mouth with hot, pearly cum. He looked expectant and slowly slid his cock out from between my lips. He arched an eyebrow at me.

My mouth closed, I smiled and swallowed deliberately.

"Fuck yeah," he said softly. "You are fucking next level, woman."

"Hell yeah I am," I said with a grin. "And you're delicious."

He groaned in appreciation.

Landon, Channing and Asher were thrusting at about the same speed. I knew all three were close to coming. I looked over at Penn meaningfully. If he could be the conductor for me...

He sat back on his haunches and nodded. "Asher, don't come yet."

Asher groaned. "But I want to."

"Yeah," Penn said, "but wait."

Asher moaned in protest, but slowed down slightly.

Zeke raised his eyebrows, but went on sucking.

"You two are close aren't you?" Penn asked Landon and Channing. "Yep, I thought so. That's it, go right to the edge."

"Asher?"

Asher made an indeterminate noise.

"Abbie wants you to come now. All of you."

Whether it was his intention or not, but when all three guys came, I came for a fourth time. This time it was so hard and intense I went all the way to infinity, stayed there for approximately a decade, then gradually floated back down through the atmosphere and back into my body.

The guys all flopped down on the floor around me, panting ruggedly and sighing.

Blazing Violet was in approximately the middle of their set.

Shit.

I was going to need to clean up and change my panties before I went on stage after them.

I barely registered Jackson sticking his head through the door, clearing his throat and then hurrying away.

Poor guy, the things he saw while just doing his job.

CHAPTER
EIGHTEEN
ABBIE

"SO... ABOUT BEFORE..."

I managed to get through my set with my knees a little weak. If I wasn't sweaty before I went under the hot lights, I was sweaty after. Thankfully the audience was receptive, with none of the attitude of the guy from the Q and A. They even shouted for an encore before I left the stage. They cheered again when I went back in sing with the guys.

By the time I was done, I was itching for a shower.

I didn't get far before I almost bumped into Jackson, who was pacing back and forth outside the green room.

He stopped to look at me, and waved a hand back and forth in the air.

"Don't worry about it," he said. "Still not the worst thing I've ever seen." And yet he couldn't meet my eyes.

"I just—" I needed to say something, if only to know we were okay after what he saw. "We didn't plan for any of that. It just happened. If we stopped to think about it for half a second, it might not have."

Jackson sighed and leaned against the wall, one knee bent, the bottom of his shoe pressed against the white painted brick. He crossed his arms over his chest and lowered his head for a moment.

When he looked back up he said, "I'm not in the business of telling any of you where you should and shouldn't, you know..."

"Fuck?" I asked.

He winced. "Yeah. But I could have been anyone. Press get past security. Fans get past security. Hell, it might have been a security officer with a phone, who decided the photo would make them more money than their job does.

There's only so much damage control I, or the label, could do if a photo like that leaked. You'd be looking at one hell of a shitstorm."

He glanced at my chest, then quickly up to my face. He'd obviously seen my bare breasts and was trying not to think about them too much. He also might have seen Landon's ass, but for the most part we kept our clothes on. That in itself was pretty amazing given everything that went on.

"I'm sorry," I said sincerely. "The last thing we want to do is create a shitstorm."

"Next time, maybe close the door," he suggested. He scrubbed a hand over his chin. "I feel like I'm talking about a group of teenagers. I know you're not that. I just don't want any of you doing anything you'll all regret."

"Taking care of our image is your job," I pointed out. "I think you're within your rights to yell at us." I didn't regret a moment of it, but he was right about closing the door. Or at least, posting a security guard we could trust outside.

Although, wouldn't that defeat the purpose? The possibility of being caught was part of the fun.

"Do you want me to yell at you?" Judging by the way he swallowed, that wasn't what he wanted to do with me.

That realisation made me swallow too. I liked Jackson a lot. He was the island of calm in a sea of crazy, even though we razzed him relentlessly. Did I think of him like another boyfriend? Would he want that? Would the rest of the guys?

All of those questions had my head spinning.

I completely understood why he kept his feelings under wraps until now. I'd told Zeke, Asher and Tully I loved them, and when the time was right I would tell the other three. Getting involved with me would be complicated for him. And an extra complication for all of us. Not to mention what happened the last time I got involved with anyone who worked for my label and was older than me. Jackson was at least a decade older.

Not that I was worried about the age gap. That was a tiny concern in the grand scheme of things.

"Actually, I'd prefer it if you didn't yell at me," I said. "Unless you're cheering me on."

"I will never *not* cheer you on," he said softly. "I'm in the top seven of your biggest supporters. Top eight if you count Levi."

"I hope I can count the boss in that number," I said lightly. My bank account was looking a lot healthier these days and no doubt so was his. Not that he was short on a dollar or two to start with.

"Definitely." Jackson nodded firmly. "He always speaks highly of you. As do I."

"That goes both ways," I said. "You two have been amazing. I couldn't have asked for better support. It's made a world of difference." I stood on my toes and lightly kissed his cheek.

He watched me with his denim blue eyes. I got the impression he was tempted to turn his face to meet my lips with his.

I was tempted to kiss his mouth and see how he tasted.

I stepped back and gave him an awkward smile.

He responded with a matching one. "Were you on your way to the shower?" he asked. "Would you like me to come with you?"

He realised what he said and his face turned pink.

My mouth went dry. Apparently after four orgasms, there was room for more. His suggestion, however innocently intended, sent a shockwave of heat through my body.

He cleared his throat loudly. "I mean, I can escort you there and wait outside to make sure no evil twins turn up."

"Right," I said. "Of course. I'd like that." Hopefully stadium security was good enough to keep out Hunter and Parker, but if anyone could slip in, they could.

"Thank you. I'd feel safer with you nearby."

We stood awkwardly for a moment or two before he gestured towards the locker rooms with a grimace.

The downside to playing in stadiums which often housed professional sporting teams was that the locker rooms smelled like old socks and sweaty feet. It was the least sexy smell ever. Maybe that wasn't such a bad thing under the circumstances.

I took my change of clothes and a towel and stepped into the cubicle. If it was one of the other guys, there wouldn't have been any question as to whether or not I should close the door, much less lock it. I trusted Jackson not to try anything with me, but it might be better to be naked out of sight.

For now. Things between us were awkward enough already.

And confusing. There was no doubt in my mind I cared about him. I couldn't imagine not having him in my life, one way or another. Would taking things a step further ruin things between us? Worse than that, would it ruin things between Jackson and the other guys? If I thought it would, then friendship would be as far as it could ever go.

Fuck, why couldn't my life be simple for a change? Apparently I thrived on chaos and hot guys. Of course that got me to wondering what Jackson looked like under his clothes. I'd never seen him with his shirt off. That didn't seem fair now that he'd seen me without one.

I shook my head to myself, stripped and left my sweaty clothes on the floor before I stepped into the warm flow of the shower.

It was strange how quickly I got used to sharing with someone else. These days, when I washed, I usually had at least one of the guys with me. We always did more than get clean, of course. Any time I was naked was an opportunity for touching and orgasms. I certainly couldn't complain about that.

About halfway through, I heard Jackson talking to someone. I couldn't hear the words; his voice was low, but he sounded agitated. Was that because of our conversation or had something else happened? Who was he talking to? I couldn't hear anyone else, so he must be on his phone.

I listened for a moment and decided he didn't sound panicked, just cranky.

I squeezed out shampoo onto my palm and started to wash my hair. Partly because I needed to and partly so I couldn't hear what he was saying. Chances were, it was about work and was none of my business. We weren't the only ones he managed.

"No," he was saying as I rinsed my hair. "Not gonna happen." He spoke in a frustrated growl. "Just—no. I haven't been able to..." His voice dropped off lower again.

I felt bad for overhearing even that little. I rinsed my hair for longer than I needed to, so my ears were under the water.

Finally, when I couldn't stay there any longer because I'd look like a prune, I turned off the water. The locker room fell into silence.

Jackson must have ended his phone call.

I dried quickly and got dressed in a clean T-shirt and track pants. And yes, dry panties. For now.

I grabbed my sweaty clothes off the floor and opened the door.

Just as I expected, Jackson was alone, leaning against the wall on the other side of the locker room. His mouth was set in a firm line like it was when he was annoyed.

"Is everything okay?" I asked. "I thought I heard you talking to someone." I quickly added, "I'm sorry, it's none of my business."

"No, it's okay." He rubbed the back of his neck. "Nothing to worry about, just work." Once again, he wouldn't meet my eyes. Was that because of the phone call or our awkward conversation from before?

"Okay, if you're sure," I said.

He pushed himself off the wall. "I'm sure. Let's go listen to the guys' last few songs. Last concert of the European leg."

After this, we had a couple of days off before travelling to North America.

Personally, I was looking forward to the small break. A tour this long was exhausting. If we didn't get a few days to rest, we'd be incoherent by the end of it.

Assuming we were coherent at the start of it. I liked to think we were, more or less.

"Let's do it," I said without thinking.

Now it was my turn for my face to heat.

"I mean, listen to them." I seemed to have sex on the brain these days. Which wasn't usually a bad thing, but it might get me into trouble if I didn't watch my mouth. Maybe I shouldn't think about my mouth, because then I might think about what I could do to him with it. That could lead down a rabbit hole I wasn't ready to jump into yet.

"I thought that was what you meant," he said. He gave me a smile but I suspected he wished I meant the other kind of 'do it'. The bulge in his pants when I lowered my gaze slightly confirmed that suspicion.

That he wasn't going to pressure me was obvious. I appreciated that. I didn't know where this would go, if anywhere, but I wanted to take my time.

He opened the door that led out of the locker rooms and gestured for me to step out first.

I was approximately a thousand percent certain he wanted to grab me and kiss me, but he didn't. He just waited until I stepped past and closed the door behind us.

"So that's how it's done?" I asked, trying to lighten the mood.

He looked at me funny before he realised what I was trying to say. "Yes, that's how you close the door. Should I demonstrate a few times so you know how to do it yourself if I'm not around?" He grinned and even gave me a wink.

I tried to ignore the way my heart flipped.

"That's not necessary," I said with a laugh. "Your demonstration was more than adequate. But if I can't do it by myself next time, I have you on speed dial."

He laughed and put a hand on my lower back as we walked back in the direction of the stage.

CHAPTER
NINETEEN

ABBIE

"SO, SOMETHING HAPPENED. KINDA," I started slowly.

Zeke and Asher both stopped with a piece of strudel a couple of centimetres from their mouths. Lucky for them I hadn't waited until they'd shoved them in.

Zeke lowered his strudel and put it back on his plate. He rubbed his thumb over his fingers to dust off flakes of pastry. "Who do I have to beat up?"

Asher bit into his strudel and nodded. "Same question," he said with a full mouth. "Just say the word and I'm there."

"That's very touching," I said dryly. "You don't have to beat anyone up. I don't think so anyway."

This wasn't going how I planned. I rehearsed every word in my head several times, but none of them came out the way I wanted.

"Is everything all right?" Landon asked gently. He touched the tips of his fingers to my wrist and gave me a worried look.

Channing, who sat on the other side of him, looked like he was ready to join Zeke and Asher in pounding the crap out of anyone I wanted them to.

"Yes," I said quickly. "Everything's fine. I..." I might as well jump straight in and tell them. "I think Jackson has a thing for me."

Asher sounded like he was about to choke on his strudel. He coughed a couple of times before he grabbed his coffee and took a gulp or two. "Ahh, fuck, hot."

Penn snorted a laugh at him. "You're such a dork."

"Love you too," Asher muttered.

Zeke patted Asher on the back until he was composed again. Once it was apparent the drummer wasn't going to choke and die, and hadn't scalded his mouth, Zeke turned back to me.

"Are you sure?"

"No," I admitted. "I mean, kinda. Maybe it was just his reaction to seeing us all together before the concert."

"That'll make anyone horny," Tully said.

"Makes me horny just thinking about it," Landon said.

"Most things make you horny," Channing told him.

Landon grinned. "That's true. Life is too short not to enjoy every minute of it."

"Anyway," Zeke drawled, "it wouldn't surprise me. How could anyone not have a thing for you?"

"What Zeke said," Asher said.

"I third that," Tully said.

"Yeah," Penn agreed.

"What do you want to do about it?" Zeke asked carefully.

"I don't know," I admitted. "I know I don't want to mess things up between you and him and him and I. If he becomes a part of this, it will change things."

"Like, we won't be able to tease him anymore?" Asher pouted.

"As if you're going to stop giving him shit," Penn scoffed.

"That's true," Asher agreed, more cheerful now. "Jackson is like a big brother to us, so it wouldn't be that weird."

"No weirder than this already is," Penn said.

"So you're okay with whatever happens?" I asked tentatively.

"Totally," Zeke said with a shrug. "It's not like we're talking about the evil twins here. We know Jackson and trust him and he knows all our shit. He's practically one of us anyway."

"What if it turns out badly?" I asked. That was hands down my biggest fear. This could so easily go all kinds of sideways.

"What if it turns out badly with any of us?" Zeke gestured around the table. Technically, three tables. The small café in Frankfurt didn't have a table big enough for us all to sit at, so we'd dragged them together. Fortunately, the staff hadn't seemed to mind. Especially after the guys agreed to take selfies with all of them.

A little bit of good will goes a long way.

"That would be bad," Asher said. "We only have to see how Violet and Blaise are to know how messy it is working with someone you hate."

"They don't hate each other," Tully said. "They just haven't figured that out yet."

"Besides, it's possible to work with somebody you can't stand," Penn said. He looked meaningfully at Asher.

Asher flipped him off. "You say you can't stand me, but I know otherwise. I'm way too adorable for that."

"Keep telling yourself that," Penn said. "Everyone knows I'm the adorable one." He pretended to fluff the back of his hair.

"You're all adorable," I said. "So much so I can't even stand it sometimes."

Jackson was adorable too.

Honestly, I shouldn't have been surprised at the guy's reactions. They'd all been very accepting of the situation so far. More than a lot of other guys would be.

"That explains the vibes I was getting from Jackson," Asher said thoughtfully. "I don't know why I didn't see it sooner. Now I think about it, it was pretty fucking obvious. He clearly adores you as much as we do."

"I'm relieved we don't have to beat anyone up," Zeke said.

Channing made a face like he was disappointed he wouldn't get the chance. No doubt something would come up sooner or later.

"Can I ask you something?" Landon asked softly.

"Of course," I said. "Anything." At this point, I had nothing left to hide, or that I would want to avoid talking about. Not that I could think of anyway.

"If you want to be with Jackson, what does that mean for the rest of us?" His eyes were a silent plea for me to be honest.

I understood why he was asking. It might be easy to assume I would either be with Jackson or with Wolf Venom.

I put a hand lightly on his cheek. "I'm not going to choose Jackson instead of you guys. He'd have to be part of this big crazy group, or not at all."

It was that simple. Every single one of these guys held a bit of my heart and that was how I wanted it. I couldn't imagine anything they would do that would make me walk away from them. We were a team, a family.

"You're not getting rid of me that easily," I added.

He smiled in relief and kissed my mouth.

"Good, because we don't want to get rid of you," Landon said. He turned to the rest of the guys. "Do we?"

"Hell no," Zeke and Asher said in unison.

"No way," Channing said.

"Nope," Penn agreed.

"Not a chance," Tully said.

I couldn't help but feel all warm and fuzzy inside. They really were basically the best guys ever.

"I guess I'll have a conversation with Jackson when I get a chance," I said slowly. "Talk about whether I was picking up on the wrong vibes or not." For all I knew, he was caught up in the moment, nothing more.

"Speak of the devil," Penn said.

I flinched, immediately assuming he meant the evil twins, who Zeke had mentioned a couple of minutes ago. If they brazenly walked into the same café we were sitting in...

"Hey." It wasn't the evil twins. It wasn't even Jackson. It was Levi, who grabbed a chair from another table and dragged it over. He sat down next to Tully. "You don't mind if I join you, do you? Good. Mr Cole, I wanted to speak to you about something."

"Yes, Mr Jones," Tully said with a smile. "This is all very formal. Am I in trouble?"

"Should you be?" Levi asked. He rested his elbow on the table and propped up his cheek with his fingertips. At the same time, he raised his eyebrow at Tully.

"Probably." Tully shrugged. "But if I am, then everyone else at the table should too."

"Did you just throw us under the bus?" Asher asked.

"Do you have a guilty conscience?" Tully cocked his head at the drummer.

"Not this week," Asher said lightly. "Anyway, I believe Levi wanted to talk to *you*."

"Yes I do," Levi agreed. "I was hoping to discuss a merger between White Wolf Records and Onyx Riot Records."

"Ohhh, are we talking about a hostile takeover?" Asher asked eagerly.

"Hopefully not," Levi said. "There's no reason for things to get hostile." He turned back to Tully. "When you get back to Australia, look through all of the records, have an accountant look over everything. I think you'll probably find Onyx Riot is a fucking mess. To put it politely. I'd like to help put it back together. Or absorb its assets into White Wolf, assuming it has any assets left. There are some good staff, producers and acts left attached to them. I think you'll agree it's best not to leave people hanging when their livelihoods are at stake."

Tully nodded. "I agree one hundred percent. They don't deserve what mess Pete left behind. I don't need to talk to an accountant and look over the books. I trust you. I'm in." He stuck out his hand to Levi. Honestly, he looked relieved. I suspected he hadn't wanted to deal with the running of the label, at least not yet.

Levi shook it, but said, "Even if you do trust me, don't sign on the dotted line until you've had a third party look it over. I won't be. But I think between us we can put something together that will help everyone. Especially our bank accounts."

"As if either of you need more money," Asher said.

"Someone has to pay for you to fly around the world and put on concerts," Levi said. "I hate to break it to you, but that money doesn't come out of thin air."

Asher stared at him. "What? It doesn't? Well shit." He shook his head in mock disbelief.

We all laughed.

"Would either of you mind if I sit in on some of that?" I asked. "I'd feel better knowing Onyx Riot was being run the way it should be."

"Are you going to hook up with Levi too?" Penn asked. He narrowed his eyes at the label's owner, then at me.

Levi and I both looked at him in surprise but Levi laughed.

"My girlfriend might not approve of that," he said.

Asher's mouth dropped open. "You have a girlfriend? Since when?"

"Since it's none of your business," Levi retorted. "I don't ask about your love life and you don't get to ask about mine." He propped his cheek on the opposite hand.

"As if saying that is going to deter Asher," Penn said.

"I can try, can't I?" Levi shrugged.

"You can try," Asher agreed. "But Penn is right. If you won't tell me, I'll ask Jackson. I bet he knows. Doesn't he?"

Levi looked back at Tully. "I think the first thing we need to do is buy those drum machines we were talking about."

Asher held up his hands. "Okay, okay. I'll be good. You're as big a spoilsport as Jackson." He pouted and pretended to look a lot more offended than he actually was.

"Yes I am," Levi agreed cheerfully. "Don't you forget it." He waggled his finger under Asher's nose.

Zeke slung an arm over Asher's shoulders. "Don't worry, I won't let them replace you with the machine. If they do that, I'll walk."

We all knew that was an idle threat, but if Zeke left, there would be no band, not really.

"That's sweet." Asher kissed his mouth, then pressed his nose to Zeke's.

"You're sweet," Zeke told him.

"Fuck," Penn said. "You two are going to rot my teeth." He grimaced at them both.

They turned to him and smiled unashamedly. Zeke put an arm around my shoulder and pulled me over so the three of us were cheek to cheek to cheek. "How's this for sweet?"

Penn snorted. "Abbie is the only sweet one."

I batted my eyelashes. "So are you." I put an arm around Landon to pull him in too. He brought Channing in with him.

"We're all sweet," I declared.

"I don't know why you want to know about my love life when you have all of this in front of you," Levi said to Asher.

"I'm a hopeless romantic," Asher said.

"You're half right," Penn teased.

"Fine," Asher said with a shrug. "I am a romantic."

That obviously wasn't what Penn was implying, but for once he didn't point it out.

CHAPTER
TWENTY

ABBIE

"SO, you think I'm sweet, huh?" Femi slipped his hand into mine as we stepped out of the cafe and started back to the hotel.

"You have your moments," I said teasingly. I smiled up at him. He was so good looking he made my breath catch in my throat. Good looking and mine.

He pouted playfully. "I have lots of moments. Some more memorable than others."

"Like your ability to orchestrate four orgasms at once?" I let go of his hand and slipped my arm around him so I could snuggle as we walked. "Those are some mad skills."

He slipped his arm around me too. "It's not rocket science. It's about watching for the signs someone is about to come. Anyone could do it if they paid enough attention."

"Maybe," I said slowly. "But there's a knack to ordering people to wait as well. Not everyone has the right tone of voice for it, I don't think I do."

"No, I don't think you do either," he agreed, much to my surprise. Fortunately, he added, "Not because you aren't as bossy as me, but because your voice makes me want to come. I couldn't stop myself."

"So..." I thought about that for a moment. "I could potentially make you come on command?"

He leaned down to nestle his face in my hair. "Sweetheart, you could potentially make me do whatever you want. I was determined to hate your guts when we met and now—"

"Now you like my guts," I finished for him.

"I love your guts," he said softly. "I love your everything. I love *you*."

A flush of warm emotion rushed through me, making my heart sing with unfiltered happiness.

"I love you too." It was a relief to tell him that. For a long time I was worried he would keep hating me, and wanting me off the tour. Not that long ago, he would have agreed with that asshole at the Q and A. Hell, he would have *been* that asshole.

Or at least, he would have *claimed* to think that way.

He must have cottoned on to what I was thinking, because he said, "I'm sorry for being such a prick back then. I'm a temperamental asshole, as anyone will tell you. I wanted you the moment I laid eyes on you. Not just physically but like this, an actual relationship. That scared the shit out of me, and I took it out on you. Plus, to some extent, I was scared the audiences would love you more than they love us. The idea of you stealing the show pissed me off."

"I understand how that would frustrate you," I said. I'd be pissed if that happened to me, but I liked hearing him admit he cared about me the whole time. That made me feel warm and fuzzy inside. "And now?"

"And now," he said slowly, "you compliment the show. You're a part of it and we all stand out. The tour is better for having you on it."

For some reason, I felt tears prickle in my eyes. "See, I said you were sweet."

"Yeah, well." His shoulders twitched. "I still would have been pissed off if you stole my solo."

I blinked away tears in time to see him grin. "Of course you would, because you're a brat." I pressed my shoulder into his chest.

"Hell yeah I am," he agreed. "Always have been, always will be."

"I don't think I've ever heard anyone say they're proud to be a brat before," I said. "Dickhead, asshole, jerk, twat, but never brat."

His chest rumbled against my arm as he laughed. "Firstly, more people should be proud of being a brat. Secondly, who do you know who is proud of being a twat?"

I thought for a moment. "Yeah, okay I don't know. I'm sure there's someone. By the way, I forgive you for being a dickhead when we first met. You kept me on my toes, but I can't expect everyone to like me."

"Believe it or not, neither can I," he said. "I know, that's hard to get your head around. I'm such a likeable guy." He gave me a self deprecating smile.

"I think you are," I said. "You're honest and funny, and sarcasm is a sign of intelligence."

"I must be fucking brilliant then," he said with a laugh.

"You're a musical genius," I pointed out. He was definitely a smart guy, and educated. He had an interesting vocabulary of insults ready to dish out as needed. What more could anyone want?

He groaned softly. "Yeah, that was my parents' weapon of choice in getting me to do what they wanted."

He put on a high pitched voice and said, "*Beau, you're a prodigy. You owe it to yourself to take full advantage of the gifts you've been given. To yourself and the whole wide world.*" He stretched out an arm.

"A big chunk of the whole wide world loves your gifts," I pointed out. "Your parents don't?"

"They hate what I'm doing," he admitted. "When they introduce me to their friends, they refer to me as, 'our son who dabbles in music these days.' As if I sit in the lounge room playing the triangle."

"Ouch." I winced on his behalf. "If I was your mother, I would be proud of you. You're an amazing guy and you've done incredible things. Even without the band, you were destined to."

"You think so?" He glanced over at me.

It was the first time I ever heard him sound insecure.

"I absolutely think so," I said firmly. "A lot of people would have walked away from music if they were pressured into it." I sighed and added, "My parents wanted me to get a normal nine-to-five job. I don't think they cared if I worked in a bank or as a teacher, or if I washed dogs for a living, as long as I wasn't doing something that wouldn't guarantee me a regular income."

"Of course, you became a singer," he said. "The definition of irregular income."

"They were disappointed, but they supported me." I slipped my hand into his back pocket. His ass was warm through the fabric of his jeans. "I think they hoped it was a phase and I would get past it some day."

"If they're anything like mine, they would have been...ecstatic isn't the word. When Onyx Riot Records broke your contract, they must've hoped that meant you would do what they wanted?" He cocked his head at me, his expression interested and attentive.

"Something like that," I agreed. "They kept saying unsubtle things like, 'Now you're not singing anymore,' like I could just turn it off like a tap. I don't think they were impressed when Levi approached me. They were pissed after what Vance and Pete both did and they wanted to protect me I guess."

"Seems like a theme around here," Penn said. "All any of us wants to do is protect you. Truth is, you're a badass. For the most part, you don't need protection from the big bad world." He gave me such a gentle, loving smile my heart did a triple flip and landed in a half melted puddle in my chest. He was so fucking sweet and gorgeous, even if he wouldn't admit to it. Deep down, he was as much a romantic as Asher.

"Just the evil twins," I said. "And people like them."

"We all need protection against them," he agreed. "Even I couldn't deal with them alone. Little assholes." His tone was begrudging. Rightfully so.

"We all take care of each other," I said. "I think it's safe to say we always support what everyone does. We certainly won't be disappointed with each other's choice of career."

He snorted a laugh. "Definitely not. We'd be hypocrites if we did."

We walked in silence for a couple of minutes, lost in our own thoughts and taking comfort in each other.

He was the one who broke the silence. "What do you think is going to come after the tour? You're not going to give up your career for us, are you?"

"You wouldn't want me to?" I stepped around a discarded pizza box and looked up at him.

"For us? No. Not until you're ready to do that, and you're not. You're taking off again and I, for one, will not be responsible for clipping your wings. No more than you would do to me or any of the guys."

"No, I don't want to do that," I agreed. "And you're right, I'm not ready to step away yet. From my career or you guys."

"I guess," I said slowly, "we spend as much time with each other as we can while none of us are on tour, and video chat a shit ton when we are. If we want this to work badly enough, we'll find a way." We had to. I knew the guys wanted this as much as I did. It wouldn't be easy, I knew that too, but it would be worth it to be together.

"Maybe I should buy you a chastity belt for when you're on tour by yourself," he said jokingly. "The kind you can only unlock with the key, which I'll keep."

I nudged him with my elbow. "What if Jackson and I go on tour without you guys?"

"Then I'll get a chastity belt for him too." Penn grinned.

"You really are a brat," I said with a laugh. "But in case there is any doubt, I would never cheat on you guys. In order for this to work, we need to communicate. And we will."

"And we'll fly out and see each other as much as we can," he said. "Whatever it takes."

He paused for a moment and grimaced.

"What?" I asked.

"I don't like the idea of not seeing you every day," he admitted. "You might be a pain in the ass, but you're my pain in the ass and I'm used to you being around. I like having you nearby, or next to me. On top of me. Or underneath me. Or on your knees in front of me. Or..."

I laughed. "Yeah, I get it. Just like you're my asshole and I like having you around."

"And they say romance is dead," he joked. He kissed my hair. "I love you so much."

"I love you so much too," I said. "I don't think we would be us if we didn't rib each other mercilessly."

"That's true, we wouldn't," he agreed.

"That's how I know you and Asher really like each other," I said. I glanced over my shoulder to where the drummer was walking hand-in-hand with Zeke. "Because you give each other hell."

"Yeah, Penn is okay," Asher said. "Even though I want to punch him in the cock every once in a while."

"Back at you, bro," Penn told him. To me, he said, "Yeah, we give each other shit but we never mean anything by it. It's just our twisted sense of humour. Or as I like to say, part of my charm." He put a hand under his chin and smiled.

"Absolutely," I agreed. A little bit of razzing between brothers was okay as long as they didn't get personal and nasty. They all seemed to know where the line was and not to cross it. Their unity was a big part of their success. And yes, part of their charm.

"So," I started, slowly and carefully as though I was about to ask something difficult or awkward, "if you didn't play the triangle in the living room, then where did you play it?"

Penn laughed. "In the conservatory, of course. Where I played all my music. And before you ask, yes, I can play a fucking good tune on the triangle. Remind me to show you sometime."

"I will," I said. If anyone could make such a simple instrument sound incredible, it would be Penn.

CHAPTER
TWENTY-ONE
LANDON

"YOU FEELING BETTER ABOUT EVERYTHING?" Channing pulled my legs over his lap and started to take off my shoes and socks. He was the only person I knew who didn't seem to be grossed out by feet. Specifically feet which were encased in hot socks and shoes for hours.

Or maybe it was just my feet he didn't mind.

When they were bare, he started to massage them, pressing his fingers and thumbs firmly into the arch of one.

"By everything, you mean Abbie?" I looked over to where she was helping the other guys sort through the shit they'd thrown on the floor.

They did this every tour, if we stopped anywhere for long enough. Pants, shirts and socks got dropped as they hurried around doing other things. Then when it came time to pack, it all had to be picked up and claimed by whoever dropped it there in the first place.

I was pretty sure half the time it ended up belonging to someone else. No one seemed to give a crap, so it happened again and again.

Channing and I, we kept our stuff in or near our cases, most of the time. I mean, sometimes clothes went flying and you had to deal with it later.

"I know you were worried she was going to walk away from us." He started to work my toes, massaging his way up each one after the other.

I leaned back against the couch and groaned. What can I say? He had magic fingers.

"She said she won't and I believe her," I said. I tried not to pull my leg away when he touched a ticklish spot. "Do you?"

He didn't answer for a while. "I think she means it when she says that, but sometimes life happens." He pulled my foot back and started on my big toe.

"Yeah, but life could happen to any of us," I said. "What if you get an offer to play for a bigger, better band?"

He frowned. "Are you saying there's a bigger, better band out there than Wolf Venom?" He pressed his thumbs hard into the ball of my foot.

"Not yet, but you never know who might break out." I closed my eyes. "You might decide to join Blazing Violet."

"According to Ryan, part of their job description is ducking to avoid getting hit by flying shoes." Channing grimaced. "At least around here, I only have to dodge flying insults."

I chuckled. "You might get danger pay working with them."

"Are you trying to get rid of me?" he asked lightly."

I opened my eyes a crack. "Never," I said firmly. "That is never going to change. Not ever. None of us are going anywhere. Except to America tomorrow. Just think, we can be eating New York cheesecake soon." My mouth watered at the thought of it. Was there a better food on the face of the planet?

Okay, pizza came a close second.

He didn't look as excited about that as I expected or hoped.

I sat up. "Chan? Are you okay? You keep getting this look on your face like you think someone is going to kick your puppy. I'm not walking away from you. Neither is Abbie. She cares about you as much as I do. As much as the rest of us do. You are our person." It was usually him reassuring me, not the other way around. But lately, he just seemed... Off.

"Are you having second thoughts about her? Or about sticking with the band?" Touring was exhausting at the best of times and it was easy to get sick of seeing the same faces day after day. Especially this tour when we couldn't get out even the small amount we usually did. I didn't mind being around my family all the time, even if they were occasionally dysfunctional, but I knew it could chafe the others.

"No," he said quickly. "It's nothing like that. It's just..." He wouldn't meet my eyes.

"Sweetie," I said softly, "what is it? You know you can talk to me about anything. Right?" I'd hate it if he thought there was something he couldn't tell me. No matter what it was, I wouldn't judge him. I loved him with my whole heart. He was, hands down, the best guy I knew.

"I know." He'd paused in massaging, but he started again now. "There's really nothing to say, and if there was I'd tell you. I think it's just the pressure of the tour and trying to keep being amazing night after night. Part of me thinks that we have to have an off night sooner or later. The more concerts we play, the closer we come to that night."

"You would never not be amazing," I assured him. "Besides, if we had an off night, chances are it would be because of me." Or Asher, but the drummer would roll with it so the audience never noticed. If I screwed up, I'd probably do it in a way the whole world could see.

Hard pass.

"It could be because Zeke fell off the end of the stage," Channing said. "Or the sound failed. Or the lights. Or the audience hated us for some reason. Or there's a tornado in the middle of the concert. Or a swarm of bees."

"I see you've given this a lot of thought," I said lightly. I didn't want to laugh at his fears, but the last two were kinda funny. Although, now I thought about it, they were more plausible than the rest of his suggestions.

"The audience isn't going to buy tickets to see us if they hate us," I pointed out. "The rest of it is beyond our control and they'll know that. I mean, if the sound fails we could still play. If the lighting fails, we can play in the dark." I smiled wickedly. "Or we could do something else in the dark and imagine fifty thousand people watching us do it."

He grinned in response to that. "I think you'd prefer to do that with the lights on, wouldn't you?" It wasn't exactly his thing, but he went along with it because I enjoyed it. The same way I took part in whatever he enjoyed.

"Well..." I couldn't deny it, because it was true. The one downside to being a rock star was having to maintain a certain image. Ours was far from squeaky clean, but fucking in front of that many people might be going a bit too far.

Maybe I would be a porn star in my next life.

"Are you sure that's all that's bothering you?" I asked. "Fear of failure? Or... fear of screwing up? I can't imagine anything happening that we couldn't come back from. We've done a pretty good job at dodging trouble so far. I mean, if anyone but us had found those heads...or if a camera recorded what Tully did to his adopted father... Things would have been different, but we still would have dealt with them. We have the best manager and label behind us."

Jackson in particular, had to manage some unusual things. And he did it without blinking, although not without vomiting. He'd do it again too, because he loved us. And we loved him, even though we gave him a lot of shit.

I was kinda hoping he and Abbie would hook up, because then I might get to see him naked. I'd imagined it quite a few times before. Not as often as I thought about Channing or Abbie naked, but I was only human. Jackson was kinda hot. I could easily picture him sliding his cock into Abbie, and touching her.

And yep, now my cock was getting hard. When was it not?

"I know," Channing said. "I'm just being paranoid. When the tour is over, I'll look back and laugh at how stupid I was to even think it."

"Of course you will," I said. I couldn't shake the feeling there was something else going on with him, but if he wasn't going to tell me, I wasn't going to push. All I could do was be here for him when he was ready to talk about it. And hope he did before it got the better of him.

I knew as well as anyone how bad it was to bottle things up inside. It would nibble and nibble at you until finally it took a chunk.

I'd done it too many times as a kid. I tried to avoid doing it now, if I could. Maybe if I opened up then, I would have got the help I needed. Or I would have gotten bullied.

I couldn't change the past, but I could make sure I learned from it.

"I never knew you were worried about bees," I said lightly.

He shuddered slightly and started to work on my other foot. "They freak me out with all their buzzing and shit. Not to mention the whole 'sticking a stinger into you and then dying' thing. I mean, what's with that? People do weird stuff, but that's pretty fucking weird, don't you think?"

"I guess so," I agreed. "On the other hand, they're just doing what they have to do to protect their hive. We can both relate to that, can't we? We would do anything for these clowns." I jerked my head towards the guys. "And Abbie," I added in case Channing thought I was referring to her as a clown.

To my surprise, Channing flinched. "Yeah, there's nothing we wouldn't do for them or each other," he muttered.

There it was again, the thought that he was worried about something in particular. Something big. My heart thudded rapidly in my chest, a combination of fear and worry.

"Channing—" I started.

"We should think about ordering dinner," he interrupted. "Maybe something typically German, like sausages." He had that look on his face like he'd moved on and wanted me to do the same.

"Yeah, okay." I tried not to be whiplashed too badly at the sudden change of topic. When he was like this, there was nothing I could do but go along with it.

"And lots and lots of German beer for Asher," I added louder.

Asher looked over and grinned. "Hell yeah. Sounds like a plan to me."

Zeke rolled his eyes and threw a folded up shirt at Asher. "I thought you were never drinking again."

Asher caught the shirt and dropped it into his suitcase.

"He was always drinking again," Penn said before Asher could respond. He seemed more relaxed after his conversation with Abbie.

I'd heard them say they loved each other. That made my heart happy. When the time was right, I looked forward to saying it to her myself.

"And then," Penn continued, "he can bitch and complain on the flight over to the states. Dibs on sitting somewhere else in the plane."

"Maybe you should get drunk with him?" Tully suggested. "Then you two can have a bitch-off."

"If that happens, dibs on not sitting near either of them on the plane," Zeke said.

"The rest of us can sit up near the front," Abbie said. "Or better yet, the back, where no one can see what we get up to." She grinned wickedly.

Zeke grabbed her hand, pulled her to him and kissed her. "I like the way you think. I also like the way you fuck."

"Back at you," she told him.

I watched them kiss and his hands started to roam over her body. Things were getting hot and heavy very quickly, but in the back of my mind I was still worried about Channing.

Something was up and I had no idea what it was.

CHAPTER
TWENTY-TWO
ABBIE

"PSST."

A hiss in my ear woke me up.

"Hmmm?" I blinked a few times and opened my eyes. It was still dark. The clock on the bedside table read three a.m. The only sounds were deep breathing and Asher snoring.

A dark shape crouched next to the bed.

I sucked in a gasp and sat up. I started to speak or scream or something, but a hand clamped over my mouth.

"It's okay, it's just me," Landon whispered. "I didn't mean to scare you." After a moment, he lowered his hand to my shoulder.

"What the fuck?" I whispered back. "You scared the shit out of me. What's going on?" Were we supposed to leave ridiculously early and I'd forgotten? No, I didn't think so.

"It's Channing," he said. "He got up, put on some clothes and left. He thought I was asleep but I wasn't. I was watching. I... I don't think he was sleepwalking."

It took a moment for my half asleep mind to get around what he was saying.

"Left? Where would he go?" I sat up a little more, not bothering to tug the blankets up over my bare breasts.

There was just enough light for me to see him shake his head. "I don't know. Something was bothering him, but he wouldn't tell me. I'm worried he might have gone and done something silly."

My heart stopped for a moment at the thought of what Landon was implying. When it started again, it was racing.

"How long ago did he leave?"

"Only a couple of minutes," Landon said. "I was going to wait and see if he came back, but…"

"You want to follow him," I finished for him.

"Yeah." He sniffed and I wondered if he was crying. He was definitely worried.

So was I.

"I'll come with you." I pushed off the blankets and searched around for some clothes to pull on. That was my bra and panties, and my track pants, but someone else's T-shirt. From the smell of it, it was one of Zeke's. It was huge on me, but it would do for now.

"Should we tell Zeke?" Landon asked tentatively.

I hesitated and shoved my phone into my pocket. "Let's see if he's out in the corridor, or somewhere close by first. If we can't find him, we'll wake up the others." I hated waking people up even more than I hated being woken up.

Channing had probably gone for a walk around the hotel to get some air or help himself sleep or something. There didn't seem much point in rousing everyone for that.

"Okay," Landon agreed. He put a hand on my arm and we opened the door as silently as we could. It creaked slightly at first, loud enough to make me wince, but slid open the rest of the way without a sound.

Asher muttered in his sleep and rolled over before he went back to snoring. None of the other guys so much as moved.

We crept out and closed the door behind us.

The corridor was lit all the way along with dim lighting. It illuminated well enough to see there was no one else out here but us. Mindful of people sleeping in other rooms, we walked silently to the elevator.

"It's on the ground floor," Landon whispered. "He might have taken it down."

"Let's check if he's in the foyer," I said. I glanced back to our door, half expecting it to burst open and the other guys to come tumbling out. It didn't. It remained closed.

Landon nodded and pressed the button.

I don't think either of us breathed much while we waited for the elevator to come up to us. It felt like an hour, but it was probably two or three minutes at most. It didn't stop anywhere else.

The noise of it coming sounded like a freight train. Surely it would wake the whole hotel?

Probably not. It sounded loud because it was so ridiculously early in the morning.

The doors slid open with a whoosh and we stepped inside.

"Does he do this kind of thing often?" I asked as the doors slid shut, closing us in.

"Taking off by himself? Sometimes," Landon said. "He needs some space once in a while to do his thing. I worry I'm crowding him. I try not to be too much." He sniffed.

I turned to face him. I pressed the length of my body to his and cupped his cheeks with my hands.

"You're never too much," I said firmly. "Everyone needs time to themselves, even if it's only five or ten minutes. We'll probably get down to the foyer and find him waiting to take the elevator back up. Then we can all go back to our room and go back to bed." I kissed him lightly on the jaw.

"Yeah, I hope so," he said. "I just wish he'd told me what was going on in his head."

"He gave you no idea what it was?" I asked. I thought back over the last few days, but couldn't recall Channing saying anything worrying, or seeming upset. Although, he was difficult to read at the best of times.

Landon scrunched up his face in thought. His cheeks, just under his eyes, shone wet in the elevator light. He dashed the tears away with the back of his hand.

"He said he was scared I would leave him for you, but I told him that wasn't going to happen. I want us all to be together. I choose both of you." He wiped under his nose.

"I choose both of you too," I said. "All of you. I would never ask you to choose me over Channing." They were bringing me into their relationship, not replacing one of them with me. Still, I understood the hesitation or insecurity. This was new to all of us and we had to navigate our way through growing relationships and big feelings. Of course there would be times when we would question things. As long as we kept on communicating, we'd get through.

"I know." Landon nodded. "I guess he had a moment of insecurity. I hoped I'd put his fears to rest, but now I don't know." In a hoarse but urgent whisper, he added, "What if I never get a chance to do that? What if he decided he couldn't—"

"You will get to tell him everything you want to tell him," I said firmly. "Channing isn't going to leave you. Neither am I."

It wasn't just tears I saw in his eyes. It was also terror. The idea of being alone was almost enough to make him fracture into a thousand tiny pieces. If I had to tell him every day that I wasn't leaving, then that's what I would do. Until he understood I meant it.

Anything else he might have said was interrupted by the ping of the elevator arriving on the ground floor. It bumped lightly before coming to a stop. The doors slid open smoothly onto the low lit foyer.

I lowered my hands from his face and laced my fingers in his. Like that, we stepped out of the elevator.

Soft music played from behind the check-in desk. Someone was on duty twenty-four hours a day, but I couldn't see them right now. Presumably they were off attending to something, or having a nap in the back and hoping no one saw them.

"He might have gone to the kitchen hoping for a snack?" I suggested.

"Right. There's always someone on duty in places like this," Landon agreed. "In case someone needs room service in the middle of the night."

Rich people problems.

Rich or not, Channing wouldn't be the first person to be hungry in the early hours of the morning. We hadn't left much of last night's dinner, between the seven of us.

"Let's go and look," I said. With any luck, someone would be taking a tray of baked goods out of the oven and we could grab some. I wasn't hungry until I had that thought. Unfortunately, none of the smells in the vicinity of the kitchen were pastry-like.

The door to the restaurant was closed but not locked. Landon pushed it open and we looked around before walking toward the kitchen.

"You hear that?" Landon tugged my hand, pulling me to a stop.

"Hear what?" I froze and listened. My mouth formed an O.

The sound of groaning and panting was coming from inside the kitchen.

"Maybe the chef is moving a side of beef?" I whispered.

"I think someone is definitely moving meat," Landon said. He looked like he was terrified one of those someones might be Channing.

If only to ease his mind that Channing wasn't cheating, I stepped over to the kitchen door and peeked inside.

That explained why the reception desk was empty. The receptionist was bent over a workbench, and the chef was pounding his meat into her. I hoped that bench would be thoroughly cleaned before any food was prepared on it. At any rate, they both looked like they were enjoying themselves. The receptionist's mouth was open and her eyes were closed in ecstasy.

Since everything seemed to be consensual, I pulled my face back before they saw me.

"No sign of Channing," I whispered. If he'd come in here for something to eat, he would have walked right past them. Even in the throes of passion, they would have noticed a buff rock star passing by. He was hard to miss.

"I'm starting to think we should go and wake up Zeke," Landon said reluctantly. "And the rest of the guys."

"Yeah, but let's go and have a look outside the front door first. He might be standing right outside, getting some air." At this point, I knew I was clutching at straws, but I didn't want to think Channing had wandered off somewhere by himself.

I mean, he was a grown man, he could do what he wanted, but I didn't want to have a box turn up outside the door in the morning with his head in it. The idea both turned my stomach and broke my heart. Of all the guys, Channing was the one I knew the least, but I didn't want to lose him.

I reminded myself Pete was dead, so Channing couldn't end up a disembodied head in a box. A tiny voice in the back of my mind reminded me that maybe it wasn't Pete who did that. Maybe it was someone else. A stalker or a crazed fan. Or someone who liked to kill people I knew and put their heads in boxes.

Shut up, I told that voice. It had to be Pete, or there was a killer still running around, and that idea was horrifying.

"Okay," Landon agreed.

I think he would have agreed to just about anything I said right now, as long as we found Channing. His hand was hot and sweaty in mine, but I didn't let it go. That contact might be the only thing keeping him from freaking out. If that was the case, then I would hold on to him until he didn't need me to anymore.

As quietly as we could, so we didn't disturb the fucking in the kitchen, we walked back across the foyer to the front door.

The street outside the hotel was empty of cars apart from one or two parked by the side of the road.

At first, I thought it was empty of people as well. Then I saw someone walking away from the hotel. I knew that walk and the way he carried himself. What the hell?

I pushed open the door and stepped outside.

"Jackson?"

CHAPTER
TWENTY-THREE

ABBIE

JACKSON STARTLED and spun around to face us. "Fucking hell, you scared the shit out of me." He put a hand to his chest. "What are you doing out here?"

"I was going to ask you the same thing," I said. "Are you going somewhere?"

"No. Yes." He shook his head.

"It has to be one or the other," Landon said.

"I couldn't sleep. I was sitting, looking out my window and saw Channing walk past," Jackson explained. "Where is he going?"

"That's what we wanted to know," I said. "Landon saw him leave the room." I didn't want to use the words 'crept out' in case whatever was going on was completely innocent.

"You saw which way he went?" Landon asked eagerly.

Jackson waved down the street. "In that direction." He looked from one of us to the other of us and sighed. "There's no point in telling you to go back to your room, is there? Either I let you go with me or you will follow me."

"Exactly," I said. "And we're wasting time. The longer we stand here talking about it, the further away he'll be."

"Right then, come on." Jackson turned back around and kept walking.

I exchanged glances with Landon and hurried after him.

"How did he look?" Landon asked when we caught up. "Was he upset or anything like that?"

"I couldn't tell," Jackson said. "He had his head down, hurrying down the road."

"Hurrying?" I echoed. "Why would he be hurrying?"

Where did he have to go that was so important? And why didn't he tell any of us he was going? Okay, I could answer that last bit. Zeke wouldn't have let him go. To be fair, the rest of us wouldn't have either. The thought of any of us wandering around Frankfurt alone, in the dark, was disconcerting and fucking scary.

"For all we know, he's gone to get ice cream and was hoping to get back before anyone noticed him leave," Jackson said. "We could be worrying over absolutely nothing."

"It wouldn't be the first time he's had sugar cravings in the middle of the night," Landon said. "Since the kitchen was out, he might have decided to go looking."

When Jackson gave him a questioning look, Landon told him about the receptionist and the chef.

"Ah, I see. I wouldn't have interrupted that either." Jackson nodded. "Maybe we should look up late night strudel cafés and head there if we can't find him soon."

"I don't think they have strudel cafés, as such," I said. "Just cafés that may or may not serve strudel."

"Are you pointing that out so you can say strudel?" Landon teased lightly. He was still worried, but obviously trying to take his mind off things a little.

"Maybe," I said. "It's a cute word." Although, I was starting to get hungry for strudel now.

"Any idea what's down this way?" We only passed a few people here and there and the occasional car zipped by.

"Hotels and a handful of restaurants," Jackson said. "The usual stuff you find in cities." He spoke lightly but he was stepping warily. Every so often, he would glance over at us like he wished we would go back to our hotel room.

Zeke was going to be pissed when he knew we'd wandered off alone. There were three of us though. We would keep an eye on each other.

"Zeke might handcuff you to him after this," Landon said. He must have sensed my thoughts.

"He can try," I said with a snort. I didn't object to the idea of Zeke handcuffing me, but not to stop me from going anywhere. Besides, it would make performing difficult and raise a bunch of eyebrows.

I glanced back towards the hotel. It wouldn't be long before one of the guys woke up and noticed we weren't there. They would wake up the rest and undoubtedly raise hell.

I pulled out my phone and put it on silent. If they tried to ring me, I would feel it vibrate, but it wouldn't wake the whole neighbourhood and scare the shit out of us. Judging by the lack of messages on the screen, the guys hadn't woken up yet.

I shoved my phone back into my pocket.

"Maybe we should try calling Channing and asking where he's going," I said.

"I did before I hurried down," Jackson said. "He didn't pick up." The potential implications of that hung in the air, but he didn't say anything more.

"His phone is probably flat," Landon said. "I'm forever reminding him to charge it. Or I take it and charge it for him. If I left it to him, it would never get done. Ironic, considering how much he loves his phone."

"Yeah, I'm sure that's it," Jackson said, sounding not at all sure.

"We'll find him soon," I said. "He wasn't that far ahead of us." He could walk faster than the slowest of us and that was me. I was shorter and had smaller legs. Long, but not as long as his. If he was hurrying like Jackson said he was, then catching up might be difficult.

For the first time, I felt bad for not suggesting Jackson and Landon go on ahead, and gone back to the hotel room. If I slowed them down and they didn't get to Channing in time...

I could be worrying for nothing. There may not be anything to get to him in time for. Nothing dire anyway. Like many things in life, it was the not knowing that was difficult.

"Only a couple of minutes," Jackson agreed. "As long as he didn't jump into a taxi or a rideshare. He could be just about anywhere if he did that."

Landon groaned. "We should tell Zeke and the others. He could be anywhere and we need us all to be looking—"

"Shhh," Jackson said. He waved us all over into the shadows of the building beside us.

I ducked in behind him and Landon slipped in behind me.

"What is it?" I whispered in Jackson's ear.

"Not what," he whispered back. "Who. I just saw the twins disappear into one of the buildings up ahead."

Sweat immediately sprung up under my arms. What were they doing here?

"Shit." I craned my neck to look around him, but saw no one.

"Fuck," Landon whispered. "If they've done anything to Channing, I'm going to rip their nuts off and shove them in their ears."

That was a new one. I had to give him credit for originality. I wasn't sure if it was physically possible but I liked it.

"I'm going to go and have a look," Jackson said. He looked at us over his shoulder. "You're not going to stay here, are you?"

"And take the chance of you being alone with them?" I asked. "No way. Either you stay here or we all go."

Jackson muttered something that sounded like, "Who is the manager here?" but he nodded. "Fine, but stay close. I don't want to have to explain to Levi how I got you killed."

"We don't want that either," I agreed.

He started forward and Landon and I stayed right on his tail. We moved silently and kept to the shadows as much as possible.

My heart was racing so hard I was sure the twins would hear it. Surely being as evil as they were, they would have some nasty, supernatural hearing or some shit.

Okay, probably not, but it sounded loud to me anyway.

"... Really useful." The voice of one of the twins came from an open window. "Reuben sends his gratitude for all your help."

Who the hell was he talking to?

It couldn't possibly be— I couldn't even finish that thought. It made no sense at all.

"Fuck off. That's all I came here to say. I'm done."

Landon stiffened at the sound of Channing's voice.

I squeezed his hand to stop him from doing anything stupid like running into the building. If Channing was up to something, the best thing we could do stay out here and listen. What was I thinking? What the hell could Channing be up to that involved those two assholes?

There had to be something more going on here.

"Be nice," the other twin said. Parker, unless I was mistaken. "This arrangement has been mutually beneficial, remember?"

I frowned. What did that mean?

"Not anymore," Channing growled. "I don't want anything to do with you and your shit. That's what I came to tell you. I'm not gonna give you any more information about your brother or the rest of the band."

"What the hell?" Landon's voice was a harsh whisper, and a rush of hot air on my earlobe.

What the hell was right. Channing was working with the twins? Feeding them information on Zeke and the rest of us? I felt like someone stuck a knife in my chest and twisted it. I could only begin to imagine how Landon must feel.

Had Channing told them when Penn went jogging so they knew where to find him? Had he told them about our date so they could crash it? Had he told them when I was alone both times they kidnapped me?

That thought knocked the air out of my lungs. For a solid minute, I could hardly breathe. My brain twisted and turned, jumping from one terrible conclusion to another.

"It's not that simple," Hunter said. "Remember, you're only helping us because we helped you."

What the fuck did that mean? Why would Channing help them? My heart squeezed. Had he been betraying us this whole time?

"Yeah," Parker agreed. "What do you think Reuben would do if he knew you were the one who killed Jonah?"

If I was breathless before, it was nothing to how I felt now. Landon and I both reeled and had to cling to each other to stay on our feet. I felt his ragged breathing on my neck, a caught sob suppressed so those inside the building didn't hear.

Channing did that? No, how was that even possible? Channing was… Channing. He had his moments, but he was no killer. Right?

Fuck, what if he was?

"Serves Reuben right for sending him after Zeke," Channing growled. "I only did what I had to do to protect the band and my brothers."

One of the twins snorted. I couldn't tell which one it was.

"Are you shitting us?" Parker asked. "You enjoyed doing it. That's why you put it in the box. So your beloved band would know what you did. It was a love letter. Classic psychotic behaviour. Right Hunter?"

"According to those documentaries you like so much, it is," Hunter agreed.

Silence fell for a few moments. "Asshole got what he deserved," Channing said finally. "And the band knew someone was looking after them. "

"How touching," Parker said sarcastically. "And we helped you to get rid of the rest of the body. How nice of us. And not just *his* body, the rest of them as well. All we asked in return was a bit of information. I don't think that's too much to ask."

The rest of them? How far did this go?

Just as I had that thought, I knew the answer.

Vance.

Poppy Newton.

Calista.

Maybe even Pete.

I don't know how it happened, but I ended up sitting on the concrete, wrapped around Landon and Jackson, trying like hell to catch my breath while my head spun faster than a tornado.

All the people who hurt me, apart from the twins themselves, who were killed, it was never Pete, or a crazed stalker. Not a deranged fan.

It was Channing.

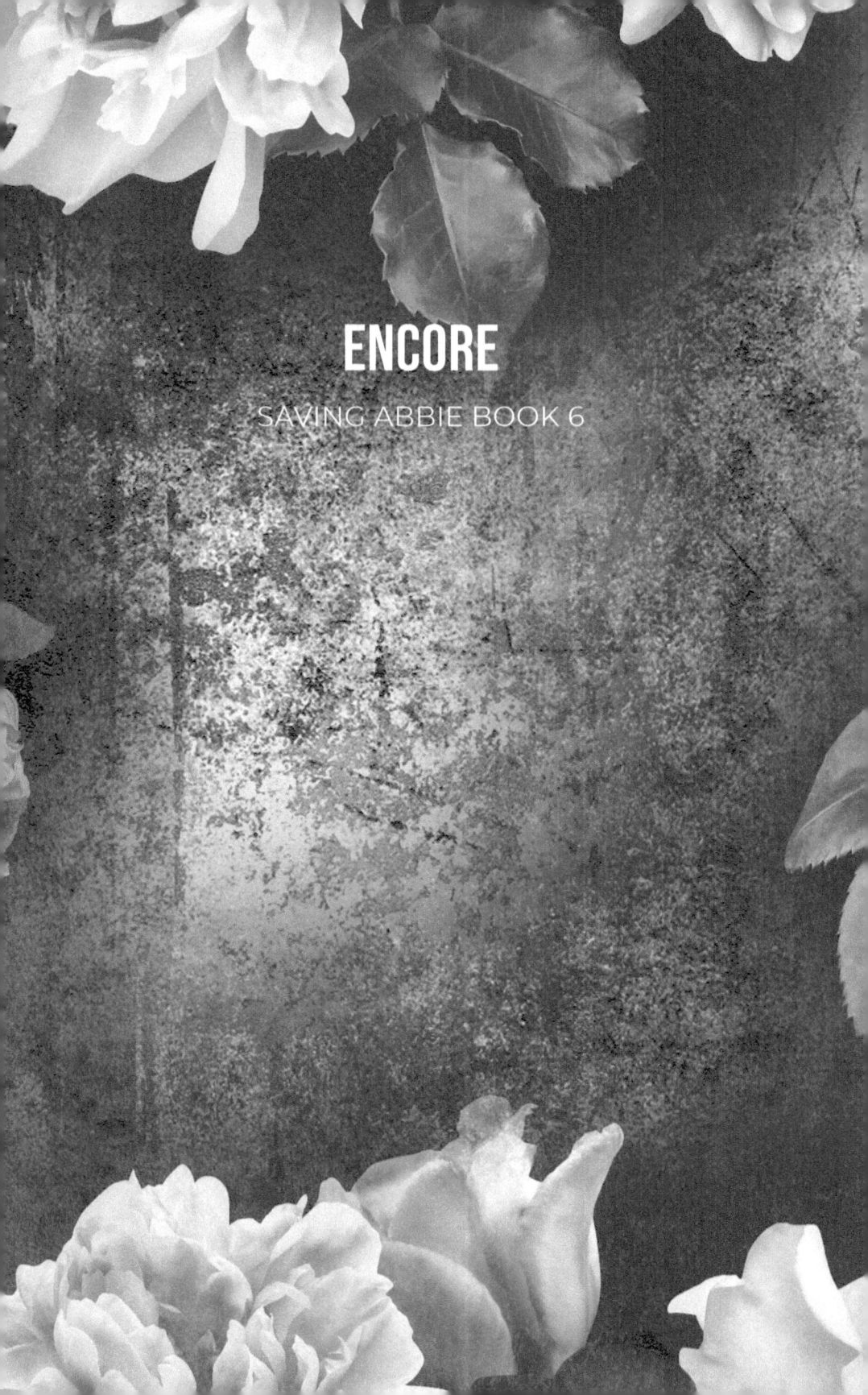

ENCORE

SAVING ABBIE BOOK 6

Bond
Written by Channing Griffin

Slip the blade,
Draw the line,
Feel the blood,
Take the end.
The end.

Step too far,
Slip too deep,
Drip too hard,
Scream too loud.
Too loud.

Take my hand,
Squeeze my throat,
Hold my soul,
Steal my light.
My light.

Love that hard,
Feel that much,
Take that step,
Tie that bond.
Tie that bond.
That bond.

CHAPTER ONE

ABBIE

BREATHE IN.

Breathe out.

I forced myself to suck in oxygen. Blood pounded through my ears. Loud as fuck. Not loud enough to drown out the thoughts that raced through my head. Not loud enough to block out the truth.

I wanted to scream until I couldn't hear them anymore. I wanted to dive under a scalding hot shower and wash them away. I wanted to go back a couple of minutes to a time before I heard what Channing and the evil twins said.

Nothing would erase it now.

Nothing.

Last night's dinner curdled in my stomach, threatening to come back up. I was living in the epicentre of a nightmare and I didn't understand any of it.

Channing was a killer.

Channing.

The saxophonist for Wolf Venom was far from innocent, I knew that, but this— this was something entirely different. Something I never in a million years would have expected to hear.

But at the same time, I knew it was true. It all made sense. What I didn't understand, couldn't get my head around, was why.

Why had Channing killed Jonah, Poppy Newton, Vance, Calista Rossi and possibly Pete? To protect us?

Fuck, did he really think—

"What the hell?" Landon whispered. He sounded gutted, shocked.

In the faint glow of a streetlight, I saw his face, pale beneath his tan, his eyes wide. He looked as horrified as I felt, as blindsided. When I thought he might deny what we heard, he didn't.

"I don't know, shhh," Jackson urged. He had an arm around each of us, his hands on our backs, keeping us down low. For once, neither of us argued.

We sat on the concrete in the dark, under the window where Channing was speaking to Zeke's evil twin brothers Hunter and Parker Brantley. We didn't call them the evil twins for nothing. If they knew we were here, we might be the next ones to die.

"Should we get out of here?" I whispered in Jackson's ear.

Before he could respond, Channing spoke from inside the building. "Yeah, you helped dispose of the bodies, but only because there was something in it for you. I'm done with doing that. I don't need your help anymore, so you're not fucking getting mine. You need to stop following us around before the same thing happens to you."

"Did you just threaten us?" Hunter's voice was amused, but dangerous. These guys were not to be fucked with. "Parker, did he just threaten us?"

"That's what it sounded like, yes," Parker agreed. He sounded less amused. "Listen here you little asswipe—"

Landon growled softly. I grabbed the back of his T-shirt to stop him from jumping up and storming into the building.

I got it, I really did. Channing was his boyfriend, his person. Although not official yet, I was their girlfriend, but I hadn't known either of them for anywhere near as long as they knew each other.

Threatening Channing was the same as threatening Landon. Honestly, I wanted to walk through the door and start tearing off some heads myself. Landon must be ready to land some punches. Or worse. But that might get him killed. I wasn't going to let that happen. He was my person. One of my guys. If anything bad happened to him… To any of them.

What even was this place? I glanced up and realised the window wasn't open, it was broken. Just another derelict building in the world. The front was covered in graffiti, but I couldn't tell if it was someone's name or words in German.

Somewhere in the back of my mind, I recognised that, if the building was empty, then no innocent lives would be lost if things went to shit.

More than they already had, that is.

"I can't let them hurt him," Landon moaned.

I had a sneaking suspicion the twins wouldn't hurt Channing. Not for very long anyway. They'd kill him and make him disappear like they had with all those bodies. The thought made my stomach twist all over again.

"We—" I started to say.

"Shhh," Jackson urged. "Someone is coming."

"They should be around here somewhere," that was Zeke's voice.

I was about to stand up and show myself when Asher spoke.

"Good. It's about time we dealt with those little shits."

I frowned. What the hell?

"Yeah," Zeke agreed. "Keep an eye out for Abbie and Landon. Fuck only knows where they are. I'm going to ring his neck when I find him."

"Probably fucking somewhere," Asher said lightly.

"Without Channing?" Zeke said. "Landon doesn't operate that way."

"Abbie has a way of changing things," Asher said.

I shook my head, trying to make sense of what they were saying. They knew Landon and Channing weren't together?

"Told you she'd be disruptive," Penn remarked.

"As if you're complaining," Tully scoffed.

"I never said I was," Penn said. "It doesn't mean I'm not right."

"Why are they all here?" Landon hissed. "I don't get it."

"Neither do I," Jackson said. "I think we should stay right where we are." His hand trembled lightly on my back.

"Sounds like we've got company," Hunter said. His voice was louder. He must have been standing right inside the window.

For a moment I thought he meant us, and ducked down lower.

"Brother dear," Parker said from the doorway. "I didn't realise we were having a party."

"You didn't?" Zeke said. He stepped inside the building and the others followed. "But I sent Channing with an invitation."

What the flying, cum-forsaken fuck? Zeke knew Channing was here?

Of course he did. He knew Channing and Landon weren't together. He'd only know that if he knew where Channing was.

My breath caught in my throat again. What else did he know?

"I didn't get a chance to deliver it," Channing said. "We were busy having a chat."

"We got the impression he doesn't like us," Hunter complained.

"Really? I wonder why that is?" Asher said. "For the record, I don't like you either."

"In case anyone was wondering, I hate your guts," Penn said. "Both of you. I'm still trying to decide which one of you is a bigger prick. So far it's a tie."

Fair enough, the twins *had* drugged him and left him where he could have drowned. He was probably itching to land a few punches himself.

"Is Landon with you?" Channing asked.

"He's out here," Tully said pausing on the doorstep. "With Abbie and Jackson."

Fuck. Of course Tully would know. He was a trained assassin. It was his job to notice anything and everything. What I didn't understand was, why didn't he keep his mouth shut? What the fuck was with everyone tonight?

"Shit," Zeke grunted.

One of the twins chuckled. "I guess they heard a bit then. I hope it was educational." Hunter stuck his head carefully out the broken window. Shame, all that broken glass could have given him a few nasty gashes.

Landon jumped up and swung, but Hunter pulled his head back before the punch connected.

"Hey, that's not nice. Zeke, call your hound off."

There was no holding Landon back now. The blue-haired bass player hurried into the building, hands curled into fists, body rigid with rage.

I looked at Jackson with wide eyes. What the hell should we do? A thousand thoughts whirled around my brain. I had no idea what the other guys knew about Channing. At this exact moment, I had no idea who to trust. Not even myself.

"It's okay, we've got you." Tully stepped away from the doorway and towards us. He reached out a hand. "Come on. It's all right."

I hesitated. I wanted to fall into his arms but I couldn't bring myself to move. Not toward him or away.

"Loveliness?" Tully crouched down in front of me. "I know this must be confusing." He put a hand on my arm.

I jerked away. "You think? What the hell is going on?"

"We'll explain everything," Tully assured me. "I'll take you back to the hotel."

I looked at him sideways, but slowly got to my feet, half an eye on the window in case something came flying out of it, like a bullet.

"The hell you are," I snapped. I wasn't going anywhere until I got an explanation for what the fuck was going on. Although... did I really want one? I thought I could trust these guys. Now...

"Sounds like your girlfriend isn't happy," one of the twins said. "We told her she should find some real men— Whoa."

That was followed by the cocking of a gun which echoed through the early morning like a crack.

"Shit." Jackson got to his feet and moved away from the window.

"You're not going to use that." I thought that was Hunter. He sounded wary. Maybe even scared. Good. It was about time he got some of his own back.

"Maybe I am," Zeke said evenly. "I've had enough of you to and your bullshit. Why don't you both take a seat?"

"See, loveliness, Zeke has it all under control," Tully said like he was talking to a wild animal. Or a child. "Everything is fine."

"No it fucking isn't," I said. "Not even slightly." I stepped past him and over to the doorway.

Hunter and Parker were sitting in two rickety old chairs in a corner, under the light of a single, naked bulb. Zeke had a gun in his hand. It was pointed at them. Where the fuck did he get that from?

Asher also had a gun, but he held it loosely, like he wasn't ready to use it immediately, if he had to. His body language said otherwise. I doubted anyone in the room was fooled.

Channing stood to one side near the wall, his hands in his back pockets.

Landon stared at him like he'd never seen him before.

Penn stood inside the door, his arms crossed over his chest until he saw me. He lowered them, but made no move towards me. "For what it's worth, I have no fucking idea what's going on either. Those two clowns left the room and Tully and I followed."

I flinched when Tully put a hand on my shoulder. "Zeke wanted the rest of us to stay out of it."

"Well we're in it now aren't we?" I said. "Does someone want to explain what the fuck is going on?"

"In a minute," Zeke said, his gaze unwavering. He shoved Hunter forward in his chair, making him hunch over. He patted him, presumably looking for a gun.

He did the same to Parker before he pulled his brother's phone out of his back pocket. "It's time Reuben and I had a little chat." He pressed Parker against the back of his seat and stepped away. The gun unmoving in one hand, he pressed the phone screen with the other. "Passcode," he snapped.

"That's private—" Parker started to say. He stopped when he found the nozzle of the gun pressed against his forehead. "Six, nine, six, nine."

Zeke snorted. "Of course it is. Very creative of you."

Any other time, someone would have joked that Zeke's pass code would be the same thing. But no one was joking now.

Zeke's thumb slid across the screen, lighting it up. "It should be about three o'clock in the afternoon in Australia. Reuben has probably just finished torturing someone for the day."

I wasn't sure if he was joking or not, but he was the one with a gun to his brother's head. At this point, anything was possible.

Parker's phone made an old-fashioned ringing sound. The video call connected a minute or so later.

"You're not Parker," Reuben remarked.

From where I stood, I only made out part of the oldest Brantley brother's face. I didn't need to see the irritation, I heard it. He wasn't getting any sympathy from me. Reuben deserved a gun to his head as much as the twins did. Maybe more.

"No shit," Zeke said. "Don't worry, he's right here. He and Hunter are doing their best not to shit their pants."

"I'm not gonna shit my pants," Hunter said. He looked like he was going to say something else when Zeke turned the gun on him. "Okay, I might pee myself a little."

"How about you shut up?" Asher suggested, his tone dangerously polite. "It's early morning and I haven't had coffee yet."

"Did you want something?" Reuben asked as though he was bored with the conversation already.

"No, just letting you know I'm going to kill Hunter and Parker," Zeke said cheerfully.

CHAPTER
TWO

ABBIE

"NO, YOU WON'T," Reuben said.

"You think not?" Zeke asked. "Is this where you say I don't have it in me to kill my brothers? Because I think you're underestimating how pissed off I am."

I'd seen him angry before, but right now he burned with cold rage. Icy, terrifyingly calm. I had absolutely no doubt in my mind he would blow the twins brains out and not regret it.

I caught Asher's expression in the corner of my eye. It matched Zeke's. They had come here to do one thing and that was deal with Hunter and Parker once and for all. I didn't know where Channing fit into all of this, but it seemed unlikely all of us would leave this room alive.

"I'm sure you're perfectly capable of killing them," Reuben said. "You might even be doing me a favour."

"What the fuck?" Hunter whispered. He fell silent again at a look from Asher.

"I think I'd be doing a lot of people a favour," Zeke said. "Especially their girlfriend, Lila Bell."

The silence that came from the other end of the phone suggested that was news to Reuben. Full points to Zeke for dropping that little bombshell at the right time.

"Fucking hell," Parker muttered. "You might as well kill us. If you don't, he will."

"As tempting as that is," Reuben said finally, his tone clipped irritation, "we have more important matters to deal with."

Zeke's eyes narrowed. "If you're trying to—"

Reuben interrupted. "One of my contacts has informed me Dante Fiorelli is planning to make a move against you once you reach American soil. All three of you. And anyone you're with."

I almost felt him trying to look down the phone to see who else was in the room and resisted the urge to poke my tongue out at him. It was a good idea not to provoke Reuben Brantley. Or any of them really. Zeke was the one with a gun in his hand.

Zeke growled. "What part of me not being involved with your business does this asshole not get?"

"The bit where we share a last name," Reuben said. "And the bit where the twins work for me." By the sound of it, that arrangement might come to an end shortly if what Zeke said about Lila Bell was true. Which, according to the twins, it was. I remember Zeke and Asher describing the Bell family as the worst of the worst, but so far they were the only ones who hadn't given us any trouble.

That I knew of.

Yet.

"All the more reason I should dispose of these two now," Zeke said. "If the Fiorellis see I'm not on your side, they might leave me the fuck alone."

"They still won't," Reuben said. "Dante is determined to eradicate all of us. As irritating as they might be, you need the twins to help you when they come after you."

"Well, that's fucking awesome," Penn said sarcastically. "I love it when we get involved in Reuben's shit. Maybe we don't go to America."

"If they don't come after us there, they'll try again in Australia," Zeke said. "We've already proven we can take care of ourselves and deal with whatever shit they throw at us. We can do it again."

"Yes, we can," Asher agreed. "What will you be doing in the meantime, Reuben? You must know by now my brother has sided with the Bells?"

"I'm aware of that," Reuben said coldly. "I'm working on an alliance between the three families to keep the Fiorellis at bay. In the meantime, the twins are at your disposal to keep you from getting killed."

"Does that mean we don't get to dispose of them?" Asher complained.

"I still haven't ruled that out," Zeke said. He was silent for a moment or two. "I'll do you a deal, Reuben. I won't kill the twins on two conditions."

"He accepts," Hunter said immediately.

"What are those conditions?" Reuben asked evenly. Apparently he wasn't as eager to accept the offer as his brother. Business before blood. What a charming family.

"First, that they never try to kill or injure me or anyone I care about," Zeke said. "Second, you stop wanting me to come back to the family. For good. Leave me alone to live my life. I know you don't want either of them dead. They're too useful to you."

"We really are," Parker said. "Very useful. Much more useful than Zeke." He flinched away from Asher's gun. "No offence or anything. Zeke doesn't *want* to be useful to the family."

"No I don't," Zeke agreed. "So, do we have a deal?"

Reuben sighed heavily. "Fine. If you want to spend the rest of your life travelling around the world playing music, then do it. You were never much use to the family anyway."

Zeke rolled his eyes. "I'll take that as a compliment."

"Hey, I just realised something," Hunter said. "Reuben can't ask us to kill each other." He offered Parker a high-five.

"I said people I care about," Zeke said.

"We know you care about us." Parker raised his hand, but instead of accepting the high-five, he eyed Hunter. "Would you do it if he asked you to?"

"Of course not," Hunter said. "My point is that he can't ask us to, that's all." He lowered his hand.

"I can still ask," Reuben said darkly. "Only if you stop being useful."

"Most. Dysfunctional. Family. Ever," Penn said.

"Ever?" Tully echoed. "It's a pretty high bar around here." He had killed his own adopted father in self-defence after all.

Landon's mother was an addict who left him alone him often as a child. Asher's family was into the same shit as the Brantleys. Penn's pressured him mercilessly to succeed. From what I gathered, Channing's family was as bad. They must have been terrible for him to end up a killer.

Yeah, the bar was certainly high.

Penn shrugged. "I stand by what I said."

"Fair enough." Tully nodded slowly.

"I thought so," Penn agreed.

"Can we go now?" Hunter asked. "We have a flight in a few hours, don't we?" He eyed the gun which was still aimed at his head.

Zeke lowered it reluctantly. "I guess so." He looked like he would prefer to poke out his own eyeballs than be on the same flight with the evil twins. Honestly, the only people in the room who didn't share that sentiment were the twins themselves, I assumed. They seemed to enjoy travelling together. Two toxic peas in a pod.

"Can I have my phone back?" Parker raised his hands to either side and rose up from the chair. He kept his eyes on Zeke and Asher.

Yeah, I would too. Neither of them looked like they'd ruled out the idea of killing the twins. Or at least, they hadn't dampened the desire to do it completely.

"Wait," I found myself saying. "Before you hang up the phone, I have another condition of these two walking out of here alive."

Nine sets of eyes turned to look at me.

Asher used his gun to wave Parker back down into his seat.

Both twins eyed me nervously.

That shouldn't have turned me on, but it did. Their fear and the fact the guys took me seriously in this. None of them laughed me off, told me to be quiet or anything like that. They were all ready to hear whatever I had to say. Yeah, attentiveness in a tense situation was hot.

"What is it, sweetheart?" Zeke asked, no hint of condescension in his tone..

"Do enlighten us," Reuben said dryly. Okay, you can't impress everyone.

"They get to walk out of here with their brains inside their heads if they leave us alone after whatever happens in America," I said. "You said you accept that Zeke isn't coming back to the family, but I don't want these two following us around, drugging us, kidnapping us, threatening us, or anything like that."

"Abbie makes a good point," Zeke said. "Unless we need their help with some other shit you bring down on us, then they stay away from us. Especially from Abbie." He jerked his head in my direction.

"And me," Penn said. "I haven't ruled out killing them at a later date."

"Condition from me," Reuben said. "You don't kill them at a later date. None of you. Otherwise, I agree to your terms. Is there anything else?"

"Can you not kill my brother?" Asher asked. "Or any of my family?"

I caught a glimpse of Reuben's expression on the screen, but I couldn't figure out the reason for it. He looked uncomfortable. Cagier than usual.

"I have no intention of killing any member of the DiMarco family," Reuben said. "Not even Dane."

"Excellent," Asher said lightly. "Then it seems like we have a deal." He lowered his gun fully and stepped away from the twins.

"Now we're gonna have to find something else to do for fun," Parker quipped. He grinned and rose again, hands still in the air.

"Get a hobby," Zeke said. He too lowered his gun and handed Parker back his phone. "Take up knitting or some shit." He didn't look like he cared, as long as it was as far from him as possible.

Hunter laughed and stood just behind Parker. "Let's deal with the Fiorelli family first, shall we? Hey, Channing, good news. We won't have to get any help from you after all." He moved past him and clapped the saxophonist on the shoulder. "Looks like you're off the hook. On the other hand, you're going to have to deal with dead bodies by yourself from now on."

Channing jerked away. "Fuck off."

"Now, now, that's not very nice," Parker scolded.

"Don't make me change my mind," Zeke growled.

"You can't change your mind, we have a deal," Hunter said. "And in case you hadn't noticed, that also means Channing can't kill us. Isn't that awesome?"

Channing bared his teeth at him.

My gaze settled on Landon, who hadn't taken his eyes off his boyfriend the entire time. He still looked scared and confused. Pretty much how I felt.

"I hate to go all manager on you," Jackson said, "but we should get back to the hotel. We also have a flight to get ready for and a shit load of explaining to do."

"Yeah, we do," Zeke agreed. "Some of us more than others."

"Some a lot more than others," Penn said, waving a hand in Channing's direction. "Right now the only thing I've got is that these two assholes a walking away scot-free, and Zeke doesn't have to worry about his family anymore. Apart from that, I don't know what the fuck is going on."

"Me either," I admitted. I caught a smile on Zeke's face and frowned. "What?"

"I just realised you're wearing my shirt," he said. "You look adorable."

I glanced down at myself. His T-shirt fell almost to my knees like a dress. My track pants peeked out from underneath. I shrugged. "I grabbed whatever I could find. And before you ask, yes, I am wearing underwear."

"There goes that fantasy," Hunter complained as he slipped out the door behind Parker.

I made a face. The only thing I wanted to do with either of their cocks was punch them. Or pull them off and shove them down their throats.

A hand slipped into mine and I turned to see Tully.

"Are you okay, loveliness?" he asked softly.

"Not really," I said. Far from it. It was nice to get the twins off our backs, but now we were facing a potential attack in another country and the reality that Channing wasn't the person any of us thought he was.

Worse than that, the possibility Zeke and Asher knew what he was doing all along.

CHAPTER
THREE

CHANNNIG

LANDON LOOKED at me like I kicked his puppy.

That was a dumb analogy; he'd never had a puppy. His mother wouldn't let him have one. And neither would any of his foster parents. Honestly, he spent most of the time looking after his useless fucking mother, trying to make excuses for the bitch, or trying to stay out of trouble. From what he told me, it only took a sniff of anything bad for a foster family to decide it was time for him to move on.

I would never understand why no one adopted him. He's the best guy I know.

And right now the expression on his face was breaking my heart.

"Sweetie—" I held my hand out to him, tentative but hoping he'd take it.

"Did you really do those things?" he asked in a hushed whisper. He didn't take my hand. Instead, he stepped over closer to Abbie and Tully, who sat on the end of one bed.

Zeke and Asher sat on another, while Penn and Jackson leaned against the walls.

The sun had risen. The glow slanted through a gap in the curtains, illuminating the room.

"Did you know about it?" Abbie asked Zeke and Asher. She looked tired and confused. Her blonde hair stuck up here and there, untamed and adorable. Now wasn't the time for me to tell her that. Later, when she understood.

Zeke shrugged. "I had my suspicions, but I wasn't sure until tonight. Um, this morning."

I expected him to look pissed off, but he didn't. Why should he? I'd only killed people who deserved it. No one innocent. Nothing he wouldn't have done, given the chance. Me—I had the chances and took them.

Landon still hadn't taken his eyes off me.

I took a deep breath and prepared to tell him everything, and have him hate me for it. That was the worst part. I didn't regret anything I did, except working with the evil twins, but if Landon didn't love me anymore, then it was all for nothing.

"Yes, I did all those things," I said simply. What more was there to say?

Abbie put an arm around Landon when he groaned.

"Why?" she asked.

Zeke was right, she looked adorable in his shirt. And out of it. Everything about her was the image of the perfect woman. Her face, her voice, her figure, the way she tasted. The way she bucked against my mouth when I licked her clit and made her come. Even the way she growled at me when I edged her. She loved it and she knew it.

I set my mouth in a line. "When Zeke told me about Jonah, I lost it," I said. "Not in an out-of-control kind of way, but I got angry. You're my family. Your enemies are my enemies. I tracked him down and... I don't know what I intended to do. Maybe just beat him up, or warn him off. The next thing I knew, I had my hands around his neck and he was dead. And it felt fucking good to know he couldn't hurt any of you again." It really had. Guys like him got off on hurting people, and they got paid for it. They were low life pieces of shit. They deserved a slower, more painful death than I gave.

I glanced down at the floor, then back up again. "I know that's all kinds of fucked up." It was, but I still didn't flinch from what I did. I owned every moment.

Penn snorted. "You think? That's at least seventeen thousand kinds of fucked up. You could have ended up dead yourself."

"But I didn't," I said even. "I got rid of a threat and it felt good." My gaze swung over to Asher. "Like it felt good to shoot that guy in Perth."

Asher gave an unapologetic half shrug. "Not gonna lie, it did feel good."

I moved my gaze to Tully. "I know it didn't feel good to kill Xavier Lang, but you did what you had to do to protect yourself and us."

"I didn't hunt him down," Tully pointed out. "But you're right. Sometimes you have to do bad shit to bad people to keep better people safe."

I noticed he didn't say, 'good people,' when he looked at me, but he didn't seem to be condemning me either.

I nodded and turned my gaze back to Landon and Abbie.

"When I realised what I did, I didn't want to throw Jonah in a shallow grave or into the harbour. I didn't have time to do either of those things anyway. And no shovel."

"So you grabbed a cardboard box, put his head inside it and put him outside Zeke's door?" Abbie asked.

"Basically, yes," I agreed. "I'm sorry I freaked you out, that was never my intention." I was wrong, I had some regrets. That was one of them. I hadn't meant to scare her, just let her know someone was looking out for her. For all of my family.

Abbie looked sceptical. "What about the rest of them?" She frowned and asked, "When Asher and Zeke were confronting Reuben over having me kidnapped the first time, Landon said you had something to take care of. Was it Vance?"

Landon's eyes were huge and his mouth popped open. I could see thoughts turning in his mind, knowing the hints were there, but he hadn't seen them. Of course, he hadn't known to look.

"Yes, it was," I admitted. "I saw how hurt you were and… I'd already fallen for you. I couldn't stand seeing you hurt like that. So I went to confront him too."

"When we went souvenir shopping in Melbourne," Landon said slowly. "You said you had a surprise for me. Something you wanted to organise."

Penn snapped his fingers. "That's right, I remember thinking Channing bought a lot less shit than Landon did. You usually buy about the same amount of crap."

I couldn't deny it, so I nodded. "I also bought a cute hat for Landon. But yeah, I might have dropped in on Calista Rossi. Then I had to stash her quickly before we moved on to Adelaide. One of the staff must have seen me with the suitcase, that was why they left it outside the hotel room."

"And Poppy Newton?" Jackson asked.

"I was going to the toilet and bumped into her doing the same," I said. "She started asking me all sorts of questions about Abbie and being nasty. I didn't plan to do anything to her, but she kept coming at me and coming at me. In the end, I shoved her into the wall and she hit her head. I don't regret doing that either." She was a pain in Abbie's ass for years. And tons of other celebrities. If I hadn't ended her, someone else would have. I did a lot of people a favour ridding the world of that bloodsucking bitch. Unfortunately, someone else would take her place. They always did.

"Did you have anything to do with Pete's death?" Abbie asked.

"Same story," I said. "I went to the toilet and so did he. He didn't recognise me, but I tripped him over. He struck his head on the sink and I left him there like that. I didn't know he was dead until you told me."

"I can't believe…" Landon said, his eyes glazed.

Okay, here it came. He hated my guts. Never wanted to see me again. If that was the case, I would be the one to quit the band. I wasn't going to force him out of it. What was I thinking? After everything I told them, they'd probably turn me in to the police. The band would be the least of my trouble. This was going to cause a shitstorm for everyone. Fuck, I hadn't meant to...

"I can't believe," he started again, "that you would do all that and not tell me about it. And not ask for my help."

I blinked.

Okay, that was *not* what I expected to hear.

"You wanted to help?" I asked. Was I hearing things? Yeah, I'd finally lost my last marble.

His mouth open and closed a couple of times. "I can't exactly say I *wanted* to, but you're my person and everything you did was to protect us. It was like one of the twins said, it was your love letter to us."

"You're not mad at me?" I asked tentatively. "For killing people?"

He sucked in a breath. "It's going to take some time for me to get used to the idea that you did what you did, but I'm upset you didn't take me along with you to do these things. I know I'm not the strongest guy in the world, but I promised a long time ago that I would be by your side always. No matter what we're doing."

All right, had someone flipped the planet upside down? None of them were looking angrily at me. Zeke, Asher and Tully all looked like they understood. Jackson looked a bit freaked out. Penn looked somewhere between bored and amused.

And Abbie— Abbie looked aroused. To be fair, she usually was. She had a bigger appetite for sex than any woman I ever met. Or man for that matter.

"If this is where you say you'll take Landon along the next time," Zeke said slowly but firmly, "then this is where I say it needs to stop. I appreciate you wanting to take care of our problems, I really do. The rest of us do too, but sooner or later you're going to get caught and then we're all fucked. Okay?"

"Okay," I agreed.

"Who's left anyway?" Asher asked. "Like the evil twins said, you can't kill them." He glanced over to Abbie. "You don't have any more enemies do you?"

"Not now Penn and I are getting along," she agreed, a smile on the corners of her gorgeous mouth.

Penn snorted. "No fucking way Channing could kill me anyway. I'm bigger than him and we all know I'm faster than him." He puffed his chest out, full of self importance.

Not gonna lie, I was still annoyed he beat me in the foot race around the stadium in Munich. We hadn't had a chance for a rematch, but I planned to kick his ass next time. Especially now I apparently wasn't out of the band. I knew these people were the best.

"I don't want to kill you," I told him, "but I'm going to beat you next time we race."

"You talk a big game," Penn said, "but you only get to crow after you win."

"You guys are absolutely nuts." Jackson scrubbed a hand over his face. "Channing killed five people and you're talking about a foot race."

My heart thudded in my chest. "Are you going to go to the police? Or to Levi?"

"I didn't tell them about Asher or Tully, did I?" Jackson asked. "No, I'm not going to tell the police. Besides, I helped you clean up one of those heads, didn't I? I witnessed what Asher did in Perth. I'm in this as deep as you guys are. But that doesn't mean you're not absolutely nuts."

"But we're your nuts," Asher said. He frowned when he realised what he'd said. "I mean, we're not your nuts. Your nuts are your nuts, but we're—"

"We get it, babe." Zeke leaned to rest his cheek against Asher's shoulder. "Jackson is stuck with us, because he knows all the shit we did."

"Exactly," Asher said cheerfully. "Manager, friend, accomplice."

Jackson groaned.

"Are you going to tell Levi?" Abbie asked.

Jackson looked over at her, a pained expression on his face. "Levi knows pretty much everything there is to know about you guys. None of this will surprise him. And I hate to say it, but at the end of the day, you guys make him a lot of money. If he went to the police, there's no way in hell we would keep this from going public. Wolf Venom would implode. White Wolf Records would implode and take Onyx Riot with it."

He sighed out pursed lips. "And at the end of the day, I can't exactly say..." He chose his words carefully. "Jonah would have killed Abbie if it wasn't for Zeke. Pete was stalking her. Vance was an asshole who used her—"

"How to say you approve of what Channing did without saying you approve of what Channing did," Penn said sardonically.

"I wouldn't say I *approve*," Jackson said. "Just that I understand. But I would prefer if it didn't happen again. Can we agree to that?" He turned his denim blue eyes to me. He looked tired, more so than usual.

"Yes, I can agree," I said. "I'm done." It wasn't like I was some kind of psychopath who got joy out of killing people. Not precisely.

I stepped over to Landon and held out my hand. I looked him right in the eyes and silently begged him to take it. He was right, I should have taken him along. I should have trusted that he would understand and keep his mouth shut. Sometimes I forgot how strong he really was. On the surface, it seemed like he was just about to come apart, but under that he was the toughest person I knew. Tougher than me.

He reached out with calloused fingers and curled them around mine and I let out a breath of relief.

"Are we good?" I asked as I pulled him towards me.

I got my answer when he wound his arms around my neck and kissed my mouth.

"That leaves another question," Zeke said. He turned and pointed at me. "Don't think I haven't forgotten about your involvement with the twins."

Everyone's eyes turned to me.

CHAPTER
FOUR

ABBIE

"WELCOME to another episode of confessions from Wolf Venom," Asher said. His tone was cheerful but his eyes were as curious as everyone else's.

"For the record, I have nothing to confess," Penn said. "What you see is what you get." He shot me a heated look, clearly suggesting he meant that literally.

As if I wasn't turned on enough right now.

Yeah, I also have a confession. It was all kinds of fucked up to be aroused by what Channing did, but I was. What he did, he did because he loved me and Landon. It was the most morbid romantic gesture I'd ever had, but I couldn't deny my life was easier without the people he'd killed.

Like I said, I knew that was fucked up, but there was a reason I fit in with these guys. We were all about each other, no matter what. Nothing and no one was going to come between us.

"Which brings us back to Channing working with the twins," Zeke said reluctantly. "I need to know what you told them."

Channing closed his eyes and leaned into me and Landon.

"I'm sorry. I shouldn't have—" he started.

"That doesn't matter now," Zeke interrupted. "What did you tell them?"

"Nothing they didn't already know," Channing said. "Or nothing they couldn't find out from other sources. I made it sound like it was inside information. You didn't think I'd really tell them shit, did you?"

Zeke looked back at him, unflinching. "There's something about disposing of bodies together that tends to bond people. Not to mention, there's something about blackmail that makes people do things they would otherwise not. So, I'd be pissed if you had, but not surprised."

"I'd be surprised," Landon said. "I know Channing wouldn't betray us. Would you Chan?"

"Hell no," Channing agreed. He gave Zeke a dark look for suggesting he would.

Zeke was as unmoved as ever. "Does anyone have anything else they'd like to admit, confess, get off their chest?" He spread his hands out to take us all in.

"Jackson, if you're going to admit your undying love for Abbie, Levi or any of us, here's your chance," Asher said.

Jackson glanced sideways at me, but instead of admitting anything, he rolled his eyes.

"I admit my undying love for coffee, which I'd love a cup of right now, and travelling around the world managing bands." He was almost convincing. "There is something you should know," he added. He looked like he'd prefer to have a tooth pulled than say what he was about to say.

Almost as though we read each other's minds, all of us crossed our arms over our chests.

"Okay, out with it," Asher said. He gave me a quick look as if to say, 'here it comes, he's about to admit he's head over heels for you.'

Jackson grimaced. "Believe it or not, Levi offered me a job behind a desk."

Zeke dropped his arms to his sides and gaped. "Come again?"

"We're all going to need a bunch of orgasms after this bullshit," Penn muttered.

Without taking his eyes off Jackson, Asher offered Penn a high five.

Penn accepted and their palms slapped together lightly.

Zeke gave them the side eye, then looked back at Jackson. "Since when, and why didn't I know about it?"

"Since Levi wants to expand White Wolf Records," Jackson said. "Including incorporating Onyx Riot into the business." He nodded towards me, since I was previously signed with the label.

"He wants me to sit in an office all day long and push paper around. That phone call you overheard while you were in the shower—"

Now all eyes turned to me. "I was trying not to listen," I protested.

Jackson offered a half smile, like he knew I wouldn't have eavesdropped on purpose.

"That was a reporter asking when I'd be taking up the job and who would be replacing me. When I said I wasn't, they asked if I had a relationship with Abbie and if that was the reason I wanted to stay with you guys. I'd been fielding calls like that all day and had enough by then."

He scrubbed a hand across his face. "Maybe I should take Levi up on his offer. I'm sure he can find someone else—"

"Are you fucking kidding?" Asher asked, looking horrified. "Who else would put up with our bullshit? Who else would hear what you've heard this morning and not freak out?"

"Everyone but us eight," I said, giving Jackson a, 'don't you fucking dare leave us,' look. "Now I know what it was about, I wish I'd made you tell me. I would have talked you out of it." I probably would have blown him into staying. I still might.

He gestured with a brief wave of his hand. "At the time, you did ask if I was all right. I could have come out with it then, but we all had enough on our plates. If I knew you were so... worried about me, I would have come forward sooner."

He glanced down at the floor and sighed heavily. "I'm sorry my secrets aren't as interesting as Channing's." Yeah, he was one of us all right, or we were rubbing off on him. His sense of humour was as bad as ours.

"No one feels bad they aren't," Zeke said. "Levi really thought he could pry you away from us?"

"Either Levi doesn't know you as well as we thought, or he doesn't know us," Asher said. "They would have to pry our manager out of our cold, dead fingers. Unless you *wanted* to leave. But please don't."

"Yeah, what Asher said," Penn said. "No other manager would put up with Asher the way you do."

With all the maturity of a professional drummer in his mid-twenties, Asher stuck out his tongue at Penn.

Penn sneered at him. "No one else would put up with me either, okay dickhead?"

"You two are doing a good job of illustrating why we need Jackson," Zeke said. "On the other hand, if you keep being assholes like that, he might be tempted to walk away from us."

"Is this where we all rush at Jackson and give him a group hug?" Landon asked.

"I think it might be," I agreed.

Jackson held up his hands. "That's not necessary—"

Of course, we ignored him, rushed at him and gathered around for a group hug. After a moment, he gave up and hugged us back.

I totally didn't miss the way his hand found its way to my ass. Or mine to his.

"You know I might not always be able to go on tour with you," he said with what breath he could get out past our squeezes. "Blazing Violet needs me too. And Abbie."

"We can share," Asher said. "As long as you remember you really belong to us." He stepped back and rubbed his hands together like he was some evil character from an animated movie.

"If that doesn't make Jackson rethink working with us, nothing will," Tully said dryly.

"Nah, he likes our special brand of silly," Asher said. "Don't you Jackson?"

Jackson made a face in response. "It's been noted a couple of times we have a flight to prepare for. I'm also going to need to speak to Levi." He ran a hand over his hair. "We're going to need additional security."

Zeke nodded. "I'll sit down with you and discuss the travel itinerary. Figure out where we need extra people and extra vigilance. Places we're more likely to come under attack and places they'll expect us to be complacent."

"Does this mean we'll be on house arrest for the rest of the tour?" Penn groaned.

"No," Zeke shook his head. "I'd prefer to draw them out and deal with them. To do that, we're going to have to act as normal as possible." When Asher opened his mouth to say something, he quickly added, "I said as normal as *possible*, not actually normal. I don't think normal is realistic for any of us."

"I hope not," Asher said. "That would suck. I don't want to be normal and boring."

"You could never be boring, babe," Zeke assured him.

"I second that," I said. "None of us are boring."

"But some of us are more interesting than others," Penn said, without a hint of modesty.

"Yes, me," Tully said. Also with no modesty.

The guys all stepped back, leaving me with my arm still around Jackson.

"How did the press know?" I asked. They always seemed able to worm their way into any situation to get information. They were nothing if not as intrusive as fuck.

"Probably someone at the label told them," Jackson said. "It's not exactly a state secret. Most of the other managers have ended up behind a desk and I've been there longer than a lot of them. It might have been nothing more than a lucky guess."

"Being stuck behind a fucking desk sounds like the worst kind of torture," Penn said.

"Exactly my point," Jackson said. "And what I've been telling him all this time. I'd rather deal with disembodied heads than paperwork."

"What can I say?" Asher said. "You have your priorities in order, that's for sure."

"I'd rather deal with neither of those things," I said.

"If we don't start getting ready, we're going to be dealing with missing our flight," Tully pointed out.

"New York cheesecake, here we come," Landon said happily.

I closed my eyes and groaned. "Oh my god, that sounds so good right now." It seemed like days since Landon and I found the hotel's chef and front desk staff fucking in the kitchen. I'd hoped to find pastries instead. I'd lost my appetite hearing what Channing did, but now Landon mentioned cheesecake, it came back with a vengeance.

"We can eat in the airport," Zeke said. He was apologetic, but it was all aimed at me, along with a soft, loving look, which I returned.

"I'm okay with that," I said. "I'd like to get the heck out of Europe."

"That seems to be a theme with us," Asher said. "Come in with a blaze of glory and go out running for our lives."

"It's a theme I'd like to stop," Zeke said. "I'm okay with a blaze of glory stuff but not the rest of it."

"I'm seriously considering the wisdom of going to North America," Jackson said. "The sensible thing might be to organise a private jet and drop off the grid. Let your family deal with the Fiorellis, Bell family, and whoever the hell else." He held up a hand. "I know you want to finish the tour, but is it worth dying for?"

"No," Zeke said. "But we're not going to die. We're going to deal with whatever they throw at us. You can come with us or you can go home and sit in an office. Or go and lie on a beach and have a few cocktails. You deserve a break. But we *are* going to finish this tour and we're going to do it in style and without dying. I can't claim we won't break a sweat."

"I guarantee I'll break a sweat," Penn said. He gave me a look that sent heat right to my clit.

I looked back at him and grinned. Oh yeah, I'd be happy to work up a sweat with him any day. And lots and lots of orgasms.

"I'm not going home," Jackson said firmly, but with a sigh. "Whatever happens, we'll deal with it together."

"If you'd like, I can field your calls for you," Penn said. "I'm good at telling those bloodsucking vultures from the press to fuck off. In fact, it would be a pleasure."

"Thank you for the offer," Jackson said graciously. "I'll keep it in mind."

CHAPTER FIVE

ABBIE

"ARE YOU OKAY?" I asked Landon the first chance we got to speak alone together.

All Zeke gave us time for was to finish throwing our belongings into suitcases and make ourselves look more or less presentable. None of that took long, but it was still a mad scramble. We bumped into each other and almost tripped over suitcases several times. The mood was light but with an edge that it might change at any moment.

Judging by the looks, the covert glances, we were all trying to get our heads around what Channing did. You couldn't drop a bomb and not expect a bang.

"Yeah." Landon pressed the palm of his hand against mine and we laced our fingers together. "I feel like I should have known somehow. We all practically live together before the tour, and we're in each other's pockets when we're on tour. No one can go to the toilet without everyone knowing. But he went off and killed people and none of us had a clue."

"Love is blind?" I suggested. "Sometimes we don't see what's right in front of our faces." I hadn't seen what Vance was up to until after I married the guy. I had no clue he didn't care about me, even though it was as obvious as fuck. He might as well have walked around with a red flag in his hand, or on his forehead.

"I'm sorry," he said softly. "I didn't mean to remind you of him. But... he can't bother you anymore."

I snorted softly. "Thanks to Channing."

"You're welcome," Channing said.

I hadn't known he walked up behind me until he spoke. I startled and looked over my shoulder. Part of me thought I should be scared of him, knowing what he did, what he was capable of. But I wasn't. He was still the same Channing, buff, hot, with an edge of mystery. He loved me enough to kill for me. What could be more romantic?

"Sorry, didn't mean to scare you." He put tentative hands on my shoulders, as though he wasn't sure if I would welcome his touch. When I didn't tell him to stop, he started to massage lightly, strong fingers ironing out tight knots.

"You didn't," I said quickly.

"Are you sure?" he asked. "Both of you. It's not every day you learn your boyfriend killed people."

"I was standing right there in Perth when Asher killed that guy right in front of us," I pointed out. "I've known right from the start you guys were into all sorts of shit. You haven't seen me running away, have you?"

"No, but I have seen you freaking out over finding a head," Channing said. "After the first time, it seemed like the right thing to do, to keep doing that. So you knew someone was looking out for you. Even though you thought it was Pete." His fingers tightened on my shoulders.

"At least we know it's not a crazed fan," I said.

His fingers loosened and he went back to messaging. "Not crazed, no. I'm definitely a fan."

He stopped and turned me around to face him. He leaned in to slant his mouth over mine and kissed me, softly but putting all of his feelings into it. If I had any doubt of his intentions, he washed them all away.

He broke off and curled his fingers in the front of Landon's shirt. He pulled him over to him and kissed him too.

Landon wound his arms around Channing's neck and kissed him like he was starving.

"Are you guys ready?" Zeke called out like a bucket of ice cold water dumped on a fire.

The guys reluctantly broke off and made a face at Zeke.

"Yeah," Channing said. He kissed Landon again quickly and made to step away.

Before he could, Landon held him there and said, "I love you." He let him go and placed a hand on the back of my head, under my hair. "I love you," he said, his breath brushing my cheek.

"I love you too," I said. I thought about saying it to Channing, but the time wasn't quite right. Not yet. I had to get my head around everything first. That would take me at least a day or two.

"Let's get our stuff and get out of here," Channing said.

I suspected he caught my vibe. We both knew we cared about each other, but putting it into words wasn't something either of us could do right now. The time would come soon enough, as long as we didn't die.

In spite of Zeke's assurances, I wasn't going to assume anything.

"As long as you promise we're not going to find any more heads," I said. "Unless they are attached to living people." There were twelve heads in the room I was pretty fond of, on shoulders and in pants. Thirteen if I counted my own.

"If we find any more disembodied heads, it wasn't because of me," Channing assured me. "I can't guarantee I won't kill anyone in the defence of my family. You guys I mean, not my biological family."

"That bad?" I asked.

"I'll tell you about them later." He crouched to zip up his suitcase and pull the handle out.

"Okay," I said softly. He'd tell me when he was ready. From what I gathered, they were homophobic. People like that didn't deserve a guy like him.

I grabbed the handle of my own suitcase and wheeled it toward the door. "Can I ask you something?" I asked.

"Sure," he said. "Now you know what I did, I'm mostly an open book."

"When Tully was talking about… What you did, he said it was rough. You asked him what he meant by that."

Channing nodded. "A guy has to have some pride in his work, right?"

Landon and I both made a face at him.

He chuckled. "No, I was curious how he knew. I mean, it's not like I have that much experience at this."

"Are you sure about that?" I asked teasingly. At least, I *thought* I was teasing. Was that something I should tease him about?

Yes, I decided, it was. Firstly, I wanted to know the answer to that question and secondly, we wouldn't be us if we didn't all have morbid senses of humour.

Channing gave me a lopsided smile. "I solemnly swear I've only killed five people." He stopped for a moment and frowned in thought. "Yeah, five. I had to count to be sure. Wouldn't want to under exaggerate."

"Or over exaggerate," Landon said. He looked like he hoped five was an over exaggeration.

"Or that," Channing agreed. He seemed lighter now, happier. Compared to how he was before anyway. Considering what he had off his chest, it was no wonder.

"Hey, Asher," Penn said, "how many people have you killed?"

Asher stopped with his hand on the door handle. "I don't know." He shrugged.

"You don't know?" I blinked at him a couple of times. Holy shit.

A slow smile crept onto his face. "Less than Channing. I'm guessing, more than Penn, Landon or Abbie."

"Fewer than me," Tully said softly.

"I haven't killed anyone," Landon said. "Just a few spiders."

"Me either," I said. Did I really need to say that? I think they probably all knew that already. Before I met them, I felt bad if I stood on an ant. Now, this whole conversation didn't even bother me as much as it probably should. Yeah, I definitely changed.

"I pissed off a few people, but I've never killed them," Penn said.

"That sounds accurate," Zeke said. He waved at Asher to open the door.

"You don't think we're going to leave without you telling us how many people you've killed, do you?" Penn asked Zeke.

"A guy is entitled to keep some things a mystery," Zeke said. "Come on, let's go."

"Either it's a shit load, or its none," Penn said. "If it's a shit load, they weigh on your mind. If it's none, it's going to fuck with your reputation for being a badass."

"If we don't leave here soon, it will be more than zero either way," Zeke growled. "I'm sure the twins have time to dispose of you before they follow us."

Penn held up the hand that wasn't curled around his suitcase handle, in surrender. "Fine, don't tell us. You're a bigger spoilsport than Jackson."

"Don't you forget it," Zeke said. The set of his mouth was grim. However many was, it was definitely a non-zero number.

Honestly, I didn't want to know. Not right now anyway. I was one thousand percent certain he wouldn't have done it if he didn't have to.

Asher looked at us over his shoulder. "Are we good? Because once we step out the door, we have to stop talking about killing people and shit like that. Because, you know we're in a hotel in Frankfurt and there are other people here."

"I'm good," I said. "Maybe we could talk about something else for a while. Like puppies."

"I like puppies," Zeke said.

"Does anyone *not* like puppies?" Penn asked. "I have the hardest heart of all of us and I like puppies. Until they piss on your leg."

"Has that happened often?" Asher asked curiously.

"I can't say it has," Penn admitted. "But enough to know I don't like it."

"Fair enough." Asher nodded. He finally turned the door handle and opened the door. He peered out one way, then the other. "It looks more or less safe."

"Okay, everyone, keep your eyes open in case Reuben's intel was wrong," Zeke said. "It wouldn't be the first time someone fed someone else false information so they get complacent." His eyes scanned the group.

As soon as he said it, I realised he was right. That was exactly what happened, at least for me. It hadn't occurred to me we might come under attack before we left Frankfurt. My little bubble shattered into a million pieces.

I was as on edge now as I was looking for Channing and listening to him speak to the twins.

"Fuck," Penn muttered. Apparently he was thinking the same thing.

My heart in my throat, I stepped out into the corridor behind Asher and Zeke. I didn't miss the fact Penn moved into place on one side of me, Tully on the other. Landon and Channing walked behind me. My honour guard. Or bodyguards. Everywhere I went since the tour started, I went with the guys surrounding me like this. I couldn't decide if it was hot, scary or both.

There were worse things to be surrounded by than walls of muscle, especially when they knew how to take care of themselves. And me.

"We'll take the stairs," Zeke said.

No one questioned him. Not just because he was our unofficial leader, but because none of us wanted to get stuck in the elevator whether an attack took place or not.

Not even with six hot rock gods. Another time maybe, but not now.

Without a word, Tully took my suitcase and carried it in his other hand. I wanted to protest, but I would have dragged it down every step, bumping noisily as I went. Nothing about that said stealthy.

"When we get out onto the street, act naturally," Zeke said. "This was planned in advance, we know nothing about any plans that would stop us from doing what we're doing. We should meet Violet and the guys outside the front of the hotel. Jackson too. The vans shouldn't be long."

The calm in his voice was almost contagious. I wanted to believe nothing bad was going to happen. That we would get on our flight, fly to North America and have a fucking good time putting on rock concerts. And then, go back to Australia and live our lives.

Maybe if I thought about it often enough, that would be what happened.

And maybe little pink, polka-dot pigs would fly.

CHAPTER SIX

ABBIE

"THERE YOU GUYS ARE," Violet said as we stepped out the front door of the hotel.

It was still early, not much past seven a.m. The traffic moving past was light. The amount of people on the street was lighter still.

When we checked out, there was someone different working on the desk. Judging by the smells that came from the kitchen, the chef got some work done after his liaison over the kitchen table.

"Violet," Penn drawled. "Did you scare all the paparazzi away?"

"Penn," she said in the same tone of voice. "I told them you were coming and they ran for the hills."

I laughed as they flipped each other off.

"Whatever has to happen to ensure they're not here," Jackson said, his expression completely deadpan. "I have to admit I hadn't thought of that. We'll have to try it next time." A hint of humour crept into his eyes.

Penn swivelled his hand to point his middle finger up at Jackson instead. "I told you the paparazzi was scared of me."

"Actually, what you said is you're good at telling them to fuck off," Asher said helpfully.

Penn swivelled his finger towards him.

"Hey," Asher protested. "What did I do?"

"I don't know," Penn said, "but I'm sure you're about to do something. You usually are."

"Just because that's true doesn't mean I don't feel attacked," Asher said.

"Are you sure you wouldn't prefer a desk job?" Zeke asked Jackson.

"I'm more or less sure," Jackson said.

"Hey, whose side are you on?" Asher asked Zeke.

"Ours," Zeke said. He snaked an arm around Asher's neck and pulled him in for a kiss. Asher made a sound like he might refuse, but he kissed him back.

I couldn't help but watch. Ever since the first time I saw them kiss, I'd enjoyed the view. They had the best friends to lovers love story, possibly ever.

"I'd tell you to get a room, but Zeke was the one who was all about hurrying us out of ours," Penn said.

Zeke broke off the kiss but kept his arm around Asher's shoulders. "If you don't want to see, then don't look." He seemed chill on the outside, but his eyes took in everything around us. Every person that went past, every car. He was a master of being vigilant without looking like it. If you didn't know him well enough, you'd easily be fooled.

At least to some extent, I was projecting my anxiety, but I knew he was on guard against everything.

I laced my fingers in Penn's. "Are you just wishing we had a room?" I asked teasingly.

He smiled down at me, then leaned to press his forehead lightly against mine. "Always, gorgeous. It's never not a good time for a nap." His body vibrated with laughter.

I slapped him lightly on the chest. "I didn't mean napping, and you know it."

"If Penn wants to nap, then it gives the rest of us the chance to fuck," Tully said. "So I say, let the man nap."

Without moving his head, Penn said, "The man will nap after a long, slow fuck." He lowered his mouth to mine for a long, slow kiss, his tongue sliding across my lips.

I closed my eyes and let out a soft moan. He was making me ruin my panties, one word and breath at a time.

He broke off and gripped my chin between his thumb and forefinger. He firmly turned my face until another set of lips found mine.

My eyes flickered open and I found myself looking at Tully. I kissed him deeply as I had Penn.

"Now who needs to get a room?" Asher teased.

"Who needs a room when you got the wall of the hotel right there?" Penn asked.

Holy shit, if I wasn't wet enough before, I was now. I broke off from Tully and looked over at Penn, who still held my chin.

"It's broad daylight," I squeaked. "And we could come under attack any minute now."

"You still want to," he stated. He slid a hand down my side and grabbed my ass.

Did I ever? I wanted him to press me back against the brick, lift up my skirt and impale me on his cock. I wanted him to fuck me until I screamed, and I didn't care who saw.

I swallowed hard.

"The van is here," Jackson said regretfully.

I didn't need to look at him to know he was turned on, I heard it in his voice. At least to some extent, he wanted to watch that happen, or wanted to do it himself. I was definitely going to have to find time to have that conversation with him. I cared about him too much to leave it for too much longer.

A quick glance in his direction confirmed my suspicion, but then we were all grabbing suitcases and pulling them forward to so they could be loaded onto the van. It was no tour bus, that was for sure. No blaze of glory. This was more a quiet retreat from Frankfurt.

Jackson and Zeke supervised the loading of the suitcases, while Penn, Asher and Tully herded me onto the bus, followed by Channing and Landon. Violet and her guys were right behind them, but they sat at the front of the van while the guys and I sat at the back. Penn manoeuvred me so I sat between him and Tully on the back seat.

"Finally, I feel like one of the cool kids," Tully said.

"When were you not one of the cool kids?" I asked him. He was one of the coolest guys I knew.

"I wasn't cool when I was a kid," he said. "I was a big nerd."

"What a shock," Penn said sarcastically.

"As if you weren't," Asher said to Penn. "I bet you were the biggest nerd of all of us."

Penn shrugged. "I never said I wasn't. I still sat on the back seat of the bus with my friends, because fuck authority."

"Penn, the rebel," I said.

He tangled his tattooed hand in the hair at the back of my neck and smiled. "You better believe it, gorgeous. Then and now." He kissed me, pressing me back until I was leaning against Tully.

Tully twisted little to the side and put his hands on my arms to hold me.

"The van has tinted windows, right?" I asked as Penn kissed my jaw and down to my neck.

"Yep," Penn said against my skin. "But anyone in the bus can see."

Good point.

I glanced around to see Violet chatting to Ryan, who sat beside her. He was looking at her like he might kiss her at any moment, if he dared.

Landon and Channing sat in front of us, talking in low voices. I caught a word here or there but not most of it. From what I could tell, they weren't discussing anything too intense.

Jackson sat across from them, his legs on the seat, his feet dangling off the side. If he turned his face a little, he could see everything we were doing.

Zeke and Asher sat in front of him, also talking to each other in low voices. Every so often, one or the other would look out the window, then they'd go back to talking. They were like a couple of soldiers making battle plans, or guards on watchful duty. Either way, the pretense of being chill was gone, unnecessary since no one outside could see us.

"See, no one is looking," Penn said. He kissed my neck and down to my chest before he tugged down the front of my shirt and peeled away one cup of my bra. He teased my nipple with the tip of his tongue.

I had a feeling I was being watched, and not just by Tully, who was still holding my arms. I looked over to see Jackson watching. I offered him a smile.

He swallowed hard in response, but didn't look away.

"You want to be with him, don't you?" Tully whispered in my ear.

I looked up towards the roof of the van. "Yes, but we're not ready yet." It wasn't just about having sex with him, that would be easy. It was about figuring where our boundaries were and where he factored into this crazy pack of ours. The guys in the band were all for it, but Jackson himself might not be. That didn't mean he couldn't watch though. If he objected, he could either look away or tell us to stop, and we would.

"All the more for us in the meantime," Penn said, his mouth full of my nipple. His hand wandered up my thigh. When his fingers grazed the front of my panties, they were covered from view by the fabric of my skirt. I was grateful for that. I wasn't ready for Violet and her guys to see my naked pussy, if they happened to look back this way. My breasts were one thing, that was another.

He tugged my panties aside and dipped his fingers into the wet well of my pussy.

I shivered with delicious anticipation.

"You like that?" he asked.

I murmured something incoherent.

"What do you say" he picked up his head to look me in the eye.

"Yes, sir," I said. "I like that very much."

"Of course you do," he said.

One of Tully's hands slipped down the front of my shirt and onto the breast which was still encased in a cup. He traced circles lightly around my nipple, then rolled it between his thumb and forefinger.

Penn hooked his fingers so they could massage my g-spot while he rubbed the heel of his hand over my clit.

"The drive isn't long, but I'm going to make you wait as long as I can."

Of course he would, because he was basically evil. Okay, that might be an exaggeration. He and Channing were the worst teases though. And I was here for every second of it.

"What if I don't want to wait?" I said breathlessly. I stuck out my chin like I really intended to rebel.

"You'll do as you're told or I'll turn you over and smack your ass until it's red," Penn growled.

I laughed low in the back of my throat. "You're going to threaten me with a good time?"

"It won't be a good time when you have to sit down for ten hours, but your ass is too sore," Penn said.

"Then I'd have to lie down," I pointed out. "That doesn't sound so bad."

"Don't tempt me, woman." He narrowed his eyes at me and worked me harder with his hand.

"If you keep doing that, I'm not going to be able to stop myself," I said.

"So you want me to stop?" He started to pull his hand out.

"No," I said quickly.

He quirked an eyebrow at me.

"No, sir," I said. "Please don't stop." Although, I had a handful of guys who would have helped if I asked them to, and we both knew it. No doubt he'd prefer to finish what he started as much as I wanted him to.

"Tully, do you think we should give her what she wants?" He looked over the top of me. "She might be too naughty to feel good."

"I think we should definitely give her what she wants," Tully said.

They must have exchanged a look I couldn't see, because Penn put his hand out and placed both of them on my hips. He rolled me over so I was face first across both guys, my face in Tully's lap.

"Hey." I grinned.

Tully tangled his fingers in my hair. "Hello there." His cock got hard under my cheek. I could feel the strain under the denim of his jeans, aroused, needy, wanting me.

Penn pushed my skirt up to my waist. "Good thing you're wearing a G string," he said. "Easier to get at bare skin."

He brought his hand down on my ass hard enough to make a loud slap. If everyone in the van didn't hear that, they would have heard my squeal.

I glanced over to see Violet look at me over her shoulder, but she smiled and went back to her conversation. I guessed she was used to our craziness by now.

Everyone else turned around to watch as Penn spanked me again. This time was harder, but made me groan in pleasure. The sharp sensation that coursed through me stoked the fire in my core and left me drenched.

He spanked me twice more, three times, each more painful and wonderful, then said, "Free Tully's cock and suck him."

"Yes, sir." With pleasure. If Tully was any harder, he'd break the zipper.

It took me a moment to catch my breath, and blink away tears from the stinging.

Penn hadn't held back and I loved that, but it was going to hurt as much as he promised. I loved every moment.

I undid the front of Tully's jeans until his erection popped out, then, my eyes on his face, fastened my lips around him and licked and sucked while he moaned.

"Penn has some good ideas," he ground out.

"Of course I fucking do." Penn slid his fingers into my from behind, two or three inside my pussy and his thumb inside my ass. "That's why you should listen to me more often."

Mercilessly, he fucked me with his hand, skilled fingers playing my saturated pussy like I was another instrument he'd mastered.

"Shit," I said around the substantial mouthful of Tully's cock. I teased his piercing with my teeth and lips, gripping and tugging gently while he groaned and fucked my mouth slowly.

"I want you both to come," Penn said, working me harder while he pinched my ass with his spare hand.

The pleasure, the pain, the wet smacking sounds of my mouth and my pussy drove me quickly to the edge and over, riding Penn's hand in almost fevered desperation.

I cried out, then clamped my lips down harder as Tully came, thrusting furiously before he stilled and squirted his salty cum deep in the back of my throat.

I was still lost deep in my orgasm when I swallowed down his release and let Penn milk my body for every drop of pleasure. He was a master at making my orgasms last for days.

"Good girl," he said when I finally came back down to earth with a lazy bump.

I turned my head to see Jackson still watching. His expression was heated, drinking in every moment.

One of these days...

CHAPTER
SEVEN

CHANNING

"WE MADE IT," Landon said.

The plane bumped lightly as it landed in LAX. The world rushed past the window in a blur. Landon preferred to sit by the window and I never argued with him. Partly because I wanted him to be happy and partly because I got to look at him and the view at the same time. That was a win as far as I was concerned. The fact he didn't hate me was the biggest win of all. I would never not be grateful for him for accepting me, flaws and all. He was the sweetest, best guy I knew.

"It's a miracle right there," I said.

He twisted around and flashed me a grin that made my heart skip and my pulse race. I was the luckiest guy in the world, in so many ways. Most of them revolved around Landon, Abbie and the band. What was I saying? All of them revolved around those three things. I think I already established that I'd do anything to protect my world.

I smiled back and when he turned away, I let my gaze slide over to the seat beside us, where Abbie had just fastened her seatbelt. She'd spent most of the flight lying over Asher and Zeke, claiming her ass was too sore for her to sit for very long.

If she wasn't cheerful about it, I'd be mad at Penn. Not the spanking, that part was all in fun and fully consensual, but I worried he'd gone a bit too hard.

Still, she was smiling as she wriggled in her seat and winced. By the look on Asher's face, he found all of this hilarious. Penn, who sat the next row over, looked smug and pleased with himself. Of course he would, he was Penn. When was he not smug and pleased with himself?

Tully, like me, looked like he wanted to get some ice to ease her discomfort.

Although, knowing him it wasn't just about discomfort. It would be about her experiencing the cold on her bare skin. He was all about heightening sensory awareness and being at one with the universe or something like that.

I don't know, it wasn't my thing, but I appreciated that it was his. He was a good guy. It kinda sucked he wasn't into other guys, but that was life. I wasn't surprised to learn Asher and Zeke were into each other. We knew it long before they did, Landon and I. We talked about it a few times and wondered how long it would take them to realise they had the hots for each other.

I got it. Sometimes it was hard to see what was right in front of your face.

The plane taxied down the runway and over to one of those tunnels we'd disembark from. This was where a lot of people like us would have insisted on getting off first. We preferred to wait a few minutes and let everyone else clear out ahead of us. It saved us tripping over them and vice versa. According to Jackson, it was good manners or some shit. Whatever, as long as we all got off the plane in one piece.

Landon's sweaty hand gripped mine as we took off our seat belts and stood. "Do you think we'll be okay?" he asked. "I'm half expecting to get shot the second I step off the plane."

"You're not gonna get shot," I told him. "There's no way I'm going to let anyone hurt you. You know I can and will do anything to stop them." I gave him a meaningful look.

He squeezed my fingers. "Not without me you're not," he said firmly. It was adorable when he got all bossy. We had long since established that I was the bossy one of the two of us. He was the sweet puppy who followed along, scared he'd get left behind if he didn't.

Yeah, I admit, that chafed from time to time. He knew I wasn't going to leave him, but sometimes he lets his insecurity get the better of him. One of these days, he'd understand and accept that he was stuck with me. In the meantime, I let him stick close if that was what he needed.

"Right, not without you," I agreed. As much as I liked to think he wasn't capable of killing anyone, he'd also do whatever he had to do to keep the rest of us safe.

Then, he'd discover that once you did it once, it was easier to do it again. Even Tully, who only killed for money once, had killed since. He claimed to hate it, but sometimes it was necessary.

"Keep your eyes open," I said.

"Not too open," Zeke said as he stepped out from in front of his seat, Asher right behind him. "Remember to play it cool. They don't know we know they're coming. If they notice us acting stranger than usual, they may try something rash. That won't end well."

"For them or us?" Abbie asked. To my surprise she stepped over to me and took my other hand. Out of all the guys, I was the one she'd spent the least amount of time with. She was busy with the other guys, I was busy with Landon, and I needed to let my boyfriend get to know her first. I was ready to jump right in from the moment I met her, but he was more restrained than that. If Abbie and I got too close too quickly, he would have freaked out.

Sometimes, you have to play the long game in life and love.

"For them," Zeke said firmly. "The only thing that worries me about that is if we leave too much mess behind. Not to mention collateral damage."

"That would be bad," Asher said.

"Very bad," Zeke agreed. He waved us ahead of him and walked beside Asher as we made our way to the door.

Penn and Tully had moved first, making sure Abbie was right in the middle of us as usual.

She was a rose surrounded by six thorns. Seven if you counted Jackson, which I pretty much did already. That was another thing I knew long before they figured it out for themselves. The way he looked at her and acted all protective of her, he didn't act that way towards the rest of us.

At first, I thought it was because she was a woman and had been through so much. Then I realised he fell for her the same time I did.

For different reasons, he held back too. For one thing, he wouldn't want to get accused of sexual harassment if Abbie didn't feel the same way he did. That kind of thing ruined careers faster than anything that ever happened to her. He also wouldn't have wanted to ruin the relationship he had with her and with us.

There was a lot at stake, but this was the way Wolf Venom did things. We jumped in hard and ran until we passed the finish line. And then we went on running. No one could ever accuse us of doing things by halves. We'd always been a driven group of assholes.

Somehow, Jackson was in front of us when we stepped off the plane and walked through the tunnel. We all ignored the flight attendants who stared at those of us who held hands. That now included Zeke and Asher. I was surprised the paparazzi hadn't picked up on that yet. They would, soon enough.

Fortunately, our fans were used to the relationship between Landon and I. They wouldn't bat an eye at Zeke and Asher.

I didn't know what they would think if they knew Abbie was with all of us, and frankly I didn't really give a shit. Our business was making music. They didn't really need to know what we did in private.

"We should be fine in here," Zeke said, keeping his tone conversational. "They won't want to try anything with all these people here. It wouldn't go unnoticed."

Penn snorted. "That's a fucking understatement. It would be headline news in about three point two seconds."

"That slowly?" Asher asked. "I would have thought at least two point two."

Penn rolled his eyes. "It takes time to record the words and upload them to cyberspace."

Asher nodded as if they were actually holding a serious conversation for once in their lives. "That makes sense," he agreed.

"You two are absolutely nuts," Landon told them.

"That's us," Asher said cheerfully. "Nuts with big nuts."

"So you admit I have big nuts?" Penn asked.

Jackson cleared his throat. "Maybe we can get our suitcases and get out of the airport sometime today? I don't know about you, but Blazing Violet is ready to put on a concert tomorrow night." He nodded to where Violet and the guys waited over to the side of the airport, watching us impatiently. "If you don't want to, I'm sure they could headline for you."

"Only if you want a riot on your hands," Penn said. "I'm pretty sure you don't, so let's go." He waved as if he wasn't the one holding us up a minute or two ago.

"Have I mentioned recently you deserve a medal for putting up with us?" Asher said to Jackson.

"I'll settle for a pay raise," Jackson said, holding back a smile.

"Poor Jax," Abbie said. She put a hand on his cheek, I think to pat it, but her fingers lingered there for a bit too long. Their eyes locked and I know I wasn't the only one holding my breath.

Just when I thought they might kiss, they stepped apart and we hurried towards customs and the baggage collection area.

We wouldn't have any trouble clearing customs, because we were who we were. They only ever glanced at our passports and made sure we weren't carrying drugs. If we were, Jackson and Levi would make the problem go away. As long as it was dealt with before the press got hold of the story. If they did, it would be more difficult, but not impossible.

The things you could get away with when you had a shit load of money.

"Everywhere I look, I feel like people are staring at us more than usual," Landon said nervously.

"Of course they're staring, we're Wolf Venom," I said lightly. "Don't get paranoid."

"Too late." His hand trembled in mine.

I stopped and turned to face him, almost pulling Abbie off her feet. I shot her an apologetic look, then turned back to him.

"You are Landon Flynn. Bass guitarist for the best motherfucking rock band in the world. Men and women all over the world have photos of you on their phones. They fantasise about you and groove to your music. You are a certified badass. You're the kid who came from nothing and is now in Los Angeles ready to play one of the biggest shows of your career. You're one of the most amazing people I've ever met, and none of us is going to let anything happen to you. I'm proud of you. I love you. Okay?"

I kissed his mouth and tasted salt and coffee. His stubble scraped against mine. I could have felt that all day long. And all night.

"Channing is right," Abbie said. "You are a badass. You both are." When I leaned back, she kissed Landon, then me. Neither was a quick peck either. She took her time, kissing us deeply with lips and teeth and tongue.

Finally, she stepped back and said, without any hesitation, "I love you both."

"I love you," Landon told her.

It took me a moment to appreciate the fact the opportunity I'd waited so long for finally arrived. This wasn't exactly how I wanted to tell her, but I would take it anyway.

"I love you too, beautiful," I said softly. That felt good. Better than good. She was gradually teasing out my deepest, darkest secrets.

And my deepest, lightest ones as well.

CHAPTER EIGHT

ABBIE

"LANDON TOOK ALL OF THAT WELL," I said.

The hotel rooms were nothing fancy, just a couple of beds in one and a couple in the other, each had their own bathroom, which made it easier for us all to cycle through the shower. The downside was that the showers were too small for more than one person at a time. Usually, we made it work, but that wasn't going to happen today. There was barely room for one person to stand up, much less two or three.

Maybe that spoke volumes about how spoilt we were. Hashtag first world problems.

"Yeah, he did." Channing lay next to me on one of the beds, my legs draped over his. With one hand, he was idly playing with my hair and tracing circles over the side of my face with his fingertips.

For once, I had him to myself while Landon was in the shower. Not that I minded spending time with both of them, but this was a rare treat.

"So did you," Channing added. He twirled a piece of my hand around his fingertip. "Most girls would have freaked out and run away."

"I'm not most girls," I said. Obviously, because he was right. Most people, when learning one of their boyfriends did the things he did, would have bolted for the hills. Me? I got aroused. "In fact, I should say thank you."

He unwound the hair, then wound it up again. "What for?" He looked at me intently with his pretty, hazel eyes.

"Wanting to make my life easier by getting rid of the people who made it harder," I said. "I've spent most of the last couple of years trying to put on my big girl panties and get past... Well, the past. But every time Vance did something, including die, the press came to me with new questions. Usually Poppy

Newton was the one asking those questions. Calista was a horrible person, and apparently Pete was stalking me. Who knows whether he had something in mind or not?"

"Stalkers usually have something in mind," Channing pointed out. "It's not normal behaviour to follow someone around and take photos of them. Unless you're paparazzi."

"I'm not sure what they do is normal," I said wryly. "But it's certainly more normal than what he was doing. You know, we were really worried about you that day. We thought you were the one who was dead in that toilet."

"I'm not that easy to get rid of," he said, not boasting, just stating a fact. "It's sweet that you were worried about me though." He leaned in and kissed my nose.

"I could say the same to you," I said. "You were worried enough to do what you did for me. How many other girls can say a guy went to those lengths for them?"

"Baby, there's two hotel rooms full of people who would have gone to those lengths for you. In fact, the rest of the guys are probably kicking themselves for not doing it before I did." He shrugged the shoulder that wasn't pressed against the mattress.

"Possibly," I said. "I mean, from what Landon said, he would have gone along with you." That was a given.

"The rest of them would too," Channing said. "Zeke and Asher would have taken part. Tully would have given advice, and Penn would have stood guard and told the rest of us what we were doing wrong. But in the end, someone had to watch over you while I was fixing things. If someone else, like the evil twins, got to you while we were busy doing that, we would never have forgiven ourselves."

"I see you've given it a lot of thought," I said. "And planning." I wasn't sure if I should find that disturbing or admirable. It was definitely hot.

"Growing up, I didn't believe in love at first sight," he said slowly. "But now it's happened to me twice. Once with Landon and again with you. Just like I don't want anything or anyone to hurt him, I don't want anyone to hurt you either. I went into protective mode."

"Have you killed anyone for him?" I asked half joking.

He hesitated.

My heart stopped. "You have?" I whispered.

"No," he said finally. "But I thought about it."

"His mother?" I guessed. It didn't take a genius to realise who he meant. What she did to him was worse than anything anyone did to me.

"Yeah," he agreed. "I didn't because I know he wants to reconcile with her. He couldn't do that if she was dead."

"No," I agreed. "He couldn't. Do you think it's possible?"

Channing frowned. "I don't know. Olive Flynn has never been the most stable person in the world. She makes Penn look like an absolute sweetheart. But when she and Landon get along..." He sighed. "Those are some of his happiest times in his life. All he ever wanted was for her to get well and for them to take care of each other. As long as both of them are alive, he's not going to give up on that."

"What about your family?" I asked gently. "Landon said they were difficult too. Let me guess, you're a long lost Fiorelli cousin?"

Nothing would surprise me anymore. Hell, I wouldn't even be surprised if I learnt I was related to them. Or the Brantley family. Or the Bell family for that matter. As long as I wasn't really Zeke's sister. That would be all sorts of complicated.

Channing laughed softly. "As far as I know, I'm not related to any of them by blood. My parents were very conservative. They don't believe people should get tattoos or body piercings or be gay. Or bisexual. Or pansexual. Or polyamorous. In their world, boy meets girl, they get married, lose their virginity to each other on their wedding night and have as many babies as they can. They didn't appreciate it when I suggested they had a breeding kink." He grinned cheekily.

I laughed softly. "They sound a bit like my parents. They weren't quite so conservative, but they expected me to be married by now and giving them a grandchild or two."

"And here you are, with seven guys who all love you," he said. "What would they think of that?"

"I'm not sure," I admitted. "I don't think they'd want to know that you guys would kill for me. I think..." I chewed my lip for a moment. "I think if they met you guys and knew how well you took care of me and loved me, they would be happy for me. Once they got used to the idea." That might take them some time.

"And the grandchildren bit?" he asked. "Would they want seven?" He wiggled his brows slightly.

I groaned and tilted my head back. "I'm not sure I want seven. That would be a handful." I looked back at him. "Would you want one of your own?" That was the first question here. Well, the second after, 'did I want children at all?'

He pursed his lips. "Yeah, I think so. I kinda like the idea of a mini me running around. Also, it would piss my parents off. Not to mention the stir we would create with having seven children with seven different fathers." He grinned.

"Yeah." I laughed. "That would raise some eyebrows. Luckily, I don't mind raising eyebrows. As long as they don't get bullied for it."

"If any of them gets bullied, they'll have six siblings, seven fathers, and one amazing mother to back them up," he pointed out. "No one would dare. Not to mention, six of those fathers are members of Wolf Venom. We're the definition of badasses." He flexed his arm.

"Not to mention me," I said, giving a flex of my own. "All those last names would be confusing though. Unless they were all Hart."

"Baby, any kid of yours will be all heart," he said. He pressed his lips to mine gently. When he pulled back, he looked thoughtful.

"I know that look," I said. "You have a song forming in your brain, don't you?"

He grinned. "It's that obvious?"

"I've seen that expression in the mirror time or two," I agreed. "Inspiration comes whenever it wants to."

"True that. Let me see..." He scrunched up his brow. "Baby, you're all heart, you got in my head. Baby, you're all heart, get in my bed." He chuckled. "Okay, needs a bit of work."

"Hey, it's a good start," I said. "And accurate, given we're already lying on one." I had a feeling he'd be balls deep inside me if Landon was here too.

As if he read my mind, he said, "Do you think it's weird that Landon and I like to be together when we're with you? I want you so badly, and if I was one of the other guys, I'd be fucking you so hard right now and making you wait to come."

"It's not weird at all," I said. "You have a special kind of relationship. Everyone has rules and boundaries, and you guys have yours. I feel like Landon would be... upset might be too strong a word, but if he walked in and we were fucking, I think that would be weird."

"But if you came out of the shower and we were fucking—" he looked at me questioningly.

"It wouldn't bother me because that's how our relationship works," I said. "I respect you and your respect for Landon. For the record, I want you too." Apart from the obvious exception of Jackson, Channing was the only one whose cock I hadn't had inside my pussy yet. In my mouth, yes, a few times. Quite a few.

"Can I ask you something?" I asked.

"Absolutely," he said. "At this point, I think you know all my secrets, so I have nothing left to hide."

"This is going to sound really weird," I said. "But when you... You know, killed and you know..."

"Cut their heads off?" he suggested.

"Yeah," I said. "What did you use? I keep wondering how you got knives past customs."

He gave me a knowing look. "You really want to know how I got knives past customs, or are you really wondering if I like playing with them?"

I licked my lips. "Both," I admitted. These guys had introduced me to a world of new things. The idea of Channing holding a knife to my throat with the same hand it used to kill turned me on way more than it should have.

He rolled me over into my back and straddled my hips. "I do like playing with them. Unfortunately, I didn't get knives past customs. I had to get rid of them before we went through the airport. But that doesn't mean I can't buy one for us to experiment with. Don't worry." He leaned down to nudge my cheek with his nose. "I know how to avoid cutting off someone's head."

"Well, that's a relief," I said. It was also a relief to know he did use a knife and not a guitar string. It might not have occurred to Landon yet, but I would bet anything Tully had thought of it. Hell, he probably knew exactly how to kill someone using a guitar string, then hide the evidence by stringing it on his own guitar.

And that wasn't even the most fucked up thought I'd had in the last few months.

"Let's call that a date," he said. "You, me, Landon and a blade."

"Lock it in," I agreed.

And there goes another pair of panties.

CHAPTER
NINE
ABBIE

"ABBIE! ABBIE!" The crowds outside the hotel shouted my name, at least as often as they shouted the guys' names.

Not surprisingly the press in LA were as hungry as they were anywhere else in the world. The tone was different though. Instead of being accusing or trying to dig up dirt, they seemed fascinated with the story of my twenty-six hour marriage and then the death of my ex-husband. Instead of being something tragic or terrible, they found it entertaining, like it was the latest Hollywood blockbuster.

I have to admit, that was the first time it occurred to me someone might actually turn that part of my life into a movie. I made a mental note to talk to Jackson about that. If anyone was going to do it, he'd know how to make sure I had a lot of say in it. Otherwise, I risked being portrayed in an ugly light and that wasn't something I was prepared to tolerate. Not anymore. I didn't expect to come out looking like an angel, but I also didn't want to be the bitch everyone ended up hating.

I waved and smiled while they took photos until Jackson herded us towards the tour bus that waited by the side of the road. Instead of saying *Wolf Venom* down the side, this one read *White Wolf Records*.

Asher nudged me with his elbow. "This is the bus the Rock Dragons tour on. When they're in the States anyway."

I nudged him back. He caught my elbow with his hand and tucked his arm through mine.

"It's adorable how you fanboy over another band," I told him. If I had to say who was bigger out of the two bands, I didn't think I could. They were both amazing and talented. Levi was lucky to have both of them on his label.

"You're never too old or successful to fanboy over someone else," Asher said. "Besides, my uncle Roman is their manager. I have to give them a little bit of loyalty."

"As long as it's not too much," Zeke said, hooking his arm through my other one. He grinned at the paparazzi as we walked past like that. "You know photos of you kissing Landon and Channing have gone viral, right?"

"Of course they did," I said. "And this will too. Maybe I should take this opportunity to make out with Penn and Tully just to round it all out."

"Don't forget Jackson," Asher said loudly. "If you're going to make out with them, then you should make out with him too."

When Jackson, who stood beside the door to the bus, turned to look at us, his face was pink. "Or we could get on the bus."

"Or both," Asher said unapologetically. He patted Jackson on the cheek on the way past. "You know you want to."

Jackson didn't meet my eyes as I stepped up onto the bus. We really, really needed to have that talk. If only to get Asher off his back if Jackson didn't feel the same way I did.

Who was I kidding? Asher would tease him anyway.

"Some people say seven is a lucky number," Asher said over his shoulder.

"And some people say *drum machine*," Zeke teased.

"Nah," Asher said, "a drum machine would take up too much room on the seat. Although, they might vibrate just right."

"Are you trying to talk yourself into being kicked out of the band?" Penn shoved past Asher and flopped down into a seat.

"A drum machine still wouldn't be as hot as me." Asher sat in front of Penn and pulled me down onto his lap. He wrapped his arms around me and nuzzled his face into my hair.

"We could put a huge photo of you on the front of the drum machine," Penn said. "Then it would be just as good."

"He has a point, babe," Zeke said, grinning. "Then you can sleep in all day."

"As long as Abbie stays with me, then maybe you guys have a point," Asher said. "We can stay in bed all day and you guys can work."

"I'm having a hard time seeing a downside to that suggestion," I said. Except the fact I was still working at building up my bank account and didn't want to rely on the guys and their money for the rest of my life. They had enough, they wouldn't care, but I did. I had some pride left, and some desire to be independent.

"Exactly," Asher agreed. "Zeke could drop in after work or whenever the band is in town." He sounded like he had it all thought out.

Zeke flopped down beside him. "You'd miss me too much. Both of you. You'd be bored after the first day or two. You thrive on challenge and applause."

"Just because it's true, doesn't mean you should come at me like that," Asher said. "I do like a good challenge. I don't need applause though, I could just download the sound of people clapping onto my phone and listen to that when I need it."

"That might be the saddest fucking thing I've ever heard," Penn said. "Also, it's bullshit. You like a live audience as much as the rest of us do." He crossed his arms over his chest and propped his feet on the seat.

Asher shrugged. "You're the ones who keep threatening me with a drum machine. I'm just trying to put a positive spin on it." Like always, he was clearly not worried about being replaced. It was the kind of running joke that would never die, even when its legs were getting tired.

"Besides, they don't need a keyboard player to sound good either. A decent quality synthesiser would do the trick." Asher made a face at Penn over his shoulder.

Penn responded by making a rude sound in the back of his throat.

"No one is going to replace you," I told him. I wiggled my hips into his groin and winced since my ass still hurt a little from Penn's spanking. If anyone was going to have to walk away when the tour was over, it was me. Not from the guys, they were stuck with me, but I wasn't a part of the band. We had yet to work out that complication. In the scheme of things, especially in the face of potential attack, it wasn't crazy important. We'd figure it out when the time came.

Asher winced too. "Tease. If you keep doing that, I'm going to come in my pants. Then you can explain to everyone why I have a big wet spot there." He twisted around in his seat and pointed at Penn before the keyboard player could say anything. "No, you can't tell them I wet myself."

Penn chuckled. "It would be accurate. Cum is wet."

"Yeah, but I didn't do it to myself," Asher said. "And anyway, they'd assume it's pee." He grimaced.

"You're a rock star, they'd assume it was exactly what it was," Zeke said. "But don't worry, if you need to come, Abbie and I have mouths you can do it in."

Asher groaned. "I knew there was a reason I loved both of you. I'm now the proud owner of a cock which is as hard as a rock." He pressed it against the side of my hip.

"I can feel it." I wriggled against him again, then slid down between him and Zeke. As fun as it was to tease Asher, the drive to the stadium wasn't long enough to ride him the way I liked to. When we arrived, we could find a place. And close the door, to make Jackson happy.

Violet and her guys piled on and the bus pulled away from the curb.

It would be nice to say we wove quickly and easily through Los Angeles traffic, but—it was LA traffic. No one in this city was going to pull over and let our bus pass, any more than they would in Sydney or anywhere else.

"Can you believe we're almost at the end of the tour already?" Asher asked. "It's gone by so quickly. It only seems like it started a couple of days ago."

"It only seems like a couple of days since I walked into the studio and met you guys," I said. And one more since I met Zeke and blew him off under the table without even knowing his name or who he was. If we ever had children, and they wanted to know how we met, we'd have to tell them it was at the label. They probably wouldn't believe the truth anyway.

Also, ewww, parent sex.

"I remember you were about to throw your shoe at Penn's face," Asher said.

"I'm not saying he wouldn't have deserved it," I said. "But that didn't cross my mind at the time. It was more fun to throw insults than shoes." Besides, I might not have gotten my shoe back from him. The way he was back then, he probably would have lobbed it out the window into the street, where it would have got run over by a garbage truck. Or, knowing my luck, an ice cream truck. Or one carrying chocolate and wine. Either way, my shoe would have been fucked and I didn't have the money to replace them.

"It still is," Penn said. "It takes more creativity to come up with an insult than it does to throw a shoe."

"Says the guy who can't throw for nuts," Asher said.

"Throwing inanimate objects is overrated," Penn said.

"As long as you don't say I'm overrated," Asher said.

"Now you mention it," Penn said slowly.

Asher flipped him off.

I turned to Zeke and said, "If I didn't know better, I'd think those two have the hots for each other. The sexual tension between them is off the charts."

"I've noticed that," Zeke agreed. To them he said, "I won't object if you to want two fuck."

"Me either," I said. "But can I watch?" I didn't think it would ever happen, but if it did, I was there for it. The idea of Penn on his knees, Asher's cock in his mouth, licking and sucking, was enough to make me drenched. The idea of Asher calling Penn sir did the same thing.

Hell yes, please. Just when I thought I'd run out of fantasies, there was always more to be had. I was here for that too.

"Absolutely," Asher agreed. "If Penn and I ever fuck, we want you both to be there. Don't we Penn?" He grinned over his shoulder.

"I definitely want everyone to be there," Penn agreed. "Because if that ever happens it's because I'm off my tree and probably need to go to hospital."

"That's a lot of words to say bring it on," Zeke teased.

"I'm starting to think you're as big a dickhead as your boyfriend," Penn said.

"That's not true," Zeke said. "You've known that for a long time."

"You said it, not me," Penn said.

I laughed and shook my head at all three of them. "And I'm starting to think you're all little boys still."

"That's more or less accurate too," Zeke said. "That's why you love us so much."

"Yes it is," I said. I couldn't deny the truth of that. Their love of life and tendency to grab each day by the balls and run with it, was part of their charm. It was addictive too. I'd done more living in the last couple of months than I had in my entire life. I worried less and less what people thought about me and enjoyed myself more and more.

"That and how adorable we are," Asher said.

He went to put an arm around me just as a loud bang sounded from the street outside the bus.

CHAPTER
TEN

ABBIE

THE MANOEUVRE WENT FROM CUDDLING, to shoving me down so my face was on Zeke's lap.

I only had time for a grunt of surprise before Zeke was dragging me down onto the floor between the seats. The rest of the guys were right behind us, pressed around us. We were jolted as the bus slammed to a sudden stop.

"Is everyone all right?" Zeke asked urgently.

"Yeah," Penn said from a metre or two away.

"We're fine," Channing confirmed.

"It was a car backfiring," Tully said. He knelt beside a window and peered out.

"Cars still backfire?" Asher asked.

"Older cars," Tully said. "But given where we are, we can be forgiven for thinking it was something else, even if we weren't expecting trouble." He made a face. "Looks like everyone else made the same assumption."

"Stay down, just in case," Zeke told Asher and I. Keeping to a crouch, Zeke moved over to the window and looked out for himself. "Shit."

Because neither Asher or I were good at being told what to do, we both scooted over behind him and looked out.

Traffic had come to a complete standstill. The door of the car next to us was open as if the driver had climbed out and ran. Same thing happened with several in front of us. Annoying, but a sensible reaction if you think you hear a gunshot.

"I thought I told you to stay down," Zeke growled at us.

"You tell us a lot of things," Penn said, slipping back into his seat. "You expect us to remember all of it?"

"Just the shit that keeps you safe," Zeke said. He got to his feet and scanned the bus, inside and out. "It looks clear, but stay vigilant."

"This traffic isn't going anywhere anytime soon," Jackson said ruefully. "We're only about a mile from the stadium."

"It would be faster to walk," Tully said.

All eyes turned to Zeke. He thought for a moment, then nodded. "As long as we're careful, we should be okay to do that. Rather than sit here on this bus waiting for something to happen."

Jackson nodded. "The driver can make sure the bus gets where it's supposed to go. We'll need it to get back to the hotel later."

"Right." Zeke waved us towards the door. "Let's go. The bus will probably get to the stadium before us anyway."

"Maybe this was all an elaborate plot so the driver could have the bus to himself," Asher said. "Hey, Jackson, did you work with him, to make sure we get more exercise? This is the kind of thing you threaten us with." He narrowed his eyes, accusing but playful at the same time.

"I know I have exceptional organisational skills," Jackson said dryly, "but this is beyond even my abilities. Even if I could be bothered to do it, which I couldn't."

"Of course not," Asher said as if he didn't believe a word, but a smile tugged at the corners of his mouth.

Jackson's brow creased, uncreased, then he rolled his eyes at Asher. "If you don't hurry up, I might stay with the bus and make you stay here to keep me company."

"Now there's a good idea," Zeke said teasingly.

"Best idea I've heard all day," Penn said.

"Sometimes I really feel attacked," Asher said to me. He pouted.

I patted his arm. "Poor baby. Wasn't it you who said you're only nice to people you don't like?"

"I did, didn't I?" He looked more cheerful now. "Anyway, Jackson wouldn't want me to stay with him. He'd rather Abbie stayed." He stepped off the bus and looked at Jackson over his shoulder.

Jackson neither confirmed nor denied the suggestion.

I shrugged at him and followed Asher out, but my eyes lingered on his denim blue ones. Asher was definitely not wrong.

"Okay, everyone—" Zeke started to say, gesturing towards me to walk in the middle of everyone else.

"No," Penn said firmly. "You're going to stay in the middle." He pointed his finger, which was tattooed with an L, at Zeke's chest. "You and Abbie. If anyone is the target here, it's you. Fucked if they're getting past the rest of us."

Zeke raised his hands to either side. "Yes, sir."

Penn's eyebrows twitched. "Huh. That works in all sorts of contexts. I like it. Right, everyone, get into place but look casual like Zeke keeps telling us to. Violet, you guys follow along at a bit of a distance. This doesn't involve any of you."

They looked only too happy to comply with that request, but no one from Blazing Violet called him sir. Penn looked a little disappointed at that, but nodded as Violet and the guys moved away.

"What we could use right now, is a pair of identical twin assholes," Penn said.

"They'd make good decoys," Tully agreed. "They're more likely to come under attack than Zeke and the rest of us, since they're closer to Reuben."

"Yeah," Asher said. "We could stick them out the front and hide behind them. Or better yet, stick great big targets on their backs."

"I like both of those ideas." Anything that kept us safe, I was all for it. Just because we'd agreed to work with the twins didn't mean we liked it, or them.

Personally, I would never forgive them for the things they did to us. Why should I? They were parasites. I wouldn't go as far as to say wanted them dead, but I wouldn't shed any tears either. Same with Reuben. Unfortunately, all three of them were probably like cockroaches—virtually impossible to kill, and often underfoot.

"Let's just not get lost." Zeke glanced at his phone and pointed. "We have to go that way."

We stepped off the street away from the stopped traffic. I glanced over at Jackson's expression as the bus door closed again. He was clearly as uneasy as I was.

Face down, heart in my throat, I followed the guys into the shade of a building.

"Should we be going straight there?" Asher asked. "Jackson might not have engineered this, but someone might have. If that's the case, they'll expect us to walk directly to the stadium."

"They know who we are," Tully said. "They'll expect us to take a different route there. If they planned this, then they planned for every possibility. The best thing we can do, is get the fuck out of the open and into the stadium."

"What Tully said," Zeke agreed. He looked over his shoulder to the bus too. He was obviously as happy with the situation as I was. He must have sensed my anxiety, because he laced his fingers in mine and said, "It'll be okay. We don't have far to go and there are people everywhere."

"You better be right," I said. "Unless you all have some power of invincibility you haven't told me about."

"Not invincibility, just caution." Zeke looked down at me as we walked. "You have it too, I've seen it."

"Yeah, I guess I do," I said. "Hyper vigilance is a symptom of PTSD, isn't it?"

"Something like that," Zeke agreed. A haunted look flashed through his eyes, reminding me I didn't know the half of what he'd been through in his life. We'd have plenty of time to find out if we didn't end up dead in the next couple of weeks. Or hours.

It wasn't just the warmth of the day that made me sweat. The whole situation had me on edge right from the moment I heard the bang. I felt vulnerable and I didn't like it.

"On the up side," Landon said more cheerfully than I'd seen him for the last day or so, "we're in Los Angeles, baby!" He swung his hand between him and Channing and grinned.

"Hell yeah we are, baby," Channing agreed. "I don't know about you guys, but I'm ready to rock the shit out of this town."

"Now that sounds like the best plan I've heard all day," Asher said. "Wolf Venom is here and were going to tear the world apart." He smiled and bowed at a couple of women who stopped to look at us as we walked past.

Specifically, to look at the guys as they walked past. They barely glanced at me.

Once, that would have pissed me off, but I was surrounded by seven hot guys whom I couldn't take my eyes off either. I couldn't expect anyone else to be any different. I could, however, be smug as fuck because all of them were mine. Let them stare, it couldn't do me any harm.

"Well, we were never going to be anonymous walking through Los Angeles," Tully remarked. He waved at a couple of young fans who squealed and took photos, eyes wide with excitement.

"It might be safer if we attract a crowd," Zeke said. "They're less likely to try something if we're surrounded."

"Less likely but not impossible?" I asked tentatively.

"No, not impossible," he agreed. "Idiotic though. They wouldn't get out of here with their butts intact if they did."

"No offence, but I'm more concerned with our butts than theirs," I said dryly.

"I'm more concerned with your butt and Asher's, because they're both so adorable," Zeke said. He slipped his hand out of mine and walked with his arm across my lower back, hand cupping my opposite ass cheek, thumb curled into the top of my skirt.

"Right back at you," I said lightly. I would have liked to enjoy this walk. It was a nice day. Like so many places we'd been to on this tour, I made a note to come back when we weren't so busy and under threat.

That begged the question... "Will there ever come a time when we don't have to look over our shoulders anymore?" It wasn't just this tour, I'd been watching over my shoulder since Vance admitted to marrying me to help his career along. It had become second nature and that wasn't okay.

His fingers squeezed my flesh. "Of course. We've already managed to get

Reuben off our backs and we know we're not being followed by a stalker anymore." He gave a slight nod towards Channing.

"We just need to sort out this last problem and we're golden."

"You make it sound so easy," I said. We both knew it was going to be anything but easy. We could be dead by the end of the week. Or the end of the day. I didn't relish either of those ideas.

"It might not be," he agreed. "But we are us and we will deal with this. We're nothing if not awesome, but we're also skilled, vigilant and we've been warned, which chances are they have no idea about. Even if they do, we have a secret weapon."

"Penn's farts?" Asher suggested. "Those things are pretty deadly."

"He's referring to the way you bore people to death when you talk so much," Penn said over his shoulder. "Maybe we should let them abduct you. You could get rid of them for us."

"Between both of those things, maybe we should let them abduct both of you," Tully said. "They wouldn't stand a chance."

"I wonder if they would tie them to each other," I mused. That conjured up all sorts of fun, mental images.

Zeke grinned. "More likely handcuff them to each other."

"I'd pay to see that," Landon said.

"How much?" Asher asked. "Because if you're gonna pay, I could arrange that."

"No you fucking can't," Penn said. "There isn't enough money for me to put myself through that." After a moment he added, "But just out of curiosity, how much?"

Landon shrugged. "I dunno. A couple of hundred dollars?"

Penn scoffed. "Nowhere near enough. For a couple of hundred million, I'd consider it."

"Everyone has their price," Tully said. "Even Penn."

"Most of us would do a lot of things for a couple of hundred million dollars," I said. What wouldn't I do? Okay, I wouldn't kill for it. I wouldn't... No, that was about the only thing I could think of right now.

Tully stopped and waved for us to do the same. "Something's off," he said.

My heart skipped in my chest.

CHAPTER
ELEVEN

ABBIE

"STAY CLOSE," Zeke said urgently.

He gripped my arm to keep me tight beside him, his hip to mine.

"What is it?" I whispered.

"Hey, there you are," a voice said loudly.

I almost jumped out of my skin. One of the motherfucking evil twins, I think it was Hunter, appeared behind me and clapped a hand on my shoulder.

"Hey, Tully," Penn drawled, "You're right, something is off. Smells worse than my farts."

"You're hilarious," Hunter said sarcastically. He glanced over his shoulder. "Oi, Parker, they're over here."

"No shit," Parker said from right front of me. He grinned when he saw my face snap around in surprise. "Lucky we're not here to attack you," he said as if he was hilariously funny. "None of you saw us coming."

"I think I speak for all of us," Asher started, "when I say none of us wants to see you coming."

I snorted a laugh. "Fuck no."

Penn offered Asher a high five. "Nice burn, dude."

Asher slapped his palm against Penn's and grinned. "I thought so, thanks."

Hunter draped an arm over Parker's shoulders. "Looks like we found the circus, bro."

"Yeah," I agreed. "We were waiting for the clowns, but you just got here."

The guys except for the twins looked impressed.

"Sweetheart, that was awesome," Zeke said. He leaned in for a quick kiss.

"It wasn't bad," Penn said. "I also would have settled for monkeys, performing bears, or freakshow acts."

"You guys should give up music and become stand-up comedians," Parker said, not looking the least bit offended. Unfortunately.

"You guys should give up breathing," Penn said scathingly. "Any number of us would be happy to help you with that."

Hunter clicked his tongue. "Have you already forgotten we have a deal? Because, if you have, we have a deal. You don't get to kill us and we don't get to kill you, or mess with you. Believe it or not, we're here to help. It took us a while to get through customs and find you guys, but here we are. Just a word of advice, you might want to be less predictable. If we found you, then they can."

"And if you hang around with us, they can find you too," Channing pointed out.

The twins exchanged a glance.

"He has a good point," Hunter said to Parker.

Parker shrugged. "Yeah, but a deal is a deal. We wouldn't want anyone to say we go back on our deals, would we?"

"Good to see you've narrowed in on the important things in life," Zeke said.

I couldn't tell if he was being sarcastic or not.

"We're good at doing that," Parker said lightly. "Hey, Abbie, ready for a real man yet?" He looked around Zeke and smiled at her.

"Fuck off," I told him.

I was tempted to tell him I didn't go for clowns, but no doubt they'd turn it into some kind of dig against the other guys.

"I think that's a not yet," Hunter said to Parker. "Give her time, she'll come around."

I grimaced at them. "Only when hell freezes over, asshole."

"The way climate change is going, that's a distinct possibility," Hunter said with a nod. "Until then, we'll wait patiently."

"I'm pretty sure there's a name for guys who come onto a girl when they have a girlfriend," I said.

"There's several of them," Zeke said. "And none of them are nice." He waved for us to get back into the loose formation we were walking in. "Let's keep going."

"I thought I was the general today," Penn said.

Zeke gave him a smirk. "Let's not have an argument over who's in charge. And don't get used to me calling you sir, either."

"Sounds like trouble in paradise," Hunter said, looking amused.

"Why do you care?" Zeke said. "It's not like you're going to replace either of us in the band. Reuben would never allow it." For some reason, he looked cheerful about that. Maybe it was knowing Reuben kept them on a short leash instead of him.

"Do we need a reason to care?" Hunter asked. He turned to Parker and said "I don't think so, do you?"

"As amusing as it is to stand here wasting time," Zeke said, his tone terse, "I'd rather get to the stadium. "Some of us have work to do." He gave the twins a meaningful look.

"Have you failed university yet?" I asked. "You're never there."

"The bitch has teeth," Hunter said. "I like that." He bared his at me.

I flipped him off.

"For the record," Hunter continued, "we're still on holidays. They end just after the tour is over. Isn't that convenient?"

"Almost too convenient," I agreed. I didn't know why they bothered going to school anyway. They had jobs working for Reuben that presumably paid well. They got to travel the world, meet interesting people and kidnap them. What more could anyone want?

"If I didn't know better, I'd think the tour was planned to coincide with the holidays," Hunter mused.

"Not fucking likely," Penn growled. "It wasn't planned for your convenience. It was planned so we could make a shit load of money."

"I thought you already had a shit load of money," Parker said. When Zeke and I started walking, he walked beside me, on the other side.

"A shit load more money," Penn said. "Enough money that we don't have to deal with dickheads like you."

"I hate to break it to you, but there's no amount of money in the world that can keep you from having to deal with people you don't want to deal with," Parker said with no hint of apology.

"Are you speaking from experience?" Tully asked. "You have plenty of money but you still have to deal with your brother Reuben?"

"Not to mention Zeke," Parker agreed. "He used to be fun, when we were kids. Now, he's all about work and telling us to go away. Not very brotherly, is it?"

"Kidnapping my girlfriend twice isn't very brotherly either," Zeke snarled. "Not to mention—" He stopped and took a deep breath. "You know what, it doesn't matter. You know what you did and why I'm pissed off at you pair of degenerate little pricks."

"Because they're degenerate little pricks?" Asher asked.

"Exactly," Zeke nodded in his direction. He pulled his phone out of his pocket and checked the screen. "It's just up ahead around the— Yeah, right there."

Like the average stadium anywhere in the world, this one was hard to miss. It looked like a cross between a low-lying spaceship and a... No, low-lying spaceship was basically it. Just past the stadium, water twinkled in the sunlight.

"You know what I wish?" Landon said wistfully.

"What do you wish, baby?" Channing said.

"I wish you could have that rematch with Penn here and kick his ass," Landon said. He gave Penn a sly look.

Channing sighed. "Me too, baby. Me too."

"In your dreams," Penn said scathingly. "I'd hand your ass to you like I did in Munich."

"Maybe," Channing said. "Maybe not."

"Do you think you could run faster than us?" Parker asked Penn.

Penn didn't break his stride as he looked Parker up and down. "I wouldn't bother. I'd wait until you started running, then walk off in the opposite direction. By the time you figured it out, you'd be a long way from me and I'd be happy."

"Sounds like he thinks he can't beat us," Hunter remarked.

"I can beat you all right," Penn said. "I'd rather use a baseball bat. Or a cricket bat. Or both, one in each hand."

"Has anyone told you you're very hostile?" Parker said lightly. "It can't be good for your blood pressure."

I hooked my fingers around Penn's arm before he rounded on them and actually started swinging. "They're just trying to get a reaction from you."

"It's working," Penn growled. He put a hand over mine and squeezed, probably firmer than he intended.

"When this is over, if you want to spank them, I'm here for it," I told him.

"Now you're talking," he said, his dark expression lifting slightly. "Not spanking them wasn't part of the deal."

"Don't bother," Zeke said. "They'd enjoy themselves too much."

"He's right, you know," Parker said. "We're into all sorts of interesting things, including that. When we were younger, we used to spank each other just to—"

Penn groaned. "Way too much information, dude. We don't want to hear about your kinky shit."

I kind of did. I mean, the mental image of the twins spanking each other was hot in all kinds of the wrong ways. I had to stop thinking about this before my mind went to cocks and mouths.

Oops, too late. Well, my panties were ruined already.

"Shame," Parker said. "I was hoping to hear about all of your kinky shit. I bet Abbie is really wild in bed." He gave me a speculative look.

I smiled back at him. "I absolutely am," I said unashamedly. "Wild like you have no idea. Wild like you're never going to find out."

Parker grinned. "Don't worry, my imagination is pretty healthy and you feature in a lot of my fantasies."

Zeke and Penn growled in unison. Zeke took a step towards his brother.

I grabbed him before he could go too far. "Don't bother. I don't care if he's thinking about me when he's jacking off. That's between him, his hand and his brain."

Parker gave Zeke a smug look.

"Does anyone know if there's a way to climb the top of the stadium?" Asher asked. "You know like, to abseil off it?"

"I don't think so," Zeke said. "Why, babe? You feel like climbing?"

"No, just thinking about where we could throw the twins where they wouldn't bounce," Asher said.

"Okay, fair enough," Zeke nodded. "I don't think we can do it there, unfortunately. Also, they probably would bounce once or twice. I'm all for finding out at some point."

"You first, bro," Hunter said. "If you survive the experience, we'll consider doing it."

"Hard pass," Parker said. "I like my feet either on the ground or on the bed."

"I'm starting to think you two have sex on the brain even more than I do," Landon told him.

"That's saying something," Channing chimed in.

Parker shrugged. "We're nineteen, we're supposed to have sex on the brain. And on the bed. And on the beach. And on the kitchen bench. And—"

"Yeah, we get the idea," Penn said. "Maybe you can shut the fuck up."

"We'll think about it," Hunter said. "In the meantime, Zeke—"

"I've seen them," Zeke said. "They've been following us almost since the bus. Don't look around," he said to me just before I did.

"Who is it?" I wasn't over my unease, but it was a hundred times worse now.

"I dunno, maybe just fans." Zeke didn't look like he believed that himself. "Let's walk a little faster."

We approached the entrance to the stadium, and security waved us in.

"My boss knew you were coming," one of them said. He was about seven feet tall with dark skin covered almost entirely in tattoos. His ears were full of piercings, including an industrial bar across the top of one. He was the kind of guy you might be intimidated by until he smiled. Then, I got the impression he was a gentle giant.

"Thanks, bro." Asher offered him a high five. He winced at what must have been a hard slap by the guard.

"Wait till I tell my kids I met Wolf Venom," the guard said. "Go on in."

Asher shook his hand and we hurried inside.

CHAPTER
TWELVE
CHANNING

"WE SHOULD BE FINE IN HERE," Zeke tried to look as calm and chill as ever, but I knew him better than to think he was actually relaxed. Once in a while, his eyes flicked towards the door.

"There's about a billion people inside the stadium," Landon pointed out."They couldn't do anything without witnesses. Lots of them."

I knew he wasn't that naive. If anything happened to us, it wouldn't go unnoticed for long, but that didn't mean it couldn't happen. Just because the security guard outside the door looked nice, didn't mean he wasn't on the Fiorelli payroll. Cleaners could pop up in toilets or someone could poison the sandwiches in the green room.

In spite of that, I said, "You're right, baby. Let's focus on the sound check."

"I thought this place would be more impressive," Hunter said, looking around the backstage area. "I suppose the stage is."

"You're not gonna get to find out," Zeke said. He grabbed Hunter's arm and pulled him aside. Whatever he said in his brother's ear, Hunter wasn't happy about it.

He sighed loudly and said, "If I have to. Come on, Park—"

"Just you," Zeke told him. "Parker can stay here with us. It's not healthy for you to spend all of your time with each other."

Both twins looked like they wanted to strenuously object, but Hunter nodded.

"Fine, I won't be long. Make sure security knows to let me back in." He strode out of the green room like he owned the place.

"I have a better idea," Penn said. "How about we tell security he can't come back in?"

I didn't always agree with Penn, but in this case I did. I'd spent enough time working with those shitheads, or trying to make them think I was working with them. They were useful up to a point. Most people wouldn't know how to get rid of human remains. The fact only they knew what they'd done with them and could put that over my head at any time made me nervous. If I hadn't agreed not to kill them, I would seriously consider it. What the fuck use were they anyway? I would have figured out something without their help if I had to.

"Did someone mention sound check?" Tully said cheerfully. "That sounds good to me."

"I'll go and see if they're ready for you," Jackson said. He glanced at Abbie, his gaze lingering a little too long, before he turned and hurried toward the stage.

"Did you finish the song you were writing?" Abbie asked as we slowly walked together towards the stage.

I looked over at her. I didn't know who I wanted to gobble up first, her or Landon. They both set my blood on fire like nobody else.

I smiled. "Not yet. I can't find a word to rhyme with threesome."

She glanced back at me like she wasn't sure if I was joking or not. "That is a difficult word to rhyme with. I'm guessing wholesome isn't the angle you're going for."

"I'm going for a bunch of angles, but not that one," I agreed. Angles, positions, I had a few of them in mind. All of them involved her and Landon. The other guys could watch and learn.

"I remember when touring used to be stressful," Landon said.

"You don't find this stressful?" I asked him.

He looked over at me and blinked. "Yes. No. I mean, I'm remember when the touring part was stressful. Now it's all the other shit. Although, there's still a threat of bees and tornadoes." He grinned at me.

I groaned softly and rolled my eyes. "It could still happen." And I was still freaked out by bees. That whole conversation felt like it took place months ago. I let my insecurity get the better of me, scared Landon would leave me for Abbie.

Yeah, okay, there was still a voice in the back of my head that had the same concern. He was sweet, and in some ways a lot more innocent than me. When we met, he was a lot more innocent. Sometimes, I blamed myself for stealing that from him. Then I remembered, the world would have done it anyway and I needed him by my side. He was the spoonful of sweetener in a bitter coffee.

"You don't like bees?" Abbie asked.

"I like what they do for the planet," I said. "But I'll stay out of their hive if they stay out of mine."

"I have the same philosophy about sharks," she said.

"I could be wrong, but I don't think sharks have hives," Landon said jokingly.

We both made a face at him and laughed.

"Honestly, a hive of sharks sounds terrifying," she said. "How would you get the honey?"

I stopped and grabbed her arm in one hand and Landon's in the other.

"Like this." I lowered my mouth to hers and kissed her long and deep before doing the same to Landon.

"Nothing could be sweeter," I said softly.

"You're going to make us jealous," Asher remarked.

All of the guys stopped to wait and watch.

"Do you want me to kiss you?" I asked him.

"I would, but then Zeke would be jealous," he said easily.

"Yes, I would," Zeke said, but his tone suggested otherwise.

I didn't think a relationship beyond friendship was in the cards for Asher and I, but if it was, I doubted it would bother Zeke too much, as long as we communicated. For that matter, I didn't think Landon would mind, if he got to take part as always.

Ever since we met, he'd been all about making me happy, and doing whatever it took to for us stay together. Sometimes, that was his insecurity talking, his fear that I would leave, but I got it. It took time for him to understand I was never, ever going to walk away from him, but every moment of that was worth it.

Landon was, and always would be, my person.

"I don't object if you guys spend more time together," Penn said. "You can even take Tully with you if you like."

Because I knew him too well by now, I said, "Here's where you say we should leave Abbie behind, but it's not gonna happen, dude."

Penn shrugged as though he hadn't just been called out. "A guy can hope." He continued the walk down the corridor as a woman who worked for the stadium beckoned us forward.

She was lucky she only saw us standing there. If we were there much longer, she would have seen someone fucking someone up against the wall.

"A guy can be an arrogant pain in the ass too," I said.

"Yes, you can," Penn said over his shoulder.

Shame he had his back to me, he didn't see me stick my finger up at him. No doubt he felt it. The guy could be such an asshole sometimes.

I have to admit, I was conflicted over the way he treated Abbie when they first met. On one hand, I wanted to do everything I could to protect her. On the other hand, he was my brother. I wouldn't have killed him, but I thought about scaring him a little bit. In the end, I decided against it because I saw the way he felt about her, and knew he'd come around eventually. Waiting for that to happen almost killed *me*, but he got there in the end.

Lucky for him.

"Hey, that's not nice," Parker said to us both. "You guys can be so mean to each other."

"Thanks," Asher said, "but we don't need your permission."

I snorted a laugh, then snorted again at the expression on Parker's face.

"That wasn't what I was saying." He frowned.

"No one gives a fuck what you're saying." I wished he would fuck the fucking fuck off and never come back.

That night in Frankfurt, I had seriously considered killing them both. Part of me regretted telling Zeke I was meeting them. In the end, I had no choice, he'd figured out I was up to something. Either way, he would have followed me. Same with Landon, Abbie and Jackson too.

Everything would have been a thousand times messier than it already was. Messy enough that it was worth putting up with the twins to avoid it. For now. The sooner they were out of our hair, the better.

"Hunter does," Parker said.

"Are you sure about that?" Abbie asked. "I mean, he might put up with you because you're twins. Or out of habit. Or because Reuben told him to."

"No wonder you hang out with these guys," Parker told her. "You're as mean as they are." He didn't look particularly offended.

"What does that say about you, then?" she asked him. "You've followed us around since before the tour began. What is it they say? Birds of a feather —"

"Fuck together," he finished for her and grinned.

"*Flock* together," she said firmly.

"You really should finish that degree, bro," I told him.

"Bro," Parker said to me, looking down his nose. "I'm not studying English literature."

"No, you're learning advanced stalking," I said. "This is your practical component."

Parker laughed. "You're hilarious."

"I'm not that far wrong," I said.

Abbie gave me a funny look.

"He goes to Brutham Academy," I told her. "Most of the students there have families like ours. They call it Brutal Academy. It's the only university in Australia where the mortality rate is higher than the dropout rate."

Her eyes widened. "That's where Asher's brother Dane works?" she asked.

"The very same," Asher agreed. "I almost went there but then I realised something. I didn't want to." He smiled with his mouth closed, all sarcasm.

"Same here," Zeke said with a rueful look and a nod. "Dad and Reuben both tried to get me to go, but I declined politely."

I took that to mean he told them to fuck off. Considering the suggestion, that was an appropriate response as far as I was concerned.

"You don't know what you're missing," Parker said.

"The students really die?" Abbie asked me.

"Yes, they do," Parker said before I could reply. "Every year before the end of the second semester, the Academy likes to test students' skills. Things have been known to get ugly."

"How is that allowed?" Abbie asked.

"When you have money and connections, everything is allowed," I said. "Bribe the right people and they'll turn a blind eye to anything. Even exam month at Brutham Academy."

"So there's a chance you and Hunter might die before you graduate?" Abbie asked. Both of her perfectly shaped eyebrows rose and I swear her blue eyes became a brighter shade.

"It's a very slim possibility, but you don't need to look so hopeful," Parker said. Now he looked offended.

"I speak for all of us when I say we're definitely hopeful," Penn said. He glanced back and gave us a meaningful look before stepping out to the stage where a bunch of people stood, watching and waiting.

His silent condemnation had a point. We should probably not talk about the Academy in front of other people. For some reason, regular people didn't understand. Yeah, okay, neither did I. Sure, families wanted their kids to be the best of the best, but to die because they weren't? That seemed tiny bit extreme to me.

As everyone filed onto the stage, I managed to grab Zeke's attention.

"Where did you send Hunter?" I asked him quickly.

He glanced at me over his shoulder. "To go and look for any sign of trouble. If anyone can find it, it's him."

"Right," I said softly. He wasn't wrong about that. The twins seemed to be attracted to trouble like they wanted to fuck it. Or they were the cause of it. Either way, trouble was both of their middle names. That and Prick from Hell.

I trotted up the steps and tried to focus on the job ahead: sounding fucking awesome for tonight's audience.

CHAPTER
THIRTEEN
ABBIE

"G'DAY," Zeke said into the microphone. "How's it going today? Thanks for coming out." It was only the sound check, but his accent was stronger than usual.

For some reason, Americans seemed to like Australians, so he might have done it consciously for that reason. Either way, it was kinda cute, although I'd never heard him say g'day before.

The handful of stadium staff who gathered around to watch clapped, and a couple cheered. It must be fun to work in a place where you got to live these moments once in a while. Most of them would probably come back tonight for the concert, but they got this for themselves.

"We're from a little island down south a ways. You might know it." Zeke grinned at Penn as the keyboardist rolled his eyes at him.

"He's laying it on a bit thick," Jackson said. He stood beside me, leaning against the wall.

"They seem to be eating it up," I said. Here we go again, tripping over innuendos.

Jackson cleared his throat. "Yeah. Zeke always has a way of knowing what the crowd likes. It's one of the things that makes him such a good lead singer."

"It is," I agreed. "Maybe I should speak with a broader accent tonight?" I looked up at him questioningly.

He looked down at me and smiled. "Just be yourself. That's plenty."

My heart skipped a beat like it was jumping a rope. It really was impossible not to adore him.

"You think so?" I asked.

His gaze lingered on mine. That look conveyed so much, without him saying a word.

"Yes, I think so," he said, his voice low but firm. "You live life unapologetically. There's no reason to change that now."

I was surprised for a moment but then I nodded. "I do, don't I?" Okay, there were moments there when I wanted to hide from the world, but we all had those. Right?

"More than anyone else I have ever met," he said. "With the possible exception of Asher. I don't think he's held back a day in his life."

"Only when it came to his feelings for Zeke," I agreed. "But that was more about him waiting patiently and coming to a realisation, than holding back. Did you know there was something between them before they did?"

Jackson chuckled. "Only from the first time I met them. I was starting to think I was wrong, but I guess I wasn't. Like I said to you once before, you helped them to connect. If not for you, they'd probably still be nothing more than best mates."

I waved a hand dismissively. "They would have figured it out."

The clash of Asher's drums echoed through the stadium. Landon was half a beat behind, but he quickly caught up. The rest of the instruments followed.

It wasn't like Landon to be off like that, but we were all under a lot of pressure. The audience wouldn't have noticed anyway, especially with them cheering and screaming. Knowing Landon, he'd beat himself up over it, but we'd help him through it. No one ever said musicians weren't temperamental as fuck. We all were, but we got each other. Most of the time.

"They might," Jackson agreed. "Sometimes it takes time to see what's in front of you." He was looking at me again.

I looked at him and swallowed. "Yeah, it does."

He leaned down to brush his lips lightly over mine. It was barely more than a graze, but it set my heart racing and made my knees weak. He tasted of coffee and something I couldn't put my finger on. Maybe with a longer kiss, I could work it out.

He straightened and leaned back against the wall as though nothing happened.

I waited, catching my breath and giving him time to gather his thoughts.

After a minute or two, he said, "I'm sorry should I have—"

"Done that sooner?" I asked, knowing that wasn't what he was implying. "Probably."

"It could complicate a lot of things," he said.

"Then we'll deal with it like we deal with everything else," I said firmly.

"With sex and alcohol?" he teased. The lines around his eye crinkled.

I laughed. "I see nothing wrong with that." I leaned against him and he placed a hand under the back of my neck, under my hair. Nothing about this felt strange at all. I'd stood like this with all the other guys dozens of times in the last couple of months. To do it now, with Jackson, felt natural and right.

"Don't tell me, you're going to have to tell Levi." I was only half-joking.

"At some point," he admitted. "Let's see where this goes first. The guys might..."

"They already know," I said. "And they're fine with it. I mean, I told them how I felt about you. I wasn't assuming anything."

"I guessed," he said quickly. "You would have assumed right. I cared about you the moment we met. Actually, before that. Would you believe I've been to a couple of your concerts with some friends?"

For some reason, I found myself blushing. "You did? Wait, did you say a couple? As in more than one?"

He grinned. "Does it surprise you so much? You're talented and gorgeous. You had fans before all the things that happened at Onyx Riot. I happened to be one of them. When Levi mentioned wanting to sign you, I might have encouraged him."

"Right," I said slowly. "So everything that happened after that is all your fault." I poked him playfully in the chest with a bright pink fingernail.

"Yes," he said ironically. "None of that had anything to do with those outside influences. It was all me."

"You would never do any of those things," I said. "You're a good guy."

He shot me a lopsided smile. "Not a very professional one right now."

"The heart wants what the heart wants," I said.

"Yes, it certainly does," he agreed. "Seeing you in concert, I never would have thought— I mean, of course not. That would be presumptuous."

"Sometimes fantasies come true." I had fantasised about this very moment a few times myself. Yes, even with six other guys keeping me busy, there was time for fantasies. What was the fun in life if you couldn't daydream once in a while?

"I'll be the first to admit I didn't think it would turn out like this," he said. "As soon as Zeke took an interest in you, I figured that was that. Being your manager, anyway, it was safer to step back and try not to think too hard about you. But then, you have a way of getting under people's skin and into their hearts. I can't say I resisted too strongly."

He paused for a moment before he continued. "Then with everything else going on, I wondered why I was resisting at all. Life is usually short. Lately, it seems like... Like if we don't grab hold now, we may lose our chance. I didn't want that to happen. For the record, I wouldn't do what Channing did, but there's a lot I would do for you. For the guys too. We might be the weirdest family, but we're still a family. One I happen to be attached to. No matter what might happen. I'll take this over a desk job any day."

"Is Levi going to be pissed?" I asked. "Does he really have a girlfriend?"

"Probably not, and yes," Jackson said. "He'll be pissed if I screw you over, and her name is Charlotte. She is a lovely woman but I don't think she is going to end up with seven partners."

"Not everyone is the sharing type," I said. "So no screwing me over, hmmm? What about screwing me?"

His face turned slightly pink. "I don't think we should rush, but…"

That was all the response I needed. If he was one of the other guys, I might have dragged him away to some quiet place in the stadium and fucked his brains out. But he wasn't one of the other guys.

"How are you single?" I asked without thinking.

"Am I single?" he asked with one eyebrow raised. He must have realised he put me on the spot, because he said, "That's a conversation for later." He stroked his thumb over the back of my neck. "I was married once and it didn't work out. Ever since then I've focused on work. Until you came along and turned everything upside down and inside out."

"Sorry, not sorry," I said lightly. He seemed sad, remembering her. Whoever she was, she must have been amazing to have caught his attention, even if it wasn't meant to be. He was an extraordinary guy.

As for turning his life upside down… I seemed to have a knack for that.

"You certainly have nothing to be sorry for," he said. "We could all use a shakeup. Wouldn't want the boys to get stale, would we?"

I snorted. I doubted that would happen. "No way," I agreed.

"It's time for you to go out there and sing with Zeke," he said with a touch of reluctance.

I felt that a little bit myself. It wasn't how I pictured having this conversation, but I felt better for having had it. It was like the last piece of the puzzle fell into place. I might have also liked the fact we were now an even eight.

"Yes, boss," I said with a cheeky grin.

He gave me a heated look. "Be careful, I might get used to hearing you call me that."

I didn't need to look down to know I would see a tent in front of his pants. I totally caught the same vibe.

"I don't have a problem with that." I brushed my lips over his. In heels, we were almost the same height. Close enough for me to look into his pretty eyes.

"Me either." He patted my ass and gave me a gentle shove towards the stage.

"All right then, boss," I said grinning over my shoulder. I barely heard him groan before I trotted up the steps and onto the stage.

Zeke caught my expression and gave me an amused smile.

"Welcome back to the stage," he said, his accent still broad.

"Thanks, mate," I said as I grabbed myself a microphone. "It's fair dinkum, bloody awesome to be here, ay?"

Zeke burst out laughing. "Yeah, mate. It's the bloody roo's pyjamas."

"Wouldn't that be a pouch?" I asked.

Zeke shrugged. "Crikey, you might be right."

I shook my head at him.

Tully grinned over the top of his hot pink guitar.

In the corner of my eye, I caught Penn cringing. Apparently not everyone appreciated our attempts to embrace our Aussie culture.

You can't please everyone.

Zeke and I started to sing "Take Me down Lower", while around a hundred stadium staff danced in front of the stage

Outside the front of the stadium, fans were probably doing the same thing. It was the perfect day for it, if it wasn't for everything else that was going on. Right now, that seemed like a million kilometres away.

I spied Jackson as he walked around from backstage to the front of it. He stayed back from the crowd until a man in a stadium uniform came over to speak to him. Whatever it was the man said, Jackson didn't look too worried. He nodded and gestured before following the man out of sight.

Presumably the bus finally turned up. Thank fuck for that. I didn't relish the idea of walking all the way back to the hotel. Not that we would, since taxis and ride shares were a thing. Still, most of those didn't fit eight of us and five of Blazing Violet. And a stray twin or two.

Parker sat in a seat off to the side, elevated for a good view of the stage. There was no sign of Hunter. What had Zeke sent him to do? I was sure I would find out soon enough. For all I knew, he sent his brother to get some chocolate. If he was going to hang around, then he might as well be useful. And what could be more useful than getting food?

We finished the song and launched into "Bump in the Night". I was pretty well acquainted with both songs before the tour, but I'd sung them so many times now I knew them as well as I knew any of my own music. Singing with Zeke was a different experience from singing by myself though. We complimented each other so well on and off stage. Like Tully would say, the universe made us all for each other and now we'd found each other.

I just hoped we weren't about to lose each other.

CHAPTER
FOURTEEN

ABBIE

"WHERE IS HE?" I glanced around the room and at my phone for the millionth time. "I haven't seen Jackson since sound check." I thought he'd be waiting for us backstage, but he wasn't. We'd decided to wait in the green room for him but he hadn't shown up yet. That was out of character for him. He wasn't our shadow but he was never far away, especially on concert day.

"Yeah." Channing leaned over to look at the screen too. "He was right there near the stage, then he walked off with some guy in a stadium uniform."

"The bus must have turned up," Zeke said, airing my initial thoughts. "But he should be here by now." He looked as worried as I felt.

I glanced at my phone again. Only a minute had passed. I sighed, then looked over at Zeke, who was draped over a chair, his ankle resting on his opposite knee.

"I'm gonna call Jackson and see where he is." He pulled out his phone and tapped at the screen. He frowned until Jackson's voice came through the line.

"Jackson," Zeke said, his phone to his ear. "Where the hell are you?" He frowned. "Oh, that sucks."

"What?" I mouthed at him.

He waved me to silence. "Well, you should have Hunter there to help you." He listened for a moment. "What do you mean he's not there?"

I sat up in my chair. "What the fuck?"

Zeke waved at me again.

I gave him a dark look, but sat in silence and listened.

"Okay, well where are you then? We can come to— What is that?" Zeke frowned. "Jackson? Jackson?" He pulled the phone away from his face and looked at the screen. "He hung up. Or the call cut out."

"Where is he?" My heart was thundering through my chest. "What did he say?"

"He said the bus broke down," Zeke said evenly. "Hunter never found the bus. I sent him to make sure it got here." He looked at Parker accusingly.

"That was what I was going to tell you," Parker said. "When he got back to the bus, it wasn't there. He couldn't find it."

"How well does anyone know the bus driver?" Channing asked softly.

"More importantly, what happened to Jackson?" Landon asked.

"Oh my god," I whispered, barely willing or able to voice the words. "You heard something, didn't you? What was it?"

"I don't know," Zeke admitted. "It sounded like a... I don't know, a muffled bang."

"Like a shot from a silencer?" Asher asked.

Zeke glanced towards the bright green carpet on the floor. "Kinda like that, yeah. I can't be sure what it was though. It might be unrelated. Just a random sound in the background."

My heart sank. I swallowed hard. "But you think it was a gunshot, don't you?"

He looked back up. "Yeah, it sounded like that. But let's not jump to conclusions, okay? It could have been anything. It might have had nothing to do with Jackson. He probably ducked, that's why the call ended. He could have—" He shook his head. "I'll try him again." He tapped at the screen and waited, a frown on his face. In spite of telling us not to worry, he obviously was.

So was I. The sound could have been nothing, but it could have been something. Everything. I held my breath and hoped like hell Jackson was okay.

The call ended without being answered.

"Shit," Zeke said softly. He glanced sharply at Parker. "Where the fuck is Hunter?"

"And why the hell didn't you tell us sooner that he hadn't found the bus?" Penn demanded. "And don't say because we didn't ask, or I will rip your motherfucking head off and use it to shoot hoops. Hoops made from your intestines."

"And I'll help," Asher said. "I've always been good at basketball."

Parker shrugged. "Because he's still trying. You guys were busy and I didn't see any point worrying you."

"Too fucking late," Tully said coldly. He looked like he wanted to use his ninja skills on Parker.

I didn't think any of us would stop him. Although, could intestines stiffen enough to be used as a hoop? No, I didn't want the answer to that.

"We need to find Jackson," Landon said. He looked like he was about ready to freak out. "The guy in uniform, he didn't really work for the stadium, did he?"

Channing put a hand on his bicep, and his arm around him, and gave him a squeeze. "We will find him." He sounded so certain it gave me a small spike of hope.

"He can't have gotten far," I said uncertainly. Channing was right, none of us knew the worker.

"Has it occurred to anyone this is a trick to get us to go somewhere?" Penn said.

"Of course it has," Zeke said. "But I'm prepared to take the risk. We're going to find him and he's going to be fine." Failing at this wasn't an option. But if it was, if anything happened to Jackson, heads would roll. Zeke would spill blood. Shit would get ugly.

"Where do we even begin to look?" I asked.

LA was huge. Even a bus with White Wolf Records written down the side in big letters could be just about anywhere.

Zeke gave me a lopsided smile. "The same way we found your phone in Perth."

"You put a tracker on Jackson's phone," Asher said. He rubbed his hands together and looked gleeful.

"I had to insist, but yes, I did," Zeke said. "He was resistant to the idea, but I didn't give him any choice." He started tapping at his phone again.

"Zeke made me give him his phone so he could put one on mine too." Penn scowled at the lead singer.

Without looking up, Zeke said, "After what the evil twins did to you, I wasn't taking any chances. But it only works if you take your phone with you when you go places."

"You're a bossy asshole, you know that?" Penn asked him.

Zeke glanced up and grinned. "Hell yeah I am. You should be calling *me* sir."

Penn snorted. "Fuck that."

"That's lame," Parker remarked.

We tried to ignore him, but one by one our gazes turned to him.

The asshole looked as smug as shit.

"What's lame?" Channing snapped.

"Needing a tracker to find people," Parker said.

"You have a better method?" The saxophonist asked. Channing looked interested in spite of himself.

I have to admit, I was curious myself. What sort of skills did these kinds of people actually have?

Parker rolled his eyes. "Of course I do," he said. "But I'm not going to tell you because none of you are interested in joining, or rejoining, the family."

"Where did you put it?" I asked.

He looked at me with his eyebrows half-mast. "I could take that so many ways, beautiful girl, but I'm going to have to ask what you mean specifically."

"The tracker," I said insistently. "Because you're full of shit, and I was unconscious in your company for fuck knows how long. You assholes put one somewhere on me, didn't you?" The idea was disgusting enough to make me physically ill.

Zeke squinted at me. "It's not your phone. There is only room for one in there and it's mine. It's still active." His eyes went to my ears.

Trying not to panic, I put my hands on my earrings and jerked in my seat.

The back of one of them was chunkier than the back of another.

Faster than I ever did anything before in my life, I undid the earring and pulled it out of my lobe. I held it in the palm of my hand. I had to squint, but something was definitely attached to my silver, heart-shaped earring.

"Fucking hell, you piece of shit—" My face hot with anger, I glared at Parker like I might skin him with my eyes. Knowing they did that while I was unconscious, I felt violated all over again, sick to my stomach.

"Here, let me," Zeke said. He reached over and plucked the earring out of my hand. He squinted at it, then rose and took it out to the corridor, where the floor was hard linoleum. He dropped the earring on the floor and ground down on it with the heel of his shoe.

The crunch of the tracker breaking was satisfying. More so than seeing Zeke destroy my poor earring.

"My grandmother gave me those," I said sadly. They were nothing fancy but they had a lot of sentimental value.

"I'll buy you a new pair," said Tully and Asher at the same time.

I looked over at them and smiled. "That's sweet." No doubt I would be inundated with earrings any moment now, but it wasn't quite the same since my grandmother died a few years ago. It was the thought that counted, I supposed. The guys were sweet like that.

"It's a shame you don't have a clit piercing," Parker remarked. "That would have been more fun to put a tracker in."

No one moved fast enough to stop Penn before he leapt up and drove his fist into Parker's face. The crunch of bone and spray of blood was almost as satisfying as the tracker breaking.

Parker let out a cry of pain and threw a hand up over his nose.

Penn swore under his breath and shook out his fist. "There, now we'll be able to tell you two apart easier. You'll be the one with the crooked nose." He looked around at all of us. "Sorry, did someone else want to do that?"

"Only all of us," Tully said. "But we wouldn't want to deprive you of the privilege."

Penn gave him a smile and a shrug and rubbed his fist with his other hand. No doubt Parker's face was as hard as it looked.

"As much fun as this is, shouldn't we be looking for Jackson?" Channing asked. He looked satisfied at the sight of blood dripping onto Parker's shirt. The sides of his mouth turned up.

"Yes, we should." Zeke looked back at his phone screen. "The tracker is narrowing it down, but there's a lot of interference from," he waved his hand vaguely, "city shit."

"City shit is the worst," Landon agreed. He managed a lopsided smile in spite of the edge of fear in his eyes. He was anxious at the best of times, and this was not of the best of times.

Parker muttered something, but the words were muffled by the hem of his shirt, which he'd pulled up to dab at his nose.

"No one cares," Penn snarled at him. "Unless you have something useful to say, then shut the fuck up or I'll shut you up."

Parker held up a hand in surrender.

Honestly, I was glad Penn punched him. If he hadn't, I might have. I was going to have nightmares about trackers, and the twins touching me. The thought of what they might have done, and the fact they knew I didn't have a clit piercing, was bad enough. Unless it was a lucky guess. I wanted to believe that, but we didn't call them the evil twins for nothing.

"All in favour of Penn shutting Parker up?" Asher raised his hand. At the same time, he stood. He had his usual smile on his face, but worry in his eyes.

We all raised our hands, but our eyes were on Zeke, waiting for him to give the word. About finding Jackson, not about Penn shutting Parker up. At least, that's what I thought we were waiting for. We might have been waiting for both. I mean, that would be fair enough, but not the priority right now. Maybe later.

He shook his head. "It's narrowed down to a block or two radius. There's too much interference to get a fix on wherever his phone is. Even then, we have to hope he's near his phone."

"This is why trackers in piercings are so much more reliable," Parker said. He ducked away from Penn, who loomed over him. "What? That's useful information. I bet Zeke will do that from now on."

"Be quiet, or I'll shove one up your ass," Zeke snapped. He raised his eyes slightly and made a face. "On second thought, no I won't. I don't need my hand anywhere near your ass." He stood reluctantly. "We'll have to try looking in the area and hope to find him. Come on."

We followed him out the door and down the corridor. Everyone fell into their usual formation, around me. Tully slipped a hand into one of mine and Asher took the other. Usually, that would give me all the comfort I needed, but today…

Today I wouldn't relax until I saw Jackson, alive and well, with my own eyes.

CHAPTER
FIFTEEN

CHANNING

"JOIN A BAND, they said. It will be fun, they said." I glanced at Landon, who walked beside me. We'd taken up the spot behind Abbie and the other guys.

Parker trailed behind us like a bad smell, dressed in a clean shirt he grabbed from someone in the stadium. He managed to wipe most of the blood off his face, but his nose was swollen. It looked painful.

Good, he deserved it. That and more.

"You're not having fun?" Landon asked. He clearly wasn't either, but he managed to cling to some of his good humour.

"To be honest with you," I said slowly, "I thought we might spend more time playing music and less time running around trying to find people while avoiding being attacked."

If I'd known how this would go, I would have taken the time to kill a few Fiorellis before we left Australia. We could be enjoying our time in LA right now. We could be having lunch in a nice little restaurant by the water. Maybe a couple of beers. We could go swimming in the hotel pool.

But no, I had to go and leave them alive to fuck with us, didn't I?

Yeah okay, I didn't know, but if I had I would have dealt with it. Hell, I would have contended with Zeke and Asher who also would have tried to deal with it, if they knew.

Tully too maybe, even though he hated killing and violence. In spite of that, I'm pretty sure he enjoyed watching Penn punch Parker as much as the rest of us had.

"If you look up, 'rockstar,' on the Internet, you'll probably find it involves a lot of playing music," Landon agreed. "And a bunch of interviews, writing songs, recording songs and shit like that. But we're Wolf Venom, we like to change things up."

"We're pretty good at fucking things up too," Asher said over his shoulder.

"Speak for yourself," Penn said.

"I always do," Asher said lightly. "Are we close?" He looked over Zeke's shoulder at the phone screen.

"Closeish," Zeke said. "Keep your eyes open. And before anyone says it, I know we're being followed." He said all of that in the same tone of voice, so I almost missed the last bit.

"Yeah, Parker is behind us," Asher said. He grinned, but clearly knew what Zeke was referring to.

"As long as he stays between us and them." I looked back and gave Parker a dirty look. Let him be killed. I wouldn't lose any sleep over it. In fact, I might throw a party. Was that morbid? Absolutely. Did I give a shit? Hell no. Bring it on.

He smiled at me and waved. "Just in case anyone was in any doubt, I'm not going to die for any of you."

"That remains to be seen," I said darkly. "Sometimes shit happens. Don't worry, we'll make it look like an accident."

Landon looked at me sharply, but I wasn't joking. We had a deal not to kill the twins, but that didn't mean I had to save them if trouble came knocking at their door. I wouldn't rule out cheering their attackers on, before we got the hell out of there.

"Channing," Landon started.

"Don't worry, I'm not going to do anything unless I have to," I assured him.

"I know," he said quickly. "Don't leave us behind this time. We're all in this together. Okay?"

I draped an arm over his shoulders and gave him a sideways squeeze. "Yes, yes we are." I managed a glance back, wide-eyed and looking around like a tourist who was amazed at finding himself in Los Angeles. Yep, we were definitely being followed. They weren't even being subtle about it.

"I get the feeling we're being herded," I said. Like lambs to the slaughter.

"Funny, I get the same feeling," Asher said, not sounding amused.

"So do I." Parker walked closer to the rest of us. "Remember, I'm more of a target than most of you are."

"That's true," I said. "Maybe we should split up. Parker can go one way and the rest of us will go another."

"If I trusted him, I would do that," Zeke said. "I can't rule out the possibility he's involved."

"Come again?" Parker asked. He shook his head and stared at Zeke. He seemed genuinely confused.

"Hunter went looking for the bus, and any potential attackers, and now it and Jackson are missing," Zeke said. "Your girlfriend is from a family that hates ours. You could easily switch allegiance and work against Reuben." He looked at his youngest brother through narrowed, accusing eyes.

"Would that be a bad thing?" Abbie asked. "If Reuben was out of the way, maybe the Bell and Brantley family would get along. They might make peace with the Fiorelli family, then everyone can live happily ever after."

"This isn't a fairytale," Zeke told her. "If they killed Reuben, Caleb would take over. And Joshua after him. Then Lucas after that. By the time they got down to him there would be blood in the streets."

"Unless they took all of them out once," Asher said. He sounded as if he liked the idea.

"Unless that," Zeke agreed. "That would still leave the twins as head of the family."

"Technically, Hunter would be the head," Parker said. "Since he managed to sneak out five minutes ahead of me. Right now, I'm struggling to see a downside to this."

"The downside is you're an asshole," Penn said. "The world doesn't need to give you any more power."

"The world doesn't get to decide," Parker said. "But now the idea is out there, it's something to think about."

"You would never do it," Asher said. "For one thing, it would mean you have to think for yourselves. Two minutes of that and your brains would implode."

"That's hilarious," Parker said dryly. "For the record, we're not working against Reuben."

"Yet," I said. Give it time, they would likely turn on him eventually. He had that way of being an absolute asshole. If I was related to him, I'd probably turn on him too. "I don't know why the Fiorelli family is bothering. They could sit back and watch you all kill each other."

"I'll bring the popcorn," Penn said.

"I'll bring the beer," Asher said. "And vodka for Abbie."

"That's so thoughtful of you," she said. "I'll wear my best little black dress."

"And the black lace bra and panties I like so much?" Asher asked her.

"Sure," she said lightly. "Or better yet, I could wear none."

"None works for me," Asher said. He slid a hand over her perky little ass.

"You know what would suck?" Abbie said.

"Apart from your mouth?" Asher asked.

"Apart from that," she agreed. "What would suck would be if the Fiorellis killed one of us, when their mission statement is actually not so bad when you think about it. Obviously not the part where they want to kill Zeke too, but the rest of it. I mean, they kind of have a point."

"You're only saying that because you haven't met any Fiorellis," Parker said.

"Or Bells," Asher said. "If you think the Brantleys suck, you ain't seen nothin'."

"The Bells aren't so bad," Parker muttered.

"All I know," Abbie said slowly, "is I've never been kidnapped by anyone from either of those other families. Or anyone with the last name DiMarco." She nodded towards Asher.

"You're welcome," Asher said. "My family has never been into kidnapping. We're more the ones who arranged transport, disposed of evidence and shit like that. We still are, I guess. We also have some renowned assassins in the family. Which I can't tell you about, because, you know, assassins."

"Yeah, I get it," she agreed. "Things don't stay a secret if you talk about them."

"Exactly." He nodded.

I half-listened to the conversation after that. The rest of my attention was on the people following us and the fact we were so good at seeming normal in spite of the fact our manager might be dead right now.

If he was, I was going to blame myself for it. We would all blame ourselves.

It wasn't just his growing relationship with Abbie, or the way he took care of us. He and Levi saw a rough group of guys and knew what we could become. They might say we would have made it anyway, but I didn't believe that. Their faith in us and their ability to nurture talent was what got us through.

From day one, Jackson knew how to handle Landon's insecurities, and my inability to keep still. He took no shit from us, but gave none back. He had a way of getting us to do what he wanted, most of the time, without having to bully or be a dickhead.

As the kind of kid who always got in trouble at school, it would be an understatement to say I had no respect for authority. Until Jackson. He taught me that you can have authority and not feel the need to step on people.

"What are you thinking?" Landon asked.

"I was thinking how lucky we are," I said. "Jackson and Levi have been good to us, you know?"

"Yeah, I know," Landon said softly. "I...don't want anything bad to happen to Jackson."

"Jackson is not going to leave you," I said firmly. "No more than I am. You're stuck with him and the rest of us. Okay, baby?"

I heard him swallow.

"I hope so," he whispered. "When this is over, will you come with me to look for Mum again?"

"I will always come with you when you ask," I said lightly. The last thing I wanted to do was see his mother again, but for him I would do anything. I hoped this time he would get the closure he wanted so much.

He glanced over and grinned. "I know you will. You're the best. You guys are all the best." After a moment he added, "Not you, Parker."

Parker huffed. "You know how to hurt a guy." He touched his face lightly. He was obviously in pain. Good, the more the better.

"I know I do," I said darkly. I wanted to hurt him badly.

"When we've taken care of all of this," Parker said slowly, "if you ask nicely, I might even tell you what we did with the rest of the you-know-what."

"I can't wait," I said sarcastically. Honestly though, it was in my best interest to know that information, in case they decided to use it against me. If they tried, then any deal we made was off, as far as I was concerned. I would kill them without hesitation. I would wrap my hands around their throats and squeeze, and squeeze. They would writhe and kick and their eyes would bulge out, but then they would go slack and the light would go out of their eyes...

I blinked a couple of times to clear that mental image out of my brain. Just thinking about it made my cock hard.

Okay, maybe I hadn't just killed those people just to protect Abbie. Maybe I did it because I wanted to. Because a little bit of me got off on it. Got off on feeling powerful.

Okay, that was fucked up, I admit it, but it wasn't like I killed anyone innocent. I would never hurt a child or a puppy. Especially a puppy. Only sick fucks hurt puppies.

"We're close," Zeke said. He glanced from his phone to the street and back again, a heavy crease in his brow.

We all knew that, if only because the people following us were closer now. The streets were getting quieter, more industrial. The less chance of collateral damage. Less chance we would have somewhere to run and hide. They knew we knew they were there, I could tell in the way they walked. They were confident we knew we were screwed.

Part of me wanted to suggest we all stop and go back to the stadium. Call the cops, let them look for Jackson.

None of us would do it. We'd leave here with Jackson or not at all.

CHAPTER
SIXTEEN

ABBIE

"WELL, THERE'S THE BUS," I said rhetorically.

We were herded into a parking area at the back of the building. The bus was parked right in the middle, at an angle across several spaces. I think the expression is, "As shit as fuck."

"That is some shit parking if I ever saw it," Penn remarked, as if that was what mattered here. "What if someone else wanted to park here?"

"Just a wild guess," Tully said, "but I think that's the point."

"On a scale of one to a hundred, Levi is going to be really pissed if anything happens to his bus," Asher said. He was squinting, trying to make out if anyone was inside.

"On a scale of one to a hundred, I'm going to be pissed off if someone doesn't explain what's going on here," Channing said.

"You and me both," Zeke said. "All of you stay back here." He turned and glared at us. "I mean *all* of you. Even you, Parker."

Parker held his hands out to either side. "I have no desire to go any closer to that." He nodded toward the bus. "In fact, I'm going to do you a favour and stay right back here, behind all of you. You know, in case it blows up or some shit."

Penn muttered something about sending Parker on ahead and us staying behind him, but no one paid him much attention.

The people who followed us here, there were only four of them, arrayed themselves behind us. None of them looked like they wanted to get closer to the bus either, but their presence suggested it might not explode. Hopefully.

Zeke walked forward as the door to the bus opened slowly.

A woman stepped out. She was dressed in a long, black pencil skirt and a red silk blouse. Her hair was dark, almost black, and pulled into a neat bun. She looked like a personal assistant in a law firm. Or maybe a lawyer.

"Ezequiel Brantley, I presume," she said smoothly. She held out her hand, long-fingers with perfect, blood red fingernails.

"Zeke," he corrected. He crossed his arms over his chest and left them there until she lowered her hand.

"I'm Renae Fiorelli." She didn't seem concerned at his rebuff. "You may be aware of the growing tension between your family and mine."

"I'm aware you want us dead," Zeke said, his tone perfectly cool. "You might be aware we have no intention of dying anytime soon. You might also be aware I'm estranged from my family and their business interests."

"And yet, you're in the company of one of your brothers," she pointed out. She gestured towards Parker. The sun glinted off a huge diamond on her hand.

Zeke didn't respond to that. Instead, he said, "Have you seen our manager? We seem to have misplaced him."

She sighed as though he was being rude for not wanting to play into whatever mind fuck she had going.

"I have," she said. "He's perfectly safe. For now."

Before she could add anything else, Zeke said, "Where is he?"

It was her turn to ignore him. "I'd like to offer you a trade. Your manager for your twin brothers."

"Deal," Penn said immediately.

"Hey," Parker protested. "No deal."

Zeke turned around to give them both a look. He turned back and said, "Why should I deal with you at all? Your family tried to kill me back in Perth. Here's a newsflash for you, it wasn't appreciated."

"Because I hold all the cards anyway," she said. "I have your manager and you're surrounded."

"And you're outnumbered," Zeke said evenly. "You have one more person on the bus watching over Jackson. There's eight of us and six of you. And you aren't armed, unless you managed to fit a gun under that tight skirt, or in one of your heels." He looked her up and down, his head sideways. "Also, stilettos are going to slow you down. Right Asher?" He glanced over his shoulder.

"I'm not speaking from experience or anything," Asher said, "but Zeke is right. You ain't going anywhere in those."

"I do have experience, and they're both right," I said. "Luckily, one of us wore sensible shoes to this... Whatever this is." I raised one sneaker-covered foot.

"Are you sure you're not speaking from experience?" Landon asked Asher.

Asher shrugged and grinned. "That's a story for later. Assuming there is a later."

"There will be," Zeke said. He turned his attention back to Renae. "You haven't shown me proof Jackson is alive."

"She also hasn't said sorry for trying to kill us," Penn pointed out.

"She hasn't, has she?" Asher said. "How rude."

A sliver of annoyance cracked Renae's calm facade.

Look, I'd be the first to admit the guys could be a handful sometimes, but in this case I suspected they were doing it on purpose. If she was angry, she would make a mistake. In theory.

She half turned and waved at someone inside the bus.

A couple of minutes later, Jackson appeared in the doorway, a man behind him with a gun to his head. He looked to be uninjured, but when his eyes flicked to me I saw real fear. Understandable under the circumstances. I would probably pee myself.

"Jackson," Zeke said cheerfully. "It's good to see you. We wondered where you got to."

"Just doing a bit of sightseeing," Jackson said lightly. "Can't say I recommend the tour."

"Maybe next time stick to reputable tour guides," Zeke suggested.

"I think I will," Jackson agreed. "Thanks for the suggestion."

"Anytime, dude," Zeke said. "If you've had enough, how about you step down here and hang out with us?"

"Stay where you are," Renae growled. "I've tried to be reasonable, but my patience is running out." She narrowed dark brown eyes at Zeke.

"That's funny," Penn said, "me too. Hey, Zeke, can we start breaking heads yet?"

"Not yet, Penn," Zeke said. "I'm still considering her offer."

"Bro," Parker complained. "On behalf of Hunter and I, I strenuously object." After a moment he squinted at Renae. "I don't even know where Hunter is right now, do you?"

A flash of uncertainty crossed her features, but she quickly pushed her mask back into place.

"Of course I do," she said smoothly.

"Bullshit," Penn said. "You wouldn't have offered to exchange Jackson for both of them if you already had Hunter in hand. That begs the question, where the fuck is he?" He looked around the parking area meaningfully. Hunter was nowhere to be seen. Knowing him, he was close by, hiding and watching.

Honestly, that's what I'd do if I were him. Actually no, I'd be on a plane to anywhere but here, but I had a sneaking suspicion he wouldn't bail without his twin. Honour amongst assholes and all that.

"Don't twins have telepathy or something?" Tully asked Parker.

"Yeah, but it doesn't include a GPS," Parker said. "I'm pretty sure he's not dead though."

"Shame," Penn muttered.

Channing made a sound of agreement.

"It seems we have a problem," Zeke said. "Even if I wanted to swap Jackson for the twins, I couldn't." He spread his hands to either side of him.

"I'm sure Hunter has a phone," Renae said coolly. "It should be a simple matter of calling him and telling him to come here."

Zeke put a hand to his forehead. "Why didn't I think of that? Let me make the call." He shoved his hand into the pocket of his track pants, but instead of pulling out a phone, he pulled out a gun and pointed it at Renae.

"Looks like you're making all the calls now, babe," Asher said. His hand hovered near his pocket.

"Right?" Zeke said. He gave Renae a sardonic smile. "You didn't think we would come unarmed, did you?"

"I expected you to be reasonable," she said evenly. "Everyone knows there's no love lost between you and your brothers. I proposed a fair exchange. Honestly, I'm surprised you didn't suggest it yourself." She arched a perfectly shaped eyebrow at him.

She must have some organisational skills if she could arrange all of this shit and still have time for the perfect outfit and makeup. I didn't like her, but I respected her style. Credit where credit is due and all that

"They annoy me, but I mostly don't want them dead," Zeke said.

"Mostly being the key word here," Asher said he moved to stand to the side of the Zeke. "Why try to exchange anyway? What sort of gangsters are you? Most of the ones I've met just take what they want."

"Ones who prefer to avoid bloodshed where possible," Renae said.

"Are you saying you wouldn't kill the twins?" Zeke asked.

"The blood of anyone who works for Reuben Brantley is an exception," she said. "We're not interested in killing anyone else."

"That's great," Zeke said. "Jackson is free to come down here with us then." He gestured with his other hand for Jackson to step the rest of the way off the bus.

Jackson moved forward slightly, his eyes on Zeke's firearm.

Renae raised her hand to stop him. "I haven't agreed to let him go."

Jackson stopped, his mouth tugged to one side. He looked like a deer caught between two lions, not sure if they'd eat him or each other.

"Consider it a gesture of goodwill," Zeke said. "Like you said, there's no love lost between me and my brothers. Parker is over there, probably with a broken nose. Do you see me taking him to hospital?"

"Good point." Parker gestured towards his face. "This hurts like a bitch." When he spoke, it sounded like he had a blocked nose. Which was basically accurate.

"Sorry, not sorry," Penn said. He opened and closed his hand which looked slightly swollen from the punch. He should get some ice on that before tonight's concert. Although, knowing him, he'd get a kick out of playing through the pain.

"How interesting that you don't get along with your brothers," Renae said. "You're very much like them." She looked at him in disgust.

Zeke pointed the gun at her head. "You want to rethink that assumption?"

"That's the same way I'd react," Parker pointed out.

"You know, maybe I *should* hand him over to you," Zeke said thoughtfully.

"I mean, we're nothing alike," Parker said hastily. "Zeke is the nice brother. The one who would never throw his siblings to the wolves. He is the kind, compassionate one in the family. Fuck knows where he got it from. Maybe he's not really related to us at all."

"I like that theory," Asher said. "Unless he's my brother. Otherwise it totally works for me."

"Me too," Zeke said. "Unfortunately, the family resemblance is too strong. Sorry, babe." He shot Asher a regretful look.

"That's okay, I still love you," Asher said.

Zeke, apparently impatient with the stand-off, said, "Here's how things are going to go. Jackson is going to step down out of that bus and we're going to leave. Nobody has to die here today."

"I'm not leaving here without at least one Brantley brother in my possession," Renae said. "My father won't care which one. He'd prefer the twins, but if it's Zeke, then so be it. We'll take the twins out on some other occasion."

"It's not that I mind being taken out by a beautiful woman," Parker said, "but I have a girlfriend."

"Now you care about that," I said.

"Yeah well," he shrugged. "She's too old for me anyway. She has to be, what, thirty-six?"

"Thirty-two," Renae said coldly. "Hardly old, but that wasn't what I meant when I said take you out."

"We all knew what you fucking meant," Penn said. "This dickhead can't keep his mouth shut." He nodded towards Parker.

"Penn loves me, really," Parker said. "Deep down, he's a big softy. Aren't you Penn?"

"No," Penn said. "Not unless you're Abbie, and you sure as shit aren't."

"He definitely isn't," I agreed. In the corner of my eye, I saw a couple of Renae's people step closer. A ripple of fear passed through me. I moved closer to Channing and Landon.

From one moment to the next, the situation turned from an amicable conversation to a shit storm.

The people to either side of us pulled out guns. The guys grabbed me and pushed me down between them.

"Zeke!" The word was ripped from between my lips.

He half turned and raised his gun.

The man behind Jackson raised his and aimed at Zeke.

A shot rang out through the parking area.

I screamed.

CHAPTER
SEVENTEEN
ABBIE

I SCREAMED.

Time slowed down.

I cowered between Lincoln and Channing, their arms around me, heads down.

Jackson threw himself the rest of the way down the steps. He barrelled into Zeke and Renee, knocking them both off their feet.

The shot aimed at Zeke missed him, slamming instead into Tully's foot.

Tully let out a yelp of pain.

"Tull!" Asher shouted. He grabbed the guitarist and they both dropped into a crouch, each with a gun in his hand.

Tully, his mouth twisted in pain, aimed at the gunman on the bus and fired.

Blood blossomed on the man's chest. His eyes widened in surprise before he fell, arms flailing. Time stopped until he hit on the ground with a thud and lay still.

One of the other attackers, a woman with a plait of long red hair, aimed at Penn. Before she could pull the trigger, Zeke, on his back, his upper body off the ground, got off a shot. It hit her squarely in the stomach. She grunted in pain and fired back, but missed by a day or two. She crumbled to the ground, gun slipping from her fingers.

A man built like a brick wall, with arms and legs like tree limbs, pointed his gun at Zeke. He squeezed the trigger.

The lead singer rolled at the last second. The bullet hit the road.

The man hit the ground when Asher shot him in the centre of his chest.

Tully took out the guy with the baseball hat on backwards, one bullet striking him in the knee, another in his wrist when it seemed the man wasn't going to give up.

Baseball Guy gave a shout of pain and dropped his gun. It was Penn who scooped it up and, apparently without thinking, shot the last guy in the groin.

The guy, eyes wide dropped to the ground, hands over his crotch.

"That's gotta fucking hurt," Asher said.

"Sucks to be him." Zeke got to his feet, pulling Renae up with him by her arm. "Kinda sucks to be you too," he told her. "Having your people attack us like that was... What's the word?"

"Dumb as fuck?" Penn suggested. "That's three words, but whatever." He tucked the gun away and crouched beside Tully. The guitarist sat on the ground and pulled off his shoe and sock.

"It's just a graze," Tully winced, his brow scrunched up. "It hurts like fuck though."

"Lucky you don't play with your feet," Asher said.

"Yeah, that's the important thing here," Tully said sarcastically. He grunted as Penn took his sock and wound it around the wound.

"Dumb as fuck works," Zeke said finally. "Is everyone okay?"

"Yeah," Channing said. He drew Landon and me to our feet. "We're fine."

"You definitely are," Landon told him. "I've never seen him move that fast."

"Yeah," I agreed. "I've never been knocked off my feet quite so quickly." I managed a small smile but I was trembling. Five people lay dead or maimed around us. Blood from one of them trickled like a glistening, red creek to the gutter. My stomach turned.

"If it wasn't for Jackson, I would be dead right now," Zeke said. "I guess I owe you a blood debt now or something."

Jackson looked pale and shaky. He stood with his back to the bus, leaning on it for support. "All in a day's work for a manager. No big deal."

I walked over to him and slid my arms around his neck. "It's a huge deal." I pressed my mouth to his in a long, slow kiss. When we stopped to take a breath, I looked at him sternly. "I was worried about you. What did Zeke say about people going off by themselves?" I would have shaken my finger at him, but my arms were busy clinging tight to him. I might not let go.

He smiled slightly. "I was told there was a problem with the bus. I didn't expect it to take this long or be this—" he searched for the right word.

"Entertaining?" Asher suggested. "Interesting? Hair-raising?"

"Fucked up?" Penn suggested.

"Fucked up sounds right," Jackson said. "I see your point about being kidnapped now. It's not as much fun as it sounds."

"I should think not," I said dryly. "It doesn't sound like fun at all, because it isn't. At least it wasn't evil twins this time."

"Speaking of the evil twins," Channing said. "Where are they?"

I glanced around, but sure enough Parker was gone. That might be the first smart thing he did since I met him.

"I don't suppose you put a tracker on him?" I asked.

"No," Zeke said ruefully. "Don't worry, he'll turn up. He always does."

"Like a shit on the bottom of your shoe," Penn said. "No matter how much you wipe, you can't get it off."

"Something like that," Zeke agreed. He turned his attention to Renae. "I hope you realise the smart thing for me to do right now would be to kill you."

"I do realise that," she said. "But that would make the situation worse between our families. Specifically between my family and you. Right now, you're not the enemy. Killing me would change that."

"That's the only reason I'm not going to," Zeke said. He shoved her away from him.

She staggered and almost fell. Heels aren't good for that either.

"I'll tell my father—"

Whatever she was going to say was interrupted by another gunshot and a bullet-sized hole in her forehead. Her eyes widened and mouth dropped open in surprise. She stood for what felt like a year, but it was probably no more than a second or two.

Then she crumpled to the ground like a broken doll.

"Fucking hell," Zeke swore. He spun around to see Hunter standing with a gun in his hand, the barrel aimed where Renae had stood seconds earlier.

"Checkmate." Hunter lowered the gun.

"You fucking idiot," Zeke snarled.

"Yeah," Penn agreed. "It's not checkmate until you've captured your opponent's queen. All you've done is take out one pawn. Anyone with a passing knowledge of chess would know that." He gave Hunter a disgusted look and shook his head.

"Penny's inner geek is alive and well," Asher remarked.

"Penn just thinks you should be accurate if you're going to use chess terms," Penn said. "Otherwise, use terms like bullseye or some shit like that."

"I'll bear that in mind for next time," Hunter said.

"Hunter!" Parker rolled out from under the bus. "That was fucking awesome."

"Park— what the fuck happened to you?" Hunter tucked the gun away and stared at his twin.

Parker grinned and then winced. "Penn happened, but it's no big deal. Just a little love tap."

"He's only saying that because you're outnumbered," Asher said. "Believe it or not, Parker was a dickhead and Penn took exception to it."

"Right." Hunter touched his fingertips to his twin's nose. "That looks painful, bro, but kinda cool."

Parker jerked his face away. "It is painful, bro." After a moment he asked, "Do you really think it looks cool?"

"Totally does," Hunter said. "Lila is going to dig the whole crooked nose thing."

"I'm happy to give you one too," Penn offered. "Although I think it's Tully's turn." He waved towards the guitarist.

Tully held up a hand. "I'm happy to miss my turn. Besides, I think I'd be fighting Zeke for that privilege."

"Hell yeah, you would," Zeke said. To Hunter he said, "What the fuck did you kill her for?"

"Because she would have killed us," Hunter said easily. That seemed to be all the excuse he needed.

"Yeah," Parker agreed. "You didn't really buy all that, 'you're not really our enemy,' shit, did you? Sooner or later, you're going to end up on the chopping block." He looked over at Channing. "Not literally, like what you do," he said. "I'm speaking figuratively."

Channing stuck two fingers up at him.

"Always charming," Hunter said. "Well, the warmup was interesting. I hate to see what they're going to throw at us for an encore."

"Maybe we shouldn't stick around to find out," Parker said. "This might be a good time to make ourselves scarce."

"The deal is, you help us," Zeke said. He gave Parker a dark look like he was about to shoot his kneecaps off. He must have been tempted. I'd bet anything he wasn't the only one either.

"If they want, they can opt out of the deal," Channing said. "That means we get to do the same thing."

The implied threat should not have been hot, but it was.

I held on to Jackson a little tighter. His body felt hard pressed against mine. Part of me, and not even a small part, wanted him to fuck me up against the side of the bus. Right here, right now, with all those bodies and all that blood...

The sensible part of me remembered the police might turn up any minute now.

Yeah, the sensible part of me was a spoilsport.

Hunter growled. "Fine, we'll stick around, but not for the rest of the day. We're taking the night off and I'm taking Parker to the hospital to have his nose looked at."

"Good, fuck off." Zeke waved him away.

"We should all get out of here," Jackson said. "Luckily the keys are still in the bus."

I leaned my head back and looked at him. "Do you know how to drive a bus?"

He gave me a lopsided smile. "It's not my preferred method of transport, but yeah, I do."

"That's kinda hot," I said.

"You think so?" he asked, his eyebrows high.

"Yeah, I do think so," I said. It wasn't a skill everyone had. To be in control of something that big was kind of sexy.

"Jackson usually rides a motorcycle," Asher said helpfully.

My eyebrows shot up. "Really?"

Jackson shrugged one shoulder. "Yeah, really. An old Triumph Bonneville, to be exact."

"That's very hot," I said. "Will you take me for a ride some time?" Yes, I meant it both ways.

He grinned. "Of course I will." So did he, I saw it in his eyes. He reluctantly unwound me from himself just enough to lead me up the steps into the bus. "Just out of curiosity, what did you think I drove? A Volvo?" He smiled wryly.

I snorted a laugh. "I wouldn't insult you like that." I stood to the side to let the other guys climb onto the bus and watched Jackson start the engine. "Maybe an SUV. But a black one. I'm sure badass people drive black SUVs."

"You think I'm a badass?" he asked.

I leaned down to kiss his cheek. "Hell yeah, boss."

He groaned.

I grinned and went to slip into the seat beside Tully. "How's the foot?"

He flashed me a smile of gratitude. "Hey, loveliness. It hurts, but I'll live. It could have been worse. It could have hit me in the hand."

"Or the groin." I jerked my head towards the window. The man Penn shot was lying still now. As far as I could tell, he was dead.

"That would be bad," Tully agreed. "I need my cock for things. Like fucking our beautiful girl."

"When you put it that way, I need it too," I said. Even after everything that happened, I was so turned on I'd probably come if someone touched my clit with a feather. Which they should totally do, because it sounded like fun.

"I'm glad you do," he said softly.

"I'm going to take us back to the hotel," Jackson said over his shoulder. He turned the huge steering wheel and the bus headed away from the carnage and onto the road. "I'll call the doctor to come and look at Tully there. Then we can all get some rest because you guys have a concert to put on tonight."

"Rest," Channing used air quotes. "Who can rest after all of that?"

"You can try," Jackson said. "A couple of nights here and we'll be the hell out of Los Angeles."

None of us was under the illusion this was over. They were going to come against us at some point and they were going to come hard.

At least this tour wasn't boring.

CHAPTER
EIGHTEEN
ABBIE

"THAT SHOW WAS EPIC," Landon said. He hadn't stopped smiling since he stepped off the stage. Even during the drive back to the hotel, he was still pumped up.

"Of course it was, you were there," Channing said to him. "And you," he said to me. He put an arm around us both and drew us to him.

On some unseen signal, the other guys went to their room and Jackson went to his, leaving the three of us alone. Maybe it was something the guys arranged in advance or maybe it was the vibe. I'd thought about Channing's date proposal since he made it, so my excitement level was off the charts. The whole day had heightened that.

Death, violence, a rock concert— yeah, I was ready for some intimacy.

"And you," I said. "No one plays the sax like you do."

"And no one plays with my sacs like he does," Landon said, still grinning.

I laughed, low in the back of my throat. "I bet." I ran the palm of my hand over Landon's groin and found him already hard. I did the same to Channing and found a matching erection.

"You don't play them badly yourself," Landon said. He took my hand and tugged me towards the bed.

I grabbed Channing and took him with us. "I've had some practice," I said.

I dragged the zip down on the front of Landon's jeans and tugged them down far enough to release his cock.

He twisted his upper body to do the same to Channing.

Both of us took a handful of cock and worked them up and down a few times.

Landon took a step back and lay on the bed. He took me and Channing down with him.

They both shed their jeans and boxers, then sat up.

Almost in unison, they grabbed the hems of their shirts with one hand and pulled them off over their heads. They dumped them on the floor on the opposite sides of the bed.

"You're overdressed there, gorgeous girl," Channing said.

I glanced down at myself. "You're right. What are you going to do about it?"

They both grinned and descended on me, helping me out of my skirt, pale pink T-shirt and white lacy bra and panties.

"That's better," Channing said. He looked me up and down and then pressed me back to the mattress. "I made a promise to you. Wait there for a sec." He climbed off the bed and went over to his suitcase.

Landon watched him with interest for a moment, then rolled over so his upper body was lying over the top of mine, his hand pressed lightly to my hip. He slanted his mouth over mine and kissed me, quick and hungry. His lips and tongue and teeth devoured mine.

"That's a hell of a view," Channing said. He knelt on the edge of the bed and crawled over to us. In one hand, he held a small knife.

I felt Landon grin against my mouth before he pulled away.

"You're a pretty fucking awesome view too, baby," Landon told him. He sat up and snaked an arm around Channing's neck, pulling him in for a kiss.

"*That's* what I call an awesome view," I said. Watching two, muscular, tattooed rock stars kiss each other was just about the hottest thing going. I would never get tired of seeing it. It didn't matter whether it was Landon and Channing or Asher and Zeke, it got me going every time. Especially when their tongues tangled.

I reached down and started to trace circles around my clit with the tips of my fingers. I closed my eyes and savoured the way it felt to touch myself while listening to the wet smacking sounds of their lips on each other's.

I was so lost in that space I didn't notice they stopped kissing until Channing said, "Why don't you let us do that?"

I opened my eyes as he grabbed my wrist and pulled it over my head.

"Keep it there," he said. "And this one too." He pulled my other wrist up to the first. "Don't move them from there, okay?"

"Landon—"

"I have an idea." Landon scrambled off the bed and over to his suitcase. He came back with a brightly coloured tie, covered in animated characters from some anime I wasn't familiar with.

"I like this idea," Channing said.

"Me too," I agreed.

Landon wound one end of the tie around my wrists and bound them together firmly enough that I couldn't spread them apart, but not so tight it hurt. He tied the other end around a lamp that stuck out the side of the headboard.

He leaned back to admire his handiwork. "Perfect," he said. "Are you feeling good, Princess?"

"Yeah," I said. I was tied to the bed between two hot guys, one with a knife in his hand. What could be better? "I'm doing fabulous."

"Can you roll over onto your stomach?" Channing asked.

"I think so." It was awkward with my hands above my head, but I managed it with a shuffling of hips and knees.

"Good girl," Channing said. "I've heard a rumour you enjoy being spanked."

I turned my head to the side and said, "I think you've seen for yourself I do."

"That's true, I have," he said. "You've been smacked by a hand and paddled by a paddle. But now I'm going to smack you with this." He held the knife where I could see it.

"Bring it on," I said. A thrill of fear passed through me. I knew he knew what to do with a knife: how to kill and how not to kill. I knew he had no intention of hurting me. I was also acutely aware of the things he had done. So aware, I was desperate for someone to touch me. I wanted, needed, a cock inside me. If this went on much longer, I might come without a touch.

Channing sat beside my hip and smacked the blade of the knife lightly on my ass. It was cold and hard, and delivered a slight sting.

Landon lay down beside me, his face a few centimetres from mine. "I think she liked that."

"Yes, she did," Channing said. He smacked the blade down, harder this time.

The sting made me wriggle my ass in a combination of pleasure and pain.

"You want to try?" Channing offered Landon the knife.

Landon shook his head. "No thanks, I'm happy to watch her enjoy herself." He ran his fingertip down the side of my face and across my jaw. "So beautiful," he whispered.

"So are you," I said.

Channing smacked me again several times, each increasingly harder. The pain became more intense with each strike.

"Your ass turns a lovely shade of red," Channing remarked. He leaned over and pressed the side of the knife very lightly to my skin. If he twisted it just so, he would slice me open.

He didn't. He pressed the cool metal to me, then lifted it up and traced a line up my back to my shoulders. His slight touch didn't break my skin, but the sensation sent lava hot heat right to my core.

A killer with a knife in his hand was scary, but his control was absolute. He was as skilled with it as he was with his saxophone.

"Roll over onto your back." Channing sat up to give me room.

Landon helped me roll, then moved down to where he could flick his tongue over my nipples.

Channing, kneeling on the other side of me, ran the tip of the knife down my cheek and onto my neck.

I failed to resist the urge to swallow hard.

He stopped. "Do you trust me?"

"I trust you," I said without hesitation. I knew without a shadow of a doubt he would never turn a knife on me. "I love you," I added.

"I love you too." He leaned forward to kiss me briefly, then continued to run the tip of the knife over my neck and across my throat.

I was trying not to tremble now, but it wasn't with fear. It was pure, undiluted need to fuck.

Landon moved away from sucking my nipples and kissed his way down my belly before lying with his face between my thighs.

"I'm going to keep the knife here," Channing said. He pressed the blade to the side of my neck, just below my chin. "You're going to want to buck and wriggle, but don't. And don't come until I tell you to."

I could barely breathe, much less move, but I managed to say, "Okay."

Landon hooked his arms under my legs and opened me out to him. He flicked his tongue over my clit and down to the entrance of my pussy. "She's so wet," he said, sounding very pleased with the discovery. "She definitely likes this."

He started to slowly devour me with his mouth, tasting and teasing.

His touch on my pussy was exactly what I needed. I was on the edge of coming after only a few laps. I headed fast to the crest of the wave but before I got there, he pulled his mouth back.

I groaned. Then again when I felt the edge of the knife prickle my skin.

"Keep still," Channing ordered.

I murmured something incoherent even to myself. Probably a sound of agreement, but frustration at the same time.

Landon lowered his face back to me now that I was no longer right at the edge of the cliff. He lapped at me and slid a finger inside me.

I moaned again. Keeping still was getting more and more difficult. I wanted to roll my hips, beg him to bury his whole hand inside me. I wanted to throw my head back and scream so loud the whole city heard me.

Instead, I kept still as Landon slid another finger inside me. Pressure built faster than a bullet leaving a gun. Before it could pass out of the barrel, Landon pulled away again.

This time, I growled at him.

"Keep still," Channing insisted.

"I can't," I said.

"Yes you can," he said. "And you will."

I bared my teeth at him but he chuckled. Asshole.

"Landon, you can make her come now."

"With pleasure," Landon said. He lowered his face for the third time and hooked his hand around so his fingers were massaging my G spot while his tongue teased my clit.

Pleasure came in an even bigger rush this time. I had to grit my teeth to keep myself still while my body was thrown over the cliff and into the hot, rushing sea of a mind-blowingly intense orgasm. When my back wanted to arch, I had to keep it stiff. When I wanted to shout, I had to grit my teeth harder. The only thing I knew in the world was the most beautiful symphony of sensation and the sharp prick of the blade at my throat.

I stayed up in that place for an eternity. I left my body for at least eight or nine minutes before floating back in a haze.

"Holy fuck," I whispered. "That was..."

"Yeah," it was." Channing took the knife from my throat and tossed it onto the table beside the bed.

He untied my arms and rubbed my wrists to make sure the blood was flowing through.

Landon lifted his face, glossy with my juices. He and Channing exchanged a look before he scrambled off the bed and over to his suitcase. He came back a minute later with a tube of lube in his hand.

"Lie down," Channing told Landon.

Without hesitation, Landon did as he said.

Channing all but picked me up and rolled me so I was lying face down on Landon, my legs on either side of his hips.

"Hey." Landon grinned up at me.

"Hey." I lowered my mouth to his to kiss him. His mouth tasted of me, sweet and salty.

Channing snapped open the lid of the lube. "We're going to need a lot of this."

A ripple of excitement passed through Landon and he kissed me more deeply.

I felt the cool of the lube on Channing's fingers as he smeared it over and around the entrance to my already wet pussy. I thought I had some idea what he had in mind, but I swallowed deeply anyway.

"Lift your belly up for a minute," Channing said. When I did, he smeared a whole bunch of lube on Landon's cock. Then a bunch on his own.

"Okay, lower yourself onto him," Channing said. "And lean forward."

I did as he asked, closing my eyes and impaling myself on Landon's thick length.

"Lean forward a little further," Channing said. He straddled Landon's legs right behind me and placed his hands on my waist. His erection bumped my ass, before he positioned himself outside my pussy.

Slowly, he pushed the tip inside, sliding along the length of Landon's cock and stretching my pussy.

"Don't tense up," Landon said.

I nodded and tried to relax. With two cocks inside my pussy, that was easier said than done. I swallowed and focused on my breathing, and the feel of being so incredibly full.

After a minute or two, I managed to relax, and Channing pushed himself a little deeper.

"Oh my god," I whispered. I'd fucked some guys with big cocks before, like all of the guys in the band, but never two at once. It was incredible to feel so full.

"Are you okay, gorgeous?" Landon asked.

"Better than okay," I said. I could barely think straight, and that was all right. Thinking was overrated sometimes. This was all about feeling.

"Are you okay?" I managed to ask. He'd be feeling the pressure too.

"Oh, fuck yeah." He looked blissed out. "If I die now, I'm gonna die happy."

Channing rumbled with laughter. "Don't die now, baby. I can feel Abbie's pussy and your cock and it feels pretty fucking amazing. I'm going to try to get in a bit deeper."

"Do it," I said.

When I thought I couldn't stretch any more, I did. He was almost all the way in now. Enough I could roll my hips and slowly ride them both.

"Holy fuck," Channing whispered. He made an unintelligible grunting sound, which I interpreted to mean he was enjoying himself too.

"Mmm, I can't even," Landon said. He rocked his hips just slightly, thrusting into me and sliding along Channing at the same time.

"Fucking hell," Channing muttered. "I knew you'd feel incredible. Both of you together is next level."

Landon thrust a little faster. "I'm going to come."

I thought Channing might tell him to wait, but he didn't. Honestly, I don't think he could have held on if he tried.

Or Channing for that matter.

They both moved with short, quick thrusts and then came almost in unison.

A moment later, I came again. I was full already, I became fuller still with two doses of hot cum, mingled in with my own.

The whole world was full of wet heat, panting and fireworks of pleasure. Who knew being stuffed fuller than a Christmas turkey would feel so good?

The guys, obviously. It didn't take a genius to realise they'd done this before. Like every other time I had that thought, I didn't let it worry me. There was no jealousy for any women in their pasts. Or men in their pasts for that matter. The only important thing was here and now, and us. And the way it felt to fall in a heap on the mattress with two amazing, loving guys.

The only thought my tired, extremely relaxed mind could think was, 'how long until we can do that again?'

CHAPTER
NINETEEN

CHANNING

"HEY," Abbie said softly.

Landon was still asleep when I woke him on one side, Abbie on the other.

After three days in Los Angeles, we were finally almost ready to head to Vancouver. A glance at the clock on the wall showed we had a couple of hours before the tour bus would turn up to collect us. Fortunately, the Fiorellis had only forced the difficult off at gunpoint and left him alive. Otherwise, Jackson would have driven us over the border. Or he would have organised someone else to do it.

Whatever, as long as we got there.

"Hey," I said back. "How are you feeling this morning?" We'd basically monopolised her for the last few nights. Judging by the sounds coming from the shower yesterday morning, no one was missing out.

"Good," she said. "You?" She seemed worried Landon and I were going to have squashed cocks from sharing her, but her beautiful pussy stretched to take us both in, like the magical creation it was.

Just thinking of that and being here with her made me hard. I rolled over and straddled her hips, my hands to either side of her face. I kissed her long and slow and deep. Her mouth always tasted amazing. Very quickly, my balls were heavy, my cock aching to be inside her.

I glanced over at Landon as his eyes opened slowly.

I smiled. He was so adorable when he was half-asleep.

"Do you want to—" I started.

"If it's okay, I'd like to watch." He covered a yawn with his hand.

"Of course you can." He usually preferred to be watched, but sometimes he liked to lie back and enjoy the show. I was happy to give him one.

I gently pried Abbie's legs apart with my knees.

She raised her knees and let me sink my eager, thirsty cock into her body. She felt amazing with Landon inside her too, but she felt just as incredible when it was just me. All warm and wet and soft. The perfect sheath for my sword. I could stay like this all day.

I slipped my hand between us and rubbed her clit as I thrust slowly. I loved the way she melted underneath me. The way my body pinned her to the bed. In this moment, she was all mine, her beautiful face, her gorgeous body. She belonged to me and Landon. No one and nothing could come between us.

Her breath came in soft little moans.

I glanced around for the knife, to enhance the experience. I thought I'd put it on the table beside the bed last night, but I couldn't see it now. It must have fallen off. I wasn't going to get out of her or off her to find it. Instead, I watched her face and rubbed harder. I could tell she liked what I was doing. She was close to coming.

I looked over at Landon. He'd pushed back the covers and wrapped his fingers around his own cock. Fuck, that was cute *and* hot.

I wanted to edge her, but just this once, I would let her finish quickly.

She must have sensed what I was thinking, because she looked at me like she thought I would take my hand away from her at any moment.

I leaned down to whisper in her ear, "You can come. Come for me, gorgeous girl."

"Only if you come for me, gorgeous boy," she whispered back.

I took my hand off her clit and slid out of her long enough to roll her over and pull her up on to all fours. Then my cock was back inside her and my hand rubbed harder.

At this angle, the piercing on my tip would work her G spot, while my fingers worked her clit and slid through her folds.

"Oh my god," she moaned. "Yes, just like that." She arched her spine and her head rolled back until she touched my hand which rested on her shoulder.

She rocked her hips back onto me, setting a fast pace for us both. Her breath came in little pants, until finally she let out a long, slow groan and ground against me.

I couldn't stop myself if I tried. A warm tingling thunder of pleasure gripped me like a noose. Pressure built until it was all I could feel before I exploded hard and fast inside her. Everything from my stomach to the tip of my cock tingled and sang. I struggled to contain a shout by biting down on my tongue.

Finally I sagged over her and we tumbled down to the mattress, side by side, sweating and puffing.

Landon grunted and came all over his hand, cum dripping from his fingers to the sheets.

"Oh, yeah," I said softly. "That was nice."

"Only nice?" she asked teasingly.

"Better than nice," I said. "It was fucking awesome."

"That's more accurate," she said. She reached over and picked up her phone from the table beside the bed. She turned on the screen and grimaced. "I need to have a shower before we get out of here. I'm sticky."

"You're welcome," I said smugly. I let her go and retreated back to the middle of the bed. That gave me a good view of her naked body as she rose. Most of her skin was smooth and flawless, unlike us guys, who had tattoos wherever we could fit them. I wondered if I could talk her into getting my name inked on her somewhere. And the rest of the guys' too, I supposed. Definitely Landon's.

I couldn't resist wolf-whistling at her before she disappeared into the bathroom. She flashed me a smile over her shoulder and, a moment later, the water came on.

I rolled over to face Landon. He was lying there watching me, looking as adorable as always.

"Good morning, baby." I scooted over to kiss his mouth.

"Good morning. That was awesome, thank you," he said.

"Any time." I dipped the tip of my finger into the cum still on his hand and traced circles around his skin with it. "I'm glad you liked the show."

"I liked it a lot. Seeing you with her is… I don't know. I could watch all day." After a moment, he added, "Okay, *some* of the day. I want to join in for some of it. Lots of it."

I gave him a slow smile. "Did you know, you're the absolute best boyfriend on the face of the planet? I'm so fucking lucky to have you."

"That's funny, I was going to say the same to you," he said. He kissed me, but I sensed he was holding something back.

"Are you sure you're okay?" I asked. "You're not just saying that because you think I want to hear it?"

Before he could answer, someone knocked on the door between our rooms once, twice, then it opened. Zeke stuck his head inside.

"Time to get up, boys and girls," he said. His hair was damp and his face was pink, like he just got out of the shower himself. He must have been up early for some reason. I always knew he had a screw loose.

"We have time for breakfast before we get picked up," he added. "Up you get, lazy bones."

I leaned over the side of the bed and scooped up the first thing I touched to throw at him. It happened to be one of Landon's shoes. It hit the wall beside his head and bounced off.

"We're awake," I said. "Fuck off and let us get up."

Zeke knelt and picked up the shoe before throwing it back at me. It hit the wall behind the bedhead and fell onto the pillow beside Landon's face.

Zeke grinned. "He shoots. He scores!" He danced back out the doorway into the other room.

"He's a fucking idiot," Landon shouted after him, but he was also smiling. It didn't quite reach his eyes.

"I suppose we better get up," I said reluctantly. I rolled off the bed. Landon followed.

I didn't even see him move, but the next thing I knew I was pressed to the wall, my back against the plaster. Landon had the knife in his hand. He put it to my neck.

I raised my hands. "Okay, this is different, but I like it." He wasn't usually the aggressive one, but if he wanted to play like this, I was all in.

"I need you to be honest with me," he said. From the expression on his face, he wasn't playing.

"Always," I said. Fuck, what had they done to make him think I wasn't? Was he actually pissed off about me fucking Abbie after all? This was a violent reaction to it if he was.

"Landon." Abbie must have finished the shower and stepped back out into the room. "What the fuck?"

"What do you want to know, baby?" I asked, my eyes on his. If there was one thing I'd learnt in life, it was never take your eyes off the person with a knife to your throat.

"Did you kill my mother?" He asked. His eyes begged for the truth.

I blinked. "No," I said firmly. "I did not kill your mother."

A flicker of uncertainty crossed his features. "You killed those people to protect Abbie. Why not her?"

"Are you jealous because I didn't kill for you?" I asked. That was all kinds of adorable.

He looked even more uncertain. "No?" He frowned. "I just—"

"I thought about it," I told him. "I didn't because it's not in your best interests. You want to make up with her. I wasn't going to take that away from you. It's something you need to do. If it wasn't, I would one hundred percent have killed her."

We could have been talking about the weather, or whether or not pineapple belongs on pizza. Somehow killing became an average part of our lives.

He nodded slowly. "Okay, I get it." He lowered the knife until it went slack on his fingers.

I took it from him. "You didn't need a knife to get the truth from me. All you needed to do was ask."

He lowered his eyes. "I know. I wasn't sure if…"

"If I would be honest?" I asked. That actually stung. "You think I'd lie to you?"

"You had a whole other life I knew nothing about," he said. "I'd call that a lie, wouldn't you?"

"Yeah, I guess so," I admitted. "I'm sorry, babe. I was trying to protect you and everyone else. I'm sorry if I didn't go about it the right way."

I handed the knife to Abbie when she hovered over closer. She took it and put it on the table over to the side of the room, then crouched beside her suitcase to grab out clothes and get dressed.

I reached for Landon's hand. For a moment I thought he wouldn't let me take it, but then he did.

"You and I have been through a shit load of things together," I said. "Your mother, my family, the band, Zeke's family. It's a long fucking list. But at the end of the day, you and I, we're solid. I promise you, I will never lie to you or keep anything from you ever again." I held out my pinky finger.

He looked at it for a moment before hooking his around it. "I believe you," he said. We shook and stayed like that for a while.

Finally, he said, "So, you liked the knife, huh?"

I grinned. "Yeah, that was kinda hot. It's a side of you I've never seen before. It was sexy as fuck."

He blushed slightly, adorably.

"Are you guys okay?" Abbie asked. She was dressed now in a cute little hot pink dress that matched her fingernails. It made her look both younger and sexier at the same time. Like a hot doll.

"Yeah, okay," I said. I looked over at Landon. "Aren't we?"

My heart stopped when he didn't respond immediately, but then he said, "Yeah. Yeah, we are. We all are." He held out his other pinky finger to Abbie.

After a moment, I did the same. She hooked her pinkies in ours and we all shook.

"For the record," she said, "can you warn me if you're going to pull a knife on each other? After everything that's happened, I wasn't sure if—"

"I would never hurt Channing," Landon said. "No matter how mad I got at him."

"You wouldn't hurt me, but would you kill me?" I asked only half teasing.

"Only if you needed me to," he said. His expression turned sad. "If you couldn't live any more, I would help you."

"I would do the same for you," I said. Fuck, this conversation got dark and morbid. Still, it was good to know we had each other's backs if pain had us but death hadn't taken us yet.

"We would all do that for each other," Abbie said. "That's stuff family does if it can, doesn't it?"

"Yes," I agreed. "And any time either of you need my organ, you only have to ask." I grinned slyly.

They both squeezed my pinky until they hurt, and laughed at the expression on my face.

"We will never not need your organ," Landon said. "It's one of our favourite parts of you."

"Along with the rest of you," Abbie agreed.

"Right back at you both," I said softly. They really were the best fucking people in the world. And I was one lucky fucking saxophonist.

"Let's go, people," Zeke shouted from the other room.

"Yes, General Brantley," I shouted back. Landon and I scrambled to get dressed.

CHAPTER TWENTY

ABBIE

"O, CANADA," Asher said as we crossed the border.

Penn scrunched up the empty paper from his ham and cheese sandwich and threw it at Asher's head. It hit him in the cheek and bounced off.

"What the fuck was that for?" Asher demanded.

Penn shrugged. "Because you say that every time we enter Canada."

"I like being consistent, okay?" Asher sneered at him playfully.

"How about you be consistently less annoying?" Penn suggested.

"It's like being on the school bus, isn't it?" I asked Jackson as I curled up against his side.

He grunted. "Yeah, but I don't remember signing up to be the teacher."

"It was right about when you signed up to be our manager," Asher said helpfully. "I'm pretty sure there's a clause in there that included you being the designated adult."

"I knew I should have read the fine print." Jackson grimaced and rolled his eyes, but he smiled the whole time.

"Always read the fine print," I said. "Although, I did and it didn't stop me from being screwed over." Thinking about Pete and Onyx Riot Records would always leave a bad taste in my mouth.

"I would suggest you only sign with people you can trust," Jackson said, "but if that clause is in there, then clearly I was wrong to trust Levi."

"I might make it a stipulation of any contracts going forward with my label," Tully said thoughtfully.

"What? That someone has to be the designated killjoy?" Landon asked.

"That's already in Penn's contract," Zeke said.

Penn flipped him off. "No it's not, I just enjoy being the voice of reason around here. Someone has to be." He shot Jackson an accusing look.

"When am I not the voice of reason?" Jackson asked. "I'm pretty sure that *is* in my contract. Spoilsport, voice of reason, adult and all around badass."

"That sounds accurate," I snuggled in closer. It was nice to get the chance to sit with him. He usually sat by himself like he was the designated nerd on a bus full of cool kids. Although, we were all self-confessed nerds anyway. Maybe that made him the cool kid, keeping us at arm's length.

He squeezed my shoulder. "I'm starting to feel like everyone thinks I'm older than I really am."

I was hoping for that opening, so I took it. "How old are you?"

He hesitated for a moment. "Thirty-six."

"So, definitely not old," I said. Twelve years older than me, but what was age anyway? Just a bunch of numbers.

"You haven't run away screaming yet," he pointed out.

"There's not really anywhere to run," I said. "I could run up the aisle, but there's only two seats behind us. It wouldn't be very satisfying."

His body rumbled with laughter. "In that case, you haven't gotten up and gone to sit somewhere else with a guy closer to your age."

"Because I don't care about age," I said firmly. "I care about *you*."

"I care about you too," he said softly. "For the record, I don't care that you're younger than me."

I looked up at him. "It hadn't occurred to me that you might. Don't guys usually dig dating younger women?"

His eyebrows twitched upward slightly. "I suppose they do. I was going to say I wasn't into that, but maybe I am and didn't know. Whatever, none of that shit matters to me."

We fell silent for a couple of minutes until I broke it by asking, "Do you want to talk about your ex-wife?"

His brow creased, then increased. "If you like. What do you want to know?"

"What happened?" I asked. "You said it didn't work out?"

He sighed. "She married a man with a bad case of the travel bug. First it was touring, then it was managing. She wanted to stay home and have babies. I wanted to see the world."

"You don't want babies?" I asked.

"I don't know," he said thoughtfully. "I didn't back then. I wasn't even in my thirties yet. I'd only just given up on the dream of making it as a muso. I wasn't ready to hang up my passport yet. I'm not old-fashioned enough to think a child can't be raised by one parent and be happy and healthy, but I think if you bring a child into the world and you're still together, you should see each other once in a while."

I snorted softly. "Yeah, I guess so, but it works for military people. You know what they say, as long as you want to make it work, you can."

"Right," he said so softly I almost missed it. "I didn't want it badly enough. Not with Carla. She was everything the people I spend all day everyday with weren't. Nine to five job, normal home life, pet dog, the ability to keep potted plants and goldfish alive. I thought I wanted something different. I thought I could fit her into my life. Turns out I need someone who gets this life. Who understands the sacrifices we've all made to be here. She never got why I wanted to keep playing and touring, or being around bands. Giving that up would be like..." He thought for a moment. "Giving up breathing."

"I can't imagine you giving any of this up," I said, waving around the bus with one hand. "Unless you get tired of being held at gunpoint, shot at, kidnapped..."

"That part I'm happy to give up," he said. "I could live without that shit in my day."

"When did you find out about the guys and all of that?" I asked. "I mean, that's not the usual thing that comes up in conversation. Does it?"

"Not really," he agreed. "Zeke didn't just walk up one day and say, 'Hey, dude, my family are gangsters.' Although, that might have made life easier." He glanced back in Zeke's direction.

"Hey, dude," Zeke protested. "That would have gone down like a lead fart, wouldn't it?"

"Not really," Jackson said. "I wouldn't have believed you."

"Yeah, there you go, that's why I didn't tell you," Zeke said.

"So, how did you find out?" I pressed. "Was it the evil twins or Reuben?"

"Actually, it was Caleb," Jackson said. "He took it upon himself to ask if I could help smuggle things over the border. When I asked Zeke about it, he admitted what was going on."

"Caleb was trying to stir up shit," Zeke said darkly. "He was lucky I didn't put his nose down his throat until it came out his ass." After a moment he added, "No, that's not completely accurate. He also wanted you to smuggle shit. Wanted us to do it. If we had, he might have gone to bat for us with Reuben, to get him to back off a bit. On the other hand, I don't want to spend the rest of my life in a jail cell somewhere on the other side of the planet, so..."

"Wow," I said. "That was really bold of him to approach you like that. Did he not think you would call the police?"

"And tell them what?" Jackson asked. "His suggestion was less direct than that and I had no proof he made it in the first place. It would have been his word against mine and the world mostly knows Caleb Brantley as a reputable businessman."

Penn snorted loudly. "Reputable, my ass."

"Yeah, well," Jackson shrugged, "it would have created a shit storm and

Zeke would have been stuck in the middle of it. And me too. No doubt the Brantley family is perfectly capable of fabricating some shit to make me look like I was the bad guy."

"Without a doubt," I agreed. They wouldn't have cared if Jackson spent the rest of his life behind bars for something they did. "That must have freaked you the fuck out."

"It was disconcerting," Jackson agreed. "But they understood quickly we weren't going to do what they wanted."

"That was right around the time Reuben started to badger Zeke about going back to the family," Asher said. "If he couldn't get to him via Jackson or the label, then he would go direct."

"Hey, Channing," Penn said suddenly. "How come you didn't kill Reuben?"

We all turned and looked at Channing.

He shrugged. "Because I wouldn't get out alive if I did that. I'd have to take out his minions as well. Don't worry, I did think about it."

"I can't believe I'm saying this," Zeke said, "but I'm glad you didn't. That would have made a shitty situation a whole lot shittier. You would have had all of our brothers, and Damon and Gianni, his most loyal minions, after your ass. Things wouldn't have ended well for you."

"Says you," Channing said. Before Zeke could respond, he added, "As it happens, I agree with you. I like my balls where they are, not shoved down my throat."

"The only balls he wants in his mouth are mine," Landon said helpfully.

"Exactly," Channing agreed. "I'm a one set of balls kind of guy."

I smiled at them both. I was glad he hadn't killed Reuben too, if only because I would have missed out on meeting him. Channing that was. I could live without having ever met Reuben.

Since Landon was always with Channing, the bad guys might have taken him out too. What would Wolf Venom be without its rhythm guitarist and saxophone player? Much less wolfie and venomous, that was for sure.

That begged another question. I seemed to have a lot of them today.

"Where did the name Wolf Venom come from?"

"Zeke and Asher came up with it," Landon said.

Asher nodded. "We thought of the two coolest things we could think of and put them together. What could be cooler than wolves and venom?"

I pretended to think about that for a moment "I can't think of anything. Although, you could have blended your names like Blazing Violet did and been Ashing Zeke, or Zekeing Ash." I held back a grin.

"The first thing that Levi would have insisted on is them changing their name if they went with either of those," Jackson said. "No offence though."

I sniffed. "Offence totally taken." Okay, they were silly suggestions, but they weren't without their charm. "Luckily I did better with my own name."

They all turned and looked at me funny.

I looked from one face to the next. "What? You didn't think my last name was actually Hart, did you?"

"Ummm..." Asher said.

"I did," Landon said. "What is it?

Penn groaned. "Please say it's not Brantley, DiMarco, Bell or Fiorelli. Or Pennington."

"I'm surprised you don't know what it is," Channing said to him.

"I know this will come as a shock to you, but I don't know everything." Penn sneered at him.

"No shit," Channing said.

"So, what is it?" Landon pressed. He frowned briefly. "I bet Jackson knows."

Jackson shrugged one shoulder "I might. It is my job to know stuff like that."

Everyone but him looked at me speculatively.

"It's Sharp," I said finally. "Can you imagine a muso going through life with the name A Sharp? It was bad enough at school when the other kids would ask if I was a sharp minor or major." It was funny now, but at the time it drove me crazy.

"I like Hart better," Landon said. "It describes you perfectly. You have a big heart."

I gave him a soft look. "Awww, thank you. That's very sweet of you. I don't know about that but A Hart sounds better to me than A Sharp."

"It's perfect." Jackson kissed the top of my head and I melted a little more. It was nice to forget all the trouble for a little while.

If only I didn't have a nagging feeling that the closer we got to Vancouver, the closer we came to being completely fucked.

Not in a good way.

CHAPTER
TWENTY-ONE

ABBIE

"I'M STARTING to feel like I could do sound checks in my sleep," Asher remarked.

"If you can't by now, then you might be in the wrong profession," Jackson said dryly.

"Was that a burn?" Asher asked him.

"If you can't recognise a burn by now, you're definitely in the wrong profession, babe," Zeke teased.

"Hold me," Asher said to me, a playful, pained expression on his face.

I gave him a hug, then a shove toward his drums. "You're a big boy, you can take it."

He turned around and grinned. "Can I ever."

"Everything is about sex with these guys," I complained to Jackson.

He draped an arm over my shoulders and tucked me into his side. "Yes, and?"

I snorted a laugh. "You're as bad as they are."

He grinned unapologetically. "It's not my fault. I was sweet and innocent before I met them."

"That is such bullshit," Penn said. "The only innocent one around here is—"

"Shhh," Zeke urged.

"What—" Penn asked.

Zeke made a zipping gesture with his fingers across his lips.

We all froze.

Jackson's hand tightened over my shoulder. He wanted to ask what it was, I saw that on his face, but when it came to matters of our safety and security, he always deferred to Zeke.

I looked around the empty stadium, but saw nothing but vacant seats and tour staff moving around fixing the rigging, adjusting lights and speakers. Nothing seemed out of place.

In spite of that, the hairs on the back of my neck rose. I might have put it down to me reacting to Zeke's sudden, wary expression, but he wouldn't look like that unless something was really wrong.

"Everyone off the stage," Zeke said. He gestured to us, but not to the stairs at the back. Instead, he waved us towards the seats.

"What's going on?" Asher whispered as he moved silently past Zeke.

"I dunno." Zeke shook his head. "It might be nothing but go."

We stepped or jumped off the stage.

Jackson jumped down in front of me, then turned to take my hand and help me down. If this was a performance, I would have been wearing heels. When it came to the sound check I took the advice I gave to Renae and wore sensible shoes. The rubber soles only made a slight thud as I hit the ground. That still made me wince.

"Where to now?" I asked Zeke.

Before he could respond, a sound came from backstage.

It sounded like a gunshot, echoing through the corridor.

"Fuck," I said under my breath.

We didn't wait for Zeke to give us any further orders, we all bolted as silently as we could into the seats.

Following Tully's lead, I stayed as low as I could and crept up through the tiers. I trusted the guitarist's instincts as well as I trusted Zeke's. A trained assassin would know how to stay out of sight.

By the time this was over, if it was ever over, I would have an interesting skill set, if not a marketable one by reputable standards.

The higher I got, the darker it was, but I saw Tully wave me over to him.

I glanced toward the stage, then slipped over as quickly and quietly as I could.

I dropped into the space beside him as footsteps sounded on the steps leading up from backstage.

"They're getting desperate," Tully whispered in my ear. "Coming after us here is…"

"Crazy?" I suggested. I startled as Penn appeared on the other side of me.

"Crazy is a good word for it," Tully agreed.

"Personally, I would accept 'fucked up' as well," Penn said. "This is not what they fucking mean when they say a band killed it in a particular venue."

I would have laughed, but it wasn't funny right now. It might not be funny later, but I'd see how things went before I decided.

Meanwhile, if whoever was after us today was that desperate, they wouldn't hold back, or stop to ask questions. Unless they were here to check our visa status. We could be overreacting.

Yeah, okay, I didn't buy that either.

Standing up and shouting, 'I'm not a Brantley,' wouldn't save my ass. Or anyone else's. None of us would do that anyway. We wouldn't throw Zeke under the bus.

"So, the little wolves have fled," a male voice said from the stage. "Let me introduce myself, since this is my shit show now. My name is Sutton Fiorelli. You might know my name. You were acquainted with my sister, Renae."

He must have had some theatre training, because he was good at throwing his voice. Of course, the acoustics in the stadium were designed for that.

Yeah, Abbie, I told myself. *How about you* don't *be impressed by the bad guy?*

"We didn't have a problem with you, only with the twins," Sutton went on. "But you had to go and wage war on us, didn't you?"

"Fucking idiot," Penn muttered. "He sounds like a cartoon villain."

I swallowed down a laugh and then bit back a cough. Nothing would give me away faster than, I don't know, making a shit load of noise.

"In case you're wondering, I brought more people with me than my sister did. We have the backstage area secured. We know you're up there. You have nowhere to go. You might as well come down. In case you think I'm joking, or that the gun I brought isn't loaded, let's have a little demonstration."

He raised the gun and turned in a slow circle, looking at each of the instruments already set up on the stage.

Penn groaned softly. "Fucking don't."

Sutton aimed the gun at Penn's precious keyboard and pulled the trigger. And again. And again. The bullets found their marks with heartbreaking accuracy, shattering the keys and sending plastic and metal flying.

"I'm going to—"

I grabbed Penn's arm before he could jump up and run back down to the stage.

It was Tully who hissed, "You have others."

Even if he didn't, his instrument wasn't worth dying for. Not the musical one anyway. I got it though. This was nothing but vandalism. Destruction of a perfectly good keyboard just because he could. I bet he had the smallest cock known to humankind.

"Don't care about that?" Sutton taunted. He nodded to one of his cronies.

Tully made a soft growl in the back of his throat as the man put his gun away and picked up one of Tully's guitars.

He said something that sounded like, "I've always wanted to do this," and smashed the guitar into the stage.

I glanced over at Tully. His fingertips were pressed to his forehead. He shook his head. He looked like he wanted to do some smashing of his own, but heads, not instruments. Obviously.

Tully lowered his hand. "Come with me." He gestured towards me and Penn.

For once, no one made a joke. If Penn noticed the innuendo, he gave no sign. He just waved at me to move between him and Tully.

I swallowed and followed the guitarist further up through the shadows amongst the seats. I don't know how he knew, but he led us straight to Asher and Zeke. Ninja skills, presumably.

Where were Landon, Channing and Jackson? I peered through the darkness, but saw no sign of them. Presumably, they were well hidden. Hopefully together.

I crept over to Asher and let him give me a quick hug.

"Thank fuck," he whispered. "I was worried about you."

"I was worried about me too," I said. Now probably wasn't the time for joking, but my remark was met with a soft chuckle.

"You're a badass, nothing bad would have happened to you," Asher said with more confidence than I felt.

"Did you miss the armed assholes on the stage?" Penn hissed. Yeah, he wasn't going to forgive the damage to his keyboard anytime soon.

"No one missed them, Penny," Asher whispered.

"Stay here," Tully said softly.

"Where are you—" Penn started to say, but Tully melted into the shadows.

"Okay," Penn whispered slowly.

The asshole finished smashing Tully's guitar. The stadium filled with silence.

"Tully is not going to let that slip by," Asher said in my ear. His warm breath became a groan when Sutton turned his attention to Asher's drums.

"You can come out, or I can keep smashing," Sutton said.

What sort of offer was that anyway? Sure the guys' instruments were precious to them, but not as precious as their own lives. Of course, it had nothing to do with the instruments or the guy's lives. It was retribution for what happened to Renae. Of course, the stupid butt plug wouldn't know it was Hunter who killed her and not one of us.

I wasn't going to be the one to tell him.

"Let's have some fun, shall we?" Sutton said slowly.

What he was doing up until now, I had no idea. He seemed as though he was having fun to me. Sick, twisted, fucking fun.

He scooped up Channing's saxophone from where it leaned against a box and drove the end of it into Asher's kick drum.

Asher looked away and pressed his face into my shoulder.

I patted his back as reassuringly as I could.

"That felt so good," Sutton said. "Not as good as hitting one of you guys with it, but close enough." For good measure, he slammed the saxophone into the stage and then stepped on the mouthpiece. Would he have done that if he knew who he was fucking with? Probably. A guy like him wouldn't be intimidated by Channing, even if he knew what he'd done.

"This is just foreplay, of course," Sutton said.

"How to say you don't know how to please your partner without saying you don't know how to please your partner," Asher said in my ear.

Once again, I had to choke back a laugh. It was one thing to use humour to get you through the dark times, and another thing to die for it. I strenuously objected to losing my life for a chuckle. I poked Asher in the ribs to tell him to stop it.

He jerked, but fell silent.

"This is my way," Sutton continued, "of killing time while waiting. Waiting for what, I'm sure you're wondering." He paced from one side of the stage to the other slowly, like he was out for a pleasant stroll in the garden. If he did that, the plants would probably wilt around him.

Whatever it was we were waiting for, I was sure we wouldn't like it. I doubted it would be anything good. It never was with people like him. Couldn't he just come to us with a box of chocolates and a pleasant conversation? Fuck no, they had to go all shooting and smashing shit.

Footsteps sounded from backstage, heading up slowly.

"That isn't ominous at all," Asher whispered.

I poked him again.

He twitched and grabbed my finger to stop me from doing it again. I had another hand if I needed to use it.

"Shhh," Zeke hissed. He peered between two seats.

Five more people stepped up on stage. Three I recognised, two I didn't.

Jackson, Landon and Channing, followed by an older man and a younger one, both with guns in their hands. The guys looked unharmed, for now, but pissed off. Channing especially, when he saw what they'd done to his saxophone. He looked as though when he was done with them, they'd be lucky to be recognisable.

Landon was sticking close to Channing's side, and Jackson, being Jackson, put himself between them and the bad guys.

"Have you warmed the crowd up?" the older man asked.

"Hey, Dad," I think they're ready for you."

I squinted at the stage. Things must be getting desperate if they needed—

"Dante Fiorelli," Zeke whispered.

CHAPTER
TWENTY-TWO
CHANNING

"THIS WAY," I said.

When Zeke told us all to scatter, I grabbed Landon and did just that. I went to grab Abbie as well, but Jackson had her by the hand and they seemed to be following Zeke.

Instead of heading into the stands, we headed out a side door, Landon's hand sweaty in mine.

"What the hell?" Landon panted.

"I don't know. I'm not sticking around to find out." I wasn't a fan of guns, especially when they were aimed at me or anyone I loved.

I pulled Landon behind a pile of boxes that would have contained some of our rigging, and tried to get a handle on what was going on. Where should we go? How many bad guys were there? After the altercation in LA, I assumed there were more of them than we faced there. They might have thought we were a pushover then, but they knew better now. None of us was going down without a fight.

I saw someone walk past and ducked down lower.

"Go out on stage and take those two with you," a voice ordered. An older man, someone with authority over the others. Asshole didn't intimidate me, but judging by the way he spoke, he was used to intimidating the people around him. He reminded me of Reuben and my father. People determined to get their own way no matter who they had to fuck over to get there.

I glanced over at Landon's pale face. He looked like he was going to pee his pants, but he really wasn't. He was stronger than he knew and now was the time for him to prove it. To himself. I already knew he was a badass.

I put my fingers to my lips and pointed forward. If we stayed behind the boxes, no one would see us. Once we got to the other end, we could figure out where to go from there. With any luck, we'd have a free run to the door leading out to the rig truck.

Landon nodded and turned to walk away in a crouch.

It was slow going, but I stayed on his tail, my ears and eyes open. On the other side of the boxes, people walked past, stopping to talk in low voices, before they moved on. I tried to get some idea of how many there were, but without being able to see them, it would only be a guess. I could safely assume they were all armed and ready to use them.

I kept an eye out for a weapon, but the fucking tour staff were meticulous in tidying up as they went. Levi and Jackson insisted on it. Right now, we could have used a pipe or something. Hell, I'd give anything for a spray can and a cigarette lighter. A homemade flamethrower would be useful. Better yet, a bazooka or even a handgun.

At times like this, we usually joked about a cloak of invisibility, but there wasn't anything funny about the situation. There would be plenty of time for joking later.

We reached the end of the boxes and I gestured for Landon to stay down. He looked like he wanted to argue, but his brow was covered in a sheen of sweat. Even when his mother was being a bitch I'd never seen him truly scared, until now.

Just hold it all together until we get through this, I thought. *You can freak the fuck out afterwards*. And then we could get nice and drunk.

I patted his shoulder for reassurance, then slowly rose.

"Hello there." I found the barrel of a gun pointed right at my face.

Fuck.

"Hey," I said. Landon would have said something clever like he'd dropped some money behind here or we crept away to fuck. Me, I couldn't think of anything smart to say. So instead I said, "What the fuck do you want?"

"Let's start with you coming out of there." He was the older man, late forties, maybe early fifties, a generous sprinkling of grey in his hair. Lines around his eyes matched the ones around his mouth. His skin looked like it tanned too often, and time was catching up with him. He was relatively attractive for someone holding a firearm in my face.

Fucker.

"Keep your hands up where I can see them," he said as I stepped out from behind the boxes. "You too." He gestured in Landon's direction. "I know there's at least two of you behind there."

"Congratulations," I said sarcastically.

He gave me a look that suggested I should probably not be a smartass to someone with a weapon, but I couldn't help myself. If I made him angry enough, maybe I could find a way to disarm him.

Landon crab walked to the side of the boxes and slowly rose.

"See, that wasn't so hard, was it?" the man said.

"I've met people like you," I said. "Doing shit like this makes them hard."

He chuckled. "That's true, but at my age you want things sorted quickly so you can go and have a nice glass of whiskey."

"We're not stopping you," I said. "If you want to leave, there's the door." I jerked my head toward it.

"Not until I've finished what I came here for," he said.

"So you know, the Brantley twins aren't here," I said. Let's be real here, they could have snuck up at any point, the pair of slippery pricks. But as far as I knew, I was telling the truth.

He shrugged one shoulder. "I cared about that before you killed my daughter."

I blinked a couple of times. "Your— Oh. So you know, that wasn't us. I mean, we were there, but it was Hunter Brantley who killed her."

"That may be true," he agreed, "and it may not. But you were there and that makes you accountable."

That was some fuzzy, fucking logic right there.

"No offence, but I think you're reaching a bit. That's like saying the audience is responsible for a football team losing." I was going to say, 'or us sucking,' but we rarely sucked these days. Not in a bad way anyway.

"I'd also like to point out, she was trying to kill us," I said.

"When she died she wasn't," Landon said helpfully. "She made peace with us, then Hunter killed her." Apparently that was the wrong thing to say, because Dante poked him in the side with his gun.

Landon flinched. His eyes were wide with fear, but he managed not to make a sound. I was proud of him, he was keeping it together.

Just a bit longer, I thought.

I desperately wanted to drive my fist into the old man's face, but I grabbed Landon's arm and pulled him to me instead.

"He's right, but we'll do as you say until we can get all of this sorted out," I said quickly.

His face red with anger, Dante said, "You can start by shutting up."

I nodded and squeezed Landon's arm. He nodded too, more vigourously than I had.

"Good, now go that way." Dante waved the gun in the direction we had come from. I sighed, but did as he asked. Right now, the best way to stay alive was to go along with their bullshit.

We only made it a few steps before one of his minions called out, "Boss, I found another one."

We all turned and I had to suppress a groan. A man about my age had Jackson at gunpoint. He looked unimpressed but uninjured. So far.

I shot him a questioning look. Where the fuck was Abbie?

He shook his head, he didn't know. Not dead then. They must have gotten separated in the scramble. No doubt she was with the other guys. They better be keeping her safe or they'd have me to answer to.

"Back inside the stadium, gentlemen," Dante said. He nodded and his minion waved for Jackson to walk beside us.

We were herded through another door into the backstage area, to the stairs which lead up to the stage. It wasn't until then I realised I'd heard some loud, disconcerting sounds coming from there.

When I stepped out onto the stage I realised why.

My fucking beautiful saxophone. It wasn't beyond repair, but I wouldn't be playing it tonight. Neither would Asher with his kick drum, Tully with his guitar and... Were those bullet holes in Penn's keys? He was going to be pissed as fuck about that.

"Hey, Dad, I think they're ready for you." The speaker was a couple of years older than me, with a passing resemblance to Dante.

Oh good, another Fiorelli brat. Another one I should have killed when I had the chance.

"I thought you would have rounded the rest of them up by now," Dante said, his tone full of condemnation. Apparently junior was a disappointment. What a shame.

Sutton's smile slipped. "I was working on it, but then I thought you might want the honours."

I glanced at Landon and rolled my eyes. And we thought our guys were full of shit. This Sutton prick failed and he knew it. The fun part was, his father knew it too. Good, let them gnaw at each other. It might give us an in.

"We have the place locked down," one of the minions said. "We know the rest of them are in here." He made it sound like it was a small deal, not a stadium with a capacity of fifty-four thousand people.

"They'll come out when we start killing," Dante said. He eyed each of us speculatively. His gaze lingered on Jackson, who stood a bit in front us. Evidently his attempt to protect us, subtle and unnecessary as it was, hadn't gone unnoticed.

I started as a grinding noise echoed through the stadium. I took my eyes off Dante's gun long enough to look upwards.

The stadium's retractable roof was starting to close. Slow at first but gradually moving more quickly, blocking out the last of the evening light. We were almost in darkness except for the lights all around the edges of the stadium, and those in the rigging.

"They must have listened to my warning about rain coming," Jackson said. "It took them long enough." He looked so irritated I almost believed him. If I didn't know him so well, I wouldn't have guessed he was stalling. What was he stalling for though?

His expression gave away absolutely nothing. I made a note never to play poker with him. Not that I played poker anyway, but his poker face was on point.

Dante looked like he wasn't sure if he should believe him, but apparently the roof closing wasn't on his list of concerns right now. He shrugged and moved around behind Jackson, his gun hanging loosely in his hand.

"Your boy tells me Hunter Brantley killed my daughter," he said.

Landon twitched at being referred to as a boy, but thank fuck, he kept his mouth closed.

Jackson's tongue darted over his lips and he nodded. "Yes, that's accurate."

"Who killed those working with her?" Dante moved around slowly.

Jackson swallowed. "It was a combination of—"

Dante stopped to kick Landon's guitar so hard we all startled. It fell and lay on the stage, undamaged as far as I could tell. Lucky for him or he would die more slowly for upsetting Landon. "Who killed them?"

"We did," Jackson said. "In self defence."

"So you admit culpability?" Dante demanded.

"I admit to people dying so we could save our asses," Jackson said evenly. "Your personal narrative might look at it differently."

"My personal narrative," Dante echoed, "has decided you can be the first to pay for what happened to my daughter." He raised the gun to Jackson's temple.

With a mechanical clunk all the lights in the stadium went out.

CHAPTER
TWENTY-THREE

ABBIE

WE WERE PLUNGED INTO DARKNESS. Not absolute, but fucking close enough.

A second or two later, a shot rang out across the stadium. I recognised the slight muffled sound made by a silencer, but it still sounded like a crack of thunder.

I had barely enough time to take a breath before I heard a thud and panicked scrambling from down on the stage.

"That's our cue," Zeke said. "Penn, stay here with Abbie. Asher, let's go."

"What—" Penn started to say.

"Tully," I said softly.

Zeke's teeth flashed in the dark. "Who else?"

I should have realised when the roof closed that the guitarist was behind it. He must have gotten into the control booth. With a whole shit ton of luck, I'd get to ask him about that later.

Strong hands pressed against my cheeks and Asher kissed me. "Love you. Stay safe."

"Love you too," I said. "You better not die or I'll..." Be heartbroken. We'd been through too much to lose each other now.

"We won't," Zeke said. "I love you."

"I love you," I said before he crept away.

Someone let out a cry of pain, but it didn't sound like any of my guys. Or maybe that was wishful thinking.

I peeked between two seats but couldn't make out anything other than dark shapes moving around. Either no one down there thought to put their phone torch on, or they didn't want to make themselves a target.

I put a hand over my mouth and leaned against Penn as realisation crept into my brain. Dante Fiorelli was holding a gun to Jackson's head right before the light went out. That thud...

I swallowed down a sob but a tear trickled down my cheek, followed by another one. Never in my life have I ever wanted to kill anyone. Until now. If I had a gun in my hand and Dante Fiorelli in front of me, I wouldn't be able to stop myself from using it.

I thought back to our band outing to the shooting range, and how the guys taught me to use a gun and told me the dangers of panicking and being emotional with a weapon in your hand. They never told me I might get emotional because someone I loved was killed, and burning rage would take over my heart.

Penn exhaled next to my ear.

"Are we really going to stay up here out of the way?" he asked.

I looked up at him and jumped as another shot rang out. That was followed by a short cry and a gurgling sound, then another thud.

"Zeke will—" I started.

"Be grateful for any help he can get if we save his ass," Penn finished for me. "You know what, you're right. You should stay here. You'll be safe out of the way. Just like I've been saying since before the tour."

He was clearly trying to get a rise out of me. It worked.

"You're still an asshole," I told him.

"Hell yeah, I am," he said. He pressed his forehead to mine. "I love you. You're a pain in the ass, but you're my pain in the ass."

"I love you too, even though you're a jerk." I lightly kissed his mouth. "Okay, let's go and kick some butt."

He took my hand and we rose. There was so much noise and scuffling coming from the stage, we didn't bother trying to be quiet. We took the stairs as quickly and carefully as we could. Nothing would reveal our presence quicker than us tumbling down the stairs. Not to mention that we might hurt ourselves. That would suck.

We were about three rows from the front when the same metallic clunk echoed through the stadium and the lights came back on.

Penn yanked me behind the row of seats. "Looks like time's up."

I grunted in pain as I fell on my knees and squinted against the sudden glare.

Either Tully turned the lights back on or the stadium staff had. Either way, we were now bathed in light.

"What's going on?" I was too scared to look for myself. With wide eyes, I looked over at Penn.

He had a grim expression on his face, but looked over the armrest in front of him. Without answering my question, he said, "Wait here." He scrambled out of the row and down towards the stage.

"What the fuck?" I said to empty space. I might have done what he said and stayed put, but by now it's well documented that I don't do what I'm told.

I snuck back to the end of the row and looked around.

The stage was packed, and an absolute mess. Sutton Fiorelli lay near Asher's drums, a gaping hole in his chest. That must have been his death gurgle.

Sorry, not sorry.

Dante Fiorelli and one of his minions had guns in their hands. So did Landon and—oh my god—Jackson. He looked a little rough and messy—and kinda hot—but he was alive.

"Looks like we have a stand-off," Zeke said. He stood at the edge of the stage, his hand around the neck of Tully's guitar. Judging by the still forms of two minions who lay near him, he'd used it on them.

Desperate times, I guess.

"They're outnumbered," Asher pointed out.

"We'll take a few of you with us," Dante said.

"How about you don't?" Penn said. He raised a hand as though shrugging, but I got the impression he was waving at something in particular.

I looked over in that direction and noticed a side door. I bit my lip. Was he suggesting what I thought he was suggesting?

No, he was just telling me to get the fuck out of the stadium.

I had other ideas.

I crawled down to the end of the row, and peeked out again.

From this angle, Dante and his minion had their backs to me. Silently, and keeping as low as I could, I snuck out from behind the chairs and darted out the door.

I found myself in an empty hallway that led out of the stadium. The other direction led backstage. During a concert, the doors would be closed and locked to prevent groupies from sneaking in. Since the tour staff were still setting up, the doors were open, a box placed in front of one to stop it from swinging shut.

Aware there might be other minions around, I trotted to the door and glanced inside.

"What are you doing here?" Tully whispered behind me.

I jumped about a thousand feet in the air and whirled around, my hand to my chest. "You scared the shit out of me."

He smiled briefly. "I could have been anyone."

"No one else would have snuck up like that without me seeing you," I pointed out.

"That's an assumption that could have gotten you killed," he said. He grabbed my arm and pulled me back and off to the side. "What's going on up there?"

I told him in a handful of words and he nodded.

"Looks like time to break up a stand-off."

"Is this where you tell me to stay here," I asked. "Because I—"

"No, I need you along on this," he said. "But I'm going to need you to do what I say. It's the only way we'll get out of here alive." He gave me a long, firm look, his brown eyes boring into mine.

I nodded. "Okay." No pressure. If I fucked up and got someone killed I would never forgive myself. A few short weeks ago, the only thing on the line was my career. Now it was my whole heart and all seven guys that each owned a bit of it.

"Good. Stay behind me and keep your eyes and ears open. I've taken care of most of his people, but there might be one or two left wandering around."

That explained the sheen of sweat on his brow. If he had any blood on him, he was hidden by the colour of his shirt. He looked good in black, and right now I was glad he wore it. If he was covered in blood, I would freak out right now.

"Do you trust me?" he asked.

"Of course I do," I said without hesitation. Maybe I shouldn't be so hasty, but I really did. I trusted whatever he had in mind, it was in all our best interests.

"Good. Come on then." He started to walk toward the backstage area, every movement cautious and deliberate. This wasn't the laid-back, gentle Tully I knew. This was Tully in stealth mode. It was sexy as fuck.

I tried to copy the way he moved, but probably looked ridiculous. Whatever, right now I was a hot pink ninja, ready to save my guys if I could.

We reached the steps and Tully dropped to a crouch. He gestured for me to do the same.

I crouched beside him and we listened.

"You know it's over, Fiorelli," Channing was saying. "You're totally fucked. Put down the gun and we might let you walk out of here alive. Your problem isn't with us, it's with the Brantley twins. We could just forget all of this and move on."

And send you the bill for all the destruction, I thought.

"You said Landon and Jackson had guns, didn't you?" Tully whispered in my ear.

I nodded and gave him a questioning look. What did that have to do with anything? Apart from the fact...

My mouth formed an O. They were the two least likely to kill anyone. Would Fiorelli know that? Probably. Predators like him were good at reading people.

Tully must have seen my realisation, because he bobbed his head quickly and turned his attention back to the stage. I could almost see the wheels turning in his brain.

"Enough of this," Dante snapped. "We both know you're not going to use those on us. You're just wasting time until the rest of my people come and dispose of you." He sounded very certain that was going to happen.

"Stand up," a voice said behind us.

I startled, but before I could move a hair, Tully had leapt up and swept the legs out from under the minion who crept up on us.

He grunted as he landed heavily on his back. The gun slid out of his hand.

I scrambled to my feet and ran to scoop it up. "You have some reflexes," I said to Tully.

He flashed me a grin and drove the heel of his boot into the man's throat. There wasn't even time for a gurgle, just a crunch of bone and a squelch I'd hear until the day I died.

I looked away as blood sprayed onto the carpet.

Holy shit.

The sound must have been audible from the stage, because I caught movement in the corner of my eye.

I looked up and saw Dante Fiorelli looking down at me. His eyes were the bluest I'd ever seen, contrasting with his black hair. He reminded me of Pete.

I didn't think.

I didn't hesitate.

I raised the gun, aimed it and fired.

An expression of shock crossed his features at the same time as blood blossomed across his groin. He opened his mouth as though he was going to shout something but then slowly, like time slowed, he fell. He landed on the surface of the stage with a thump and a groan.

I was vaguely aware of another shot and Fiorelli's minion joined his boss on the floor.

The gun dropped out of my hand and my knees gave way under me. Tully caught me before I hit the ground, my mind churning, the world a haze around me.

Blood pounded through my body.

The only thing I could think was— *I killed a man.*

CHAPTER
TWENTY-FOUR

ABBIE

"I'M GUESSING that wasn't what you had in mind?" I asked.

"Not exactly." Tully raised his glass to me. "But it got the job done."

I raised my glass back and swallowed a gulp of wine.

We all looked over as Jackson entered the hotel room. He rubbed a hand over his face and blinked a couple of times. He looked rumpled and tired. Basically how I felt.

"The press and fans have accepted the bomb scare excuse," he said. "Fans are disappointed, but they understand why police are swarming all over the stadium. We should be clear for you to play tomorrow night, if you're up to it."

"We'll be up to it," Zeke said. "If Asher is over his hangover by then."

"Hey," Asher said in protest. "I haven't had that much to drink."

"Yet," Penn said. He reclined against a wall, half of his attention on us and the other half on the news that was playing on the TV. I caught a glimpse of the stadium on the screen, and the faces of disappointed fans.

"They're the real victims here," Asher said. "I still can't believe you shot Dante Fiorelli in the cock."

"I was pretending it was Penn," I joked weakly. I glanced over at him and smiled, remembering his comment at the shooting range. He accused me of thinking about his cock while hitting the target in the groin. He was right, but I'd never tell.

"Remind me to teach you to aim for shoulders instead," Zeke said. "Shooting a guy in the cock is a dangerous reflex for a girl to have."

"It looked like a painful way to die." Landon still looked slightly freaked out from the evening's attack. He was snuggled up to Channing, but something in the way they sat looked comfortable, not like Landon was scared he was going to leave, and needed to hold him down.

"It couldn't have happened to a better motherfucker," Penn said.

"What Penn said," Channing said.

Penn raised an eyebrow at him. "Did you just agree with me?"

"Just this once," Channing said. "I still want that race do-over. The sooner I can kick your ass, the better."

I slipped out of my seat and walked over to put my arms around Jackson. "They're never going to change, are they?"

"You wouldn't want us to change," Tully said. "Either of you."

"I guess not," I agreed. I turned back to Jackson. "Are you okay?"

"For someone who was almost shot in the head, I'm doing fine," he said. "How about you? You must be… Conflicted?"

I thought about that for a moment. "Kinda. I mean, he wasn't walking out of there alive and he would have happily taken as many of you with him as he could."

"It was awesome," Asher said. "I wish I'd done it, but it was still fucking epic. Hey, Jackson, how did you not get shot?"

"He threw himself into us," Channing said. "Dude has one move, but it's a good one."

I glanced back at Jackson as he shrugged.

"I think it's a good idea to get out of the way of a bullet and get you guys out of the firing line at the same time. Wouldn't every manager do that?" He gave me a lopsided smile which made my heart flip.

"That's a resounding no," I said dryly. "Hopefully it's nothing you'll ever have to do again."

"The Fiorellis will be in disarray now," Zeke said. "Reuben can take care of the rest of it. They should leave us alone now to enjoy the rest of the tour."

"I'll drink to that," Asher said, raising his beer bottle high.

The rest of the guys matched him.

I sighed. "What happens after the tour?" I asked Jackson. I searched his denim blue eyes, hoping he had some answers.

"After the tour is IslandFest," he said. "Levi expects you to join the boys there. I was thinking maybe you and I could… I don't know, I'll arrange something."

I felt my face heat. "I'd like that."

"Good, because I hear you were talking to Levi and suggested we get our band back together for one last concert there too." He raised an eyebrow at me.

"I—" I blushed a little brighter. "I just thought… You two might enjoy playing again. If only one more time in front of an audience."

He smiled. "I can't wait. I wish I thought of it myself. It's exactly what I need after all this craziness. I'm not surprised you know what I need more than I do." He sounded a little choked up.

I kissed his mouth.

He kissed me back but then reluctantly broke off. "I have to go and speak to Levi. He needs to know what went on here. I was thinking I might suggest that nothing changes."

I gave him a funny look. A confused glance over shoulder showed all the guys were looking at him the same way too.

"What do you mean?" I asked softly.

"I mean, you touring with the guys is unorthodox but it's working. I don't see a reason not to do it again. Without all the killing and stalking and shit."

I grinned. "I like the sound of that." We could have our break time together and travel the world together. What could be better than that?

"Or she could officially join Wolf Venom?" Penn suggested.

Everyone looked at him in surprise. He'd come a long way from the guy who claimed he didn't want me around at all.

"Or that," Zeke agreed.

I thought about that for a moment. "I'd love to, but I still have my career to rebuild. I've just started getting that on track. There's still a ways to go." Plus I wanted to keep my creative freedom. I'd have more of that as a soloist than I would as a part of the band. And I'd get to jam with them. Win-win.

Zeke and Penn both nodded. Neither looked surprised, or annoyed. I didn't think they would be. They supported me and my career one hundred percent. That was just another reason I loved them. One of so many.

"We will need to work out where we're all going to live," Zeke said.

"I vote one big house with a cuddle puddle," Asher said.

"And a sensory room," Tully added.

"And recording studio," Landon said.

"And a gun range," Channing said.

"And a soundproof room where I can go to get away from you motherfuckers," Penn said.

"And a pool," Zeke said. "I've always wanted to live somewhere with a pool."

"I'll leave you to work that out." Jackson gave me a quick kiss and slipped back out the door.

"In the meantime," Penn turned off the TV and stepped over to me, "I don't know about you guys, but I'd like to celebrate being alive." He slipped his arms around me from behind.

EPILOGUE

ABBIE

I GLANCED around Reuben's library while the guys talked. He had more books than he had the last time I was here. I'd like to think someone with so many books couldn't be irredeemably evil, but it was Reuben we were talking about. He'd always be an asshole.

"And so you ran when you saw Fiorelli coming?" Asher asked Hunter. He looked like he was trying not to laugh at him.

Hunter gave him a look. "We were on our way, okay?" His eyes flicked over to Reuben, who sat in his big leather chair, looking unimpressed.

"Would you believe we got lost on the way?" Parker asked.

"Nope," Zeke said easily. "I'm with Asher. You took one look at them and ran away."

"We did not—" Hunter started to protest.

"That sounds accurate," Reuben said, his tone as dark as his expression.

"At least I got rid of Renae Fiorelli," Hunter said sulkily.

"Yes, at least you got rid of an unarmed woman who basically surrendered," Zeke said.

"She would have come after you again anyway," Parker said. "Having her there might have tipped the scales against you."

I could tell from their expressions no one believed a word the twins were saying. Whatever. That was firmly in the, 'not my problem,' basket. They made their beds, now they got to lie in them.

Reuben turned to Zeke. "I commend you for dispatching Dante Fiorelli and his son Sutton."

"It was Abbie who killed Dante," Zeke said evenly. "We don't know exactly who killed Sutton. With the lights out, it could have been anyone. Including Dante."

We'd discussed this a couple of times since that night, so I wasn't surprised by the suggestion. Dante certainly hadn't seemed impressed by his son. But to kill him? That was another thing that wasn't my problem. These people were all kinds of fucked up. If they wanted to take each other out, then so be it.

I was distracted by the sound of footsteps in the corridor outside the library. They stopped just outside the door.

Without moving, Reuben said, "You can come in."

I wouldn't have believed he was capable of talking in such a soft tone if I hadn't heard him myself. I found myself blinking at him in surprise before I glanced toward the door.

A woman around my age, stepped into the doorway. She looked tentative, nervous. Dark hair hung to her waist. Her large blue eyes had a hint of green. She was at least six or seven months pregnant.

Asher shot out of his chair. "Mina?"

It took a minute for that to register. Mina? As in his *sister* Mina? What had he said about her? *'We used to call her Mina Sunshine, because she was always smiling.'*

She wasn't smiling now. She looked anxious, like a scared rabbit looking at a fox. Or a den of foxes.

"Hello, Asher," she said softly.

Asher's gaze dropped to her belly. "Whose baby is that?"

Silence fell except the slow, heavy tick of a clock on the wall.

It was broken by a single word from Reuben. "Mine."

———

VENOMOUS

A SAVING ABBIE NOVELLA

So Good
Written by Abbie Hart

My love was a dark place,
Betrayed, denied, and broken.
I was shattered,
Over and gone.
Over and gone.
So gone.

One night I saw you,
And everything changed.
You put your arms 'round my world,
Broke all the chains.
All of the chains.
The chains.

Nothing can hold me back,
When you're holding me.
So many become one,
So hard, yet so easy.
So fucking easy.
So easy.

You have my whole heart,
Soul and body too.
Forever, I'll have,
Every one of you.
So fucking easy.
So fucking good.
So good.
So incredibly good.

CHAPTER
ONE

ABBIE

"I THOUGHT you said we were arriving in style." Penn looked over the back of his seat at Jackson, his eyes narrowed. "If this tin can rocks any harder, I'm going to puke on your shoes."

"This tin can," Jackson said slowly, "is worth a year's worth of wages. Yours, not mine. For the record, a small commercial aircraft would have bounced much worse than this one. If you prefer, I'll organise a boat to take you back to mainland North America?"

Penn made a rude sound in the back of his throat and turned away.

I put a hand on Jackson's thigh and squeezed, but my eyes were on the back of Penn's head.

"I think you should organise a *rowboat* for Penn." I couldn't resist teasing the keyboardist. He'd do the same to me if I was the one feeling sick.

Without looking back at me, Penn raised his hand and flipped me off. "It's not my fault if I get travel sick on small craft."

"No, but it's your fault we have to hear about it," Asher said from across the aisle. "Jackson finally organised a private jet for us and you're still not happy."

"I think it's awesome." I leaned my head against Jackson's shoulder and smiled up at him.

"I'm glad someone thinks so." Jackson lightly kissed my forehead. As manager of Wolf Venom, the hottest rock band in the world right now, and me, the slightly less popular soloist, he had enough on his plate without Penn complaining about everything.

Sometimes I wondered if Penn wasn't happy unless he had something to complain about. I loved the band's keyboardist as much as I loved the other six guys, but sometimes he could be a pain in everyone's ass.

"I think it's awesome too," Asher said. The band's drummer was an easy-going jokester, who usually put a positive spin on things, even the worst situation. His inappropriate humour at the wrong moment almost got us killed a couple of times in the past, but we got through. We always did.

"I agree." Zeke Brantley was the band's lead singer and unofficial leader in times of danger. When we came under attack by gangsters who were after him and his mobster family, he was the one we followed. If not for him, we'd all be dead right now. Especially him.

Good times.

He was also Asher's boyfriend as well as mine. "I think the label should spring for a private jet more often. Although, maybe with a king-sized bed next time." He grinned as Jackson turned to frown at him.

"Rowboat for two," Jackson said wryly. "Maybe you and Penn could race the plane back to Florida."

We all laughed, except Penn, who turned around to give him a dirty look.

"Don't encourage Zeke," he said. "That's exactly the kind of challenge he'd take."

Channing, the band's saxophonist, twisted around in his seat. "Are you afraid you'll lose?" he taunted.

"Rowboat versus a plane, what do you fucking think?" Penn retorted. "But you reminded me, it's past time we had that rematch. You, me, sandy beach. Let's see who can run fastest then. It'll still be me." He beat Channing back in Munich, weeks ago, but that was on paved ground. Sand would be a lot harder, given that it's a lot... you know, softer.

"You're on," Channing said. "I look forward to kicking your butt this time. Maybe we should make it interesting."

"You don't think this whole tour was interesting?" Landon asked. The rhythm guitarist's eyes were wide.

"He has a point," Tully said. The lead guitarist sat alone in front of Zeke and Asher, stretched out across two seats. "We almost died a time or two."

"Don't remind us," Jackson said. "Let's just enjoy IslandFest and put all of that behind us."

"Good idea," I said. "But I'm curious what Channing has in mind for a bet." Neither of them needed money, but they were so competitive, bragging rights wouldn't be enough.

"I'll think of something," Channing said.

"I can see the island," Asher said, drawing everyone's attention to him. He pointed excitedly at the window, his face pressed against it like he was a five-year-old boy, not a man in his mid-twenties. Whatever, we'd all agreed growing up was probably overrated anyway.

I looked out the window beside me at the sparkling ocean. It was dotted with boats, most heading in the same direction. IslandFest was going to be enormous.

Five days of rock music, partying and more music. Two hundred thousand concert goers would descend on the island. A hundred and fifty of the best bands in the world, and who knows how many up-and-coming artists, ready to perform in different locations around the island.

It was going to be incredible. I could hardly believe I was a part of it. Me, Abbie Hart. This was dream come true stuff right here. I wouldn't pinch myself in case I woke.

Without warning, the plane dropped a few metres. I made a face and swallowed hard to hold down my breakfast.

Penn groaned and his head disappeared. I peered between the seats to see him bent double, head between his knees.

"Are you—" I groaned as the plane dropped again. "That rowboat is sounding better and better."

"Sorry folks," the voice of the pilot came over the speakers. "An offshore breeze is creating turbulence. We'll be landing in about ten minutes, so buckle up."

We all hurried to do as he suggested, right at the same moment the plane dropped for a third time before rising again.

Penn popped back up long enough to say, "Was this plane made by one of your asshole families? It seems to hate me as much as they do." He disappeared again.

I smiled. He liked to pretend he was an asshole, and he wouldn't agree if he heard me say this, but he was sweet at times. All of the guys were. Besides, he had a point about the plane. Or at least, the turbulence. I didn't think even mobsters could control the weather. Yet.

"Maybe that offshore breeze is Penn's farts," Asher said. "He might be causing it."

Muffled words came from Penn's direction that sounded a lot like, "Fuck off," followed by, "It's probably bad air from Asher's ass."

"At least they haven't lost their sense of humour," I said to Jackson.

He laughed softly. "I've never known them to lose that. Other things, yes, but never that." He and I only became close in the last couple of weeks and we were still trying to sort out where he fit in with the rest of my boyfriends. He was their manager and their friend but he was also their family, with or without me.

It was…awkward, but we'd figure it out. Hopefully IslandFest would give us the chance we needed to do so. Including finding time to be alone, just the two of us. We looked for opportunities for the last couple of weeks but none had arisen, so to speak. With the world tour coming to an end, we were all busy and exhausted. A couple of days on the island before the festival started might be just what we all needed.

Sun, surf and sand, cocktails and my guys. Sounded like heaven to me. After this, we'd be off home, back to Australia. Back to our normal lives. The new normal that was, in which I was dating seven guys. Yeah, mind blowing isn't it?

"I can see the runway," Asher said. He looked around and frowned. "I just realised something."

His expression made my heart race. What the hell was wrong now? Hadn't we been through enough?

Evidently I wasn't the only one thinking exactly that. Everyone turned to look at him with more or less the same expression on their face. Worried with an air of freaked the fuck out.

"What did you realise, babe?" Zeke asked. His gorgeous face was creased in concern, laced with barely contained violence. He always seemed on the verge of punching the shit out of someone, or blowing their brains out.

"I realised," Asher said slowly, "that we should have parachuted down. Think of the entrance we would have made." He threw his hands up and raised his eyes like he was watching us fall from the sky towards him. A smile tugged on the corners of his mouth.

Penn sat up. "Who votes we throw Asher out right now?" He raised his hand. "We could open the festival with a splat instead of a bang."

"I know you love me," Asher told him. "That's why you wouldn't do that."

"I wouldn't do it because it would put the rest of us in danger," Penn said. "Otherwise, I'd totally do it. I bet Tully would help me."

Tully raised both of his hands, palms forward. "Leave me out of it, dude. I'm not throwing anyone out of a plane unless they're trying to kill one of us. If they are, then all bets are off. And so are they."

I believed him. If he had to, he'd kill to protect us. And he had. Most of us had. I didn't want to dwell on that anymore. The nightmares were enough.

"No one on this plane is trying to kill anyone else on this plane," Jackson said firmly. "Including the pilot, who is an old friend of Levi's."

The owner of our label, White Wolf Records, certainly knew some interesting people. But then, if anyone was going to know someone with a private jet, it would be Levi Jones. To say he was connected was an understatement. He also gave me a chance when I needed it more than anything. He signed me after my former label terminated my contract and no one else would touch me. Without him I wouldn't have my career or any of my guys.

"That's good to know," I said. "I'm almost certain the turbulence is a natural occurrence." After everything I'd seen and done in the last few months, I wouldn't rule out anything anymore. Even something as crazy as that.

He curled his fingers around mine. "It's one of those things, that's all. We'll be fine. I promise. Nothing bad is going to happen to you. It can't, because I have plans for us." His deep, rumbly tone left me in no doubt what he meant. A jolt of pure fire lanced right down to my core.

I looked up into his denim blue eyes. "You do? What is it?"

His eyebrows twitched and he smiled. He was clueless how hot he was. That was part of his charm.

"I'm not telling you. If I did, that would ruin the surprise. Trust me, you're going to love it."

"I do trust you," I said. "I'm sure whatever it is, it will be amazing." My heart stuttered at the thought of being alone with him. With six other boyfriends, I had no shortage of orgasms, but that didn't make me want him any less. If anything, waiting so long for this made me want him more. Semi-forbidden fruit and all that.

The lines around his eyes crinkled slightly as he frowned. "Now I'm worried I oversold it a little bit. Should I have just said you'll like it?" His eyes shone with humour.

"Always start low," Zeke said. "Then no one has high expectations."

"Are you speaking from experience?" Asher asked. "Because you always start with a high bar."

"That's because I know I can meet those expectations," Zeke said smugly.

"Thanks," Jackson said sarcastically. "You think I can't? You have that little faith in my organisational skills?" He made a face but clearly wasn't offended. We all knew his organisational skills were second to none. That was one of the reasons he was such a good manager. One of many reasons.

Zeke grinned. "Of course not. On the other hand, if you do something amazing, that's going to make it harder for the rest of us to impress Abbie." He looked totally unconcerned that might be an actual problem.

"I don't need to try to impress her," Penn said. "She's seen my cock. She's already impressed."

I couldn't argue with that. His cock *was* impressive. They all were, just like the guys they were attached to.

"If she's impressed by your cock, then the bar is really low," Asher teased.

"At least she can see mine," Penn said. "Unlike yours, mine is bigger than a pencil."

Asher laughed. "I've never seen a pencil as big as my dick. How would you write with it? It would be too long and thick."

"Long and thick, sounds like an accurate description of your head," Penn said.

"It sounds like an accurate description of both of your heads," Channing teased. He lightened up in the last few weeks, and joined in the teasing more often.

I shook my head at them all. They wouldn't be them if they didn't give each other hell. At the end of the day, all of the guys were closer than brothers. Their bond with me and with each other was unbreakable. Even when the situation was difficult, or deadly, we pulled through together.

We could survive a week of drinking, partying and music on a tropical island in the Caribbean.

I mean, what could go wrong? Right?

Okay, plenty.

CHAPTER
TWO

ABBIE

"THIS IS AMAZING." Landon's eyes were huge as he looked around one of the rooms. We had two, with a door between them, and a bathroom for each room. The door would stay open and we'd gather in one room, like we usually did. Not many hotels accommodated polyamorous groups of eight. Yet. Give the world some time.

"Yeah, it's not bad," Channing agreed. He dragged his suitcase to the corner and left it beside Landon's. Give it five minutes, there would be clothes strewn around everywhere.

"How to say you've been in a lot of five-star hotels without saying you've been in a lot of five-star hotels," Asher teased. He left his suitcase in another corner, with Zeke's and mine. "I think it's amazing."

"It really is," I agreed. The resort was one of many on the island, and not even the biggest or fanciest, but the view of the ocean a couple of metres from the front steps of the villa was incredible.

"I'm not that easily impressed by places." Channing shrugged. "As long as you two are here, I have all I need."

"Thank you," Zeke said as if Channing was talking about him.

"He means me," Penn said, dragging his suitcase into the other bedroom.

"He means all of us," Asher said. He draped an arm over Channing's shoulder. "Right?"

"Sure." Channing gave him the side eye. "If that's what you want to believe."

Asher patted his back. "It totally is." He lowered his arm and stepped away. "Who's up for a swim?"

"Not you," Jackson said. "You all have an interview in half an hour."

We all turned and gave him a look, including me.

He raised his hands. "What can I say? Have you forgotten you're not here for a holiday?"

"Forgotten, no," Asher said. "In denial, yes. Surprised you couldn't give us a few hours to unwind? Not really."

"Trying to keep your careers on track? Definitely," Jackson retorted. "It shouldn't take long, then you can do whatever you want for the rest of the day. Within reason," he added quickly. "Don't forget I'm the designated killjoy around here."

I hooked my arm through his. "No you're not. You're just doing what's best for us, because you care."

"And because he gets paid for it," Penn said.

"That too," Jackson agreed. He kissed my nose. "Just so you all know, Abbie and I are going on a date tonight. Try not to burn the resort down while we're gone."

"So much for doing whatever we want for the rest of the night." Asher snaked an arm around my waist and pulled me away from Jackson and to his chest. "I was looking forward to a bunch of fucking." He kissed my mouth, long and slow. His tongue swept across my lips, hungry as always.

Zeke stepped up behind him and wrapped his arms around Asher's neck. "You can still have a bunch of fucking, babe."

"Hell yeah," Asher said. "Although, it's fun when it's three of us. Or more than three."

"I'll pretend there's two or three of me," Zeke said. "By the time I'm done with you, you'll forget there's only one of me."

Asher looked over his shoulder. "I knew there was a reason I loved you. You're epic."

"Fuck yeah, I am," Zeke agreed. "So are you two." He kissed Asher and then me.

"If we keep doing this, we're going to miss that interview," I said. Which was tempting right now, with both guys wrapped around me and each other. The breeze generated by the ceiling fan above me did nothing to cool my blood. With seven guys around me, there was no shortage of stimulation, no lack of fucking either. They always got me going with just a look or a touch anyway. And all of them knew it.

"They won't notice if we're not there." Asher nuzzled his face into my hair.

"They won't notice if *I'm* not there, but they'll notice if you're not," I said firmly.

"They'll notice if *any* of you are missing," Jackson said. "They want to speak to all of you." He gave me a long look when I turned my face to look at him. "You too. I know you haven't had a good relationship with the press in the past, but we're working on changing that. Okay?"

That was the understatement of the year, but I wasn't going to let them get me down anymore. I'd dragged myself up from a black hole with the help of the guys, and the support of my fans. If the press didn't like it, they could get fucked.

Not by me.

Honestly, most of them were nice these days. Of course they were. They caught a sniff of the relationship between me and the guys and wanted to be the ones to break the story. Considering the boost it would give to their careers, they might do almost anything for it.

Good luck with that. We had no plans to discuss it with anyone other than ourselves. As far as we were concerned, it was our business, no one else's. At least until we were ready to make it someone else's business. For now, we'd keep it amongst us.

Although we weren't exactly going out of our way to be discreet. Photos of me with Channing and Landon, and with Asher and Zeke, had all gone viral. Sooner or later, someone would take photos of me with Tully, Penn, Jackson or all of them.

Whatever. If that was all people had to talk about in their day, then maybe they should get themselves a life.

"I know you wouldn't arrange interviews with anyone who would act like a prick," I assured Jackson. "And if they do, that's on them. Not you."

"The label's publicist has been carefully vetting everyone that might want to talk to any of you," Jackson said. "They know if they screw up, they won't get access to you again. Levi is big on giving second chances to people who deserve it, but not those who don't. And he has a *long* memory."

"To match his long bank account balance," Asher said.

"Exactly," Jackson said lightly. He didn't say any more, but we all knew what he was thinking. The guy's bank balances were healthy too. Healthier than his or mine.

When I first met the guys, I was down to my last couple of hundred dollars. I was better off now, but I had a long way to go to catch them. Not that it was a competition. They made it clear on more than one occasion that what was theirs was also mine. Naturally, the opposite was true as well.

On the other hand, I liked to have my own money and not rely on them for anything other than support and orgasms. Lots and lots of orgasms.

I glanced at my phone. "Do I have time to make myself pretty?" I asked.

"You're already pretty, sweetheart," Zeke said immediately.

"It's Asher who needs the help." Penn was leaning against the wall, looking out at the ocean. "But there's not enough time in the day to make him look pretty."

"Fuck off," Asher said cheerfully. "I am pretty. On the outside and, unlike you, on the inside too." He flashed Penn a sarcastic smile, showing no teeth.

Penn shrugged. "I don't want to be pretty on the inside. That would interfere with my reputation as a badass and an asshole."

"Nothing will interfere with those," Zeke assured him. "You've firmly established yourself as the band asshole."

"Thank you." Penn nodded as though that was an actual compliment. "Don't anyone go forgetting it."

"How could we forget, you keep on reminding us, sir?" I told him. When we first met, we hated each other. Or at least, we gave each other a lot of shit. At the same time, we wanted to fuck each other. Okay, not much changed, but I loved him like crazy. He was an asshole, but he was mine. And loved when I called him sir before I sucked his cock dry.

Penn shrugged and gave me a look so heated it was lucky my panties didn't melt right off .

Whether or not I was pretty was a matter of opinion, but right now I was as wet as hell.

"I might go and fix my make up." By that I meant, change my panties. These guys were all dangerous in the best possible way. They loved driving me wild as much as they liked playing music.

I was one hundred percent here for every moment of it.

Asher gave me a knowing glance of his own and reluctantly unwound his arms from me.

"Okay, but Zeke and I get to take you out for lunch tomorrow. I'd say breakfast, but it sounds like you might be busy with Jackson." He gave us both a lopsided smile. Not one hint of jealousy. If anything, he looked ready to herd everyone out the door so we could be alone.

Tempting, but even if the interviewer didn't notice my absence, they'd notice Jackson's. They'd probably take it as a cue to ask questions they were already told not to ask. At the very least, they'd push their luck as far as they could take it.

That would probably lead to Penn telling them to fuck off. As much as I wanted time alone with Jackson, I didn't want to miss that. Penn was never shy about sharing his feelings, especially when that feeling was irritation, anger or annoyance.

"If I'm lucky," Jackson agreed.

My heart did a triple somersault.

Jackson usually played his cards close to his chest. Today he looked at me like I was the last piece of chocolate, saved just for him. A piece he'd thought about eating for a long time.

Honestly, that was probably accurate. I thought about him eating me for quite some time too. Pretty much since we met. I couldn't wait to see what he had planned. Whatever it was, it would be amazing. Even if it was a simple picnic on the beach, watching the sun set. That sounded perfect to me.

"I won't be long." I stopped to give Jackson a kiss on my way to my suitcase, then pulled out what I needed and stepped into the bathroom.

"Let us know if you need any help," Tully called out after me.

I opened the door and peered back out at him. "You know how to fix makeup?"

He grinned. "No, but I know how to mess it up." Before I could respond he added, "I also know how to avoid messing it up." He winked and wiggled his eyebrows.

I shook my head at him and closed the door again. If we weren't in a hurry, I would take him up on that offer. At this rate, I was going to need shares in a panty factory.

I regarded my reflection in the mirror while I added a little extra mascara and eyeliner, and redid my lipstick.

A few months ago, I would have seen a down and out, desperate singer looking back at me. Now, I looked happy. Happier than I ever had. Never in my wildest dreams could I have imagined living the life I was living right now.

Okay, no one would have imagined the mobster part, or the seven boyfriends, but if anyone even told me it was possible, I would have told them they were out of their minds. And yet, here I was, in a tropical resort, living my best life.

I was a lucky girl. And very much looking forward to a nice quiet night alone with Jackson.

CHAPTER
THREE

JACKSON

"OH, WOW, ARE YOU KIDDING ME?"

The way her eyes widened, and the smile on her gorgeous mouth, were exactly what I hoped for. What I imagined a hundred times since I thought this up.

"Whose—"

"I borrowed it from the resort manager." I led her over to the back of the vintage motorbike and handed her a helmet. "According to her, it still runs." I knew enough about bikes to know this one was in nearly perfect condition. Perfect for a bike which lived in a place where salt sooner or later attacked everything.

"If it breaks down, we don't have far to walk." I picked up my own helmet and pressed it down onto my head.

We could have walked there to begin with, but how would I impress her if that was how our date started? After all, I was trying to stand out when her other six boyfriends were all famous rock stars. I still wasn't sure what she saw in me—a former bass player turned manager twelve years older than her. I wasn't as buff as the other guys or as cool. I could drive a bus and ride a motorcycle, so there was that. A guy had to use what skills he had.

I had a few more up my sleeve before tonight was done.

She gave me a doubtful look, which I probably deserved, and slipped on her helmet.

I helped her onto the back of the bike and straddled the seat in front of her. "Hold on tight."

My dick was twitchy before she slipped her arms around me. Feeling her pressed hard against my back…

Down boy, I told myself. We had plenty of time for that later.

Who was I kidding? Abbie was absolutely gorgeous and my cock was right to respond to her.

Fortunately, with a couple of days before the festival and being later in the afternoon, the narrow road that circumnavigated the island was almost empty. Apart from a few people walking, and a man riding a bike, we had it to ourselves.

"Do you know we're going?" she said in my ear.

I laughed. The wind dragged the sound away.

"I have some idea," I said over my shoulder. The island wasn't big enough to get lost, and the directions I was given seemed simple enough. Ride past all the resorts until we reached a part of the island that wasn't developed yet. Our destination was right at the end of a spit of land. Everything should be waiting for us.

"This is beautiful," she said as we flew across a small bridge over a stream. On one side was forest, on the other ocean.

"You're beautiful." The view might be jealous of her, but it was a gorgeous part of the world.

"No, you." The breeze swept her laugh away too, but not before it tickled my ear, making me even harder.

"I'm not beautiful." I slowed the bike as we rode onto the spit and headed to the very end. We stopped under a stand of trees and I killed the engine.

"That was amazing." She slipped off the bike and removed her helmet. "I've always wanted to learn to ride like that."

"I'd be happy to teach you." That, and a whole bunch of other things.

She smiled. "Will you also teach me to ride a motorbike?"

"Did you read my mind?" I asked. Yeah, okay, it was probably obvious what I was thinking. Partly because we both knew what this time alone was for, and partly because I was a hot-blooded guy.

"I didn't need to, it's what I'm thinking too." She slipped her hand into mine and I led her away from the bike and toward the beach.

"Is that rowboat for Penn?" She smiled teasingly at me.

"Don't tell him, but yes," I joked. "We're going to use it first though."

"Are we going fishing?" she guessed.

"That depends, do you *want* to go fishing?" I asked.

She frowned slightly, like she rolled the question around in her mind before she responded. "I mean, if that's what you organised, then I'd love to." That was very diplomatic, but I couldn't tell what she was really thinking.

"And if I didn't?" I asked.

"Did you?" She was never one to hold back for long.

"No, I didn't." I grabbed the end of the boat and started to drag it towards the water. It wasn't too heavy, and slid easily over the perfect sand, leaving a gouge behind it. The tide would swallow it soon enough, making it look like we were never here.

"Thank goodness, because I hate fishing," she admitted. "I'm not very outdoorsy. I'm more of a city girl."

"Me too," I said. I paused for a moment and laughed. "Except the girl part." *Smooth, Jax*, I told myself. She probably thought I was an idiot and she hadn't known until now.

Thankfully, she laughed too, and moved to grab the end of the boat beside me.

Together, we dragged it down to the sand and into the shallows.

"Do you know how to row?" She twisted the front of her skirt in one hand and held it up out of the water.

"Would you believe I rowed competitively in high school and university?"

She regarded me for a moment. "I think I would believe that, yes. Were you any good at it?"

I took her hand and helped her to climb into the boat. "Not Olympic-level good, but not bad. Mostly it was just fun and good exercise. Then I met Levi and we started the band and I got too busy for it. Hopefully it's like riding a bike, you never forget how." I climbed in and sat facing her, my back to the front of the boat.

I gripped the oars and started to row.

She watched me for a couple of minutes then said, "It's kinda hot that you know how to do all these things. Row, ride a bike, drive a bus."

"A manager needs all sorts of different skills," I said. "Sooner or later, they come in handy. This one in particular. You never know when you might need to row a beautiful woman around on a tropical island."

I watched her when she smiled. I wasn't lying when I said she was beautiful, but when she smiled, it was like the whole universe exploded into fireworks. And the best thing? She had no idea how gorgeous she was. If she did, she'd have a bigger ego than all of Wolf Venom put together. All the bands who were here for IslandFest put together.

Instead, she was humble and sweet, but not scared of her own sexuality. Perfect.

"Just a wild guess, it doesn't come up often?" she said.

I cocked my head at her. "You know, you're right. It doesn't happen nearly as often as it should. I'll make a note and mention it to Levi the next time I talk to him."

She laughed. "So, where are we rowing to?"

"Who says we're rowing anywhere?" I asked. "We might just be rowing for the fun of it." And it was fun, but it wasn't the point of this date.

"The lack of any food on the beach, and in this boat, suggests you're up to something," she pointed out. "And the fact we seem to be headed straight for that yacht." She nodded forward.

"Maybe it's in our way and we're about to run into it?" I suggested.

"If that's the case, then I suggest you turn *really* soon." She only looked slightly worried. She knew, after all we'd been through, that I wouldn't risk her life, not for anything.

I smiled and turned my head to gauge the distance between us and the yacht. At the last moment, I put down the oars and stood to grab a rope on the side of the bigger vessel. I pulled us in until we were hull to hull and tied the rowboat to the side of the yacht.

"Yours?" She looked impressed.

I snorted a laugh. "I wish. This is a bit above my pay packet. It belongs to the resort." It was a beautiful vessel. One day...

I checked the line was secure and gestured towards the ladder on the side of the yacht. "Ladies first."

"I don't see any ladies, but I can go first." She grinned at me and gripped the bottom rung to pull herself up. Lucky I'd told her not to wear heels, those would have gotten in the way, big time.

I watched her cute little ass and firm, inviting thighs as she climbed the ladder, then followed her.

The sun was just starting to set as we stepped onto the deck of the yacht.

"This is lovely," she said softly. Her gaze swiveled, taking everything in.

A blue tablecloth covered a table that was bolted down to the deck. The top of the table was decorated with flowers and candles. Beside the table, two boxes sat, one with food and the other with wine.

The rest of the deck was decorated with flowers and of course a wide mattress, blankets and pillows. Music played from speakers around the deck. Not hers, or Wolf Venom. The playlist was full of soft rock songs, carefully chosen to be background music, to set the scene.

Yep, classic seduction stuff. Why screw with what works?

"You thought of everything," she said.

"Probably not everything," I said. "Hopefully]enough to get us through the night." All I really needed was a little bit of food and her. Maybe not even the food.

"It's beautiful," she said.

Her tone distracted, she added, "Thank you." She glanced around carefully, eyes narrowed in a frown. She peered below decks, into the small living area and bedroom. She might even have looked under the table.

I waited until she finished, my arms crossed over my chest. Finally, she stopped looking and nodded, satisfied.

"No sign of any evil twins?" I asked.

"Not that I can see," she said. "We might get to enjoy an uninterrupted night."

Zeke's identical twin brothers had followed us around on the entire world tour. I wouldn't be surprised if they turned up here, on the island. If they turned up on this yacht, I wouldn't hesitate to throw them back overboard. The pair did nothing but cause trouble for everyone.

We didn't call them the evil twins for nothing.

"Good, then let's have some wine and something to eat." I pulled two glasses out of the box and poured one for each of us. I handed one to her and offered her a toast.

"To not being interrupted," I said.

"I'll drink to that," she said. She raised her glass to mine and we clinked. She sipped and smiled. "Delicious."

"Not as delicious as you." I looked forward to finding out exactly how tasty she was. Better than the wine, I'd bet.

"You're going to give me an ego the size of Penn's," she said.

I laughed. "There's no way you could have an ego that big. That's not who you are. But if you did, I'd still love you."

Her expression softened. "I love you too," she said softly. "This night is going to be perfect, I can tell."

"No pressure," I said jokingly. I slipped my arm around her.

We stood watching the sun dip toward the horizon. It glittered off the water, all pink and yellow and gold, like the world painted a special work of art just for us. The headwind that created the turbulence in the plane had dropped to just a slight breeze. The air was warm, but clear and fresh. For a little while, we could pretend we were the only two people in the entire world.

CHAPTER
FOUR

"THIS WAS INCREDIBLE." I leaned back against Jackson. He wrapped his arms around me.

The yacht bobbed on water illuminated by moonlight and distant lights from a resort on the island. Every so often, the sound of distant music, and shouts of people having fun, whispered on the breeze. Aside from that, it was just us.

Being away from all the guys and the hustle and bustle of the tour was a strange but lovely change.

"I'm glad you liked it." His breath brushed the side of my neck.

I shivered deliciously.

His voice low and husky, he said, "I wasn't sure if I could compete with the other guys. You've had some memorable dates with them."

"This was memorable because it's lovely and no one has crashed it," I said.

I waited for a moment, but no evil twins appeared out of nowhere. "And because I got to spend it with you."

I turned around and wound my arms around his neck. "Also, you don't have to compete with them. I love all of you equally."

He hesitated for a moment and glanced around. "Sorry, I was waiting for Asher or Penn to say you love them the most." His teeth flashed white in the moonlight.

I laughed softly. "That is something *both* of them would say. Then they'd flip each other off."

He chuckled. "Lucky for everyone, we all get along so well. As much as I'm going to miss managing Blazing Violet, I can live without their blazing arguments. It's a miracle Violet and Blaise haven't killed each other yet."

"Or fucked each other," I said.

"Or that too. I'm sure that will happen soon enough." His grimace folded into a smile. "But let's not talk about them."

"Let's not talk at all." I pulled his mouth down to mine and kissed him lightly, barely more than a brush of my lips over his.

"I can do not talking." He kissed me more deeply, but still soft and tasting of wine and the chocolate mousse we had for dessert.

I swept my tongue over his lips and inside his mouth to meet his.

He ran his hands up and down my back a couple of times, then slipped under the hem of my shirt. His fingers were calloused but gentle against my bare skin.

"You feel amazing." He broke off from my mouth and kissed his way down my neck, while his hands wandered up higher.

"No, you." I brought my hands down to rest lightly against his chest before I started to undo the buttons of his shirt. I hadn't seen him without one, and I was intrigued about what I would find. I expected tattoos and I wasn't disappointed. He had a dragon with outstretched wings across his chest, and several other mythological creatures on his shoulders. His chest and stomach were as firm as any of the guys', his abs clearly defined, even if he wasn't quite as ripped.

I slipped his shirt off to reveal the delicious V of his hips, and a couple more tattoos on his sides.

"What does this one mean?" I lightly touched what looked like an arrow bent into an infinity symbol, done in simple, black ink.

He glanced down. "It means sometimes you have to go through shitty times to get to good times."

I couldn't suppress a snort. "That's disturbingly accurate. Did you add, 'seeing the future,' to your list of skills?"

He smiled. "No. It's just a general rule the universe seems to have. It puts you through shit and then you come out the other side, stronger than ever." He brushed a stray bit of hair off my face. "Just like you did."

"Shame, I was going to ask if you have the numbers for next week's lottery draw," I joked. "I would have bought a ticket." Although, with seven amazing boyfriends, hadn't I already won the lottery?

He chuckled. "Sorry, I can't help you with that. I'm sure sixty-nine is one of the lucky numbers." He leaned in to kiss me again.

I laughed against his mouth. "That would be a very lucky number."

He worked his hands higher up my back and pulled my shirt up over my head. I raised my arms and broke off our kiss long enough to let him tug it off. He dropped it on the deck and unhooked my bra. After he slid that down my arms and over my hands, he stepped back to look at me.

"Holy crap, you're gorgeous," he said. "How in the world..." He shook his head and kissed me again. His hands wandered around to my front, sliding slowly over my skin until he cupped my breasts.

"You feel even better than I imagined." He rubbed his palms up and down my nipples until they pebbled under his touch.

I hummed softly. Every touch was making me wet as hell.

"Jackson," I said just to say his name. "I want you so much."

"I want you too." He walked backward to the mattress and lay back, taking me with him. He helped me to shed the rest of my clothes and let his mouth and hands wander all over me.

He kissed his way down my body, over my stomach and down between my thighs. He slipped an arm under each one, opening me up to him.

"I've been wanting to taste you like this for so long." He lowered his mouth to my pussy and, with a feather light touch, traced circles and patterns around my clit and folds, like he was drawing musical notes with his tongue. "Just as I suspected, you're delicious."

I could only respond with a soft moan, because his delicate licks had me going crazy. I wanted more, I wanted everything, but I also wanted this to last forever.

He slowly, and as gently as he did everything, slipped a finger inside me.

"Woman, you're so wet," he said like he'd never felt anything like the inside of my body before. He added a second finger to the first, and hooked them around to massage me inside.

"Fuck, Jackson, that feels so good." I rolled my hips, bucking against his hand, wanting to feel everything, all at once, but trying not to rush.

"You really do," he agreed, his voice muffled by my pussy.

I laughed slightly, but it was cut off by a groan as pleasure built, stammering through my blood like a drum roll. "I'm going to come."

He licked and stroked me harder than ever, pushing me, driving me to the edge hard. He said something that sounded like, "Come for me, beautiful."

And I did. I came so hard my back arched and I lifted halfway off the mattress. My cry of pleasure shattered into a million different notes, which echoed across the water. They probably heard it back at the resort. Good. Let them.

I started to come down, but Jackson didn't stop. If anything, he worked me even harder than before, his determined, persistent, slow touch pushing me to another, even more explosive orgasm.

I bucked against him frantically, muscles clenching everywhere. I held my breath until I saw stars in a hundred different universes, ignited by the blood pounding through me. When I finally managed to breathe, my shout was louder than the first time. I threw back my head and screamed out his name.

I felt like I was floating down from the atmosphere, but he still didn't stop.

"One more," he said. It wasn't a suggestion. It wasn't a demand either, not exactly. It was a statement of fact. One he expected could happen, would happen.

"I don't think I can," I said. "Please—" I didn't know what I was asking for. Maybe for him to stop, and maybe begging him never to stop.

"You can," he insisted. "One more for me." His hand and mouth worked me with expert, precise touch. I was his instrument and he knew exactly how to play me. Precisely how to get my body to do what he wanted. What we both wanted.

I started to shake my head, but the pressure rose again.

It was slower this time; Adante, not allegro. A rising tide instead of a flash flood. Although I'd probably covered his hand with a flood of my juices.

When I came for a third time, his name was ripped from my lips louder than before. So loud it left my throat almost raw. I bucked and rolled against him so hard the yacht rocked with me. Honestly, I was so lost in pleasure I didn't care. The whole world disappeared and the only thing that was left was one long, intense orgasm that swallowed me whole and slowly slithered me out the other side.

"Holy shit," I said once I finally managed to get my breath back. "That was insane."

"In a good way, I hope." He slipped his arms out from under my thighs and scooted up until he was lying beside me. He smelled of me and, when he kissed me, tasted of me.

"In a very good way." I rolled onto my side and unfastened the front of his jeans. His erection was so eager to escape, it was a miracle he hadn't broken the zipper, or split the seam of his boxers.

I blinked. My eyebrows rose.

"Okay, I wasn't expecting that."

Four bars, parallel to each other, were pierced down the length of Jackson's cock.

"Babe, you get hotter and hotter," I told him. Landon had thought about getting a Jacob's ladder, but I had no idea Jackson already had one. I lightly ran my finger across each one, and the skin in between. Both were deliciously warm to the touch.

"You know what they say, it's always the quiet ones." He grinned. He grabbed me and rolled me until I straddled his hips.

I smiled back. "They do say that, don't they? I guess when it comes to you, I need to learn to expect the unexpected." I positioned myself so my pussy was over his cock and lowered myself down slowly.

His eyes widened. "I could say the same about you." He exhaled slowly. "You feel so fucking incredible."

"So do you." His piercings massaged my insides, teasing, sliding against sensitive flesh. I definitely had at least one more orgasm in me, maybe more. He felt so ridiculously amazing, how could I not?

He gripped my hips in firm, gentle hands, but let me choose the rhythm. "I thought about this so many times, but this is at least a billion percent better than anything I imagined."

"I'm so glad I didn't disappoint you," I teased. I started slowly, rising and falling up and down his hard cock.

He laughed softly. "You could never do that. Not even if you tried." He looked up at me with a combination of bliss and love that both melted my heart and heated my core.

"I love you," I said, as the pressure slowly rose yet again.

"I love you too." He thrust up into my body, hips working. "I'm the luckiest guy in the world right now."

"I'm the luckiest girl in the world all the time." I locked my eyes on his and watched his face as I rode him, slow then fast then slow again. His piercings massaged my insides like nothing I ever felt before. As it was, his cock was big enough and thick enough to fill me to absolute ecstasy.

"Come with me," he said. "Come with me, beautiful girl."

I pressed my palms to his rock hard stomach and drove us both with deliberate rolls of my hips, in perfect rhythm with him.

My eyes not moving from his, I came harder than ever. At the same time he stilled and came inside me. In that moment, there was nothing but me and him, love and pleasure, fireworks and hot blood, release and breathless panting.

We finally slumped together on the mattress sweating and trying to catch our breath. For the longest time we just lay there tangled around each other, lost in the perfect moment.

CHAPTER
FIVE

ABBIE

IT WAS STILL DARK when I woke. Jackson and I had managed a shower before falling asleep on the mattress on deck, his arms around me.

I opened my eyes a crack. As far as I could tell, neither of us had moved. What woke me then? Specifically, what woke me that made the hairs on the back of my neck rise? Maybe it was latent paranoia after the four, and all we dealt with.

That's in the past, I told myself. There's nothing there.

And yet, all my senses were on high alert. Something was definitely wrong.

Jackson twitched and his hand curled around my arm. He felt it too. His hand was a warning not to speak, not to move.

I squeezed his arm in return to indicate that I understood.

I trusted Jackson completely, but if anything was up, we might wish Zeke, Asher or Tully were here. They had the skills and the background to deal with all sorts of shit. Fortunately, both of us were quick learners.

I hoped.

Something bumped against the side of the yacht.

It's just the rowboat, I told myself.

Only… The rowboat was on the *other* side of the yacht. Shit.

I hardly dared to breathe.

Something moved on the side of the boat. Or some*one*. Or several some-ones. Whatever it was, it probably wasn't a friendly dolphin come to hang out with us. It could be the other guys, fed up of waiting for us to come back. It would be like them to crash this party. If they did, I would…

"He's up there," a male voice said. Not one I knew. On the upside, it wasn't the evil twins. On the downside, it wasn't any of the guys either.

Wait, did he say 'he'? Were they after one of us, or was it a case of mistaken identity?

I twisted around enough to whisper in Jackson's ear. "We need to get out of here."

I barely finished speaking when the night was lit up by a burst of light. I threw my hand up in front of my eyes and blinked like crazy.

"What the fuck—"

"It's him all right," a voice growled.

Jackson sat up, also shielding his eyes from the light. "Who are you and what the hell do you want?" He pulled me behind him, placing himself between me and whoever the fuck it was.

Another voice said. "We'll take her too. You have thirty seconds to get dressed or you're going like that."

"She looks fine just how she is," the first voice said. "Easier to have some fun with her before—"

"She's not going to live long enough for any fun," the second voice snapped.

I looked over Jackson, my eyes wild. Rule number one of any kidnapping or potential kidnapping: don't let them take you to another location.

On the other hand, the sound of a cocking gun was loud so close to my ear. Holy fucking shit.

I grabbed my clothes, which were still scattered around the deck, and dressed with about five seconds to spare. Go me.

Jackson did the same, but still managed to keep himself between me and... whoever they were. That was a very Jackson thing to do, protecting someone he cared about. He did the same with the guys in the past. He always joked he was just being a good manager, but he was more than that. He was a good guy. One of the best.

"Get in the boat," the first man ordered. He waved us over to the side of the yacht, a gun in his hand.

"I feel like if you're going to kidnap us, you should at least tell us who you are," I said. That seemed only fair to me, although I doubted they were going to be that forthcoming. People didn't sneak up on you in the night and then tell you all about themselves. Right?

"You'll find out soon enough," he said.

"Okay, well... For the record, I hate being kidnapped. It's getting to be really annoying." I swung a leg over the side of the yacht and started down the ladder on the opposite side to the rowboat.

"I agree," Jackson said. "Being kidnapped sucks. You could just tell us what you want. Maybe we can work something out. It sounds like it's me you want anyway. Leave her here. She—"

"We want you to shut up," the second voice snapped predictably. Whoever they were, they weren't chatty. Honestly, I didn't want their life story anyway, just the reason they were doing this and what they wanted from us. It might be something we could resolve over leftover lobster. Oh, right, we ate it all. There might be some bread left.

"We don't need you with all your body parts intact," the first man said.

Since I preferred to have my body parts intact, I pressed my lips together and fell silent.

I stepped down to a boat bigger than the rowboat but smaller than the yacht. Another man grabbed me around the waist and pushed me onto a seat. Jackson was plopped down beside me a moment later.

"Please tell me this was part of the date," I whispered. "Just to spice things up a bit." I wasn't sure if I'd be relieved or pissed off if that was the case. He might earn himself a one way trip overboard.

"No," he whispered back. "Should it be? I could have—"

"Fuck no," I said quickly. "Everything was perfect up until now. Any idea who they are?"

He looked thoughtful. "I'm hoping there's a competing festival who really, really wanted you to sing there."

"The chance of that seems kinda slim," I pointed out.

He sighed. "Really slim. My other guess is much worse. "

"Please tell me your other guess is a rival *label*," I joked weakly. "I'll also accept a practical joke." Since they seemed to know who he was, mistaken identity was probably off the table.

"It's more likely they have to do with one of our families," Jackson admitted. "Unless you accidentally pissed someone off recently?"

"If I did, you'd know," I said.

"That's true." Nothing happened that he and Levi Jones didn't know about, or find out about pretty quickly. Or know before the rest of us knew. Or— Yeah, they were well informed.

The first two kidnappers jumped into the boat and a man moved to start the engine and peel us away from the yacht.

We sat in silence for a few minutes, until I said, "As soon as the guys notice we're missing, they'll come after us."

"Yeah," Jackson said. "They—"

The kidnapper piloting the boat picked up something from beside the steering controls and pointed it over his shoulder towards the yacht.

A couple of seconds passed and nothing happened.

Then the yacht exploded into a huge fireball that lit up the night and all the water around it. Flames and debris flew into the sky. The blast sent huge waves that threatened to swamp the boat we were on. We crested one and slid down the other side. My stomach made approximately the same motion and I groaned.

Jackson gripped the seat in front of him with one hand and me with the other, while I held onto the seat with both hands, knuckles white.

"Worst carnival ride ever," I growled. Thank fuck Penn wasn't here, he'd probably be throwing up already. I was close to doing it myself.

"This is bullshit," I said once the ocean settled again. Tears ran down my cheeks at the sight of the yacht. It quickly burnt down to the waterline. "What if they think we died on there?" The yacht was going to be on the bottom of the ocean within an hour or two. By the time they brought it back up to the surface, if they did, and realised we weren't there, days could have gone by. Or longer.

"Hey." Jackson put an arm around my shoulders and pulled me to him. "You have met them, right? They'll figure it out. And you know us, we're resourceful. We're badasses. We've gotten ourselves out of worse situations than this, and we've done it in style. Well, you've done it in style, I'm just the manager."

"You're very stylish," I said firmly. "And you're not just the manager. You're one of my boyfriends and a guy I love." He was right though, we had gotten ourselves out of some terrible situations, but we'd had all the other guys with us, and all their skills. This time, it was just the two of us and I didn't even have a pair of heels to stab someone in the eyeball with. If it came to it, that was. It seemed kindly likely that it might. This was so fucked up.

"I love you too." He pressed his nose to mine.

"We told you to shut up," one of the kidnappers growled. "Maybe we should separate them."

"Just keep an eye on them, Leopold," the man piloting the boat said. "As long as they cooperate, we have no need to make this unpleasant."

"Yes, Nikolai," Leopold grunted. He didn't look happy at being told not to throw his weight around.

Me, on the other hand... I nodded towards Nikolai. "I like this guy. I mean, for a kidnapper, he seems kinda reasonable. Don't you think?"

Jackson shrugged one shoulder. "I've been kidnapped by worse."

"Actually, so have I," I said. "How about that?"

Nikolai turned and gave us a funny look. He probably thought we were completely insane.

Maybe we were, but this was how we dealt with stress around here. We made silly jokes and kept things as light as we could.

"Any idea where they're taking us?" I whispered.

Jackson shook his head lightly. "Another yacht or another island would be my guess, but I could be wrong. For all I know, they might have a submarine around here somewhere."

"I've always wanted to go in a submarine, but not against my will," I remarked.

"Really?" Jackson asked. "I can't say it's on my bucket list." He scratched the back of his head. "They seem like they're all about really enclosed spaces and underwater and all that shit. But if you want to do that someday, I'll see if I can organise something. The other guys might want to go too."

"I bet they would," I agreed. "We could have a band outing on a submarine." Of course, we had to live long enough to do it.

"Is there anything else you want me to organise?" he asked. "Just, you know, while we're on the subject."

I thought about that for a moment. "I've always wanted to go in a hot air balloon. I hear they have really nice ones over Canberra." If I remembered right, they flew at sunrise over the small Australian capital. It sounded beautiful and serene. I could use a bit of serenity right now.

"That should be easy to arrange. I'll pencil that in. When I get a pencil." He looked like there were other things he wanted to do with that pencil, namely shoving it into the eyeball of Leopold or one of the others.

"You're the best," I said. "I bet Asher would be ecstatic if you organise a skydive too."

"I wonder if Penn would jump," Jackson mused.

"If the others do, then he definitely will," I said. Penn wouldn't let his fear get in the way of his ego, even if he was shit scared.

"That's true," Jackson said. He squinted up ahead at the rising sun.

I looked in the same direction but didn't see anything but open waters. Wherever we were going, this could be a long boat ride. At least they didn't make us row. Yeah, that's me, thinking about all the important things. Whatever got us through the next couple of days. And kept me from freaking the fuck out.

CHAPTER SIX

ZEKE

"CAN'T SLEEP?" Asher flopped down on the sand beside me and sat with his arms around his bent knees.

I glanced over at him. My oldest friend, and now boyfriend, I couldn't remember a time when he wasn't a big part of my life. Once in a while, we talked about what we would have done if we hadn't formed a band. Whatever it was, we would have done it together.

"Neither can you, by the look of it, babe." I looked back towards the dark waves. The sun would be up soon, but for now there was only moonlight and pathway lights to illuminate the resort. It was beautiful, but I was too on edge to appreciate it right now.

"Looking over our shoulders is an ingrained habit," he said. "I'm not sure I can outgrow it, as much as I want to."

Those were my thoughts as well, but there was something else. Call it a sixth sense, instinct, whatever. Something was wrong. Or I was being paranoid.

"I shouldn't have let them go out there by themselves," I said.

"Firstly, I don't think you could have stopped them," he said. "Secondly, you know where they are?"

"I made Jackson tell me before they left, in case something happened." He wasn't happy about it, but he understood. I planned to be too careful for a long time. Possibly forever. Whatever it took to keep us all safe, even if it meant overstepping a whole lot.

"They're on a yacht out there." I waved in a vague direction.

"And now you think something's happened?" Asher asked. "What is it?" He didn't question my instincts, or tell me I was crazy. He got me. He'd also grown up in a mobster family. And he knew when I thought something was up, it was. I'd never been wrong yet. I hoped like hell I was wrong this time.

I shook my head. "I don't know. It might be nothing more than Abbie breaking a nail."

"But it might also be that Jackson fell overboard and got eaten by a shark," Asher said lightly.

"That would be bad," I said. "But we would have heard Abbie screaming from here if that happened. Unless it ate her too."

"Talking about eating her makes my cock hard," Asher commented.

"What doesn't make your cock hard?" I teased.

"Thinking about pineapple." He dug his toes into the sand. "I don't know how people can eat that stuff."

"Because it's delicious?" I suggested.

"You're delicious." He leaned his shoulder against me and rested his head against mine.

"That's funny, I was going to say the same about you." I sighed softly and took a moment to enjoy the way it felt to sit here like this with him. It was almost enough to put my nerves to rest. With a hint of breeze and the sound of the waves lapping on the beach, it was peaceful here.

"You're right about that, I am," he said jokingly. "We should go to resorts like this more often. It's nice to sit here doing nothing and not think about too much. Live in the moment and all that stuff."

"It is nice," I agreed. "I love you, babe."

"I love you too." He nestled in a little closer. "You know what would make this perfect?"

"What's that?" I asked.

"If—"

The night exploded.

A bang echoed across the waves. A fireball flew into the sky. The yacht, previously invisible in the dark, was now lit up like a bonfire.

I shot to my feet, almost knocking Asher aside.

"Fuck!"

He got to his feet. "Please don't tell me that's where…"

"Of course it fucking is," I said. "We need to get out there." A hand on the back of my head, I looked around frantically. Between the burning yacht and the rising sun, there was enough light to see a lot of sand and no boats. No jet skis. Not even an inflatable hippo.

"The surfboard shed is—" Asher raised his hand to point.

"It will have to do." I headed off at a run, him on my heels.

We passed the villa door just as it opened and a sleepy Penn stuck his head out, Tully right behind him.

"What the hell, dude?" Penn asked.

"Get the others and come with us," I shouted as I bolted past. I didn't need to look back to see if they did what I told them to. I knew they would. This wasn't our first rodeo, as they say.

I sprinted to the surfboard storage shed and grabbed hold of the handle. I tugged, but it was locked.

I swore under my breath. Of course it was locked, but the door didn't look very sturdy. I took a step back and kicked the door in. The door frame splintered, parting it from the lock easily. It was the kind of security only designed to keep out honest people, not to keep desperate people from breaking in. They could send me the bill for the repairs later. I might recommend an upgrade, if they didn't want people helping themselves to surfboards.

I grabbed the closest board and swung it around, almost throwing it at Asher. I didn't stop to see if he caught it before I grabbed another and tucked it under my arm.

We stepped out of the shed when the other four guys arrived. Without more than a quick, questioning glance, they stepped past and grabbed their own boards. I made a mental note to thank them all later for not wasting time asking what the fuck was going on.

Asher was right beside me as I hit the water, board out in front of me, and started to paddle. It was a long time since I'd been surfing, but I'd done enough of it to move quickly through the water. I kept my eyes open, looking for any sign of Abbie and Jackson in the water, or the sharks we'd joked about minutes earlier.

None of that seemed funny anymore.

I cursed myself for not going out to the yacht sooner. I fucking knew something was up. If I acted when my instincts first twitched, I might have prevented this. Whatever *this* was. Yeah, okay, I might also have gotten caught up in it. The speculation was pointless, so I pushed it aside.

The yacht still burned ferociously. It sat heavier now, sinking towards the water line as it got more and more swamped. There was no sign of Jackson or Abbie treading water. No floating bodies. If they were on that yacht when it exploded…

No, I couldn't think like that. They were fine. They had to be. If they weren't, I was not going to be okay. And if someone did this to them, I was going to rip their heads off and shove it up their asses.

"There's a rowboat." Asher pointed.

I followed the line of his gesture and nodded. He was right. The small craft floated maybe twenty metres from the burning yacht, bobbing on the swell.

I turned my board and started to paddle toward it

"Abbie?" I called out. "Jackson?" I couldn't see anyone in the rowboat, no movement or sound. It wasn't until I reached the side and peered in, that I saw it was empty. A length of rope trailed in the water. I grabbed it and hauled it up. The end was singed. It must have burned through letting the boat drift away.

"Fuck." I flung the rope away and turned back towards the yacht.

The sun was a finger above the horizon by now. If Jackson or Abbie were anywhere nearby, we'd be able to see them.

Unless...

I paddled faster towards the yacht. A glance back over my shoulder showed the other guys right behind me. They all looked as worried and scared as I felt. Landon, in particular, looked like he was ready to pee his pants. Like always, he stayed close to Channing.

"We'll find them," Asher said.

I looked over at him and nodded. "Hell yeah, we will."

Closer to the yacht, the heat was more intense. I ignored it and kept paddling until I reached the side. I grabbed hold of an un-burnt section and pulled myself over and onto the deck.

"Zeke? Is that a good idea?" Asher asked.

I glanced back. "Probably not, but someone has to do it. Stay there and keep an eye out for them." I looked away before I could see whether he nodded or not.

A hand in front of my face to shield my eyes from the heat, I stepped carefully. The yacht wobbled dangerously underneath me. If I wasn't careful, someone would die on board. Me. Hard pass.

I saw what looked like the edge of a blanket and the remains of a mattress to the side of the deck. Near that was what might have been a phone an hour or so ago. Now, it was a twisted piece of metal and plastic.

There was absolutely no sign of Abbie or Jackson. No remains, no stink of burning meat. Nothing.

I turned around slowly, taking in everything, before I stepped back to the twisted railing. Wincing from walking on the hot deck, I slipped into the water. In a few strokes I reached my board and reclaimed it from Asher, who had hung on to it with one hand.

"They're not there," I said. "If I had to guess, I would say they were gone before that exploded."

"Not a coincidence then," Tully remarked. He looked the yacht over with all the attention I'd given it. If I missed anything, he'd pick it up.

Asher too. He seemed as though he was nothing more than a jokester, but he was as meticulous and observant as me. He likes to say that no one suspects a drummer who's always laughing and messing around, and he wasn't wrong. It got him places the rest of us couldn't go. Trust that wouldn't be bestowed on me. People liked to confide in him. Some regretted it later.

"Empty yachts don't usually explode by themselves," I said. "Someone did this. Whoever it was, they probably thought we'd assume Abbie and Jackson are dead and not go after them."

"Or this is a distraction," Tully said. "They wanted us out here."

"What the fuck for?" Penn snarled. "Some up and coming band wants our spot in IslandFest?"

"Fuck that," Channing said.

"What he said," Landon agreed.

"I know some people get desperate to be famous, but this is going too far," I said.

"You don't think that's what this is though, do you?" Asher asked.

"Not for a moment," I said. "I think someone took them, and we're going to get them back."

"Of course we are," Asher agreed.

"Definitely." Landon nodded. "Where do we start?" He looked at me with absolute trust that I had all the answers.

That would be great if I had any. Right then, I was drawing a blank.

"We need to get back to the resort and let the authorities deal with the yacht," I said. "Then we'll figure things out." I hoped, because I didn't know who would have done this.

Rattling around in my brain was a few possibilities, but I ruled most of them out one by one. That left a very small list. Even a small list was better than nothing.

"Can't the universe give us a mother fucking break?" Penn snarled.

"At least life is never boring," Tully said with a sigh. If he was trying to pretend he wasn't as worried as the rest of us, he failed. I knew him too well for that. As well as he knew me, so when he looked at me and gave a slight nod, I knew he wasn't fooled by my calm façade either.

"I'd like some fucking boring." Penn kicked to turn his board around and started back to shore.

"Me too," I said to his back. "Me too."

CHAPTER
SEVEN

ABBIE

"NICE PLACE FOR A RESORT." If I had to guess, I'd say we were on the boat for at least two hours. We passed a few other watercraft, but never got too close.

Each time, Leopold or one of the other kidnappers—George or Nikolai—would point a gun at us and remind us that calling out for help was a bad idea.

Personally, I thought it was a great idea, unless it got us, or any potential rescuers, killed. Then it was a really crappy idea. If only to keep anyone innocent from being dragged into this insanity, I said nothing, but it chafed.

Eventually, a purple bruise appeared on the horizon. It soon became a small landmass, then an island. One which looked unoccupied until we followed the shoreline around to a bay, which held a small building and a dock. Both of them looked relatively new.

"Or a private tropical home," Jackson said. "We should bring the guys here and see if they want to buy it. It would be a nice place to drop out of civilisation."

"It really would," I agreed. Since Nikolai was the most reasonable kidnapper up until this point, I said to him, "Did you bring us all the way here just to show us a nice island we can buy? Because you could have just asked."

"Can we kill them now?" Leopold asked. "She's a mouthy bitch."

I had a few words which would describe him perfectly, but I decided not to share them, on the grounds they might get me killed. I'd save them so I could insult Petr with them later. He'd get a chuckle out of them. Or he'd tell me to fuck off, and to get on my knees and suck his cock. Which I would happily do. Our relationship was complicated.

"Not yet," Nikolai said.

George hopped out of the boat onto the dock and tied up the vessel before the rest of us got off. Nikolai led the way off the dock and up a path that led through some trees. The rest of the kidnappers walked behind us, Leopold with a grumpy scowl on his face. He seemed like the kind of man who needed to kill someone before breakfast, or he couldn't start his day.

I preferred coffee.

The trees opened to a section of lawn which led to a long, low house overlooking the ocean.

"I've seen enough movies to think this looks like the lair of a supervillain," I said. I glanced over at Jackson when he didn't laugh or agree. For the first time since we met, he looked tense. And I'd seen him when someone was holding a gun to his head. This was more than fear. He looked as though he knew exactly what was going on. And he didn't like it.

"Is this where you tell me exactly what's going on?" I whispered.

"I don't know exactly what's going on," he said slowly.

"But you have a reasonable idea, right?" I cocked my head at him and silently begged him to give me some answers.

"Yeah," he agreed reluctantly.

"And it's not good, is it?" Okay, I knew that already. Nice people didn't kidnap others at gunpoint. Not without their consent anyway.

"No. I apologise in advance for getting you dragged into this." He shot me a look of regret.

"What is *this*?"

"You'll find out soon enough," Nikolai said over his shoulder.

"I've always hated cryptic crosswords," I said. "Because I hate cryptic *anything*. If you're going to kill me, the least you can do is tell me why." Okay, the least they could do was tell me nothing and just kill me, but if I didn't get any answers I would find a way to haunt all of them, including Jackson.

None of them said a word.

They marched us up to the front of the house and in through a side door.

I was expecting a compound inside. Maybe some torture devices, or a man sitting in a chair stroking a fluffy white cat.

Instead, it was an ordinary, if tastefully decorated, island home. Hardwood floors, wicker furniture, lots of shiplap on the walls. Everything was white, blue or oatmeal coloured. There wasn't even a single person chained to the wall, or a table covered with a map and plans for world domination.

Okay, I admit it, I was slightly disappointed.

In spite of that I said, "I like what they've done with the place. It just screams Caribbean relaxation. Doesn't it?" I watched Jackson carefully. His eyes were on the door down the end of the house.

"You've been here before?" I asked him.

His tongue slid over his lips, a sure sign of nerves.

"Not for a long time, but yes."

"Sit down." Nikolai waved to a couch which faced a window.

The view was incredible, but I was in no mood to appreciate it. Right now, I was too scared, and getting more so by the minute.

I sat, but didn't take my eyes off Jackson. It occurred to me how little I really knew about him. I knew he was my manager and Wolf Venom's manager. I knew he was a longtime friend of Levi Jones. I knew he was the bass player for Levi and the Rips—which as band names went, was pretty epic. I knew he knew about the guys' gangster families and didn't bat an eye at any of it. I knew the sight of disembodied heads made him vomit.

He wasn't alone in the last one.

Apart from those things, and the fact he could row and drive a bus, what else did I know? It never occurred to me for a moment that he might come from the same background as most of the guys. Or worse.

I loved him, but I felt like I was looking at a stranger. One who seemed to be trying to keep himself from unravelling around the edges.

"It's me you want," Jackson said softly. "Take Abbie back to the island. She has to be there for IslandFest. They're going to notice her absence."

"I'm not going without you," I said firmly. In spite of everything, he was still one of my guys and I wasn't walking away and leaving him here.

"If we don't need her, then we can kill her," Leopold growled.

"I'd like you a lot more if you stopped talking about killing me," I told him. I already knew they weren't going to take me back, not after all their effort to bring me here in the first place.

"Also, I think you do need me. If you didn't, I'd be dead right now." That begged the question, what did they need me for?

Yeah, okay, I could figure that one out. If this was about Jackson, then I was here for leverage. Oh goody. Although, that meant we weren't completely powerless. Right?

Jackson rubbed his forehead with his fingertips. "It's probably best you don't antagonise them any further. Let me do the talking. I'll do the best I can to get you out of here safely."

"Not without you," I said again.

He turned his face to look at me past his fingers. "You might not have a choice. If you get the chance to get out of here, you need to take it. No matter what happens to me. Promise me."

"Jackson—"

His denim blue eyes looked right at me, like he was trying to see into my soul. "Promise me," he insisted. "We don't both need to die."

"You're not—" I started. I sighed in frustration. "Okay, I promise. If I can get out of here I can, but if we can both get out of here, then that's what we'll do."

He nodded, but he didn't look convinced that would happen. Honestly, I wasn't too convinced either.

"Who owns this place?" I asked. "If there's any chance of us buying it, we should at least have some idea of its history." Okay, it might give me a clue as to what the fuck was going on too.

As expected, no one answered me. I decided to take Jackson's advice and be quiet for a while. I'd spent enough time with the other guys to know that sometimes you need to listen and watch in order to figure out what's going on and what to do.

I made a note of all the entrances and exits, the windows and the furnishings, and the way our kidnappers stood around us. Even if they weren't armed, we were outnumbered. I knew how to use a gun if I could get my hands on one, but I had nothing in the way of hand to hand combat skills and nothing more than basic self-defence. The guys promised to teach me more when we got back to Sydney, but that wasn't for another week.

The kitchen probably held knives, but those were no good against guns.

I sighed out my nose in frustration and sat against the back of the couch, my legs crossed at my knees.

What were the rest of the guys doing right now? They wouldn't have missed the yacht exploding. Zeke should know we're not that easy to kill, but then what? How would he and the other guys know where to find us or even where to start looking?

They wouldn't, I admitted to myself. They saved me from a few things early in the tour, but as it went along, I got the confidence to save myself. I was going to have to do that now. Jackson and I, we'd have to find a way out of here and back to the guys.

If there was anything I learnt in life it was that sooner or later an opportunity would arise. I'd have to be ready to take it. Of course, it would be a lot easier if I had a fucking clue what we were up against. The odds this was a practical joke was getting slimmer by the hour.

Just in case, I glanced around for hidden cameras. Or obvious ones. I saw no sign of either. Shame, I would have enjoyed flipping them off and telling whoever was behind them to fuck the fucking fuck off. If there was anything I hated more than cryptic crosswords, it was practical jokes. Especially ones that involved guns and kidnapping. This would make a great adventure holiday experience, but in reality it sucked all kinds of hard.

The door at the end of the house, finally, opened.

Beside me, Jackson's whole body tensed even more. That was saying something, because he was pretty damn tense to start with. At least he wasn't shouting or trading insults with the kidnappers like Penn would have been.

Tully probably would have killed them all by now and they wouldn't have seen him coming. Asher would have tried to make them laugh and probably got himself killed with too many silly jokes.

I could only guess what Landon and Channing would have done, except that Channing would do anything to protect Landon, even if it meant spreading kidnapper blood all over the house. People had different ways of expressing their love for other people.

As for Zeke, he wouldn't have let them take us to begin with. He probably would have pulled a couple of guns up from under the mattress and shot them before they stepped on deck of the yacht. Yeah, that was a hot mental image. I might cling to that for a while to keep myself sane.

Jackson rose when a heavyset man stepped out of the doorway. He held out a hand to indicate that I should stay sitting.

"Jasha," the man greeted, rubbing his hands together. He started speaking rapidly in what sounded like Russian. Jackson seemed to understand every word.

I stared at him. Who the hell was he?

CHAPTER
EIGHT

ABBIE

JACKSON RAN a hand over his face and shook his head. "Not a chance, Yuri. And it's Jackson. I left the other life behind a long time ago."

I was done sitting down and shutting up. I rose to my feet and looked from one guy to the other. "What's going on? I didn't know you could speak Russian."

Yuri looked at me, his eyelids heavy under bushy brows. To Jackson he said, "You should explain. A woman like her isn't the kind to back down."

"You're right, I don't." I also didn't like the suggestion he had a clue about me after sixty seconds, but whatever. "Someone should explain to me why we got kidnapped at gunpoint by someone who seems to know you." Was this the fourth time now, or the fifth? The fact I was starting to lose count was not okay.

The part where Jackson could speak Russian was kinda hot, but the rest sucked.

"It's a long story," Jackson said wearily.

"Let me guess. Bratva? KGB? Russian royalty?" I knew they didn't have one anymore, but if Jackson was a motherfucking prince, I was going to lose my mind.

Yuri chuckled. "She is something else."

"I am, aren't I? Maybe you shouldn't kill me then." That seemed reasonable to me.

"That depends on Jackson," Yuri said unhelpfully.

"Jackson doesn't want me dead."

"No, I don't," he agreed.

"Then we have a deal," Yuri stated.

"We definitely do not," Jackson said.

"If you start at the beginning of the long story, you might get to the end sooner or later," I said. Otherwise, I might skip over to the kitchen and look for a knife. At this point, I wasn't sure who I would use it on.

"Would you like some coffee?" Yuri offered.

"I'd love some." That was the most civilised thing anyone said all day. "As long as it's not poisoned."

Yuri waved at the couch. "Sit. Make yourselves comfortable. Jackson can tell you everything."

"Yeah, someone needs to." And let's face it, he was the only one here I trusted to tell me the truth.

I perched on the edge of the couch and crossed my arms.

He sat down heavily beside me. "You probably guessed by now my family is Russian. They moved to Australia when I was five and changed our name to Beckett. They wanted to put the past behind them. My mother worked in a bakery but my father worked for the government. Specifically, getting intelligence on other world governments."

I blinked. "Your father was a spy? That's kinda cool."

He snorted softly. "Yeah, kinda. One of those other governments didn't think it was very cool though. They put a price on his head, so we had to run. My father's former employers kept track of us. He was one of the best they had and they wanted him to go back eventually. He refused. Australia was a lot safer. He got a job driving a bus. He was happy."

"Was?" I echoed.

"Somehow, someone from Bratva found out who he was and where he was, so my parents went into hiding. Yuri wants to know where they are."

"Why?" I looked over to Yuri, who was leaning against the kitchen bench, waiting for the coffee machine to heat up.

"Because his whereabouts are worth a lot of money," Yuri said. "What Jackson didn't tell you is that his father was a double agent and an enforcer. His loyalty was not to Russia either. He tortured a lot of innocent people for enjoyment."

"So he pissed off a lot of people?" I guessed. "And a lot of people want him dead."

"I don't want him dead," Yuri said. "I want to collect the bounty on his whereabouts. What happens to him after that..." He shrugged his broad shoulders.

"I'm guessing that's a lot since you've gone to all this trouble," I said.

"Several million dollars," Yuri said. "I even offered to share some of it with Jackson."

"Just a wild guess here, but he told you to fuck off?" I looked back at Jackson as he nodded.

"He did some shitty things, but he's still my father."

"Of course he is." We'd covered up plenty of dubious things over the last couple of months, what was one more?

"Let me get this straight," I said slowly. "If you tell this asshole where your father is, your father ends up dead. But if you don't, then he's going to kill me? That's why I'm here, isn't it? They need you alive, or they won't find out where he is." That was awesome, wasn't it now?

Fuck.

"If they kill you, I'm definitely not going to cooperate," Jackson said firmly.

"We don't need to kill her to get you to cooperate." Yuri poured a coffee and took a sip. "Mmmm, this is good."

"You're going to torture us by withholding coffee?" I asked. "You're more evil than you look." What kind of asshole does that?

"I'll start by withholding coffee. Where it finishes is up to you. But don't think you have to decide now. I'll give you a couple of hours to talk about it. I'm sure your woman is very persuasive."

Talk about putting me in an impossible situation. I didn't want to die or be tortured, but asking Jackson to give up his father's whereabouts was a whole other story.

"Leopold, Nikolai, take our guests to the guest suite," Yuri said. "Leopold, don't kill anyone until I tell you to. And don't hurt them either. You'll get your chance soon enough if they decide not to cooperate."

Leopold didn't look happy at that, but he nodded and waved his gun at us. He really did seem to enjoy that part of his job. I wondered if he was a bully at school too.

Nikolai, being slightly less of an asshole, gestured with his hand. "This way."

They led us through the door Yuri had come through, and into a corridor at the back of the house.

Nikolai opened a door and nodded for us to step inside.

I glanced at Jackson, who also nodded. He looked at least as troubled as I felt, but seemed inclined to cooperate with them for now.

I shrugged and stepped into the room, Jackson right behind me.

Nikolai pulled the door shut and I heard the lock click into place.

"Well this is great," I said with a deep sigh. My brain was twisting and turning in a million different directions and none of them were good.

The room was as tastefully decorated as the rest of the house, with a wide bed and windows overlooking the ocean, but it was still a cell.

I stepped over to a window and looked out. "I was hoping to see a fleet of ships, with Zeke standing at the front like that scene in *Titanic*. But maybe armed. To the teeth. With rocket launchers." Instead, all I saw was empty sea.

Bummer.

Jackson walked up behind me and wound his arms around me. "I'm sorry you got caught up in this. I haven't heard from them for months. I thought they'd given up. I should have known they wouldn't."

I leaned my head back against his chest.

"When it comes to money, people tend to be persistent. Why does he need it if he owns this place?" The island alone would be worth more than five million dollars.

"He probably doesn't," Jackson said. "It's borrowed, or maybe the owner doesn't know he's here."

"We can add breaking and entering to his list of crimes." It was a minor felony compared to kidnapping and threats of torture and murder.

"And withholding coffee," he said.

"That might be the worst thing of all," I joked weakly. Honestly, I could give up coffee for the rest of my life if it meant I didn't get tortured or killed. It was a small thing in the scheme of things.

"At least we have a view," he remarked. "He could have locked us away in a room without one."

"He's completely redeemed then," I said sarcastically. "This would have been a lot easier if you were a prince."

"This would be a lot easier if my father wasn't who he was," Jackson said. "That includes being a king. Although, I think I'd make a pretty crappy prince. I'm not a big fan of publicity or cutting ribbons."

"Yeah, that doesn't sound like you at all," I said. "Plus they would have wanted you to marry a princess. One who doesn't have six other boyfriends."

"In some cultures, that would be exactly who they'd want me to marry," he said. "A warrior princess with six warrior boyfriends to protect me. That sounds pretty perfect to me."

"Princess Abigail," I said. "That does have a ring to it. Are you sure you're not secretly royalty?"

He chuckled. "I'm pretty sure I'm not. Does it matter?"

I pretended to think about that for a moment. "I suppose it doesn't. Unless it would mean an army is coming to rescue us. Otherwise, I'm okay with being ordinary, and being with you, manager, bass player Jackson." I looked over my shoulder at him and smiled. "I love you."

"I love you too." He kissed my cheek. "But there's nothing ordinary about you. You're my smart, gorgeous, amazing, talented girlfriend. I'm beyond lucky to know you."

I turned back to the window and sighed. "So if there isn't an army of your loyal subjects, or a fleet captained by Zeke, then what are we going to do? Do you really know where your father is?"

"Sort of," he said. "Not his exact location, but I could find him if I had to."

I realised by his cagey response that he assumed someone was listening in.

That made sense. They might have hoped we were dumb enough to give them answers by accident.

Nice try, assholes, I thought. They were going to have to try harder than that. Or better yet, let us go and forget about it all. That sounded like a good idea to me.

"Am I really supposed to ask you to tell them where he is, just to save my own ass?" How could I possibly ask Jackson to choose between me and his father? That was an impossible choice, even if he did horrible things in the past. It wasn't as though I was perfect either.

"That's exactly what most people would do," he said. "I wouldn't blame you if you did. Why should you go through all of this for someone you don't know?"

"Why should you go through this for someone you *do* know?" I asked. "This won't come as a surprise to you, but some people suck."

He laughed bitterly. "Yeah, they do. But people like you and me, we're tough. We'll get through this."

"I hope so, because I don't want to die on a tropical island, kilometres from anywhere, and have my remains thrown to the sharks to cover up my death." That would be absolute bullshit if it happened. I would definitely haunt them if they did that to me.

"That's why we're going to get out of here," Jackson whispered. "If you're ready to leave, that is?"

"I'm very ready to get the hell out of here," I whispered back. "But how?"

"Do you trust me?"

CHAPTER
NINE

ABBIE

"I'VE DECIDED TO TALK," Jackson stated.

He'd knocked on the door until Nikolai unlocked it and opened it. Both he and Leopold looked at him doubtfully. Leopold, in particular, looked pissed off. Presumably he misses out on his fun if Jackson cooperated and gave up his father.

If he felt that strongly about hurting people, there were three other kidnappers and Yuri on this island. He had my blessing to kill any of them. In fact, he'd be doing us a favour.

I considered suggesting it but figured he'd probably decline my kind offer. His loss.

"Come this way then," Nikolai said. He stepped back from the door and kept his gun on us while we walked out of the room. "I suggest you don't waste Yuri's time. He's a very busy man."

He couldn't be that busy if he had time for kidnapping and threatening innocent people. I kept that thought to myself. Jackson suggested I not speak, but keep my eyes and ears open and let him do the talking. Whatever it took to get us out of here alive, I'd happily do it.

We walked back out to the kitchen and living area. Yuri was sitting on a couch reading a book. I liked to think people who read weren't too evil, but I'd more or less been proven wrong about that in the past. Besides, I knew that book. I read it a year or two ago. One of the guys likes to torture people for fun. He could have been looking for inspiration in the pages.

"I hear you're ready to speak," Yuri said without looking up. "I should tell you, even if you do divulge your father's location, I intend to keep you here until the information is confirmed as correct."

"That doesn't work for me," Jackson said. "I'll give you the information you want and then you let us go."

Now Yuri looked up. "It's adorable that you think this is a negotiation. It's not. In case you hadn't noticed, I hold all the cards."

"Except the one with my father's location written on it," Jackson said. "I think they call that the ace card or something." He glanced over at me but I shrugged.

I had no idea about cards. It sounded about right though.

"If I kill her, he might realise we're not playing games," Leopold said. He sounded way too excited at the idea.

I forced my gaze over to the setting sun, visible through the window. It was beautiful, and helped me to remember to keep my mouth shut when I wanted to tell Leopold to fuck off.

Yuri clicked his tongue. "Leopold has some anger issues, but he's loyal."

I swung my eyes back to see Leopold give Yuri a glare that didn't look particularly loyal to me. I had a sneaking suspicion he'd happily put a bullet in his boss's brain just to satisfy the urge.

Do it. Do it.

Unfortunately, he didn't.

"It shouldn't take more than a day or two to confirm your information," Yuri said. "If you're being honest, you might get back in time for your little festival."

Little festival? I choked back a response. He might be a reader, but he clearly had no idea about musical events. That moved him up a notch on my scale of evil. On the other hand, I suspected he knew exactly what IslandFest was, and he was trying to get a rise from me.

"Your girlfriend is quiet all of a sudden." Yuri cocked his head at me. "Nothing to say, little wildcat? I bet you love leaving scratch marks all over dear Jackson here."

I couldn't stop myself. I said, "Him and my other six boyfriends."

His eyebrows shot up. Then he laughed. "You really are quite the woman. Maybe I should keep you here when Jackson leaves."

Jackson bristled visibly. "Not a chance. You couldn't handle her anyway."

"That sounds like a challenge to me," Yuri said. "Unfortunately, my wife would not approve. I'm so sorry to disappoint you, dear."

"I'll try to contain my heartbreak," I said sarcastically.

"So, do you want to know where my father is or don't you?" Jackson asked. "Because if you don't, we'll be on our way." He made to step toward the door we'd come in through.

"Nikolai, take down the details," Yuri said. To Jackson he said, "Know this. If the information is wrong, I'll start by having Leopold remove your girlfriend's tongue. Then one breast, and then the other. Then he can decide if he wants to remove her fingers or her toes one by one."

"Fingers are more fun," Leopold said.

"You're a sick fuck," I told him.

He actually grinned at me. Apparently the idea of cutting me up into little pieces appealed to him.

Honestly, the idea of cutting him up into little pieces was sounding more and more enticing. Just the idea. I'd never act on it, but I could think about it. The reality was, if I wanted him in pieces, I had six guys only too happy to do it for me. And Jackson could watch.

Nikolai approached with a tablet in his hands and nodded to Jackson. When Jackson spoke, he tapped the information into the screen, then stepped away.

"It seems to be a real place," he said.

"Good. Dispatch a team there," Yuri said. "And return our guests to their room." After a moment he added, "And supply them with some food. And coffee."

"Yes, sir," Nikolai said. He gestured for us to return back to our fancy cell.

I glanced at Jackson, reassured by his calm expression. Not even the promise of coffee was going to settle my nerves. Only getting out of here would do that.

Preferably alive and intact.

The door clicked shut behind us, only to open again ten or fifteen minutes later for George to bring in a tray of food and coffee. While Nikolai and Leopold watched, guns in hand, he placed it on the table and backed out the door. He barely gave us more than a glance.

"You think it's safe to eat?" I cast a dubious look at the plates of food and steaming mugs.

"I think if Yuri wanted us dead, we'd be dead," Jackson said. "Why bother to poison us?"

"Shits and giggles?" I suggested. "Easier cleanup?"

"We're going to have to take the risk. We don't want to come this far and die of starvation." He picked up a sandwich and bit into it. He made a face, like he wanted to spit it out.

"What is it?" Fuck, if that asshole poisoned Jackson, I was going to find a way to shove the sandwich down his throat. I didn't know how I would do it, but I would. "Are you okay?" I put a trembling hand on his arm.

He shook his head, then nodded. "There's raw onion on this sandwich. Why would someone put that on there?" He opened the bread and pulled off the rest.

I sagged with relief. "Evil people?" I suggested. Personally, I didn't mind raw onion, but I checked my sandwich for anything strange before I bit into it.

It was nothing more terrifying than cheese, lettuce and tomato. It wasn't exciting, but it was filling enough. I washed it down with coffee, which was strong but surprisingly good.

I waited, but I didn't die, so that was a bonus.

"It's almost dark." I nodded toward the window.

It felt like a hundred years ago since we rowed out to the yacht, had a lovely meal and fucked out on the deck. As dates went, this was certainly unique.

Unfortunately.

With any luck, we'd get a second chance at being alone together. Although, knowing Zeke, he'd make sure we weren't as far away next time. Or he'd put a tracker in my earring like he did with my phone. And I'd let him.

"Let's get some rest," Jackson said. "It could be a long time before they confirm my father's location."

"I'm sorry you had to do that," I said regretfully. "Things could end really badly for him, couldn't they?"

"They could," Jackson agreed, his brow furrowed. "But he'd agree I made the right choice. If it was him or you, he would choose you too."

"No one should have to make that choice." I waited until he put down his coffee cup and wound my arms around him. "This is all kinds of fucked up."

"Yeah, but it was all kinds of fucked up before either of us were born." He grabbed his arms around me and pulled me to his chest. "The past had to catch up with him sooner or later. He knew that."

"What would he think when he knows you were the one who told them where to find him?" I inhaled the warm, musky scent of his body. Often, I found dangerous situations arousing, but I wasn't going to fuck him here. There was no way either of us would let our guards down that far.

"He'll understand," Jackson said. "He'll know I wouldn't have done it without good reason."

"Are you close?" I asked.

"Pretty close. He was the one who taught me how to drive a bus. He said you never know when you might need skills like that."

I looked up at him and smiled. "That skill certainly did come in handy. And it was hot too."

He smiled faintly. "If I get a chance to see him again, I'll let him know you think so. He'd think that's hilarious."

"He sounds like a good guy, except the whole torturing people for fun part. Do you think any of that is true?" It wouldn't be the first time someone made up something to falsely incriminate someone else.

"Honestly, I have no idea," Jackson admitted. "Believe it or not, it never came up in conversation. How would I even start that anyway? 'Hey, Dad, did you torture people for the hell of it?'"

"Sometimes the direct approach is the best approach," I said. "But it's not something I would ask my father either."

His eyebrows dipped briefly. "Is there any suggestion your father was involved in anything dubious or illegal?"

I thought about that for a moment. "Seriously, once upon a time, I would have laughed at that suggestion. But now, I've come to realise people can surprise you. Maybe you never really know a person completely. Sometimes that's a bad thing and sometimes it's a good thing. If we knew everything there was to know about each other, then where would you go from there? Wouldn't things start to get boring eventually? Having some guesswork keeps things interesting. Spicy."

"Things with you will never get boring," he said firmly. "Interesting and spicy are two fantastic words to describe you. I can't imagine a day going by when you wouldn't say something or do something that takes me by surprise. And with eight of us in this relationship now, we have eight times the surprises."

"Maybe we can stick to pleasant surprises after this," I said dryly. I'd had more than enough nasty ones for one lifetime.

"I'm all for that." He kissed my forehead, then led me over to the bed and settled us both down on top of the covers.

"Get some sleep. I'll wake you when the time is right."

I didn't think I could sleep, but when I closed my eyes I was out within a minute or two. I'd need my rest for the coming hours.

CHAPTER
TEN

ABBIE

"ARE YOU SURE ABOUT THIS?"

Jackson blew out a breath through pursed lips, but said, "I'm sure. It's the only way we're getting out of here."

"When you put it that way..." I gripped the end of his top cock piercing between the thumb and forefinger of one hand, and the ball with the other. While he carefully held his cock, I started to rotate the ball, unwinding it from the bar.

He was still as I slowly slid the bar out of his cock.

"Lucky I needed extra long bars," he said, looking smug.

Men.

"Don't make me stab you in the eyeball with this." I wielded the bar in front of his face before I handed it to him.

"Death by cock piercing," he mused. "It would be a unique way to go."

"Don't sound so cheerful about it." I shook my head at him and followed him over to the door. The only light in the room was the moonlight. Hopefully that would be enough for him to do what he needed to do.

"When this is over, I look forward to letting you put this back." He held up the bar for a moment, then slipped it into the lock.

"I look forward to putting it back while you explain how you learnt how to pick locks," I said.

"Deal. We should probably be quiet now." His brow creased in concentration for a minute, two minutes. Finally, his teeth flashed white and he straightened up. He handed me the bar and I quickly screwed the ball back on loosely before tucking them into my pocket. Wouldn't want to lose a perfectly good cock piercing.

"Stay behind me," he whispered. He eased the door open a crack and peered out.

My heart raced like crazy. Loud enough I'd swear someone would hear it.

The door swung open silently before he crept out. He gestured behind him, for me to stay put. A moment later, a grunt was followed by a soft thud, then Jackson stuck his face back into the room.

"Come on," he hissed.

Walking silently as I could on the hardwood floor, I followed him out, almost tripping over Leopold, who was lying just outside the door.

"Is he..."

"Just out cold," Jackson said. "No idea how long he'll stay that way."

Right. If Jackson was one of the other guys, Leopold would be dead right now. Okay, maybe not Penn or Landon, but one of the others wouldn't have hesitated to kill him.

Hoping like hell I didn't wake him, I slipped the gun out of Leopold's fingers and held it loosely in my hand. I hoped I didn't have to use it. I knew how, the other guys made sure of that, but I didn't want to kill or injure anyone if I didn't have to. But if it came down to them or me, I knew which one I'd choose.

Jackson grabbed my other hand and we walked down the corridor toward the kitchen area. Yuri and the other assholes must be asleep, because the place was dark and silent. Apparently they'd underestimated our ability to use a cock piercing to escape. Their bad.

To be fair, it's not something I would have guessed would happen either. I mean, who does shit like that? Us, apparently.

We were halfway across the room when a sound made us freeze. Jackson pulled me down behind the couch just as someone stepped into the kitchen. They opened the fridge, pulled something out and closed it again.

Okay, they wouldn't be the first person in the world to have a midnight snack. I might have done it once or twice myself.

I held my breath and waited while they ate their snack.

After what felt like a decade, they finally walked out of the kitchen and back down the corridor. The door at the end opened and then clicked shut.

I let out my breath in a silent whoosh and rose when Jackson tugged my hand.

We crept over to the door and he put his hand on the lock. The sound it made when it unlocked seemed as loud as thunder.

I winced and waited for the bad guys to come running.

No one did until we stepped out into the humid, predawn air. If I had to guess, I'd say we were three or four hours from sunrise. The only sound was the ocean lapping on the beach, and the buzz of some kind of insect.

That was, until Leopold came lumbering toward us, murmuring something incoherent. I couldn't tell if it was rage or if he wasn't speaking English.

He shouted something and raised his hand.

I acted without thinking. For all I knew, he had more than one gun or had stopped long enough to grab one. Either way, I wasn't going to wait to find out. I raised the gun and fired, getting him square in the centre of his chest.

My first thought was, *Fuck yeah, the guys would be proud of me.*

The second thought came as Leopold flew backwards and crashed to the floor. *Fuck, was he dead?*

"We need to get out of here," Jackson said urgently. "There's no way they didn't hear that." After a moment he added, "Freak out later. Come on."

I nodded and let him drag me out and away from the house. Lights blazed on inside, and assholes started shouting. They must have found Leopold already. And the open door. With any luck, they'd check our room before they looked out here. They might assume a rescue party turned up to save us and was on their way to our gilded cell.

Whatever, we couldn't assume anything so we ran, stumbling every few steps over bumps and hollows in the lawn, or stray sticks. Somehow, we managed to keep each other on our feet before we slipped into the trees a few metres from the beach.

"We need to get to the dock." He tugged me in that direction.

I glanced at the house. A couple of baddies stood out the front, silhouetted in the light. It wasn't going to take them long to figure out which way we were headed. They had the advantage of knowing this place much better than we did. We had desperation on our side, if nothing more.

We hurried toward the dock, not bothering to stay quiet. Speed was what mattered now, not stealth.

No one was at the dock when we skidded to a stop there. Two boats were tied up, the one we'd arrived on and a small rowboat.

To my surprise, it was the rowboat Jackson gestured for me to jump into.

"Wouldn't the other one be faster?" I asked.

"Faster, but louder," he said. "Stay here." He stepped up to the other bollard and started to untie the rope that tethered the bigger boat to the dock.

In about fifteen seconds flat, he had it undone and threw the rope onto the deck of the boat. He leaned to press his hands against the hull and gave it a shove. Just when I thought he would fall face first into the water, he straightened up and followed me into the rowboat.

He grabbed the oars and started to row, keeping out of the way of the other boat that was now floating free on the tide.

I was almost blinded as the dock was suddenly illuminated with floodlights. I threw a hand over my face and ducked down lower.

Lucky I did, because a bullet whizzed right over where my head just was. If I hadn't moved, I would be dead.

I won't lie, I didn't want to kill anyone, but when they shot first, then all bets were off.

I straightened enough to get off a shot, narrowly missing getting Nikolai in the leg. So much for being the reasonable kidnapper.

He aimed at me again but missed my shoulder by a hair.

"I'm starting to dislike this guy." I aimed at his groin, since I seemed to have a knack for hitting that part of the body, and got him square in his thigh.

He growled and got off another shot, this time grazing my upper arm.

Pain blossomed through my bicep and I cried out.

"Abbie? Are you all right?" Jackson's eyes were wild with worry, but he didn't slow his rowing for more than a beat.

"I'm fine," I said quickly. It hurt like a bitch, but I'd live.

Nikolai tried again but we were too far away and the bullets only hit the water with a spray, before they sank uselessly to the bottom of the ocean.

I snorted a laugh, but only a small one. We weren't safe yet. I wouldn't relax until we were.

"You're a badass," Jackson said approvingly. "Are you sure you're okay?"

"It's just a graze," I said. "Don't dudes dig chicks with scars?" If they didn't, then they should. Especially since I got this one helping to save our asses.

"I dig you, with or without scars," he said. "But I prefer you alive and unhurt."

"You too," I said. And me too. I much preferred myself alive and unhurt.

I looked back at the house. All of the baddies, including Yuri, were gathered on the dock. If I had to guess, I'd think they were trying to figure out how to get the other boat back so they could come after us. Someone was going to have to swim out to it and that would take time. Time for us to get the fuck out of here.

"It's going to be a long way back to the island this way," I said. "Do you want me to take a turn rowing?" I pressed a couple of fingers to my wound to stop it from bleeding. Rowing would hurt like a bitch too, but I'd do it if he needed a break.

"I'm good," he said. "We won't need to row all the way back, unless I'm wrong."

"Wrong about what?" I frowned at him.

"Wrong about how Yuri got here." He jerked his head behind him, toward a dark shape that bobbed on the swell. I hadn't noticed it until now, but it grew bigger and bigger by the moment.

"Another yacht?" The question was rhetorical. What else would be floating around out here? It certainly wasn't a huge, inflatable unicorn. It wasn't even a huge, inflatable penis. That sucked, because one of those would be fun. Okay, maybe not out here in the middle of the ocean, in the dark. Another time maybe.

We slid across the water towards it, silent except for the dip of the oars every couple of seconds. When we were about twenty metres out, I saw how big the yacht really was. Superyacht might be a better name for it. Low lights glittered here or there, for the convenience of the crew. If anyone stood watch, I couldn't see them. Presumably Yuri thought his little toy was safe out here.

"Do you know how to drive a yacht?" Was drive the right word? Whatever, he knew what I meant.

"Everything is operated with computers these days," he said. "How hard can it be?"

"That would be no then," I concluded. He was right though, how hard *could* it be? The bigger problem might be dealing with the crew, who could very well be innocent.

About ten metres from the superyacht, another sound echoed across the water.

"Shit," Jackson said softly.

I looked back the way we came to see the lights of the other boat, Yuri and the other kidnappers on board. They headed towards us with all the speed of a vessel with an actual engine. As fast as Jackson was, he couldn't out-row a motorboat. And now we were stuck between that and the yacht.

"Shit is right," I said softly.

CHAPTER
ELEVEN

ABBIE

"GRAB THE LADDER," Jackson said. "We need to get on board before they get close enough to shoot."

I grabbed the closest rung and pulled, until the side of the rowboat bumped against the yacht. Climbing with a gun in one hand wasn't the easiest thing I've ever done, but I wasn't going to let it go. I sure as hell wasn't going to put it in my pocket and risk shooting myself in the foot. With my luck, that would be exactly what happened.

I pulled myself over onto the deck and dropped down lightly. I turned back to the railing as Jackson grabbed the ladder.

They were almost in range.

George raised his gun and peppered the other side of the rowboat with bullets. It quickly started to take on water, but Jackson was clear by then.

"Come on," I urged him. "You're nearly there."

Another shot rang out and Jackson grunted.

"Jax!" I called out frantically. "Come on, babe."

His breathing was laboured. He was obviously winded from the effort of rowing, and in pain, but he kept on climbing.

George aimed again, but I pointed my gun at him and squeezed the trigger. George ducked and the shot missed him, but hit Nikolai in the stomach. He went down like a bag of potatoes.

"Give it up," Yuri shouted over the water. "You have nowhere to go. I know you're both injured. Surrender now and you might get to live."

As offers went, that was pretty crappy. Why would I surrender when all he could give me was a maybe?

Jackson reached the top of the ladder and I leaned down to help him up. "Where did he get you?"

"In my ass," he said with another grunt of pain, mixed with one of frustration and a sprinkle of humiliation.

I frowned. "Bummer."

He gave me a faint smile. "Yeah, just a bit. At least he didn't shoot me in the cock."

"He wouldn't dare," I growled. I helped him over the railing and down to the deck. "Maybe we should take a leaf from their book."

I ducked down low and peered over the railing. The rowboat was already half full of water. No one was using that ever again.

I raised the gun and aimed at the hull of the other boat. My aim was off. I missed the hull and hit the engine instead.

Unfortunately, it didn't burst into flames like it would in the movies, but it did sputter and die.

"Looks like someone's going to have to get out and swim," I remarked.

"Sucks to be them." Jackson was looking around like he might actually be able to see his own ass. Blood already coated the back of his pants and seeped down his leg.

"We need to get you to a doctor," I said. Me too, because I was also covered in blood. "Preferably before anyone tries to stop us." Voices sounded from inside the yacht and a couple of lights flickered on.

"Are we going to be able to steal this thing?"

"I have a better idea," Jackson said. "Come on."

"Please tell me it's not another rowboat," I said.

He grinned and let me around to the back deck of the yacht. Was this the poop deck? What even was a poop deck? I didn't know, I'd look up later. After I dealt with what I was staring at.

I blinked.

"Are you out of your mind?"

"You have a better idea?" he asked.

"No, but do you know how to fly one of those?" Had he hit his head at some point, or was he even more of a badass than I thought?

"My father also thought flying a helicopter would be a useful skill I might need some day." He ushered me towards it and opened the door. "In you get."

He closed the door behind me and trotted around to the other side. He winced as he slipped into the seat and clicked in his seatbelt.

"Normally I'd do a pre-flight safety check, but we don't have time for that." He pressed the button to turn on the helicopter's engine and the rotors started to turn.

"This isn't going to go unnoticed." I slipped on the set of headphones he handed me before he put on his own.

"Probably not," he agreed. "Keep your eyes open."

I took that to mean, 'be ready to shoot anyone who comes along and tries to stop us.' I had no idea how many bullets I had left, if I even had any, but I could wave it around and potentially deter people.

The rotors were turning faster now, just a blur out the window, barely visible in the early light of the morning.

With a jolt, the helicopter lifted up off the yacht's helipad and into the sky.

I held my breath. We were a very clear, very obvious target right now. A target for assholes who probably knew where to aim to make the helicopter explode or crash back down to the deck.

Goody.

Jackson banked the helicopter slightly and flew in the opposite direction of Yuri and George. By now, several people appeared from below decks and watched us take off.

We quickly rose to a height beyond the range of a handgun, and Jackson took us in a wide circle around the superyacht.

I spotted George in the water, pulling a rope behind him, towing Yuri and the smaller boat to the yacht.

"Who says it's hard to get good help these days?" I asked.

Jackson laughed. "It's funny the things people do if you pay them enough."

"That's true. You definitely deserve a pay raise after this. Maybe Levi will let you keep the helicopter."

"Then I'd spend half my life taking Asher on joy rides around whatever city we're in." He pressed a couple of buttons, the use of which I could only guess at.

"That doesn't sound so bad." I waved at Yuri as we passed overhead. He might have waved back and he might have been flipping me off.

Sorry not sorry, asshole.

"Yeah, but he'd want to fuck in the back seat, instead of enjoying the flight." Jackson looked over at me and smiled a panty melting smile.

"Is it wrong that this is really, really hot?" I said. "I mean, we're both injured, we got kidnapped at gunpoint and shot at. I shot a couple of people and all I can think is how sexy it is that you can fly a helicopter."

"Priorities," he said with a firm nod. "It should also bear in mind that IslandFest starts in a few hours. If we're lucky, we'll get you back there in time."

I swore under my breath. "I forgot all about it. I was kind of busy trying not to die." If I didn't turn up, something else would die—my career. I hadn't worked my cute little butt off to throw it away now. Or have it taken away from me by asshole kidnappers.

"What's going to happen to your father?" I asked.

"The location I gave them was an old one," he said. "He and my mother are long gone from there. It'll look like he just left, but they won't find him." He pressed a couple of different buttons and switches. "It was never going to be that easy to find him. He's like a fox."

"But they'll keep looking?" I guessed.

He looked over quickly and nodded, before turning back to the controls. "Yes, they'll keep on looking. They'll look until they find him or he dies of old age. Whichever happens first."

"And they're not going to stop asking you where he is, will they? Yuri is going to keep on coming."

"Yuri will go underground after this," Jackson said. "Someone else might pop up, but I'll make it known that I don't know where he is. At this moment, I really don't. It's safer for him and me if it stays that way." His denim blue eyes looked sad at the idea of never seeing his father again. Or his mother, for that matter.

"I'm sorry about that," I said sincerely. I couldn't begin to understand how that would feel. Knowing they were out there somewhere and never knowing where that was. Always wondering if they might turn up alive or otherwise.

He shrugged one shoulder. "I have another family now anyway. You and all the boys. And Levi is like another brother to me." He hesitated for a moment, then said, "Both of my families have almost gotten me killed in the last few months."

"Several times," I agreed. "What is family for if they can't put you in danger from time to time?"

He chuckled. "They're pretty good at getting me out of danger as well, so there's that."

"At least life is interesting." A little peace and quiet might be nice for a while. But it was kinda cool to be in a helicopter, flying over the Caribbean.

"It certainly is." Jackson shifted in his seat. He was clearly in a lot of pain and if I had to guess, I'd say it was getting worse. That was understandable, since he was probably sitting on a bullet. That probably hurt like a mother-fucker. It just went to show how much of a badass he was, that he didn't complain. He just got on with the job of flying the helicopter like some kind of action hero.

"You know, they should make a movie out of this." I kept a close eye on him, although what the fuck I'd do if he passed out, I have no idea. The best thing I could do right now was keep him talking and alert.

"Hemsworth can play me," he said immediately. "They'll have to find someone smoking hot enough to play you."

"I'm sure there are lots of actors who could play me." Maybe that blond one who won an Academy Award that time. What was her name? I couldn't remember.

"Asher is going to be really disappointed he missed all the excitement," I added. Zeke was going to be pissed. He always was when someone kidnapped me, and he didn't have family ties to Yuri to keep him from ripping the guy's head off. He'd just go ahead and do it. Tully too. Penn would give Yuri a piece of his mind first.

What would Landon and Channing do? Whatever it was, it wouldn't be pretty.

"We can act it out for him," Jackson said. "Although, he'll probably take one look at the helicopter and forget all about what he might have missed out on."

"That sounds accurate." I realised I still held the gun in my hand. "Should I get rid of this?" The last thing I needed was to have it used as evidence against me. Even if everything I did was in self-defence.

"Absolutely," Jackson agreed. "Jettison that bitch."

I carefully opened the tiny window beside me and slipped the gun through the crack. I opened my fingers and let it slide away into the air. I didn't see it land or be swallowed by the waves, but no one would find it out here.

"We should reach the island in half an hour or so," Jackson said. "Luckily the bad guys stocked the chopper with enough fuel." He pressed a button in front of me and talked into his headphones.

"This is the island airport," a voice came through both of our headphones. "I see your approach. I'll clear you for landing."

I realised that, as hot as seeing Jackson fly a helicopter was, I was looking forward to having my feet back on solid ground and the other guys' arms around us both.

CHAPTER
TWELVE

ZEKE

I CURLED and uncurled my hands to keep from punching something. Or someone.

"Absolutely, fucking nothing," I growled. "It's like they disappeared off the face of the planet. I don't think the authorities believe me when I say they weren't on that yacht."

Levi nodded, his expression grim. "It's been how long? About thirty hours?"

"Too fucking long." I stalked from one side of the room to the other. "I've had everyone I know looking into this Yuri guy, but so far nothing on him either. You said he was after Jackson's father?"

I should have known Jackson was into some shady shit. The rest of us were, and he rolled with it. Whether it was being ambushed or having to dispose of disembodied heads, he dealt with it. It never occurred to me to question why.

Levi sipped his coffee and looked way too cool under the circumstances. "He didn't tell me much, but that was about the gist of it. He's dropped by Jackson's house a time or two, but I don't think he expected it to escalate."

I rubbed a hand over the back of my head. "I wish he'd come to me. I might have been able to do something to prevent it." If this guy was the one behind Abbie and Jackson's disappearance. There were still some dubious players in the game, like the Bell family, but this didn't feel like any of them. They would have waited until we were all together and taken us all out. And, as far as I knew, the Bells had no argument with Abbie or Jackson. Unless...

I shook my head to myself. There were too many ifs and buts, and right now it didn't matter who did this, as long as we got them back.

"You can't fucking babysit all of us all the time," Penn snapped. He gave me a look like he thought I was overreacting, but he was as worried as the rest of us. I saw it on his face and in every agitated movement. More agitated than usual.

"Can't I?" I retorted. "I don't remember you objecting when I saved your ass a couple of times."

Before Penn could respond, Asher stepped in between us and slipped his arms around my neck. "Fighting with each other isn't going to get us anywhere. We need to support each other right now. We're all worried about them. We would all do anything to get them back."

I closed my eyes and pressed my cheek to his. Neither of us had shaved for a couple of days and our stubble clashed and scratched, but I drew strength from his touch.

"I wish I knew what we had to do, that's all," I said. "Who do we have to kill to get them back to us? Point me in the right direction and I'll go."

"And we'll go with you," Landon said. "Right, Channing?"

"Without doubt," Channing agreed. "We all feel as helpless as you do."

I looked over at him and wanted to dispute that, but I couldn't. The expression on his face, on all of their faces, were a match for mine.

"I don't suppose the label got a ransom note?" Tully asked. He looked very sure the answer would be no. And it was.

Levi shook his head. "No, which is just as well because I don't think the label has enough money to pay what either of them are worth." He sighed heavily. "No, I might not have the background you guys do, but thinking back at the way Jackson talked about Yuri, it makes sense that he or someone like him was behind this."

Which brought me back to wishing Jackson confided in me. I would never have let him and Abbie go on that yacht if I'd known there was this kind of risk out there. Which was exactly why he didn't tell me. Like Penn so eloquently said, I couldn't babysit them all the time.

"The ocean is a big place," Asher said. "It will take a bunch of boats to cover it."

"A fleet," Penn said. When we all turned to look at him he said, "A bunch of boats is called a *fleet*."

Asher shrugged, his chest rising and falling against mine. "Whatever."

Penn muttered something about accuracy, but otherwise fell quiet.

Asher shook his head. "What was I saying?"

"Well if you don't know, babe..." I teased lightly. I kissed his mouth before he could retort, then pulled back. "What were you saying? Something about a bunch of boats." I shot Penn a warning look before he commented.

"Right." Asher frowned adorably. "Maybe we need something better than a bunch of boats. Like a plane. Or—"

"A helicopter," Landon said.

Asher snapped his fingers and flicked a finger gun at Landon. "Exactly. A helicopter."

"No," Landon said. "I hear a helicopter. Maybe they know something."

I listened. He was right, there was a helicopter headed towards the island. If I had to guess, I'd say it was coming in fast and low.

"The airport is on the other side of the island." Tully frowned.

I nodded and headed out the door without another word, my fingers curled around Asher's.

We trotted out to the field where the organisers were still setting up for the festival. A stage sat along on one end, wide enough and deep enough for even the biggest bands. Speakers were arrayed around it, big enough that the music would be heard on the other side of the island.

The centre of the field was open, but ringed with portable toilets and other amenities. Right now, it was also full of people. Many lay around on blankets or towels, claiming the best vantage point for themselves.

On the other side of the amenities was a sea of tents. This was usually were one of the guys would have mentioned how much fucking would go on inside, and outside, those tents. Not today though. Today, we stood with our hands shielding our eyes, watching the helicopter approach.

I was right, it was coming in fast, and wobbling now and then, like it was either on the breeze or the pilot couldn't keep it straight.

"Um..." Asher said.

"Right," I said. I put my hands around my mouth and shouted, "Clear the field!"

For a solid thirty seconds I thought everyone was going to ignore me. Then they noticed the big ass fuck helicopter headed straight for the field and scattered like scared sheep. Several tripped and almost fell, but managed to get out of the way right before the helicopter bumped down onto the grass.

It rose again, did a half-turn and then came to rest before the engine died.

"What the fuck?" Penn muttered.

For once, I agreed with him. I hurried towards the helicopter, eyes wary, expecting trouble.

I didn't expect the passenger door to pop open and Abbie to slip out. She kept her head down, away from the still turning rotors and hurried around to the other side of the helicopter.

"He's injured," she said, her voice and eyes as wild as her hair.

"So are you." One of her sleeves was covered in blood.

She glanced at it as though she'd forgotten all about it. "It's nothing. We need to get Jackson to hospital." She put a hand on the pilot's side door and yanked it open.

Jackson looked pale. He was also covered in blood, but he was alive. He even managed to say, "Hey, it's good to see you," before he almost tumbled out of the helicopter.

I managed to grab him and with Asher and Abbie's help, stop him from falling onto the grass. The pilot's seat was covered in blood. Not enough to kill him, but enough that he was going to be out of it for a day or two.

The other guys, without having to be told, arrayed themselves around Abbie and Jackson to shield them from the people gawking. That didn't stop people from trying to look, or taking photos. No doubt there were at least a dozen videos of the helicopter landing and Abbie getting out being uploaded to the Internet as we spoke.

"There's a medical tent over here," Levi said, waving a few metres away.

"Can you walk?" I hooked one of Jackson's arms over my shoulder and, to my surprise, Penn did the same on the other side.

"I'm all right," Jackson protested.

"He got shot in the ass and hasn't slept since we got taken," Abbie said.

"Yeah, all I need is some sleep," Jackson agreed.

"You're in the wrong place for that." Penn snorted. "No one is going to be sleeping around here for a couple of days."

Jackson gave him a sidelong look. "Thanks. Love you too."

Penn shrugged his other shoulder. "Didn't say I don't love you, just saying—"

"We get it," I said.

We helped Jackson into the medical tent and down onto one of the low camp beds. While a nurse tended to his ass, I finally got a chance to turn to Abbie. I pulled into my arms and kissed her, long and deep.

Then I pulled back and said, "Where the hell were you? We've been going crazy trying to figure out how to find you."

"Out and about," she said lightly. "Would you believe we went for a joyride?"

I raised my eyebrows at her. "I fucking hope not, because most joyrides don't end up in blood, or with landing a helicopter in the middle of a field of people."

"Jackson was going to land at the airport but he was getting faint," she explained. "It was that or ditch in the ocean."

"I'm glad he chose that." Later, he was going to have to tell me how the hell he knew how to fly a helicopter. I kissed her again before I was all but shoved aside so Asher could kiss her. Then Tully. Then Penn. Then Landon and Channing together.

Levi even managed to give her a hug. "If you wanted to generate some extra publicity, you could have asked." He grinned.

"I thought I'd surprise you," she said sarcastically. "What do you think?"

"Best fucking entrance ever," Asher said. "I think we should arrive that way for all of our concerts from now on. Minus the injuries."

"Asher is paying for the use of the helicopter," Penn said dryly.

"I'm actually tempted," Asher said. "Just because it would be that awesome."

"You're an idiot," Penn told him.

"Love you too," Asher told him.

Penn rolled his eyes in response.

"Excuse me, but your manager will be fine," the nurse said. "Nothing I couldn't fix up myself and he only needed a handful of stitches." She looked like she pulled bullets out of asses often enough that she didn't even think twice about them anymore. Maybe she did. I bet nurses saw all kinds of things on a daily basis, so nothing much was new anymore.

"He's going to need something for the pain the next day or so, but otherwise I recommend rest. As much of it as he will get here anyway." She nodded and walked away to tend to somebody else.

"He's lucky," I said slowly. "This way, I can't kick him in the ass."

Abbie placed her hands on her hips. "None of this was his fault. If it wasn't for him, we'd still be there. Or dead."

"If it wasn't for Abbie, we'd be dead," Jackson said, stepping towards us, a pained expression on his face. "Be careful around her when she has a gun in her hand." He added that last bit low, so no one else could hear.

"Sounds like we missed all the fun." Asher looked rueful.

Abbie put her arm around him and rested her head against his chest. "Trust me, you didn't miss a thing. And we didn't miss IslandFest. But what I need right now is a long, hot shower."

We stepped out of the medical tent to a loud round of cheers from the concertgoers gathered there. Most of them had their phones up, filming us. Specifically, filming Abbie.

"That was fucking epic!" someone shouted.

Someone else started to chant and one by one everyone took it up. "Abbie! Abbie! Abbie!"

"Oi! Oi! Oi!" Asher shouted in reply.

The crowd laughed and changed the chant to, "Venom! Venom! Venom!"

"No one knows how to please a crowd like Wolf Venom and Abbie." Levi grinned.

"We're definitely a hard act to follow," I agreed. "But you know what, I'm sure the band after us will be just as awesome."

To the shouts of the crowd, we headed back to our hotel rooms. We had some unfinished business to attend to.

CHAPTER
THIRTEEN

ABBIE

"BEST FESTIVAL EVER," Ashton declared.

We walked back to our hotel room after the last band of the festival finished. The exhausted, but still hyped, crowds cheered almost as loud as they'd played.

"It really fucking was," Landon agreed. "I hope they invite us back next time."

"I hope next time I don't go yur'at for arriving in a helicopter." I glanced over at Jackson and smiled. He was still walking a little stiffly, but a lot more easily than a couple of days ago.

The guys hadn't let the poor guy sleep until they heard every detail of our kidnapping and escape. According to Zeke, Yuri was long gone before any authorities arrived. As we suspected, the house didn't belong to him. Neither did the superyacht. If anyone else was involved, no one had any answers.

"Do you know how many bands have approached me to be their manager?" Jackson asked.

"Is it zero?" Penn cocked an eyebrow at him.

Jackson pretended to look insulted. "No, it wasn't zero. There were three, but they were very insistent."

"You told them no though, right?" Zeke asked. "I hope so, because I'd hate to have to hurt anyone."

"You're stuck with me," Jackson said. "If only to keep people safe from you." He gave Zeke a faint but affectionate smile.

"Whatever it takes, bro," Zeke slapped him on the back.

"You guys are all idiots," Penn said.

"Yeah, but you're all my idiots," I said, including him in the insult.

"I knew there was a reason I still hate you." But the look Penn gave me was loving and, for him, soft.

"I hate you too." I returned his look.

Moving so quickly he made me squeal, he scooped me up in his arms and carried me into the hotel. He lay me down on the bed and lay over me. Before he kissed me he said, "If anyone else wants in on this, we don't mind."

He claimed my mouth in a searing kiss that made me forget everything, and slid his hands up under my top.

"We're in," Asher said. He grabbed the hem of his shirt and tugged it up over his head with one hand, then reached for Zeke and dragged him down beside us.

The bed dipped on the other side and I expected to see Tully, but it was Jackson who lay down next to us. He looked nervous. That wasn't surprising. His experience of us fucking as a group, was walking in on us one time in one of the stadiums. He gave me a lecture about closing the door. I'd always suspected he'd wanted to join in.

"Are you sure?" I asked softly.

"I am if you guys are," he said carefully. This would change his relationship with the other guys forever. I think on some level we all knew that. Hopefully it would be for the better.

"The more, the merrier," Tully said. He sat near the end of the bed and started to pull off my skirt and panties.

Between Penn and Jackson, they helped me out of my shirt and bra, then stripped off their clothes.

I heard the sound of scraping and picked up my head to see Landon and Channing push the other bed over so we had one long bed. Then they were also naked.

Everywhere I looked, there was a naked hot guy. Not just that, but naked hot guys who loved me. Whom I loved. Lucky me.

I lay back and Penn kissed me while Jackson ran his hands around and over my breasts, touching and feeling like he wanted to memorise every centimetre.

Tully gently parted my thighs with his hands and lowered his face between my legs. He circled my clit with his tongue, teasing and tasting, but not quite touching.

"Please," I groaned. "I need…"

"We know what you need," Penn said. "Let's not rush it." Before I could glare, or retort, he slanted his mouth over mine and kissed me, cutting off words before they were formed. He thrust his tongue between my lips like he was fucking my mouth with it.

I sucked eagerly, like it was his cock.

The warmth of Jackson's mouth clamped lightly over one of my nipples. He grazed my sensitive, pebbled peak with his teeth.

Tully chose a moment to slip one, two of his long fingers inside me and draw my clit in between his lips.

I shivered with delight. My whole body was on fire with all the sensations all at once. Every one of my senses were stimulated almost to the point of overload. The taste of Penn, the feel of Tully and Jackson, the smell of desire, the sight of Penn's bright blue eyes so close to mine, the sound of sucking and licking and kissing.

Every single one of us was a part of this.

It was divine.

Penn loved to tell me when I could come and when I couldn't, but there was no way he could have stopped me, nothing he could have said. The orgasm pounded through me louder than any of the bands at IslandFest, harder than the hardest rock song. I shattered into a million little pieces and cried out against Penn's mouth.

Tully didn't stop working me, teasing until I came back down and flopped against the mattress. Only then, he pulled away his face and slid his fingers out of me.

Penn leaned looked at me like I shouldn't have come without his say so, but he said, "My turn."

He swapped places with Tully, the lead guitarist coming to lie beside me. He kissed me, tasting my juices. "You're so delicious."

"I could say the same about you." There was something about a guy who tasted of my orgasm. Especially when he was the one who made me come.

"You're so fucking wet," Penn said. "I'm starting to think fucking is your favourite thing."

I gave him a husky laugh in response. "It definitely is. That and music. And you guys."

"I'm glad you added that last bit." He wasn't gentle when he thrust three fingers into me, not even a little bit. He worked me hard with his hand and mouth, like he was determined to push me to the edge as quickly as possible.

That was exactly what he did, but before I tipped over, he took his hand away and kissed up and down the insides of my thighs.

At the same time, Tully and Jackson took turns lavishing attention on my breasts and kissing my mouth. I felt like the centre of the universe. Or at least, their universe.

Just before I went completely crazy, Penn started to work me again, harder this time; relentless.

"Good girl, come, right now," he ordered.

Whether it was his words, his actions or a combination, I did exactly that. I arched my back and dug my nails into Jackson's arm. I closed my eyes and pressed my lips together. I rocked my body so hard I didn't know how my spine didn't snap. I cried out so loud most of the island probably heard me.

I finally flopped down and lay panting, letting the blood return to the rest of my body.

"Good girl," Penn said again. "Now you're all witnesses to the fact she can do as she's told once in a while." He looked smug.

I snorted breathlessly and said, "Fuck off."

He just grinned. "Jackson's turn."

Jackson looked like he wasn't sure if he was going to do it Penn told him to do, but apparently making me come again was worth being bossed around for.

I wasn't sure I *could* come a third time, but the sight of Asher with his mouth around Zeke's cock, Zeke's fingers tangled in his hair, and Landon and Channing lying head to feet with each other's cocks in their mouths drove me to the edge a third and then a fourth time.

Apparently it had the same effect on Zeke, because he came too. "Fuck, fuck, fuck. Yeah."

Penn scooted up next to me. "Open up, you dirty bitch." He liked to mix up his praise with his dirty talk. He tapped my lips with his cock.

I gave him a look like I might disobey, but then opened to let him slip his cock into my mouth.

Jackson, mouth shining, eyes on me, knelt between my thighs and carefully slid his cock into my body.

Someone, I don't know who, handed around a tube of lube. The guys rolled me over so I straddled Jackson.

"Lean forward," Penn ordered.

Jackson raised his eyebrows. I smiled reassuringly at him. He knew if he wanted us to stop, he only had to say so. We were all about consent and respect.

I leaned over Jackson while Tully lubricated my rear hole. His finger was cold, making me shiver before I took a deep breath and relaxed, appreciating the way he opened me up, readied me for him.

He tossed the lube to someone else, placed his hands on my hips and slowly slid himself inside.

On one side of me, Channing did the same to Landon, while on the other Asher did the same to Zeke.

Holy shit.

I managed a glance at Jackson's face at the point where Tully's cock must have touched his. His eyes widened, but then half closed again. Yeah, this might change everything for all of us, but it was definitely a change for the better. Jackson was very much one of us now.

All around me, and inside me were the slow steady thrusts and pants of seven guys. The whole world was gone and everything left was this moment and all eight of us.

One by one, the guys came, a series of grunts and moans and the occasional, "Fuck yeah."

I came again, right at the point when Jackson and Tully both did. They both stilled inside me, only a narrow wall of my body between their cocks. They were so close, they must have felt each other's rush of warmth, the squirt of pearly cum into me. That might be the hottest thing yet. It was followed closely by Penn slamming between my lips and spilling his salty release into my mouth. I waited until he pulled out before locking my eyes on his and swallowing down every drop.

"Good girl. You're not so bad after all."

I slapped Penn on the chest with the back of my hand, but it was a half-hearted effort at best. "Neither are you," I said. "Mostly."

He chuckled and lay next to me, his hand on my hip.

Tully and Jackson lay on the other side, with all the other guys spread out around us.

We all sagged together in a heap of arms and legs and satisfaction. We snuggled down together and finally slept.

One big crazy, blissed out family.

———

For a FREE short story set in the same world as Abbie and the Wold Venom guys, grab your copy of No Accident

For more dark mafia hotness, the next stop is Bait.

ALSO BY MAGGIE ALABASTER

MM Romantasy

Shadow and Steel

Drop-Dead Lethal

Dead Cute

Bloody Sweet

Pretty Psychos

Best Served Cold

Heart Stopping

Heart Rending

Heart Breaking

Heart Beating

Aurora Hollow duet

Take Me Slowly Part 1

Take Me Slowly Part 2

Ruck Boys

Filthy Ruck

Hard Ruck

Twisted Ruck

Bad Ruck

Dirty Ruck

Deadly Ruck

Sparrow and the Mafia Kings

Possessive

Ruined

Corrupted

Pucking Dark Hearts

Pucking Hearts Collide

Pucking Forbidden Hearts

Pucking Hardened Hearts

Dusk Bay Demons

Puck Drop

Breakaway

Power Play

Brutal Academy

Book 1 Heartless

Book 2 Cruel

Book 3 Vengeful

Court of Blood and Binding

Book 1 Song of Scent and Magic

Book 2 Crown of Mist and Heat

Book 3 Sword of Balm and Shadow

Book 4 Whisper of Frost and Flame

Dark Masque

Book 1 Bait

Book 2 Prey

Book 3 Trap

Novella A Very Dark Masque Christmas

Saving Abbie

Book 1 Pitch

Book 2 Pound

Book 3 Session

Book 4 Muse

Book 5 Rhythm

Book 6 Encore

Novella Venomous

Saving Abbie books 1-4

Saving Abbie books 4-6 + Venomous

Ruthless Claws

Book 1 Ivory

Book 2 Crimson

ABOUT THE AUTHOR

Maggie Alabaster writes reverse harem romance.

She lives in NSW, Australia with one spouse, two daughters, one dog, and countless birds.

Shop direct from Maggie! Store

Sign up for Maggie's newsletter! Sign Up!

Join Maggie's reader group! Join here!

Follow Maggie on Bookbub! Click here to follow me!

Check out Maggie's website- www.maggiealabaster.com